PINNACLES OF POWER

THE MAXWELL CHRONICLES

PINNACLES OF POWER

MICHAEL PHILLIPS

MOODY PRESS
CHICAGO

2 3 4 5 6 7 8 Printing/BC/Year 96 95 94 93 92 91

Printed in the United States of America

To John Ward

one of those special comrades in the Spirit
with whom God has joined my heart in unity

About the Author

MICHAEL PHILLIPS is one of today's prolific and versatile Christian authors. As an editor (chiefly of the works of George MacDonald) he has produced some thirty titles. As a co-author (with Judith Pella), his Stonewycke, Highland, and Corrie Belle Hollister historical series number twelve books. In addition, Phillips has written twelve books on his own, and as a publisher has produced still another score of titles. His books, with total sales of three million, have won a number of awards, have appeared on numerous best seller lists, have been chosen upon repeated occasions as book club selections, and have been translated into several foreign languages.

Phillips, 44, was raised in northern California, educated at Humboldt State University, and presently makes his home in Eureka, California, with his wife, Judy, and their three sons, Gregory, Robin, and Patrick.

Introduction

It is not generally customary for the author of a book of contemporary fiction to introduce his own work. There are, however, several factors concerning the volume you are holding that may interest you. Foremost among them is the fact that this book was written close to ten years ago.

At that time, though I had begun editing MacDonald in earnest, not a single word of original fiction had yet passed through my typewriter. *Pinnacles of Power* had the dubious distinction of being my initial foray into that world—my first novel. Upon completion I promptly sent it around expecting—as does every hopeful young novelist—to see finished copies and rave reviews pouring in within no time. What I received instead were rejection letters—literally, as the months, then years, passed, by the dozen.

Needless to say, there were no raves. The chief objection did not seem to be with the writing itself, but rather with the delicate nature of the subject. Nobody exactly called Jackson's probing "controversial," yet it was clear the editors reviewing it were uncomfortable with the whole idea of calling into question the finances, motives, and whole foundational veracity of a national ministry and its leadership.

You have to remember when this took place. During the early 1980s, fundamentalist ministry, televangelism, religious broadcasting, and Christian book publishing and the parallel recording industry were *all* in the midst of huge growth and unprecedented worldwide impact. Everywhere you looked public evangelicalism was exploding. Money was pouring in. Churches and universities and student groups and bookstores and TV and radio stations and publishing companies and networks and singing groups and talk shows and training centers and outreach programs were springing up throughout the country. It was a season of unimaginable world impact and great optimism. Evangelicals possessed political and social clout. They had just helped elect a president, and that was only the beginning. The pundits were saying the conservative Christian right was the next huge constituency that could dynamically change everything in the social and political landscape. By 1986, out of this huge wave of activity, evangelicalism put forth another major presidential candidate and in the early months helped set the focus for the whole election. It seemed we were on the verge of truly influencing the world for Christ in a massive way. Evangelicalism was, in a sense, in the midst of its euphoric season of Camelot.

Throughout all this, without motives of malice or an axe to grind against any specific man, ministry, or movement, I believed some cautionary notes needed to be sounded with respect to our foundational priorities. The political and financial emphasis concerned me, as did many other subtleties I could see creeping into the overall evangelical outlook. Thus was Jackson Maxwell drawn into the fray.

Those publishing houses, however, who read his story did not apparently share my premonitions of concern. How was I to know, as Jackson's creator, that I would encounter the very obstacles he faced in his quest to make public *his* sense of disquiet? This was a story, it seemed, that the Christian media—in the form of evangelical publishing—did not want exposed to the public. The whole idea that indiscretion and sin might lie among the unseen roots of one of America's most well-known and visible ministries was just too . . . well, it was inconceivable! They couldn't publish something like that. It would be injurious to the cause of Christ.

Thus, the responses I received were in themselves probing: "Who do you mean here . . . who does Such-and-such represent . . . what is the *real* name of this ministry you mention?" There were five or six prominent figures at whom they were certain I was pointing my finger.

I vividly recall a conversation with an editor at one of the large publishing houses (one, by the way, with whom I have *not* recently published).

"Do you mean . . . ?" I was pointedly asked, as a certain name was mentioned.

"No, of course not," I answered. "He's a man I respect and admire."

"Then is it . . . ?"

"No," I insisted, repeating as I'd already emphasized, "nothing here is modeled specifically after *anyone*. It's simply a broad look at leadership and ministry in general."

"Then what exactly is it you are trying to do here?" the editor went on. "What is your design . . . your agenda?"

"There are no hidden motives," I answered again. "I simply think there are some issues we as concerned Christians should be thinking and praying about, that's all. We mustn't have our heads in the sand and assume these kinds of things can't happen. Satan is prowling around, and we have to be on our guard."

The upshot of the conversation was, "Well, we wish we could do Jackson's story. We kind of like it. But . . . well, you see—we just can't risk it. It's too pointed. There could be offense taken. Certain people could . . . I'm sure you understand—our readers might get the wrong idea. We can't take the chance."

The message was clear: Don't intrude upon Camelot.

In the end, the book was rejected between many times, and Jackson's saga was destined to wind up in my file of mothballed titles I assumed would never see the light of day. Having had, I must admit, my writer's enthusiasm severely dampened, I decided to try my hand at less controvertible and contentious subject matter. Thus I have spent the past decade almost exclusively in the genre of historical fiction.

When certain events with which you are familiar rocked evangelicalism several years ago, it was with a certain sadness that I thought of Jackson. Suddenly everything was altered overnight. The euphoria was gone. The bubble of optimism was burst. Suddenly we were brought face to face with the reality that we were not living in a fairy tale after all. For some it became almost an embarrassment to be associated with the stained movement called evangelicalism. It was not that I realistically thought that Jackson's story might have been able to make a difference in the unfolding specifics of that unfortunate time. Yet I was saddened that the perspectives generated by Jackson's inquiry had not been able to be a prayerful part of the milieu within which we attempted to place events into a meaningful perspective vis-a-vis our commission to

11

spread the gospel into a world suddenly grown skeptical and suspicious.

Years marched on. And now, after all this time, I must confess almost to surprise, that there suddenly *is* interest in making Jackson's investigation known. Yet I find myself thinking, "But it is too late for any good Jackson might have been able to accomplish."

My hope, however, is that it is *not* too late. For though the one half of the story is told—the public drama, the details of which we all know only too well, *and* this story of Jackson's private quest—another half yet remains to be told. That is what we might call the follow-up, the completion of the story—an ongoing sequel of healing and restoration. It is a sequel yet awaiting fulfillment within the body of God's people, and for which the world—though it scarcely realizes it—is eagerly watching. In one sense, one might say that the fulfillment of the Great Commission has been temporarily put on hold until the world witnesses how we handle these hurts and falls and divisions within our family. Only after those troubles have been scripturally attended to will the world again be ready and eager to listen on a widespread scale.

Perhaps it will be in this area of healing and rebuilding and renewal that Jackson Maxwell will yet—even after all these years—exercise the impact it was my hope he would have ten years ago. For this book begins a series in which a number of issues crucial to restoration and unity will be explored.

So, with all that as background, I introduce you to Jackson Maxwell, a composite, perhaps, of us all as we search for truth and integrity within the Christian body, and within our own selves.

The book remains 95 percent as it was first written, with only a few additions and minor corrections made to bring it up to date. No details of plot have been added, as it were, after the fact. All the things in this novel you may find similar to occurences that have in one way or another come to pass in factual lives and ministries were in print, as I said, almost ten years ago. I say this, not to claim any sort of oracular insight, but merely to emphasize again that none of the characters, none of the fictional ministries mentioned, and none of the situations involved are in any way intended to represent actual persons or organizations.

I do indeed hope and pray that Jackson and Jacob and all the characters you will meet here will be capable, each in his own way, of exercising impact within God's body and within *your* life as you come to find your unique place in it. If they cannot now alter what has already been, perhaps they might yet influence "what is to come" as God's people discover how to put restoration to work. Only thus will we discover how we are to step into and live within the unity for which Jesus prayed. In so doing, the *power* of the gospel to realistically impact the world will be unleashed—not through our programs and our agendas and our political maneuverings, but through the recreative power of God to transform individual hearts.

MICHAEL PHILLIPS

Cast of Characters

News with a Vision

Jackson Maxwell—reporter, staff writer (*NWV*)

Ed McClanahan—editor *National Profile* newspaper, asst. editor *Christian World Magazine* (*CWM*)—both owned by *News with a Vision* (*NWV*)

Linda Provionni—a friend of Maxwell's, advertising staff of *NWV*

Jerry Ziegler—staff writer, *NWV*

Bill Andrews—staff writer, *NWV*

Gilbert Dillow—executive VP, *NWV*

Fred and Ellen Maxwell—Illinois farm couple, Jackson's parents

Evangelize the World

Jacob Michaels—evangelist, Christian leader, and head of Evangelize the World (ETW)

Hamilton Jaeger—assistant to Jacob Michaels

Elizabeth Michaels—Jacob's wife

Henry Michaels—Jacob's father

Lance Michaels—Henry's brother

Diana Michaels—daughter of evangelist

Richard Michaels—son of evangelist

Sondra DeQue—PR spokeswoman for ETW

Robert Means—longtime friend of Michaels, ETW correspondence department

Liz Layne—Michaels's secretary

Harriet Steadman—finance department, ETW

Cooper Graves—now ETW staff, formerly on the staff of *NWV*

George and Sarah Haley—retired Texas farm couple

Marsha and George Haley, Jr.—son and daughter of George and Sarah

Sebastian Elliot—Dallas realtor, friend of Hamilton Jaeger

Jefferson Montgomery—U.S. Senator

Sydney Wilson—aide to Senator Montgomery

Other Characters

Harmon LeCroix—singer

Barry Harrison—*Christian Organizations and Ministries* (*CO&M*)

Carson Mitchell—Sonburst Ministries, best-selling author

Anthony Powers—head of Students Committed to World Evangelism (SCWE)

Jerome McGrath—Word of God Publishers

Jeff Bahnes—Evangelism Radio

Neil Pierce—Jericho Recording

Jeremy Harper—*Moody Monthly*

Sylvia Blissick—Distressed Persons Anonymous (DPA)

Sybil Macon—adoption agency

Jerome Bullinger—former assistant to Hamilton Jaeger

PART 1

Beginnings

1

"I don't care how it's done, just take care of it!"

"It could come out—there may be questions."

"Blast it, Bruce," exploded the other, adding several abusive expletives in a rare outburst of profanity, "of course there may be. That's why we're here—to prevent that, nip it in the bud."

"What would you suggest then . . . that I—?"

"For crying out loud, Bruce, take whatever measures are needed. This isn't a church social. You're in the big league now. I hired you because you seemed an ambitious and resourceful young man. And frankly, I've not been disappointed. You've shown initiative. You've been valuable to me. And now that you have the power of my position behind you—and the finances to match—you've got somehow to make it happen."

"I understand, sir," he replied with a soldier-like snap in the voice. His crew cut, hard-featured face, and steel gray eyes heightened the impression of resolute toughness. He was one ready to give his all for the cause, with powerful will and deep convictions to match.

"Do you? Do you really understand . . . ?"

The voice trailed off as he gazed out the window toward the distant lights of the city. His eyes, after a moment, were diverted to a pulsating spotlight illuminating a billboard that proclaimed, "Nixon's the one—a man you can trust!" Only a few yards away, a "JFK" sign sought to counter the flashing message.

A brief silence followed. The fifth floor office was but dimly lit. No other soul was present in the building. It was late.

"Funny, isn't it, Bruce?" resumed the elder of the two, musing to himself more than addressing his young disciple. "People all over this city, all over the country, trying to decide whom to vote for. But what difference will their decision really make in four, or in eight years? What faces us is so much larger. People are depending on us. Much is at stake. We've been placed in this position of responsibility for a reason. Ours is a sacred obligation to fulfill. Just imagine what the scandal would mean! We can't let this—this unfortunate occurrence—taint the image, if you know what I mean."

"Yes, sir."

"They look to him for guidance, Bruce. For support, strength—for meaning. We can't take that away from them . . ."

The words grew softer. Another pause. The sound was of a man attempting once more to justify the confused motives of his own mind rather than trying to convince the youthful corporal awaiting his orders.

"—the vision must move forward, Bruce, we've got to see to that—you and I. One momentary lapse, one little slip musn't . . ."

He sighed deeply.

Then as if his resolve was finally settled, he spun quickly from the window and looked his young accomplice firmly in the eye.

"He need not know, you understand. Just take care of it, Bruce—behind the scenes as it were. Make sure the young man is paid well for his silence. As far as I know, the young woman has no idea what she's stumbled into. Keep it that way. Any problems, come directly to me. No one else is to be told anything. Are you with me, Bruce?"

"Yes, sir. It seems our duty is clear enough."

"Good. You have the organization behind you. Whatever it takes. You have carte blanche."

"I'll do my best, sir."

"I'm depending on you, young man. And so are millions of the flock."

PART 2

1991
Jackson Maxwell

2

As Jackson Maxwell strolled into the editorial room, the aroma of fresh coffee assailed his eager nostrils. How could he anticipate that he would look back on this moment as the turning point—the day everything began to change? For now it felt like any other morning.

He greeted familiar faces as he worked his way through the maze of desks and tables to his own personal cubbyhole toward the rear of the expansive open area. The day was in full swing by 8:15, and already computer keyboards were resonating to the beat of busy fingers throughout the room. Here and there, an old teletype machine or typewriter could also be heard clacking out its messages.

He sat down at his desk in a small cubicle of workspace piled with books, file folders, magazines, and newspaper clippings. In a twenty-four-inch semicircle clearing sat his typewriter.

Where was I last night? he thought.

He pecked out his name and the day's date on top of a blank sheet. Then his fingers fell silent.

"Cup of coffee, Jackson? I'm headed that way."

"No, thanks," said Jackson.

The other began to walk off, then turned and added, almost as an afterthought, "You still using that ancient thing?"

"Yeah," answered Jackson, "I just can't get my fingers used to the feel of a terminal keyboard."

"Makes rewrites easier, that's for sure. I wouldn't write any other way than on a computer."

"That's what everyone seems to say, Jerry." Jackson laughed.

"Why don't you make the switch then?"

"I suppose I still feel more creative at an old fashioned Underwood, or a not-so-old-fashioned Selectric. Something about pounding those keys—metal on rubber. It *feels* more like writing."

42917

"Well, all I've got to say is you're a dying breed." Jerry laughed, continuing on to the coffee bar.

Jackson returned his stare to his typewriter—neither an Underwood nor a Selectric, but a new state-of-the-art electronic IBM Wheelwriter—wondering how he'd ever get started again on the article. He wondered the same thing every morning.

Maybe a cup of coffee would help, he thought.

"Hey—Maxwell!"

No one mistook the voice of his editor. The booming voice filled a room almost like his six-foot, four-inch frame overwhelmed his small swivel chair on those rare occasions when he chose to occupy it.

"—you got anything important going on?"

Jackson turned to see Ed McClanahan leaning toward him out his office door. Though the morning had just begun, already the editor's sleeves were rolled up, top button unfastened, and an unfashionably outdated tie loosened, creating a generally disheveled air.

"Not too much," Jackson replied, "I'm about halfway through what you might call an investigative book review."

"What's it on?"

"That controversial best seller Hal Lindsay and the Hunters collaborated on. You've heard about it, surely. Somebody connected with the Hunters had a vision that ties in with a project Lindsay had going in Jerusalem concerning the Temple. Quite a stir among evangelicals over it. It's going pretty well and isn't due till next month's deadline."

"Good. I've got a little piece I need for tomorrow. Can you tear yourself away?"

"Sure," said Jackson, glad to be relieved from his silent typewriter.

"I'd like you to get out to Wheaton. The Wade people are cooking up some new sort of display. They've come across some old manuscripts. You know, by Lewis or Tolkien—one of those fellows they have to do with. I think some relative donated them. I thought it would make a good three- or four-inch box for next week. Find out what you can, write it up. Two hundred fifty, three hundred . . . maybe four hundred words max."

Jackson picked up his briefcase, shoved his chair back under

24

the desk, and headed for the door. Leaving the third floor editorial room, he walked to the elevator and pushed the "down" button. As the door slid open, before him stood a tall, thin black woman, mid-thirties, carrying an armload of papers and looking in a hurry.

"Jackson, I haven't seen you for weeks!"

"I've been out and about, a lot of writing. Several stories coming out in the next six months. What about you, Linda?"

"They keep me busy down in advertising. Not that I don't miss the writing. But I get in less trouble over what I say. And it's a steady job—which I need. Joe isn't working right now—hurt his back."

The elevator stopped on the first floor, and the two emerged.

"We've got to get together, Jackson. I'd really like to hear what you're working on."

"How about lunch tomorrow?"

"Sure. I've got nothing going."

"I'll come down about quarter till twelve. Do you know that German deli down the street? Great sandwiches, a few tables."

Linda nodded in agreement and hurried toward the advertising office.

"It's a date then," said Jackson waving over his shoulder as he made his way toward the parking lot.

The drive out to Wheaton was one Jackson Maxwell always enjoyed, especially at this time of year. So much, in fact, that on occasions like this one he'd take a longer route northwest and then south through the country just for the scenery. The fall colors exploded on the hillsides, and the farmlands never failed to inject him with a dose of peaceful refreshment, a needed counterbalance to the usually hectic pace of the city and the newsroom. He found Wheaton assignments a pleasant diversion from ones that took him into downtown Chicago or off to New York.

The interview on this particular day and two drafts of the 335-word story took him the rest of the afternoon.

The next day, he and Linda squeezed into a corner table amid the congested lunch-hour throng.

"Where were you headed yesterday?" Linda asked, knifing a glob of mustard onto her roast beef on rye.

"Over to Wheaton College," said Jackson. "A cousin of Tolkien's sent them some papers last month no one had seen before.

25

Couple manuscript drafts, several original letters from Lewis, a critique of *The Hobbit* by Owen Barfield dated 1933—fascinating!"

"You doing a story on it for the magazine?"

"Don't I wish! I'd love to be assigned a feature story like that. Think of it—a trip to England for 'background.' Unfortunately, it's only a small news piece for the paper."

"I thought you were on the magazine staff."

"I am—officially. But you know McClanahan. He'll take who he can get for anything. The paper and the magazine work pretty much together. He needed a piece for next week's *Profile,* and I had nothing pressing. Besides, I'll take a trip to the Wade Library anytime."

"I've never been," said Linda.

"You ought to! Every edition of the books published by Lewis, Tolkien, MacDonald, Sayers, Barfield, Chesterton, and Williams, plus letters, old manuscripts."

"I guess I've just never been that enthusiastic about any of their writings."

"I'll have to busy myself converting you!" Jackson laughed.

Jackson Maxwell and Linda Provionni worked on the staff of *NWV,* International—*News with a Vision*—headquartered in Chicago. *News with a Vision* was the publisher of *Christian World Magazine,* a monthly, and the *National Profile,* a Christian biweekly newspaper. Linda, thirty-six, originally had joined the *Profile* as a reporter. But her opinionated ideas and discomfortingly incisive journalism had stirred up more problems in controversial areas than her editors deemed "edifying." So rather than letting her go, they shuffled Linda off to advertising, where she had been for two years. Jackson had worked his way onto the writing staff of *Christian World* by way of a part-time research assistantship while attending Wheaton College. At the time, he had been preparing for the mission field, but now writing had become his consuming interest. He'd never studied journalism as such, but with practice and experience had grown into a reasonably competent writer. Though young, and still toward the bottom of the *NWV* ladder, he was viewed by some as one of the up-and-coming whose mark would eventually be felt. Ed McClanahan, the *Profile* editor, had his eye focused on young Maxwell and knew that with proper seasoning he would mature into a recognized Christian spokesman.

"What else have you been working on?" asked Linda.

"Oh, you know. The usual. Celebrity interviews, book reviews, covering the 'happenings' in the Christian world. The specifics change, but the major magazines accentuate a similar style of journalism."

"Do I detect a trace of boredom?"

"Maybe so. Seems there's not much meat in it. Just once I'd like to sink my teeth into something that fights back, a genuine investigative piece of reporting."

"What is there to investigate in the Christian body? No murder mysteries, haunted houses, or secret treasures there."

"I suppose so," he replied slowly. "I don't know what I'm after."

A pause followed.

"Have you ever read *Scuffy the Tugboat?*" Jackson asked at length.

Linda shook her head.

"It's a children's storybook. I remember it vividly from my childhood," Jackson went on.

"Tell me about it."

"There's a little bathtub toy tugboat who wanted to get out into the real world. The bathtub was too small for him. He kept saying over and over, 'I was meant for bigger things!' That's sometimes how I feel, like I'm caught in a sheltered little spiritualized world writing only superficialities."

"And you feel destined for bigger things?" queried Linda.

"Yeah, I guess I do. It's not that I feel *I'm* too important for the kinds of things I usually work on. It's not me, it's the nature of the stories themselves. I long for significance. I'm hungry to write something that will make a difference, that will have some impact. It sometimes seems to me we're involved in a gigantic Christian entertainment industry—magazines and books, crusades and compact discs, interviews and TV appearances, music concerts, speaking tours, autograph sessions all destined to amuse and entertain and divert our attentions. We live in the era of the 'famous Christian.' We're not looking for godliness, for Christlikeness from our leaders. They're performers, celebrities, personalities. How often are we brought face to face with the real guts of the gospel, ghetto ministries and gutter-level problems and issues? Rarely. It's

27

all glitter and tinsel. Christianity in this country has become show business—a Hollywood hype—promoting big-name Christians and their products and ministries and ideas."

"Give you a soapbox and you jump right up and go to it!"

"Sometimes I tend to get rather heated when I think about all this," said Jackson with a smile.

"A writer's got to think, or he goes stale," said Linda. "I was only joking."

"I know."

A short pause followed.

"I don't want to write to entertain," Jackson went on after a few moments. "I want to stimulate people so that growth happens in their lives, and so that they are turned to focus on the truly critical matters."

"You don't feel you're doing that? I've read your articles. They're good, Jackson. You've become a gifted writer. Certainly people are helped to grow."

"Maybe. But competing for the readership is tough. People want to read gossip about the stars more than they want to confront serious questions. I study all the magazines and Christian media stuff. There's some good writing going on; some of the magazines are committed to trying to be significant. And I would rate ours as one of those. But then on another level, sometimes I think we're no different from the *National Enquirer* or *People* magazine. It's all properly spiritualized, of course. We put the right words and phrases and motives over everything so it looks and sounds different. But isn't it just a gloss spread across the top? Down deep aren't we essentially doing the same thing? It's just that we offer the inside scoop into the lives of the stars using all the acceptable spiritual jargon. Look at the covers of the slicks. You'll see an Amy Grant or a Frank Peretti or some other famous personality, nice smile on his face, with a caption inviting you inside to get to know 'the real' Amy or Frank or whoever. Isn't it just the Christian *People* magazine syndrome?"

"You're asking me? Don't forget, Jackson, I'm the one who practically got kicked out of journalism for trying to get people to look at things they were uncomfortable facing. You're starting to sound like me!"

"Yeah, I suppose you've been here too," sighed Jackson. "But

I'm just getting tired of not feeling like anyone out there's listening to people like us. I may write a good article, a sensitive piece of serious concern, but who's going to care? The public clamors after the sensational more than the significant. So we get assigned similar stories over and over. The subject matter never changes. I guess I'm suffering from the Christian superstar syndrome. I'm weary of the same stale interviews:

CWM: And what do you think of drugs?
Superstar: I never touch them; a real threat to our nation.

CWM: What word do you have for the Christian body?
Superstar: Oh, I'd just tell everyone that we have to be unified and love one another and tell the lost about Jesus.

CWM: What's your favorite part of performing for the Lord?
Superstar: Standing in front of the thousands of people, feeling their love, singing praises to Jesus, knowing that we're all going to be in heaven together. It's just wonderful!

CWM: How did you get your start?
Superstar: I went to Nashville and, well, the rest is history.

They both laughed.

"You sound cynical. Better not let your editor hear you or you'll get transferred to advertising," said Linda, revealing sparkling teeth with a wide-mouthed laugh. Her classic Afro, dark skin, and pleasing cheerfulness blended attractively, making her a favorite on all floors of *NWV*. It was no wonder Jackson often sought her company when he was pensive or uncertain.

"I suppose it's not really that bad," he added. "Most of the so-called stars we interview are fine people and do have important things to say. Still, I'm longing for a new approach. Something to knock the apathetic part of the Christian body out of its complacency."

"What do you think of Jacob Michaels?" asked Linda.

"Funny you should bring him up. Talk about your superstar of superstars! He was the cover story for our December issue. Can you believe it: 'Jacob and Elizabeth Michaels Share Their Most Unforgettable Christmas Memories'?"

"What's the matter with that?"

"It's bland, hackneyed, unimaginative. How will it really change anyone's life? Just like their being named 'Family of the Year' last year. How do we *really* know what their family is like? They're only chosen because of their visibility, their fame."

"He's coming to Chicago in the spring."

"I know. I heard a pitch for money on the radio yesterday on my way out to Wheaton. 'Do something for Chicago. Let us help bring morality back to your community with your donations.' I couldn't believe it. Such a flagrant appeal for money grates on me."

"There's a story for you, Jackson. A scoop. *The* exclusive interview with Jacob Michaels! If you could land an hour with him, direct the questions—maybe you could write something notable, uncover the *real* man, something with genuine force and impact."

"Maybe."

"Why so disinterested? He's the biggest Christian name since Billy Graham. He's *the* leader of Christianity these days. If you could get an audience with him, it would be the reportive coup of the decade."

"I see your eyes igniting, Linda. The reporter in you is rising."

"It is a thrilling possibility."

"I don't know . . ."

"Promise me you'll think about it."

"It's not really up to me anyway. There's my editor, not to mention Michaels himself. He doesn't grant many interviews."

"I know. Just promise me you'll think about it. If the Lord's behind it, the doors will open."

"OK, OK—I'll think about it!"

3

"You mean we don't actually have a file on him as such?"

"No. We just keep track of any issues that mention him."

"Then I'd have to run down each on film individually?"

"That's it."

"A lot of work."

"If we had a larger staff and a more sophisticated computer system like a big daily, we'd probably have complete files. As it is . . ." The keeper of the archives shrugged.

Jackson cast a hurried look about the small room. Cabinets and boxes lining the walls were stuffed to capacity with manila folders. On a table in the corner sat several stacks of magazines and clippings still to be sorted, categorized, and then filed.

"I don't relish a day in front of the microfilm reader."

"Guess it depends on how badly you want the information."

"Well, give me that list of issues."

"Might take me a while to sift through and find. How about if I run a copy up to you in about an hour?"

"OK. Thanks, Sherry."

Jackson took the stairs back from the second-floor records office, eased into his chair, and then propped his feet up on the desk in front of him. His six-foot, 170-pound frame let out a long, quiet sigh. He was well dressed, but casually, in comfortably fitting blue slacks with a blue patterned shirt and brown tie. He rarely wore a jacket of any kind except outdoors.

The magazine that had prompted his unscheduled visit downstairs lay where he had left it—still open to an article titled "Michaels Assets Pegged at Half Billion." Jackson subscribed to nearly a dozen magazines to keep abreast of what others were doing and to keep his idea chest well stocked. Over lunch he had been skimming through the current issue of *Christian Organizations and Ministries* when the article on Michaels had jumped off the page:

A report released recently revealed that the Jacob Michaels organi-

organization, Evangelize the World, Inc., has surpassed the half-billion dollar mark in total assets. According to reliable sources in ETW, several recent acquisitions in the South pushed the asset total over the $500 billion mark. Michaels's financial adviser and top assistant, Hamilton B. Jaeger, could not be reached for comment, but spokesperson Sondra DeQue confirmed the accuracy of the news release. "Mr. Jaeger has recently negotiated the purchase of a sizable section of Texas farmland on which Mr. Michaels intends to construct a 24-hour television broadcasting station and a training center," Ms. DeQue said. "There have also been a number of other recent purchases in other sections of the country which tie into our vision for world evangelism. Unfortunately, I am not able to give further specifics at this time."

The nonprofit organization, brainchild of Michaels's evangelist father, Henry, in the late 1950s, has in recent years come to represent a powerful force in the political arena as well as in the spiritual . . .

Reading the *CO&M* article a second time, Jackson rocked back in his chair, replaced the magazine on his desk, and did not continue.

His Lindsay/Hunter story was all but completed and not due for another week. It was a good thing, for this afternoon his typewriter sat tranquil and his thoughts wandered far afield.

Staring vacantly toward the ceiling, his hand fidgeted unconsciously with his trim brown mustache. Something gnawed at him—what, he couldn't put his finger on. Christian organizations all over the world were amassing assets and holdings worth millions of dollars and were building churches, training centers, colleges, and missions. Nothing so unusual about that.

Then what about the Michaels article troubled him?

Was it the secular tone in which the words were cast? Was it Sondra DeQue's ambiguous reply? Was it the Ms. reference? Was he too puritanical in the modern age of the nineties still to be annoyed at women calling themselves Ms.? Maybe it was the vague "could not be reached for comment." Who was Hamilton B. Jaeger anyway, the shadowy figure behind the scenes of every major Jacob Michaels event?

Jackson's thoughts trailed off in no particular direction.

It had been such a subtle series of fragmentary questions called up into his mind by the *CO&M* article that had for the first time in three weeks recalled to Jackson his conversation with Linda.

"Promise me you'll think about it," she had said.

And he had so promised. Unfortunately he hadn't done so.

Until today. Suddenly, with the article before him, Linda's words raced back out of memory: "If the Lord's behind it, the doors will open."

After finishing his lunch he had walked downstairs to make his inquiry about a Jacob Michaels file. The following afternoon he spent in close contact with the microfilm reader, reviewing two years of stories in *Christian World Magazine* and *The Profile* having to do with Jacob Michaels and his ETW, Inc.

He discovered nothing to relieve the burr stuck under the saddle of his brain: simply factual reports, coverage of evangelistic campaigns, statistical summaries of ETW work throughout the world. Evangelize the World was, on the face of it, carrying out a significant work affecting people the world over. It spent vast sums in what Jackson considered a wasteful manner. But on the other hand, millions went toward seemingly worthy causes— sending radio messages to previously unreached corners of the globe, making monetary donations to distressed nations, training young people to be sent throughout the world with Christian literature, conducting church-organization seminars, and sponsoring innumerable retreats, conferences, and symposiums on various topics. All in all, ETW had compiled an impressive track record.

Finally he picked up his phone and dialed the advertising extension.

"Linda—Jackson here. I've got to talk to you. Have any time tomorrow morning?"

"I can make some. Why?"

"It's the Michaels thing. I have been thinking about it like you told me to. But let's save it for tomorrow."

4

The next morning Jackson Maxwell and Linda Provionni were seated in a small interview room, as private a place as existed at *NWV.*

"Linda," Jackson began immediately, "something's chewing on me."

"Jacob Michaels?"

"Since you brought him up three weeks ago, my subconscious must've been at work, digging up all my old superstar prejudices. Two days ago, I picked up a little article about his organization and really reacted."

"What upset you?"

"I don't know—there was nothing 'wrong.' Just the tone—so much like big business. I followed up by reading a batch of articles and news releases. Actually, they're doing a lot of good, you know."

"I've never really followed him that closely. Just another Billy Graham, isn't he?"

"In many ways, I suppose. But Billy Graham is a transparent man, solidly spiritual in everything he says and does. I admire him. I know he comes under criticism from time to time. But anyone who bothers to look deeply into his personal and family life and his character would easily see the consistency. His life lines up with his message. But with Michaels, the real man never surfaces. It's all organization oriented. And the organization is into some pretty far-reaching stuff—real estate, buildings, schools, radio and TV, businesses, political lobbying. They even own a bank and investment company. At least they don't have a Christian theme park yet, but it seems like they have just about everything else! Billy Graham's vision is evangelism, and that's what he does. But it's different with Michaels—too much a blend of the secular and the sacred. I should say, too much as far as *I'm* concerned."

"I've never thought of that before," said Linda.

"Remember in the seventies when the talk shows were so

popular? And then political involvement became the big thing, The Moral Majority and so on. Now all those divergent approaches are embodied in Jacob Michaels. You've got Graham, Bakker, Robertson, Falwell, Swaggart, Schuller, Humbard, Roberts, and Hal Lindsay all rolled into one. He's preacher, teacher, evangelist, author, popular singer, and prophetic spokesman. He speaks out on politics, investments, the economy, not to mention ideological matters of doctrine and belief, and people take his every word as gospel. He's held in such high esteem he can do or say literally anything he wants and people will follow. How can one man occupy that position and retain his perspective and balance? People eat it up because of who he is. But something is missing. I've read his books. The words are right. But you never find out *who* Jacob Michaels *is*—as a flesh-and-blood human being. We nominate him for Man of the Year—yet do we really *know* the man?"

"Sure, Jackson, but you could say that about dozens of writers. That's their style, they just don't intrude themselves into the forefront. And besides, the other day you were criticizing the public's always wanting to know 'the real person.' "

"I suppose," returned Jackson thoughtfully, then went silent. He opened his mouth to speak again, checked himself, and fell to thinking.

"It's just that . . ." he began once more, probing aloud, "someone in Michaels's position, going around the world speaking as one with God's mandate of authority, should be a person you can trust."

"What can't you trust about him?" asked Linda.

"There we are again. There's *nothing* I can put my finger on exactly."

"Jackson, don't you think you're suffering from the Woodward and Bernstein syndrome, looking for skeletons in the closet?"

"Maybe that goes with being a reporter. I'm not out to undo anyone in a religious Watergate. I'd be satisfied to find Jacob Michaels a sensitive and compassionate man. I just want to know, that's all. I just suddenly find myself drawn to him, and I want to know what sort of man he is."

"I told you before. Get an interview. Find out—on a personal level," said Linda.

"That would be something."

"What have you got to lose?"

"I'd never be granted one," said Jackson. "I've heard the red tape and secretaries and assistants you have to wade through are really something. That is if you can even find out when Michaels is in town. A young unknown reporter like me wouldn't stand a chance."

"But you've got a certain assertiveness that gets you into those sorts of situations. Remember your story on the merger of Zonberg and Voice?"

"My first major story. It was pretty good, wasn't it?"

"You'd have never found out about it before everyone else if you hadn't vigorously taken the offensive and weaseled your way right to the top."

"Linda!" said Jackson. "Are you saying I'm pushy?"

She laughed. "Maybe in a good sort of way. You are sensitive, dedicated to do the upright thing. Yet once your way is clear, watch out. At that point, you become downright forceful."

"An odd mixture, that's me!"

"For a reporter, though, both essential qualities," added Linda.

"If you keep your job long enough!"

"Well, that's true. Just look at me. You've got to mellow the aggressiveness without compromising the dedication—not an easy assignment."

"Hey—I've got to get back. McClanahan's going to have my hide. Thanks for the ear. I needed someone to listen."

5

Though nearly an hour remained before eight, the huge football stadium was already 80 percent filled. The final night of every Jacob Michaels crusade offered something distinctive. Often as many as five or six top-name celebrities were flown in for the occasion. And tonight Fulton County would not be let down.

The low-pitched buzz of anticipation continued to heighten. At length when the announcer walked onstage and reached for the microphone, he had to shout to be heard: "Ladies and gentlemen, welcome to the final night of Jacob Michaels's Atlanta crusade. As you know, it is our custom to make our final evening together memorable, and we want you to participate with us. So won't you begin with a warm Southern welcome to a man whose recently recorded album release shot to the top of all best-selling charts last month, the incomparable Harmon LeCroix and his sister Pamela!"

The stadium echoed with frenzied cheers and applause. The spotlight exploded into brilliance, revealing Harmon at the piano and his sister on stage. Sensing the current of enthusiasm, Harmon opened with a spell-as-you-go cheer. "Give me a J!"

The crowd roared it back.

"Give me an E!" Again the crowd responded, louder this time. He proceeded to spell, "S—U—S!"

"What does it spell?" he yelled into the microphone.

"J—E—S—U—S!" roared the frantic crowd. "Jesus, Jesus, Jesus!"

As the light softened and shifted to Pamela, Harmon began playing on the piano as his sister sang, "Jesus . . . Jesus . . . the name we all sing is Jesus . . . ," and the spectators resumed their seats and slowly quieted.

Following their two numbers the next singer to be introduced went simply by the name Charla, a beautiful five-foot, four-inch, twenty-four-year-old soprano with four successful record albums to her credit. Her ability to blend traditional style with contemporary appeal had given her popularity not only among Christians of varied ages throughout the country but also in the crossover secular market. One number from her praise video had been aired on MTV. She sang two songs, one slow, the other upbeat, at the end of which most present were clapping.

Once again the announcer returned to center stage. As every performer was well known, his introductions were minimal. "Now, ladies and gentlemen, won't you welcome the top-rated religious country-rock group in America today, from Nashville, the Upward Connection!"

Once more the stadium pulsated with wild cheering. The first song was equally vibrant, the drums and loud guitars pumping emotions still higher. Then the group's leader, to introduce the final preliminary number, asked the crowd for silence. "We'd like you all to close your eyes," he said, "and listen intently to the Savior's voice as we sing. Then on the final verse, if you're so led, please join in with us."

The number began, the crowd gradually responded and began to sing as the tone shifted toward an attitude of worship. At its conclusion, thousands of hands were in the air. "Praise the Lord," shouted some, whispered others. "Thank you, Jesus!" "Hallelujah!" The unrestrained exclamations of praise continued for some thirty seconds, brought to an end by the voice of the announcer, once more on stage.

"And now here's the man you've all come to see," the announcer began one final time, "Jacob Michaels!"

Stadium-wide applause rang out, and the evangelist walked briskly onstage under the focus of bright spotlights.

"Thank you!"

The applause continued. "Thank you very much," he said again smiling broadly and waving, both hands in the air. "Thank you!"

Though the spontaneity of the diverse assembly of young and old, rich and poor was unrehearsed in its outbursts, there was yet present, for those with eyes to see it, a carefully orchestrated mass media presentation with Jacob Michaels at its center. Massive television crews were in evidence with cameras and technicians located in every corner of the stadium. The crusade, being shown worldwide, commanded greater viewership than any Super Bowl ever, and its sponsors were hardly oblivious to what that audience signified in dollars.

"I regret my wife could not be with me this week," Michaels was saying, "especially tonight, for we dearly love singing together during these wonderful crusades. Nevertheless, I would like to sing a number for you now which I hope will continue our attitude of worship and will set the tone for my remarks later in the evening."

The orchestra played an introduction followed by Michaels's contemporary country style as he sang:

"Speak to us now, Lord;
    your people are waiting.
Your servant is ready, Lord;
    no need for hesitating.
Give us your word, Lord;
    take us to the mount,
    and show us our new promised land."

The stadium had been darkened as Michaels stood bathed in light on center stage. As he sang, cameras zoomed in for close-ups, side angle shots, and fade-outs. Nothing was left to chance. His tie was perfect, make-up flawless, not a hair askew. The lines of his face were well cut, even handsome, his smile captivating. His black hair, flanked above each ear by conspicuous streaks of gray, blended in distinguished fashion with his tailored blue suit and tan face. All eyes rested upon him, and the effect was powerful.

Jacob Michaels, if such could be said, more closely resembled an evangelical Pope than any other comparison that could be drawn, with a popularity nearly unparalleled in the annals of Christianity. The great evangelists of the nineteenth century had commanded huge followings. But Jacob Michaels's popularity was massively widespread culturally, even in areas with no spiritual inclinations. He was no mere religious powerhouse. His influence extended into politics, world affairs, socioeconomics, and finance. As had been said of Great Britain a century earlier, the sun never set on the empire of Jacob Michaels. His regular Sunday morning television broadcasts had transformed that largely neglected time slot into a commercially viable opportunity for enterprising stations. The national networks fought over rights to his crusades. His financial contributions to worthy causes were always highly publicized in the media and not infrequently amounted to sums greater than entire nations were themselves able to offer.

Never had there been one so like a prophetic spokesman for such a huge majority of Christendom. Following recent meetings with Michaels, the Pontiff himself had declared, "Jacob Michaels is indeed God's man for today. I salute him, his dedication, his organization, and I look forward to working with him to seek healing for the world's distressing problems."

How appropriate was the borrowed truism—when Jacob Michaels spoke, people listened.

The song ended, and Michaels walked to the podium.

"I have a message for you tonight," he began, "which may prove unlike anything you've heard before. A message of hope—a message concerning the future—a message from God. As the words in that song indicated, I do believe God speaks. And upon occasion, He communicates to one man on behalf of many. In the Old Testament are found many instances of God's speaking to His prophets for the benefit of all the people . . ."

As he continued to weave the scriptural basis for his discourse the congregation of tens of thousands sat with eyes transfixed. Michaels's charisma and charm wove a spell on every listener. The introductory music had set a tone, and emotions were now receptive, minds open. The schedule and numbers had not been chosen unintentionally. Everything pointed toward preparing the assembly for Michaels's words. And it had worked with great success.

"And so now in these days," Michaels was saying, "God's voice also breaks through. God still gives certain of His servants messages for the greater body. I believe this is such a time—and I believe I possess such a prophetic manifesto."

He paused momentarily, seeking maximum impact for his words.

"God has shown me in recent months that new times are coming when God will expect us to see the world evangelized. Times are coming when God will expect us to remove barriers between ourselves. I believe God is saying that organizational walls will have to go . . ."

Of course urging unity between Christians and Christian groups was nothing new. Such had been the topic for many a sermon since the 70s. Yet when Jacob Michaels spoke out so definitely, he usually had more in mind than generalities. Especially when he spoke of organizational unity as head of the largest Christian organization in the world.

"The solidification of our talents and resources will become increasingly necessary," he went on, "even merging of them. We are one body, and to achieve the impact in the world, I am certain that may mean a coming together unheard of previously."

He continued for another thirty minutes, speaking indefinitely but with emotion. His presentations were always spellbinding, and tonight was no exception.

"I will be articulating in more specific ways the sort of unity toward which I feel God is leading us in the coming months. But rest assured, new times have arrived. Therefore, expect the new, expect the challenge of untried ideas. Do not reject what seems out of place.

"In conclusion, I would like to remind you that God's voice has broken through to me. I continue to seek Him about what He would have me say to you, to the church of America, and to the world. I recognize I occupy a focal position in which my words are carefully scrutinized. Therefore, I want you to know that when I do speak out and make recommendations, I do so prayerfully and seriously.

"Therefore, in whatever form ensuing messages come to you, whether it be in crusades, radio or television broadcasts, or books, I urge you to consider my words as from the Lord no matter how unprepared at the outset you may be for them. For I will not speak without the confidence that God has prompted me in what I say.

"And now let us join our hearts together, close our eyes, and sing from memory the first verse of that wonderful old chorus 'What a Friend We Have in Jesus.' "

The orchestra began softly, and soon the thousands gathered were singing in unison as the altar call was given. Many walked forward, and several dozen boxes of evangelistic literature were given away.

The stadium was not empty and quiet until well past 2:00 A.M.

6

Elizabeth Michaels turned from the blazing fire and walked back into the kitchen.

The sautéed chicken was about ready. She added the zucchini slices, stirred them, sizzling, in the butter sauce, poured the rice into a boiling pot of water, turned down the burner, and returned once more to the cozy warmth of the living room. Outside, the wind howled and a bitter rain pelted against the window panes.

A perfect night to be home, she thought. Even better that her husband would soon be joining her. Just the two of them, a quiet dinner, his favorite, and then the warm fire. No deadlines, no engagements, no decisions, no reporters, no speeches, no television cameras. This sort of evening had been rare in their marriage.

He'd called to say he'd be home by 7:30. She wandered into the family room to look at the clock. 7:22. She adjusted her dress again, glanced in the mirror, and nervously fidgeted with her hair one last time, then almost as an afterthought hurried into the bedroom and dashed a few small drops of Emeraude, Jacob's favorite perfume, onto her fingers and dabbed them behind her ears.

She wanted this night to be perfect!

"I've got to relax," she told herself. "He's only been gone a week. I've been alone longer many times."

Yet something about this trip had been harder on the evangelist's wife. At forty-nine, the concerns of aging pressed ever closer. The solutions of L'Oreal were needed with increasing frequency. In public, she found herself hiding the brown spots on her hands. More and more she found that the demanding schedule of appointments, photography interviews, charity luncheons, recording sessions, and speaking engagements did not satisfy her. She was finally coming to realize that being a celebrity was not as glamorous as it appeared from the outside.

Elizabeth Michaels craved the affection she had known all too infrequently.

Back in the kitchen, she poured herself a half-glass of Chenin Blanc, turned off the rice, and put the chicken and zuchini on simmer. Then she sank into her favorite chair, took a sip from the glass, and waited.

There had, of course, been compensations. Her marriage to Jacob had been a good one. The early years had been especially happy, when the children were young and before Jacob had hit the spotlight. Before Henry's retirement, they had managed to keep somewhat out of the limelight while still recording albums periodically. But at that point the taxing speaking schedule and enormous financial growth were still in the future.

Yes, she admitted, she missed those early years. But she was not one to hold her husband back. His career was important to her. She was proud to be his wife. He was God's man for these times. She felt fortunate to be allowed to share in such a ministry even if it meant subordinating her personal needs to public demands.

She rose, went back to the kitchen, turned off the skillet, covered both dishes, returned to her chair, laid her head back, and closed her eyes, thinking.

Suddenly, the clock struck eight. She started up, surprised to find she had dozed off. *The wine must've relaxed me too much,* she thought.

She rose and checked the dinner once more; it was growing cold, and the zucchini was getting soggy and limp. She turned the stove on low and stirred both dishes again, then put another piece of wood in the fireplace.

Ten minutes later she heard a car approach up the driveway. The headlights glared momentarily through the curtains, then went black. In another few moments Jacob Michaels came through the door, an icy gust of wind seizing the opportunity to enter with him unbidden.

"Miserable night!" he muttered. "Hello, dear. I'm home."

Elizabeth walked toward him, embraced him firmly, and laid her head on his damp chest.

"What's all this?" said Jacob. "Quite a passionate home-coming!"

"I've missed you," said Elizabeth softly. "I just need to hold you for a minute."

"Yes—well, I missed you too, of course, dear," he said, kissing his wife on the forehead. "But now let me get out of this wet coat." He was caught slightly off guard by her advances.

She released him, feeling a twinge of disappointment, and stepped back. "How was the trip home?" she asked. "When did you get in?"

"The plane touched down at O'Hare about three. We just slid in under this storm." Jacob went immediately to the bedroom, removed his overcoat, suit jacket, and tie, then reemerged. "We've been over at the headquarters since then, Hamilton and I. But that's over, and I'm free tonight and all day tomorrow. How about a sail on the lake if the rain clears?"

"Oh, Jacob, that'd be so nice."

"I'll call and arrange it right now, if the boat's free," he said. "Say, what's cooking?" he went on as he dialed the phone. "Smells delicious."

"Chicken and zuchini. I thought you'd like it on your first night home."

Forty-five minutes later, Jacob Michaels sank comfortably into his favorite overstuffed chair, pulled a footstool nearer, and lifted both feet onto it. His wife put on a light Mozart recording of *Country Dances*.

"Would you like a small glass of wine?" she asked.

"Thank you, dear," he said. "A perfect way to finish off that wonderful meal."

Then she sat on the couch, shoes off, feet hooked back underneath her.

"Ah, Elizabeth, this is the life, isn't it? You and me—nobody else." He sighed deeply and sipped the wine.

Elizabeth smiled faintly. "We should try it more often."

"We will, we really will," he said earnestly. "This hectic pace won't last. It's just that with the acquisitions and plans for the station and the training center and the crusade schedule—it's been a fast-paced time. It'll settle down soon, I promise."

Elizabeth said nothing. How many times throughout the last ten years had she heard those same words? She understood. But she wondered if he did. The lure of importance and power and the clamor of the public she knew would never let up. He was doing God's work—an important man in one of life's high places.

Then, his tone changing, Jacob said, "But I've some news. Remember the transmittal station we were negotiating on? The one in Arizona. The call came in yesterday. Hamilton pulled it off.

With the satellite capability we're planning into the Greenville site, we'll be able to beam radio and television programs anywhere in the world."

Elizabeth smiled.

"And," he went on, "we've managed to add another three hundred twenty-acre parcel adjacent to the Greenville property. That'll enable us to go ahead with the conference and recreational facilities. It's really going to be something! You should see the master plan Hamilton is devising—TV studio, evangelism training center, the Jacob Michaels Foundation University—all there in one place."

"I'm happy for you," said Elizabeth, "and Hamilton."

"Yes, I suppose it is his baby in a way, isn't it?"

She said nothing further. A silence followed.

The fire had burned low. Jacob rose and threw on a fresh birch log. The bark caught with a crackle and burst into flames.

"I was thinking the other day," Elizabeth said at length, "about that time when your father found us after church. Remember?"

"You don't think women are the only ones with nostalgic recollections, do you?"

It had been thirty years before in the Michaels's home in one of the more well-to-do sections of Philadelphia, he the twenty-four-year-old son and heir apparent of the by then famous evangelist Henry Michaels. He had graduated from Temple (with modest marks and taking six years to do so) in sociology two years earlier and had since lived with his parents taking odd jobs in the ministry. Henry's critics enjoyed calling attention to his lounge-about of a son. But Henry steadfastly maintained that "he was just getting a breather before gearing up for seminary."

One Sunday evening before church, the two of them had secured the library to themselves. They were embracing with mounting passion when Henry entered in search of his Bible. He had made no comment at the time beyond a muttered "Excuse me," followed by a hasty exit. But later during the evening meeting at which he spoke coincidentally on the parental obligations to raise up standards of godliness in their children, both Jacob and Elizabeth noted that he seemed to be a little off his usual form.

"I don't think I'd ever seen your poor father so flustered," said Elizabeth with a chuckle.

"It was a wonder he made it through that sermon! What an

oddly timed set of circumstances. But you know, he never mentioned the incident to me. I always expected some kind of verbal drubbing."

"Maybe he hoped you were listening to his words more than a bit casually."

"I don't actually remember what I was thinking as he spoke."

"I do," said Elizabeth with a smile. "We were sitting in the back and could hardly keep our faces straight. You must remember—I had to go to the ladies' room part way through, just to settle the titterbug."

"I do remember now," said Jacob with a hearty laugh. "My poor father! What I must have put him through in those early days."

"But he got his wish, didn't he? The evangelist's son taking up the banner and carrying the message forward."

Elizabeth and Jacob had married several months later, and the following term Jacob entered seminary—to his father's great delight—and soon thereafter predictably received "the call" to the evangelistic pulpit. Nothing could have pleased the sixty-year-old evangelist more than to have his own son follow in his footsteps. Especially so since Jacob's pledge to serve in the family tradition came at the climax of a highly publicized crusade in Los Angeles. Jacob had unexpectedly joined his father at the podium to say a few words and had then, with the aplomb that was to serve him well in later years, made his public declaration to the throng, which had then applauded him enthusiastically.

From that moment on, the sometimes wayward son of one of the country's top religious personalities began to receive much more favorable press. His devout devotion to his studies and wholehearted zeal for the crusade tour life aided his cause. As did his amiable nature and charismatic charm. Nor was his image in any way hindered by a covert positive-publicity thrust conceived by the elder Michaels brother and confidant, Lance, and engineered by his young aide, Hamilton Jaeger. As his brother's business manager until his death in 1969, Lance often found himself in a position to further his brother's cause and, some said, his own in the process, in ways and with means which remained hazily obscure to Henry. That the evangelist himself never caught wind of the efforts of Lance and Hamilton on behalf of Jacob during his early years on the tour after seminary did not imply that they were not eminently successful. It was not many years before Jacob's somewhat rocky start was all but forgotten and the focus of public attention became more and more directed on the son who would inevitably inherit the reins of ETW, Inc., and take it to still greater heights.

And why not? The public loved young Jacob. His recording albums were popular, boosted no doubt by his regular TV appearances during every crusade of his father's, and he would soon author two books—rather hastily written, it is true, and containing more platitudes than serious content—which would sell more than 100,000 each. His career as a public figure and religious spokesman was off to a flying start. Henry eventually retired to his home in the suburbs with his wife. When she died several years later he became more reclusive than ever. But Jacob scarcely took notice.

The silence in the room had grown heavy, both husband and wife lost in their private reminiscences.

"I was lucky to nab you," said Elizabeth. "If I'd have come along any later, you'd have been too hot a commodity for a commoner like me."

Jacob laughed, staring at the fireplace. "I don't know," he said. "Your charm would have won me at any time."

"Hardly!" said Elizabeth with mock seriousness. "I've heard those stories about your days at Temple." Her eyes caught his, teasing. "As much as your father's publicity people tried to hush it up, you were said to be quite a lady's man."

"Aagh!" he growled with a smile. "Vicious rumors! Nose-to-the-grindstone, that was me. I spent my nights in the library."

Another silence followed. Elizabeth had inadvertently stumbled into a known sore spot and regretted it. Now she feared the mood of the evening would be broken. It had been going so well. She and Jacob hadn't talked, really talked, or joked or laughed together for a long time. It had been a good evening. He had seemed relaxed, off guard.

She glanced over at her husband, deep in thought. *Where was he?* she wondered. His eyes were transfixed on the fire, once again dimming to embers. Dare she intrude?

Elizabeth rose, walked over to him, barefoot, and smiled. "It's late—time for bed."

She knelt at his feet and embraced him around the middle,

head on his lap. Emeraude was the one perfume that always used to intoxicate him. She took his hand, stood, and with as inviting a look as she could muster, murmured softly, "The rain's pounding on the roof. It's so cozy inside, and we've been apart for over a week—quite romantic, don't you think? Come to bed with me."

He hesitated momentarily, then said, "Go ahead, dear. I'll be there in a few minutes. I've got some planning to do. There's never enough time during the day. I'll be just a little while . . . wait for me, OK?"

Climbing the softly carpeted staircase, Elizabeth wondered how many times in her married life, especially the last half-dozen years, she had spent solitary evenings or had gone to bed this way, alone. It was undoubtedly well she did not count them. In recent years particularly it had become a pattern for her husband to stay up late, brooding on organizational affairs or preparing a speech or message, and usually when he came to bed Elizabeth was asleep and seldom woke. She tried to say she did not miss the intimacies of their bedroom. Those energies, in any case, had become channeled into other areas years before. But companionship at the close of the day was a warmth a woman cherished. There had been good things about their marriage, but there had been an aloneness too.

Something about this particular night had left Elizabeth with an unaccustomed sense of sadness. Tears filled her eyes and a temptation seized her to return downstairs, to ask that for just one night, at the hour of sleep, she need not be alone.

Then she said to herself, *I'm being silly. Jacob would be kind, but he would never understand.*

7

The early October storm, the first of the season, lasted four days. There was no clearing, and no sail on the lake. It rained all weekend.

Chicago's once posh Bayview district was quiet on Sunday afternoon. Most of the downtown shops had by now adopted the practice of opening for business between noon and five. But the financial district, of which Bayview was a neighborhood reserved primarily for professional offices and executive suites, remained tranquil from Friday night until Monday morning.

Hamilton Jaeger quietly rode the elevator to the sixth floor of the Luxor Towers building, where Evangelize the World, Inc., leased three full floors for the headquarters of their international organization. They had been there since 1959, an arrangement initiated by Lance Michaels when the building was one of the district's finest. He had rented two modest offices on the fifth floor, one for himself, one for his brother. His consideration at the time was that a growing ministry such as ETW should occupy a prestigious address. Such could only heighten its esteem in the public eye, which would encourage—he hoped—generous donations.

Through the years, as ETW had mushroomed, it had gradually taken over the entire fourth, fifth, and sixth floors, one section at a time. Three decades earlier the seventeen-story, reinforced concrete Luxor building had been modern and fashionable. Top flight brokerage firms and advertising agencies resided there, some occupying more than one floor. Now, however, like other structures of its era, the signs of seediness were becoming apparent, and a number of the first-class tenants had moved on to newer buildings. But though aging, the Luxor remained on the edge of Chicago's most exclusive lakefront property and continued to suit the organization's needs, a decision inestimably aided by the fact that now both Jaeger and Michaels themselves possessed a stake in the conglomerate ownership of the building.

Jaeger exited the elevator and walked crisply to his office and unlocked the door. His walk and appearance, down to his closely-cropped short hair and well-pressed slacks, spoke of his deft, nononsense approach to life.

With military precision, he flipped on the lights, turned on the coffee pot, and sat down at his desk—not to relax, but to get organized. He was not a man who *ever* relaxed.

There was much to do. The architect for Greenville would be in town to see him next week. Then he had to fly to Phoenix on the twenty-third to conclude the escrow arrangements on the transmittal station. Then of course there were the financial considerations to review. And though months away, he knew it was not premature for advance preparations for the meeting scheduled for March 18 with Senator Montgomery. He glanced down at his calendar at the date. "DC-JM-9AM" was all it read. Best it remain that way for the present. Not even his secretary need know. The trip to Washington was ostensibly, and in fact, to make final preparations for an ETW crusade in early summer and had been on his docket for months. The private brunch with Jake was merely an unpublicized meeting with an old friend. For the moment, if anyone asked, it was just a renewal of an old acquaintance. No need to mention the subject of their discussion.

His thoughts turned to finances once again.

He reached for the thick black ledger and thumbed through it. Here was ETW. For him, this ledger told the story. For one such as Jacob Michaels, the financial balance sheets, projections, charts, and various funds amounted to nothing but accounting mumbo jumbo. But to one such as Hamilton Jaeger, they were the bread and butter, meat and potatoes all rolled into one. Five minutes with a financial statement and Hamilton Jaeger could distill the relative health or instability of any organization—be it profit or nonprofit.

He was thus particularly well suited for his present position in the Michaels camp. Not an accountant himself, he yet grasped enough of the spiritual vision on the one hand and the nuts and bolts of finances on the other to bridge the gap with unusual resourcefulness. He interpreted spiritual direction from above to the accountants, directing them in the handling of the money itself. And he interpreted the monetary jargon to Jacob Michaels in a way he could understand, without bothering him with every petty detail.

In short, Hamilton Jaeger occupied a position of great responsibility and power in ETW. He sat at the fulcrum of a vast empire that now exceeded half a billion dollars. And no one perceived the inner workings of that domain quite as he did.

The Greenville acquisitions represented the summum bonum of his career. For years he had dreamed of an expansive property that could house many facilities and become the headquarters of a greatly upgraded ETW from which any number of additional ministries could be launched. He thought back to the many successful Christian groups providing spark and substance to his vision—Campus Crusade, PTL, ORU, CBN's Virginia Beach complex, YWAM. But now he envisioned something beside which the efforts of all those paled in comparison: an enormous complex that ultimately could serve not merely as the headquarters for one Christian organization but as the center and heartbeat for organized evangelical Christianity itself.

His mind soared with the possibilities!

He poured himself a cup of special imported Gevalia coffee blend as he continued to ruminate on how far the concept had come.

He had initially conceived of the Greenville Project more than ten years earlier. At first, he'd said nothing to Jacob other than gradual hints that ETW should "expand and diversify" its holdings in order to broaden the basis for ministry. Sensing Jacob's progressive acquiescence, he quietly directed that purchases be made, which he considered first-rate investments. Thus over the years ETW had proliferated. They'd bought out dying Christian radio stations and revitalized them. Jaeger had organized the purchase of several nonprofit Christian businesses, nursing homes, schools, conference centers, and the like and had turned them into efficiently run and profitable operations. Simultaneously he had begun setting money in reserve for the purchase of raw land to one day house his dream. Jacob had been brought along slowly enough and skillfully enough that Hamilton was able to subtly carry himself as though the whole concept of a unified Christian center of ministry was Jacob's idea rather than his own.

At every step of the way, he had been discreet so as not to attract too much public interest. His motives, after all, were noble. But the public would have a difficult time understanding the complexity of what he was trying to do and his methods for achieving those goals. He saw no need to add confusion to the situation.

At the same time, most of the enterprises purchased began

to flourish under his leadership. Many which remained officially nonprofit did so well in fact that he had to ingeniously devise methods to adjust the books so that the ledger always showed no profit where none was supposed to exist. The IRS was happy; all the legalities were strictly observed. ETW's accountants were happy, confident that high spiritual concerns dictated the motives behind every decision and never questioning the legitimacy of certain creative bookkeeping operations. And Jacob Michaels was happy, knowing from the reports reaching him that ETW was broadening its field of service to the community, the Christian body, and the world.

Meanwhile ETW thrived. The various businesses prospered. Donations had never been higher. Crusade attendance was soaring. Television audiences were attracting a greater and greater percentage of total viewership, enhancing advertising contracts. Jacob Michaels's books and records (boosted by frequent TV plugs) were selling in the hundreds of thousands and significantly added to the total revenue.

As Jaeger rocked back in his high-leathered chair and sipped his coffee, his thoughts were not so much occupied with obtaining the capital to realize the scope of his dream. Rather his concern was how to utilize the funds he knew were available. Nonprofit status often involved walking a financial tightrope between regulation and suicide. Thus far he had managed to see that ETW prospered while keeping inside the law. But doing so was ever a more complex undertaking. Greenville was the biggest game he had tackled yet. He would have to be sure of himself. The reserve account, the contingency fund, the discussion with Jake—it all tied in.

He thumbed through the ledger further, paying special attention to the various "Cash in Bank" entries under the assets section. Then there were the several "Assets in Reserve" accounts that could be activated. There was a way. It could all be done—Greenville, Phoenix, and the scheme involving Jake. He just had to find the most expedient method to draw the strings together.

But he had to be particularly wary. The press had been on them recently. More and more they were noting ETW's widening spheres of endeavor and using the opportunity to take potshots at Jacob's motives. They'd like nothing better than to make media hay over what looked like a financial blunder. They wouldn't care how accurate their charges were. If it made a good story, that's all they cared about.

The CO&M *article didn't help the image much,* reflected Jaeger. True, it had been factual enough. The total assets *did* now exceed $500,000,000. But that was only one side. What about the liabilities? The printed figure by no means signified ETW's worth as anything close to it. Like most news stories, it implied a monetary motive without making the charge openly. That irritated Jaeger. The article was well disguised as objective reporting, simply a statistical summary of where things stood. But the insinuation was clear—that ETW was pulling down millions in profit and expanding like any other multinational corporation.

The press! Distorted half-truths—always focusing on the sensational aspects of the news—sniffing everywhere for scandal and wrongdoing—creating it by innuendo if no facts were forthcoming. Anything for a story! Glossing over or ignoring serious points made in briefings or press conferences—operating on its own double standard.

Jaeger set down his cup and stood up. He walked about his office and slammed the fist of his right hand into his open left as his lips exploded in an unuttered expletive.

He resented it!

Evangelize the World was out to evangelize. But in this complex world where money was the oil that ran the machinery there wasn't any other way to accomplish it than with huge amounts of capital. Money didn't grow on trees, even for Jacob Michaels. It had to come from somewhere. That was his job!

Why couldn't the press appreciate what they were trying to do? He could understand secular news services running statistical and biased reports. But Christian magazines? They were doing a disservice to the cause!

Still, there they were. And he had to find a way to work around them while maintaining his positive public demeanor.

Calming, Jaeger returned to his chair and once more picked up his cup of coffee. The next two years would be pivotal, he thought. If they could make it through this transition period, get the Christian public used to the idea, get the miscellaneous balls rolling before anyone really knew what was up, then by the time they stopped to wonder, they'd have become sufficiently accustomed to the whole thing never to question its motive.

"I've got to maintain a tighter rein on Sondra," he mused. More sticky articles could be on the way. He had to know what she was going to say in advance. More, he had to gain a greater control over what she said. But plenty of time for that.

He downed the remainder of his lukewarm coffee, rose, and briskly strode to the drafting table. There a 24 x 36-inch sheet revealing his master plan for Greenville awaited him. He sat down on the stool, picked up a sharpened pencil, and went to work.

He remained alone in his office far into the evening.

8

Meanwhile, in another corner of the Luxor, one floor down, another was quietly engaged this Sunday evening in the affairs of ETW. That which occupied the heart and mind of one Robert Means, however, was business the likes of Hamilton Jaeger, notwithstanding his expertise with money, ledgers, and blueprints, could never begin to understand.

Never considered much of a good churchman, Means often retired on Sundays to the quietness of his office, there to conduct not the business of ETW, as he did the rest of the week, but the business of the Sabbath. He was one of those few souls who found true worship a thing easier to grasp in aloneness with his Master than in conglomeration with two or three hundred other hearts less hungry than his own.

On this particular Sunday, as he sat in a threadbare easy chair in one corner of the small room, his well-worn Bible in his lap, a sheaf of papers upon which he had been jotting down notes lying on the coffee table to his right, the eyes of Robert Means stared blankly ahead. He had been trying to study but could not keep his mind focused on the Scriptures he had been attempting to decipher. The commentary on the gospel of Mark lay open on the table where he had set it an hour ago. He could not think about the old evangelist's gospel just now. His heart was heavy with matters much closer to home.

Something was wrong.

He had had misgivings about the direction of ETW for years. But lately a sense of urgency had crept into his prayers, an indescribable feeling that things were about to go badly wrong, that suddenly far more was at stake than at any time in the past. It was nothing he could put his finger on. And of course he wasn't close enough to the centers of power to have the slightest notion that would give substance to these recent qualms. But he had learned over the years to trust the quiet whisperings of the Spirit. And thus he did not take this present foreboding lightly but rather with a deep sense of prayerful caution and vigilance.

Means had been with ETW almost as long as Jacob Michaels himself. The two had practically grown up together, and even though Jacob had been the heir of the empire, he and young Robert had been full coequals in nearly everything during their early years. Roommates at Temple, the two had lived together, studied together, planned and schemed and dreamed together—and even upon occasion prayed together. They had been young, and neither had possessed what could be called a developed faith. Yet Robert had, even then, been seeking to deepen his own spiritual roots. There were times when the two would fully open their hearts to one another and each would share his dreams, his worries, his hurts. And when they did pray together at such moments, the communion was genuine, for they truly loved one another in a way in which only young men can.

It had been only natural, then, for Means to join ETW also, and during their first years on its staff together, despite the fact that Jacob was the heir and Robert a mere hireling, their friendship continued. Robert believed in his friend and was gratified to both serve with him and be his servant as well. He saw God at work in Jacob and truly prayed that ETW might be effective in doing what its name proclaimed.

For the first several years following Jacob's dramatic announcement of his "call" in Los Angeles, Robert had been his assistant and valet and man Friday all rolled into one. Even though the public had never heard of Robert Means, in private Jacob always talked about his hopes for the future as if the whole thing was a joint effort. It was always "we," never just Jacob alone. The two of them would rise side by side, just as it used to be, brothers and friends and fellow warriors in the Lord's army!

There was one in ETW, however, who was not so enthusiastic about the presence of Robert Means so near the apex of power. That one was Hamilton Jaeger, assistant to the late Lance Michaels and at that time assistant to Henry Michaels. There could be room for but one trusted lieutenant who had the Michaels's ear. Jaeger was determined that that one should be he. As he had served Lance as a faithful private and as he was then serving Henry as a seasoned captain, he was even then looking ahead to the day when he would rise to the summit of his generalship in service to the rising next Michaels generation. As Jacob's right-hand man, he would stake his claim to destiny. He would not have that destiny undermined by divided loyalties or by influence he could not twist to serve his own purposes. Somehow he sensed in young Robert Means a hidden strength he would never be able to dominate, and in his heart he determined to remove him from proximity to the reins that guided ETW.

No one could say exactly how Means's gradual distancing from his friend had been effected. The process had been so slow and cunningly devised that not even Jacob was aware of it. A string of secretaries were brought in for Jacob, which initially served to lessen his dependence on Robert. One thing led to another, with the result that Means was taken out of the loop of meaningful work. As the years progressed Jacob and Means saw less and less of one another, and as Jacob rose more and more into the spotlight, Robert was shunted further and further off onto insignificant sidetracks within the huge corporate structure.

Neither man ever realized what had happened. Robert took the changes with grace and humility, never doubting for an instant Jacob's intentions nor doubting the necessity of the different directions things had now begun to move. He lived in the reality of the words of the Baptist, "He must increase, I must decrease," and continued to view himself as not only the Lord's servant but also the servant of Jacob Michaels, his friend.

Years went by. When the two men met in the hall or saw one another from a distance, Robert had to admit the old sparkle of friendship just didn't seem to be there. A few times he tried to strike up a conversation, to rekindle the common vision. There were hints at such moments that the old love still was alive someplace. But sadly for Robert, those hints were all too infrequent and came as irregular intersections of divergent lifepaths. In his deepest heart he feared he and Jacob were moving in different directions. Once or twice he sought out Jacob's office, hoping perhaps they could pray together. But after being told to schedule an appointment, the first available slot being two weeks away, he went away disheartened. He told the secretary to tell Mr. Michaels he had been by and to call if he wanted to see him. But no call came. How was Robert to know that the message had been intercepted by Hamilton Jaeger with the words "No need to mention this to Jacob. I'll see to it myself."

Robert occasionally thought of leaving ETW. Yet he still believed in world evangelism as the cause to which he had chosen to dedicate his life as a Christian. And he still believed in ETW, and in Jacob Michaels. True, he was himself not out in the forefront where lives were being impacted by the thousand. But he had enough of a servant's heart to realize that the work of managing an organization the size of ETW required hundreds of small people doing invisible jobs. All taken together, everyone was involved in the vision. All parts of the body worked in harmony, from the visible and significant down to the man or woman who pushed a broom or emptied the trash. He knew the lesson of 1 Corinthians 12 concerning the body, and he was not so proud as to covet recognition or to resent being one of the little people behind the scenes.

So he had remained with ETW all these years, quietly doing the jobs that had been given him, believing in the cause, believing in Jacob, and believing that he was an intrinsic part, however small, in an effort that was out in the forefront of carrying out Christ's Great Commission.

In actual fact, Robert Means was not at all a small or insignificant part of ETW. He—along with scattered others here and there, mostly unseen—had helped to hold the fabric of the structure together over the years. For along with everything else he had done, Robert Means had learned to pray. And years of practice had made him a warrior on that ancient and unseen battlefield.

As he had prayed for Jacob and the entire staff, and for the direction of ETW, for probably five to ten years now Robert had sensed hints of disquiet in his heart. He had continued to pray, and continued to lift up his old friend. But although he had grown profoundly through the experience, he could not feel that he was any nearer to understanding what the Lord might be trying to direct through his prayers.

Now, in just the last couple of months, the burden had grown suddenly heavier. This Sunday, as he sat in his chair staring straight ahead, his Bible study on Mark all but forgotten, the only thing he could think was that something was at hand. A change was coming.

His spirit felt heavy. Thunderclouds were approaching, and he feared Jacob stood directly in their path. Rarely had he felt such a prayerful weight on behalf of his old friend as he did this present hour. He drew in a deep breath, then let out a long sigh. There was only one thing to be done, and he had delayed it too long already.

He took his Bible from his lap and set it on top of the papers on the table, then slid from the chair onto his knees. Even as the man who had relegated him to this insignificant office to answer correspondence all day long was scheming with plans and calculator and numbers one floor above, Robert Means clasped his hands, bowed his head, and began to pray.

"Oh, God," he whispered, "I have no words, only a heavy heart full of compassion and concern for Jacob. Accomplish Your purposes within his life, Lord God. Open his heart to You and all You would do not only through him but within him. Perform Your surgery in his soul. Draw him deeper and deeper into communion with You, Father. Whatever influences You are bringing into his life toward this end, may he be receptive to them. Open his heart and mind to receive the fullness of all You have prepared for him. Do Your work in his life, Lord."

He paused, sighed again, then continued.

"Do Your work in *my* life, Lord. Accomplish Your pruning and purifying work in my heart. And to whatever extent You ordain that I be a part of the answer to this prayer I have prayed for Jacob, O God, I am willing and eager. Reestablish brotherhood between us, heavenly Father! Let me be not only his servant but once again his friend."

His lips fell silent.

For a long while, however, the knees of Robert Means remained bent to the floor. He stayed in the building late into the evening. But when he left, the gleam in his eye and the warmth in his heart were of distinctly different origins than those in the eye and heart of Hamilton Jaeger.

9

"There are limits."

"What specifically, then, would you suggest we do?" asked Michaels.

"That's hard to say. On the one hand, we do need to cultivate better relations with the religious media. But on the other, when you get too intimate—"

"Hamilton, for pete's sake! That's one reason we have the press on our backs. You and Sondra and sometimes I think the whole PR staff talk around issues so much you never say a thing."

"It's just that we have to be careful. There are two sides to this—lots of options. We have to choose our moments for openness while guarding our privacy."

"Why do we have to guard our privacy I want to know, Hamilton? What do we have to be private about? We have no secrets."

"It's just that in an organization of this size, the decision-making process is a delicate matter. We have to retain some degree of seclusion here, especially at the top where policy originates. I mean just look at this Dallas situation. If we leaked our plans at this point, the locals would be up in arms. Other Texas-based ministries would become immediately defensive. There'd be a move to block us from coming. Certainly, Jacob, you see the complications involved?"

"I see it—partially. Still, if what we want to set up is a center for Christian ministries and communications, for heaven's sake, we're hardly helping our cause by being closed mouthed and *not* communicating about it."

"The problem is that things get blown out of proportion when only part of the story comes out. I needn't remind you, do I, of the occasional—should I say, expediency—of not telling all?"

He looked at his companion intently. Michaels glanced up, then his eyes sought the window for an escape as a moment of silence followed. Maybe he did need reminding. How he despised Hamilton's bearing.

"That is not to say, of course," Jaeger continued, "that there aren't times for frankness. It's just that you have to select them with precision. The press must be coddled, led, used, so that their reporting works to our advantage as well as their own. You remember the trouble Nixon had with the press. So much of it could have been avoided if he'd taken the time to utilize—"

"I understand, Hamilton," interrupted Michaels, able to tolerate no more of the other's soft-spoken argument. "I trust your judgment. I'll leave it in your hands—what to tell, and when."

Just then the intercom sounded in the office.

"Yes, what is it, Liz?"

"Mr. Jaeger's secretary just rang me. He has a telephone call— long distance—Washington. I thought he ought to know."

He glanced over at Jaeger. "Tell her I'll be right there," said Jaeger. "It shouldn't take but a minute. Then I'll be back. I really think, Jacob, we ought to nail down some specific news releases so we can remain coordinated."

"Fine, Hamilton, I'll be here," said Michaels without enthusiasm.

Jacob sat down on the couch bordering one wall of his spacious office. Outside the picture window, Chicago was bustling with activity. Beyond, the lake was made barely visible from the afternoon lifting of the clouds. Maybe the rain would finally let up.

In the privacy of his office he took a deep breath and exhaled slowly. With no cameras, no crowd, and no microphones to demand from him inspirational vigor and cheerful bouyancy he could now let down. It felt good not to smile for a change. At fifty-three, the years were starting to tell on him. Still a trim figure with an athletic six-foot one-inch, 190-pound build, his face nevertheless bore traces of the strain that usually accompanies a fast-paced, successful life.

He laid his head back on the cushion and fell to thinking. He found pensive moods coming more and more frequently these days. Why, he wondered, couldn't the press and other Christian ministries handle the size and expansion of ETW? Why was money always a stumbling block? Just once he'd like to level with everyone—put all the cards on the table and call on brotherly trust to carry the day.

Unrealistic? Perhaps.

Hamilton was right. The press did twist the truth. Maybe not intentionally. It just happened. Pure statistics, without the meaning behind them, could be devastating.

Just then the buzzer sounded once more.

"You're wife on the phone, sir."

"Thank you, I'll take it . . . Hello, dear," he said into the phone a moment later.

"Jacob," said Elizabeth on the other end, "I was just wondering when you'll be home tonight?"

"Why, anything special going on? I didn't forget an engagement, did I?"

"Oh, no. I just thought maybe we could have dinner together. You'll be heading for Seattle in a few days. There aren't many times left—"

"That sounds good. How about seven? I'll be home by then. On second thought, make it seven-thirty."

"Promise? Hamilton will try to keep you later."

"I can handle him. Yes—I promise."

"I love you, Jacob."

He returned to the couch and fell to musing about their marriage. It had been a busy one. Too busy, he had to admit. Now that the children were grown, he regretted he hadn't given them more. And he wished he'd given Elizabeth more, too. But with her there was still time. Maybe tonight!

Hamilton walked brusquely back into the room unannounced, interrupting Jacob's reverie. "Now, where were we?" he said, then went on without waiting for Jacob's reply, "I really think we need some mode of attack on this publicity difficulty. If Greenville's going to be accepted by a wide cross section of the religious community, we need to introduce it gradually, on our terms. What I've been considering—"

"Hamilton," interrupted Michaels, "I think you're overreacting. There is no publicity difficulty, as you put it. And besides—I'm not in the frame of mind right now to come up with a publicity campaign."

"But," insisted the other, "the news is already leaking out, and we must retain control of the manner in which—"

"Just take care of it, Hamilton. I don't care how. You don't have to tell me the details. Use the means you think best to make it come off like we want. Just don't exaggerate it out of proportion."

"I understand."

Once more the intercom sounded. "I'm sorry to interrupt you again, sir."

"That's fine, Liz," said Michaels, "what is it?"

"There's a young reporter here, by the name of Maxwell. I told him you didn't consent to interviews without some sort of prior arrangement, but he's quite insistent about scheduling something. Any chance you'd want to make an appointment after the Seattle trip?"

Jacob glanced hurriedly at Jaeger vehemently shaking his head. He turned his eyes toward the window and sighed, trying to scan the pros and cons. Something in his mind told him there had to be a change. He swung back around and in an uncharacteristic moment of hasty decision, began to straighten his tie and said to his secretary, "Show him in, Liz."

"But, Jacob," Jaeger implored, "this is no way to—"

"It's all right, Hamilton. I'll be reserved. What better way to improve relations with the press than to demonstrate that we're available and have nothing to hide?"

"Sir, I simply must urge you to reconsider. This is no time to—"

"Too late, Hamilton, I've made up my mind. Besides here comes the young gentleman now."

The heavy birch door opened and in walked Jackson Maxwell, hesitant at so unexpectedly finding himself in Jacob Michaels's office. This was fortuitous beyond his wildest hopes.

He hid his awkwardness, sucked in deeply, marched forward with what he hoped would be viewed as an air of confidence, and extended his hand. "Sir, I'm Jackson Maxwell from *News with a*

Vision. I appreciate your seeing me."

"Certainly, son," returned Michaels with his most polished professionalism. "I'm happy to meet you. Those of us involved in public ministry owe a great debt to the religious media, especially to fine magazines and newspapers such as yours."

"Thank you, sir," returned Jackson warily. He vowed to be on guard and not be taken in by soothing words. "We try to faithfully promote God's truths."

"And a fine job you do, I might add," said Michaels. "We're all behind you—oh, forgive me, Mr. Maxwell, this is my associate Hamilton Jaeger."

The two shook hands with stiff formality, Jaeger forcing a smile, Jackson sensing the reluctance on the edge of his grasp.

"Now, Mr. Maxwell, what can we do for you? Would you care for some coffee?" asked his host.

"Thank you, no," answered the reporter. "I'm considering a possible feature story, maybe a couple of stories, having to do with the preparation for the Chicago crusade in the spring. I just wanted to meet you and ask if you'd be willing to work with me."

"That sounds fine, Mr. Maxwell. May I call you Jackson? Now, Jackson, is it community preparation, involvement of the local churches, and that sort of thing you're interested in? If so, I'm certain Hamilton here—"

He glanced over at Jaeger with a sweeping gesture of his arm.

"—could readily supply you with the files and back-stories. We go about this pretty much the same everywhere. Works quite well."

Jaeger, visibly relieved at the nonthreatening direction the interview seemed to be heading nodded his assent, smiling for the first time.

"Well," said Jackson, "that would of course be helpful. And I certainly appreciate your willingness to cooperate. However, I was hoping for an 'inside look,' so to speak, at *your* arrangements. Something different, something the public hasn't heard before."

The two older men flashed a brief glance toward one another, each probing the other's eyes for some hint of where to proceed.

"I don't know," began Michaels slowly. "Of course we could probably have our PR staff put together something like that. If I could just refer you to—"

"I'm wondering, Mr. Michaels," pressed Jackson, "whether you wouldn't be agreeable to simply letting me ask some questions and we could see where it went?"

"I suppose—" he hesitated, cleared his throat. "Yes, I think that would be all right. Sure, go ahead, Jackson."

"Thank you, sir. One of the first things that comes to mind is finances. It obviously takes staggering capital to stage a major city evangelistic crusade?"

"Yes, certainly. We do rely on local volunteers to a great extent. All the counseling is done by church people from the area. That cuts down on the costs for personnel."

"There's your staff though, quite large I understand. And the rent for facilities must be gigantic—a week in the city's largest stadium?"

"That's where the faithfulness of our thousands of generous supporters comes in. If it weren't for them we'd never be able to carry on the work we do."

Michaels was conducting himself in his most genial manner.

"I wanted to ask you about that," said Jackson, turning a leaf of his notebook, beginning to tire of the pat formulas he was being fed. He decided to push a bit harder. "Is there any correlation between specific gifts and specific expenditures? What I mean is, do people earmark their donations in order to assist with a specified campaign, so that when it is all over you know where you stand, in the red or the black, as far as a certain crusade is concerned with respect to the giving that has come in explicitly on its behalf?"

"Not in a precise way. You see, there is so much overlap in what we do that there's not always an attempt to differentiate every expense item."

"In other words, the donations all go into the coffers, and then the money is spent wherever needed?"

"That's something like how it works."

"So if a lady here in Chicago, say, wanted to do something to help your upcoming crusade here and sent you one hundred dollars, she would have no way of really knowing whether her money was spent to further the gospel here in Illinois, or whether it went somewhere else, to publish a book perhaps, or—maybe to buy some land in Texas?"

Jaeger shifted uncomfortably in his chair, then said, "Really, young man, I fail to see what bearing all this has on our preparations for—"

"It's all right, Hamilton," said Michaels. "Mr. Maxwell is asking a legitimate question." Then, smiling broadly, he turned toward Jackson and went on. "You see, Jackson, in a strict way, what you've said is correct. But at the same time, neither would your imaginary lady know that her money was *not* being spent right here. What you must remember is that the people who give are doing so because of their faith in us to represent the Lord's ways in all we do. So that lady's money is used to further the gospel, wherever it goes."

"My point is," insisted Jackson, bearing down to make his point, "what happens if there is *more* donated for Chicago than is actually spent there? In a case such as that, many people would be donating to causes they might know nothing about, possibly didn't even support."

Michaels forced another smile, then answered. "Yes, but Jackson, you see those people aren't giving *just* for the Chicago crusade, they're donating to the ministry, to see God's Word spread in many ways and in many places."

"I'm sure that's often true. And that's fine, Mr. Michaels, as long as that is a person's intent. But what about those people who feel they're giving to a distinct phase of ministry to further the gospel in a certain locale? What I'm concerned about is the ambiguity involved here. Just a few days ago I heard of your radio ads asking for money—"

"I would not say we were *asking* for money," interposed Jaeger half rising again.

With exasperation Jackson glanced his way, then said, "Well, whatever you want to call it, what was said was something to the effect of, 'Let us bring morality back to the community with your donations—' "

He paused and looked at the other two momentarily.

"—and that certainly contains the implication that you intend to use people's money in response to that ad for Chicago only. Now you're telling me otherwise. It seems a trifle deceptive to me."

"I can assure you," began Michaels, then stopped briefly, choosing his words with care. But before he could continue Jackson began once more.

"And this raises another point. That is, if you have what might be labeled a 'General Fund' where the proceeds of all your various enterprises land, what guidelines are there for each specific aspect of it?"

"I'm afraid I don't follow you."

"For instance, say you publish a book. Then over here you operate a school. You conduct evangelistic crusades. There are a number of businesses. You regularly send donations to many mission organizations. On the other hand, you are involved in certain investments that I would think bring in substantial dollars. I understand some of your enterprises are quite lucrative and in fact have provided the capital for the rapid expansion of the past several years."

"Well, yes, the Lord has prospered us for our faithfulness."

"What I'm getting at is, aren't some of these things actually making a profit? Don't some of the crusades actually come out significantly ahead when you tally up giving alongside actual expenses incurred?"

"Again, it's very difficult to ascertain that precisely. Hamilton," he said, turning to the other, "would you perhaps like to try to shed a little light on Mr. Maxwell's question?"

Michaels sat down, visibly relieved to be spared the hot seat momentarily.

"Mr. Maxwell," Jaeger began, "it is not customarily our policy to talk about finances in such a manner. We quarterly publish a complete financial statement which details everything very thoroughly and is available to the public—"

"Yes, Mr. Jaeger, I obtained a copy before coming," Maxwell said with a touch of sarcasm. "Yet I must say it was reduced to such broad generalizations that there was hardly much concrete information to be gained from it."

"Really, young man," Jaeger shot back, running low on reserve, "we allowed this interview with the understanding that we'd be discussing preparation for the upcoming crusade. In an organization of this size, we cannot hope to convey to you the delicacy of certain negotiations and the methods by which our accounting is done. There is nothing either side could hope to gain by going into it in more detail. With your background, it would be impossible for you—"

"Excuse me, Mr. Jaeger," interrupted Jackson with rising

boldness. "I'm sure you're probably right. But let me just ask again, how do you, as a nonprofit organization so highly dependent on donations from thousands of people, justify that many facets of your operation do in fact bear considerable monetary fruit?"

"You have to look at the total picture, which you're refusing to do."

"I'm trying, Mr. Jaeger," said Jackson, his face reddening. "All I want to know is how you can spend money for one thing when the person giving it may have intended it to go elsewhere?"

"I tell you, Maxwell, the question's too complex for a simplistic answer!"

"It would appear, from one perspective, that you are using the gifts of persons who think they are contributing to God's work in one area to expand your holdings and profitmaking ventures in others."

"Your statement smacks of accusation, Mr. Maxwell! If you are hinting that anything unethical is going on, I can assure you—"

"Hamilton," said Michaels, rising calmly and smiling amiably, "Mr. Maxwell intends nothing of the sort. He is just letting his reporter's imaginative spirit get the best of him." Then turning to Jackson, he said, "Let me say this, Jackson, your line of inquiry is interesting—*if* you were reviewing a secular corporation whose motive was the profit line. But we all know such is not the case here. Even if we do show—I use the term advisedly—a 'profit' occasionally from some particular phase of ministry, the determining factor for nonprofit status is the whole complete spectrum of endeavor. I can affirm that we work very closely with the IRS, on a very congenial level I might add, to maintain our rigid adherence to their standards. And Hamilton here," he laughed good-humoredly, "though perhaps a bit high-strung when talking to reporters, is as fine and upstanding a financial adviser as I could imagine having."

"I'm sure of that, sir," said Jackson, "and I apologize for any intimation to the contrary on my part. My intent is not to snoop around for something amiss. I simply thought an 'angle' for my story might be to follow a monetary donation for the purpose of helping a certain community through from start to finish. But it appears my idea isn't possible since such a would-be gift might as well be spent financing rent on this office, your next record album, or a chunk of ground outside Greenville."

Jaeger sprang from his chair. "Mr. Maxwell, your insinuation is not taken lightly!"

"No insinuation intended," said Jackson calmly, but with a hint of arrogance in his voice.

"If people heard that sort of thing, with the obvious bias you seem to be taking, it would be—it *is*—simply distortion. And how did you hear about Greenville? The site location was never revealed to the press."

"I called a friend on the staff of *CO&M*. Someone there knew, though they weren't allowed to use the information in their story."

"On my direct orders! And I forbid you to reveal it also. You could compromise—"

"Forbid! Mr. Jaeger?" said Jackson, nearly losing himself. Hamilton Jaeger's attitude was beginning to unnerve him. "I needn't remind you that the press has complete freedom to print the truth."

"Gentlemen, gentlemen!" said Michaels in a slow-paced tone. "No need for raising our voices. We're all brothers here, on the same side. Hamilton, sit down, calm yourself. Mr. Maxwell here will be discreet. He understands our position." He glanced at Jackson with a friendly nod, as if to confirm his words.

"Mr. Maxwell," he resumed, "you do grasp our need, at least temporarily, for some measure of confidentiality on this thing? I can assure you we'll contact you when we're ready to release more details." Then glancing at his watch, "It's getting late. I'm sorry, Jackson, Hamilton and I have a meeting to get to. If you'll excuse us we are going to have to call an end to this most productive interview."

"I understand, sir," said Jackson rising, concealing his frustration while he gathered his notepad and jacket. "I thank you for your time and seeing me unscheduled like this. You've been very gracious."

"Any time, Jackson, any time. And we'd be happy to help further with that article of yours, as long as we can steer clear of finances." He laughed good-humoredly, but with a trace of nervousness in the tone. "Make an appointment with my secretary. We'll see if we can't put something together for you on a different sort of 'inside' look at campaign proceedings."

10

Jackson was upset.

No doubt he'd sabotaged his sole opportunity for possible future interviews with Jacob Michaels.

If only Jaeger hadn't been there! He was certainly a live one.

Of course his own line of questioning had precipitated the heated tone, and he chastised himself for going too far. He hadn't intended it.

Jackson took his time getting back to the office, driving along the lakefront, then parking for a while, just to think. The sun was out, and joggers, taking advantage of the opportunity, had swarmed to the park's trails and the nearby streets.

Why were Michaels and Hamilton so jittery about a discussion of finances? Could there really be something shady going on? He doubted it. But if Michaels's designs were honorable, then why so closemouthed? Didn't honesty demand openness? Wasn't truth compromised by secrecy in any form?

Instinct told Jackson he was onto something, possibly even a major story, though at this point it was totally shapeless and insubstantial. As he reflected he admitted that there were problems with trying to pursue it. After the disquieting interview he really had no idea what he might be looking for. Then there was the practical matter of his regular assignments, which limited the time available for a nebulous quest "inside" the hallowed walls of ETW. Making it even more difficult was the fact that he had not confided in anyone yet. Ordinarily a reasonable man, his editor was nonetheless caught in the bind of constant deadlines, which created an unending mad rush for results. It was sometimes difficult for him to understand that finesse and patience were important tools for a good writer.

Jackson started up the engine of his subcompact Ford and headed back to the office.

It was time to tell McClanahan.

"You did what!" boomed the editor.

"I went to interview Jacob Michaels," said Jackson once more.

"And what did his secretary say? Did she give you an appointment?"

"Better than that. I talked to Michaels himself, for probably twenty minutes."

"I don't believe it! I've sent people over there dozens of times, never gotten a thing. How—but Maxwell, what's the idea of jumping into something like this without your editor even knowing it?"

"I had an idea I wanted to explore further before I involved you. Besides, I had no idea it would turn out as it did."

The editor regarded him quizzically. He was a graying veteran of newspaperdom and good at his job. He'd worked his way up through the ranks, mostly on large city dailies, before joining the staff on *NWV* at its inception as the first editor.

"Well? How did it turn out?" he asked.

"I've been in more comfortable circumstances. Hamilton Jaeger was there. He and I tangled over my probing of finances. I doubt he'll talk to me again."

"What were you doing questioning their finances?"

"They've been buying up land in Texas, and I was moderately curious. And I had a right to be. That's a reporter's job. I was within my proper journalistic guidelines. But he was angered that I brought it up."

"You should have known that finances are always a sore spot with these big organizations. Haven't I taught you better diplomacy than that?"

"Yes, but I wanted to know. Besides, that wasn't my original intent."

"What was?"

"I had a brainstorm—a series of three or four stories leading up to their Chicago crusade next spring. You know, progressively looking at preparations. I was fishing for an approach and backed into the money issue. I'd read an article on their finances, and it probably kicked the dust up in my subconscious. Then once we were moving in that direction, they were so evasive, how could I not pursue it? Double-talk is a clear invitation for a reporter to probe, you know. And I went for the bait."

The editor did not reply for a moment, then said, "I know you were just thinking this through preliminarily. But you're supposed to be a part of a team. I realize you prefer to be a loner

70

when you're hatching a story. So far you've gotten away with it. But you can push that game too far and get yourself and the paper into hot water."

Jackson nodded. He knew McClanahan was right.

"Actually, the idea of a short series isn't bad," the editor went on in a new vein. "But it'd have to be positive and upbeat."

"I'd like to give it a try. Something about Michaels intrigues me."

"But nothing the least bit questionable!" McClanahan warned.

"I'll be careful," said Jackson. "But I don't want to recite meaningless drivel from their PR files either. How about an original article that's pretty tame, just general, followed by something more probing? Maybe the second article wouldn't even have to do with ETW especially."

"OK. Write up a short initial article for the November *World*. Then if it's suitable, we'll follow it up with two more, a second one, say, in January. The Chicago crusade's the first week of May, isn't it?"

"Yes."

"All right. Show me what you have in a few days, and I'll work it into the spacing budget."

Jackson walked slowly back to his desk and sat down. *What to focus on?* he thought. He liked the idea of a personal touch, a different approach. For now he'd put his reservations about Michaels and his dislike of Jaeger on hold.

Of course, he'd explore further. If he intended to bring in finances he'd have to read, talk to people, and make sure he had his information straight. But most of all he'd just have to allow time for his thoughts to distill until an approach for the article presented itself.

11

Jackson unlocked the door and walked slowly into his apartment. It was chilly. He turned up the thermostat, glanced through the pile of mail on the floor, and headed for the kitchen. Sometimes he enjoyed spending an hour preparing a complex salad or baking a potato to go with a thick, juicy, hamburger steak. But not tonight. He was tired and just wanted to flop down and rest.

He pulled out a canister of granola, an open carton of milk, a banana, a knife, and a spoon and headed for the living room where he flipped on the TV and sat down in his favorite easy chair. The news was just underway. He still missed Cronkite and Severeid after all these years but liked to stay informed nonetheless. CNN filled the bill nicely. If the day's events were boring or gruesome, he could always catch a rerun of Bob Newhart, Magnum, or MASH.

Jackson enjoyed TV. He had definite scruples about what he watched. He knew what he liked and wouldn't waste an hour in front of a program he had no taste for. But what he watched he heartily enjoyed.

Maybe it was an escape. But Jackson saw no problem with that. His was an energetic mentality, even a passionate one, ever alert, always sizing up people and situations, incessantly sifting through life's out-of-the-way corners for meaning. Jackson was no phlegmatic. He tackled decisions and circumstances with a mental vigor that would have rendered him exhausted had not every day contained moments when he could let up and allow his mind to drift.

Jackson was not, however, a fast-paced and frenzied person. To observe him carrying out his many routine assignments at *NWV*, one would scarcely suspect the fervency brewing beneath the surface. But the more sensitized one became to the deeper levels of his nature, the more awakened one was to the bubbling cauldron of energy and fiery dynamic that drove him.

Even Jackson himself continued to discover new layers of feeling and motivation within. Toward what he was driven he was often uncertain. Was it knowledge of the truth that pulled at him so relentlessly, compelling him to follow? Was it depth of relationship? Justice? Accomplishment? Success? Was it even possible to pin down the core of his being?

Jackson was one of those rare persons in whom emotions and logic were fully operative at peak levels. His intellect was driven to understand and his emotions driven to feel everything around him. He could never "let things be." He could tolerate no compromise. In him was no capacity for apathy. To Jackson, *everything* mattered. And mattered a great deal!

Thus when evenings came, Jackson was usually emotionally and mentally drained, even after the most routine of days, and ready for something that required little from him. He often found himself unable even to summon the wherewithal to tackle a book. But after a good night's sleep, Jackson Maxwell was always prepared to rush headlong into another day with everything it could throw at him.

He watched television until nine and then went to bed, where he lightly read until falling asleep at about nine-thirty.

There was another phase of Jackson's life that worked to energize him and heighten his intensity while at the same time providing a physical outlet for it. He was a fitness buff and prided himself on keeping in shape. Whether it was cycling, swimming, handball, tennis, jogging, or lifting weights, at least four times a week Jackson suited up to enjoy himself in a workout of some kind. A master of none, yet he derived great pleasure from athletics in any form.

The next morning, therefore, he left his apartment at six-thirty and headed up the sidewalk on his lightweight ten-speed. He lived five miles from *NWV* headquarters and only a mile from a city park consisting of various playgrounds, picnic areas, and several miles of running and cycling paths. On the mornings when Jackson had nothing scheduled later in the day at the gym or courts, he either jogged or cycled through the trails.

He pedaled slowly to the park. The day was cold but bright and promised to turn out beautifully. He circled the park once and was starting around it again when he heard footsteps approaching from behind.

"Jackson!" a voice panted. "Wait up!"

He turned and slowed.

Running toward him was a young woman, perhaps twenty-eight, clad in faded Levi cutoffs and a gray sweatshirt, with blonde hair, of medium build but very short, her face flushed and beads of sweat just beginning to form on her forehead. She and Jackson had met several months earlier at a fund-raising breakfast sponsored by a number of local churches for a new Christian high school in the area. Jackson had been flipping pancakes, she serving tables. Afterward he'd given her a ride downtown, they'd discovered several shared interests and since had run and biked together three or four times. Though their interest in one another already surpassed what could be termed a casual acquaintance, they each still knew little about the other. Their conversations till now had mostly been limited to recreation.

"Diana—hi. I wondered if you would be here."

"Wouldn't miss it, four times a week you know. But why the bike? I thought you ran on Thursdays."

"Usually. But I banged up my knee last Sunday—a game of touch football with the guys at the office. I thought I'd lay off it for a while."

"Well, I'll never keep up with you. I've been sprinting to catch you for a quarter mile just now."

"Sorry. But I'll take it easy for a lap or two around the park."

"Thanks," said Diana regaining her breath, "but I didn't know you worked in an office. For some reason I pegged you as a graduate student, DePaul maybe."

"Why's that?"

"I don't know. I suppose because you're always talking about working out, I just assumed you had the sort of flexibility in your schedule that would come from the university life."

"No, I've been out of that for some time—I'm a reporter."

"No kidding! With what paper?"

"Not a paper actually. I work for a magazine. Ever heard of *Christian World*? We're not gigantic, that's for sure."

"Sure I have—you do a paper too?"

"That's us!"

"Must be fascinating, meeting important Christians and traveling all over."

"It's interesting all right. But I hardly travel all over, and I haven't met that many big names. Matter of fact, lately I've found a certain frustration in it. That's why I work out regularly and why it probably seems I'm always talking about the other side of my life. I try to forget the work when I'm out running or biking or playing handball. Helps me find a balance. But hey, I didn't come here to get weighed down about all that. How about you? You told me you were a student. You didn't say where."

"It's only part time—over at Cosmopolitan. I have this crazy notion of being a singer someday."

"No kidding?"

"Yea. Probably a pipe dream."

"I don't know. Nothing's crazy. You just have to be willing to pay the price."

"You're right," said Diana with a sigh. "It's just that—" she hesitated, then went on "—in my case there's a lot involved."

Jackson waited, thinking she would go on. But a quick glance at her face told him the subject was closed. He said nothing for another moment, then, "Well, here's my trail out of the park. I have to get going. I'm going to put in about five miles before the streets get too congested."

"Thanks for the company," she said. "I've got to be heading home too. See you next Thursday?"

"I'll try," said Jackson. "If my knee's better, I'll try to go about four miles with you."

"It's a date then!"

12

"Barry . . . ? Jackson Maxwell calling again," said Jackson into the phone after dialing the number of *CO&M*.

"Two calls within a month. Jackson, I'm flattered."

"I know, . . . inexcusable." Jackson laughed. "Say, Barry, I'm following through on some writing I'm doing on the Michaels organization. Is this a convenient time to ask you a few more questions? Am I pulling you away from anything?"

"No, this is an OK time. I'm doing a story on YWAM, Vets with a Mission, Agape Force, and Focus on the Family—a comparison of methods and ideologies. It's going to be a good one, I think. They're helpful, great people to work with. Certainly more accommodating than the Michaels people. But right now I'm in the middle of a section of rewrite and would welcome the diversion."

"I'm trying to nail down more on that Texas acquisition. You told me before that you got into that in your interview."

"We only skirted the edges of it," said Barry.

"You said the site was near Greenville. When I mentioned that in passing, Jaeger practically exploded. He made a dramatic point of forbidding me to mention it. I don't understand what's going on, and I have to be clear on it."

"That's how he was when I interviewed him—really jumpy."

"How did you find out in the first place?"

"We had a piece scheduled for updating the status of ETW. It's a regular thing we do for *Organizations and Ministries*. Most of the leading Christian groups go along. That's part of our purpose, to report changes. So Jaeger was more or less obligated to talk with me. Anyhow, the interview was progressing along very normal, uninteresting lines when Sondra—"

"DeQue?"

"Yes—you know, 'Ms.'?"

They laughed.

"She really loves that label—makes sure everyone respects it too!"

"Anyway, Ms. DeQue apparently blundered and mentioned

the recent acquisition of a large Texas estate. That's when the whole thing about the half billion in assets came out. Jaeger was noticeably perturbed but maintained his composure. He hadn't been planning to reveal that figure. But when I pressed he relented, knowing, I suppose, that I would print it anyway."

"And would you have if he'd held his ground?"

"I would have tried to verify it. But—sure, I think I would have. That's why our magazine exists—to keep the Christian public informed of such things."

"So he allowed you to say they had bought a chunk of Texas and the size of the assets total?"

"Begrudgingly. Then they told me about the training center and TV station."

"And that's all you got?"

"Not quite. A few minutes later, Sondra let slip that the site was just outside Greenville—do you know the place, northeast of Dallas? Boy, Jaeger hit the roof—really furious! Read her out something fierce. I couldn't see what the ruckus was all about, but it was important to him. He instantly banished me to silence, and considering what I already had, I consented."

"Why the hostility?"

"I can't imagine," said Barry. "And when I finished the draft of the article and tried to contact him for a final comment on what I had written, he wouldn't talk to me at all."

"When I was interviewing Michaels and him two days ago he implied that if the exact site were known, other Christian organizations would feel threatened, as if ETW were infringing on their turf. There are quite a few setting up shop in Texas. Jaeger apparently thinks they would think Michaels was encroaching on what they were doing."

"I can't imagine any other organizations fearing that, any more than I can foresee Michaels trying it."

"True. But Jaeger is a suspicious guy. He's probably interpreting the situation from the perspective he'd adopt if he were in their shoes, unless he does have more in the hopper than he's telling."

"You're not suggesting—"

"No. I'm just thinking out loud. I'm certain Jaeger does what he's told. Michaels seems to run a pretty tight ship."

"But no captain knows every little detail of operation down in the boiler room—Reagan, North, Poindexter, and the boys. You know the principle."

"With something of this magnitude, though, Michaels would have to be calling the shots—hey, we're getting pretty far afield. I just wanted to confirm Greenville. I may want to mention it."

"With Jaeger's prohibition?"

"Jaeger told me not to publish anything about it, but I didn't agree to that prohibition. My whole life as a journalist is to *dig*, to find out what's *really* happening. Yours too. We have an obligation to our readers, to the public. Certainly we owe them our allegiance far more than we do the secretive likes of Hamilton Jaeger."

"'That's true, but—"

"I know it's a fine line we walk ethically between giving people like Jaeger the benefit of the doubt and our public duty to uncover the story. It's not easy. I'm not always sure I am doing the right thing. But if there's something there, I *have* to unearth it, no matter how much it upsets Jaeger."

"How can you justify that position?"

"How can I justify not printing the truth? By the very nature of writing and reporting, our responsibility is to get at truth. And sometimes that truth is well concealed. So it seems to me we are within proper moral guidelines to push for the facts more strongly than someone with lesser motives might."

"That's a pretty risky position."

"I know. It's hard. But I am bound as a writer and as a Christian to get beneath the surface of a critical story. I'm not saying I should always do that, or that I should do it without serious thought beforehand. But there are times when a reporter has to go forward with an investigation, even if he knows people will be hurt by what he finds."

"That's easy for you to say," Barry countered.

"Walking the line between protecting a subject and exposing what needs to be unearthed is a sacred trust we've been given. Getting at the truth requires placing a higher regard on the public's need to know than a desire not to cause pain. Besides—my story's going to be complimentary. If the story runs in November, you'll see why I wanted to be certain. It will contain nothing Hamilton

Jaeger will mind, I'm sure."

"It's your byline—and your head!" Barry laughed on the other end of the line.

"Nothing that serious. Thanks again, Barry. Talk to you later."

13

"Hey—Maxwell!"

There was McClanahan again. Jackson hadn't been in the building five minutes.

"How's that Michaels piece coming? Time's short for November. I'm squeezing it in as it is."

"I'll have you the final in three hours."

"Great! How many words do you think?"

"Seven-fifty—nine hundred. How does that sound?"

"I'll give you nine hundred max. Then we'll use a picture—figure two pages."

"OK."

"Now what about follow-up? They're working up the January issue for space. You still thinking about three stories?"

"I'm inventing a fictitious person who makes a pledge to the Michaels crusade in Chicago. That's the one you'll see today. After that I'm not exactly sure, but I'm thinking of a broader look at the whole foundation of Christian finances."

"I like it."

"Do you mind if I editorialize a bit?"

"No. How else is there sometimes to probe beneath the surface?"

"Might ruffle a few feathers."

"It won't be the first time. But the Michaels people are sticky about what's said. We don't need them on our backs. So try to be somewhat objective. And be up-front about the fictitious part."

"When's the deadline?" asked Jackson.

"I ought to have it by Thanksgiving. A week sooner would be better," said the editor.

"I can make that. Having the first two pieces off my back will make Thanksgiving that much more enjoyable."

"What are your plans?" asked McClanahan.

"I'm heading down to my folks' place. Haven't seen them since March."

"Where are they?"

"Down just outside Quincy. They used to have a pretty fair-sized farm—wheat, corn, lots of hogs. But they've sold off their land bit by bit. New highways, industrial development, housing sites—same old story."

"Anything left?"

"They're down to about ten acres. But that's OK. They're getting too old to farm that much anyway, and the income from the property keeps them in fair shape financially. Still, it's been hard on them to see the farm die a few acres at a time, especially my dad. That land goes way back with him."

"You raised there?"

"Yeah—and I do miss the old place."

"Roots, huh?"

"In a way, I suppose. Not like Dad though. He was raised there too. The land's part of him. I love it, but I can remain somewhat detached. When I was a kid I loved that land. The fields—used to romp through them by the hour. Summers were great! But ever since I was a teenager something about it changed for me. It just wasn't the same anymore. It might be different if I were flesh and blood tied into it."

"What do you mean?" asked McClanahan.

"I'm adopted."

"Jackson, I didn't know. How old were you?"

"Right out of the cradle. My folks raised me from the start. They're just like real parents to me. I never knew anyone but them."

"What's it like—any regrets?"

"How do you mean?" asked Jackson.

"Ever wish you weren't adopted or maybe knew your blood parents?"

"I haven't really thought about it that seriously in years. When I first found out, it hit me pretty hard. I suppose I submerged it.

80

I was young and impressionable then. And afterward Mom and Dad never brought it up again. If it did come up, Mom would quickly get us talking about something else. There seemed to be a pain, and I didn't want to probe. Maybe I should have—I suppose I had a right to know."

Jackson went silent for a moment, then sighed. "But then again I suppose Mom had a right too."

"Well, that's interesting," said McClanahan at length. "I'm glad you told me—but we'd better get to work. Cup of coffee?"

"No thanks, Ed. I never could get used to that stuff, even early in the morning."

14

Jackson completed his first article. Usually the gap between deadline and finished printed product was so wide that he enjoyed reading over what he'd written. But since McClanahan had rushed this first one through into the November *World* in the space vacated by a canceled eight-hundred-word piece, when the issue came, Jackson scarcely glanced back over his work. He sensed no foreboding about it. *Surely,* he said to himself, *Michaels and Jaeger will appreciate what I've written. I've given them a solid piece of favorable exposure.*

But Hamilton Jaeger was anything but pleased when he snapped open his copy of *Christian World* and took in what Jackson Maxwell had written.

Mrs. Ada Windenberry pulled the drapes, turned up the heat, and sat down at her small antique oak secretary. *Winters in Chicago are always so cold!* she thought. *And blustery—the wind never lets up!*

She pulled her knit sweater tightly around her shoulders,

opened the drawer where the checkbook was kept, and proceeded to write a draft for $100.

I hope this does some good, she thought. *This city's headed downhill, and somebody's got to do something. On television he said our donations would bear fruit right in our own city. I just hope his crusade will help slow down this moral decline.*

Only last week, a close friend of Ada's had been mugged just three blocks away from where she sat at this moment. When Ada had heard that there would be a special youth rally during the week, aimed particularly at street youth, she had decided right then to be part of that ministry. *If my $100 will help a few more kids to that meeting, I want to give it, even if I can hardly afford it. Who knows,* she thought, *maybe my donation will play a role in the salvation of that poor young man who robbed Gwen the other day.*

She prayerfully filled out the middle portion of the check first, then on the top line wrote: "To Jacob Michaels." *It'll be more personal that way,* she thought, and then placed it in an envelope on which she wrote Evangelize the World, Inc., Chicago, Illinois.

She immediately felt better.

Ada Windenberry had a sense down inside of doing something tangible to forward the Lord's work in her own community.

A thousand miles away, in another city, in another small apartment Edna Howden sat reading the newspaper. Somehow on this particular evening she was struck with the violence more prevalent in Dallas every day. It disturbed her. How she longed to do something meaningful. But what could a poor widow on social security hope to accomplish single-handedly? She herself was as afraid to go out nights as everyone else.

She'd remembered reading of Jacob Michaels's plans for a massive Christian outreach center based in Greenville. *That's so nearby,* she thought. *Having an evangelistic organization like that practically in Dallas is bound to have a positive impact. Maybe there is something I can do! Maybe I can contribute in a small way to his coming here and carrying out that needed work.*

And with that Edna wrote out a check for $50, placed at the bottom the note "For Dallas outreach," and sent it to ETW, Inc., in the envelope they had provided. She was on their mailing list.

Two women whose paths will never cross in this life, motivated out of concern for God's work in their area, prompted by their faith in ETW and Jacob Michaels, each giving to support a worldwide ministry whose message to its faithful followers is simply "Help us to evangelize the world." Surely these two fictional vignettes cannot help but remind us of Jesus' words to His disciples after seeing the widow deposit her two mites in the Temple treasury, "She has given more than all the others . . . for she gave out of her poverty." It is the thousands of persons—much like Ada and Edna—who make an enormous ministry such as ETW functional on a daily level.

This was the point made by Jacob Michaels himself in an exclusive interview for *Christian World*. In discussing preparations for ETW's upcoming Chicago crusade, Michaels was quick to give credit to "the faithfulness of our thousands of generous supporters. If it weren't for them," Michaels added, "we'd never be able to carry out the work we do."

And what exactly is that work as it relates specifically to dedicated followers such as Ada in Chicago and Edna in Dallas? Where do their gifts of $100 and $50 actually go?

Following a specific gift from donation through to expenditure would certainly be an impossible task. But Ada can confidently know that because of many gifts such as hers, from all parts of the country, ETW will indeed stage a significant attempt to reach people for Christ in Chicago. And should more funds actually be received for the Chicago crusade than is required, the surplus will then be spent in other avenues of evangelistic endeavor by ETW. It is faith in the vision of ETW that is at the root of Ada's desire to be part of that ministry, whether her $100 is actually spent in Chicago, to support some other phase of the organization, or contributes toward the purchase of property in Greenville, Texas, that ETW has been accumulating over the past several years.

And at the same time Edna can rest assured that she is playing a significant role in the expansion of ETW's ongoing vision. Her $50, spent to further the Greenville project or spent in some other way as needed by ETW, will bear fruit in God's kingdom.

Thus, as the Jacob Michaels evangelistic staff gears up for the week-long Chicago crusade four months from now, one of the most vital aspects of their link to potential success involves the faith that thousands of their supporters will be led to contribute toward that common cause they all share. As the gifts come in—large and small—they pool together to make eternal things happen.

Ada and Edna, you do make a difference in God's work.

"Greenville!" Jaeger snarled under his breath as he threw

down the magazine. That Jackson Maxwell would have to be stopped.

15

Several weeks passed. Thanksgiving approached, and Chicago was treated to one final glimpse of summer past with a stretch of sixty-five degree days. Sailboats dotted the horizon, aromatic lawns revealed fresh mowings, and throughout the city final hurry-up bits of pre-winter yard work was done. And wherever there was space, sparsely clad runners, bikers, walkers, and picnickers enjoyed it while they could.

"Jackson!" he heard. The familiar ring of Diana's voice could not be mistaken. They'd agreed to meet at the park at three that afternoon for a run.

He turned. "What a day, huh?" He looked around with outstretched arms and let the gesture complete the sentence.

Settling into a comfortable jog beside him, she said, "I haven't seen you on Thursdays lately."

"I haven't been out recently," said Jackson.

"Losing interest?" asked Diana.

"I've been playing tennis a bit more. But the main problem's been time. I've been involved in a project that's been hanging over me. I had to get out and let off some nervous energy in this glorious sunshine."

"I know. It's great, isn't it? What's the project about?"

"I'd rather not say—just yet."

"Oh, OK. Sorry. Well, then, how about pushing the mile loop once with me—around seven minutes? Can you go that slow?" Diana asked.

"Slow? Seven minutes is fast! Remember, I'm just a recreational jogger, not serious like you."

"You're pulling my leg, Jackson. You're a man. Men can go

faster."

"Are you trying to bait me into an admission of male chauvinism?"

"A liberated nonfeminist like me?" said Diana. "Never. But come on, let's go." She darted off in front of him.

Jackson dug his toes into the grass and took off after her. Other joggers were everywhere. Parents and children feeding the ducks, families enjoying picnics. No one would have guessed it to be mid-November.

At the end of the mile Jackson was breathing hard. His once or twice a week running was no match for Diana's five miles a day.

"How about a breather?" asked Diana as they completed the circuit.

Jackson flopped down on the grass, and the two lay back and filled their lungs with the succulent springlike air.

"How's the musical career coming?" asked Jackson at length. "Any contract offers, nightclub engagements?"

"Hardly! I'm just taking my classes, practicing, and waiting."

"For what?"

"I'd rather not say . . . sorry, but I have my reasons—just like you."

"Two strangers keeping secrets from each other?" quipped Jackson.

"It's not like that," said Diana seriously, "it's just that—"

"Diana, I was just being sarcastic," broke in Jackson, anxious lest he'd offended her.

"Oh," she said, seemingly confused. "I couldn't really tell from your voice."

"I meant nothing," said Jackson. "Besides, I kept the first secret. Hey, let's tackle that loop again—but slower this time."

"No, thanks, Jackson," said Diana. Her forehead knitted slightly as her eyes looked away. "I think I'll be heading home." She rose and jogged off without another word.

Jackson stared after her in silence. Why had she grown so suddenly withdrawn? The brief interchange clearly signified more beneath the surface than he'd been aware of.

He got to his feet slowly, jogged the loop once more, and walked back to his apartment where he jotted his folks a brief note concerning his Thanksgiving plans.

16

Fall passed. Jackson finished the final draft of article two, and with relief deposited it on McClanahan's desk. He didn't want to think about ETW or finances for a month!

December proved a slow time for Jackson. The first Midwestern snows fell. Running and cycling became more difficult. He played handball several times. He did not see Diana. Once or twice he'd been tempted to drive over to the Cosmopolitan School of Music campus and try somehow to find her, but thought better of it. On reflection he knew it was a crazy notion. He knew nothing about her schedule and didn't even know her last name! Yet he still longed to rectify what had been an awkward last parting.

Christmas Jackson planned to spend in Quincy. He was to drive down on the twenty-third. When the day arrived menacing black clouds blew in from the north. Hoping to beat the downpour he left as soon as he was able. But before he'd driven ten miles down the interstate huge pellets of rain began to pound on the windshield. Something in the atmosphere's solitary gloominess cast a somber melancholy over his spirits.

He was prone to random fits of dejection. It was the one thing in his personality he could hardly tolerate. Over most of what came his way he was able to exercise some degree of control. But his moods held him at their mercy. It was fine if his disposition was upbeat. But when he felt empty and cheerless he would have given anything for the internal capacity to pull his emotions up by the bootstraps.

Alone. That's what he felt. But why now? Things had been going smoothly. He had good friends and a job he liked with sensitive people. He had a family that loved him. Then why did he feel so unsettled about driving down to visit them?

His thoughts trailed back to the conversation he and McClanahan had had several weeks earlier. Had McClanahan's questioning about the effect of a past with no birthright stuck like a burr in his subconscious all this time?

He'd always accepted his lot, taken it for granted. But now

his apparent rootless history had been turning itself over in his mind. Had those few questions of McClanahan's, so innocent on the surface, triggered the same emotions that had so rocked his world as a thirteen-year-old some eighteen years earlier? To cope then, he'd buried his true feelings and hadn't allowed them to surface. But now those feelings seemed determined to come back and haunt him.

In fact, this was one of the rare times in the last eighteen years that he had recalled that decisive day when he first learned the truth about himself. Suddenly it was like yesterday. His thoughts drifted back . . .

The tall stalks of ripening corn looked the same. But somehow they invited no exploratory play on that day. All was suddenly changed. The world had grown hostile. He felt alone.

The boy was feeling the first bitter sting of the awkward transition into manhood. Until thirteen his life had been largely sheltered. His friendships at the nearby rural school had been satisfying. He'd faced none of the upheaval he'd have otherwise been thrust into had he grown up in the inner city. His mom and dad had given him all the love they had the power to bestow. The tranquil pace of the small farming community had worked its calm into the young man's soul.

Until today.

Perhaps his thirteen protected years had prepared him for this moment. On the other hand, perhaps the pain bit so deep because he'd suffered so little. The experience of pain carves depths into the soul, depths from which character emerges. If he had few resources to fall back on, today's pain would deepen his future reservoirs of compassion.

He would never know the anguish his parents felt over their decision. They so desperately wanted to do the right thing for their son. They'd put off telling him when he was young; the time never seemed quite right. As the years quietly passed, possibly they had even hoped to block it out of their own minds. Maybe he would never have to know.

But ultimately truthfulness prevailed; they would have to tell him. When he was a teenager, they decided, he'd be on the way to manhood. That would be the time.

The boy walked on, out into the fields. How many hours he'd played here with his friends—crawling among the four-foot-high stalks, piling up bales of hay to make forts in a nearby field left fallow. He could not recall a time in his life when this cornfield was not a part of him. How special were the times here with his dad, being shown how to tell when the young ears were ripe and, later, helping with the harvest. As much as anything in the world, this field was him.

But now all was confusion. The cornfield seemed alien and distant. The world that had been comfortable and warm was now far away.

Who was he? That was the question, though his young mind would not formulate it so succinctly for many years. All he knew now, today, was that something hurt deep inside. He had to be alone in his place of solitude. The cornfield would minister its pacifying effect on his troubled heart.

So he walked—far from home, far from any other being, his fists bunched before his face for protection from the sharp edges of the blades of corn. In his isolation was his agony. Yet he was compelled to bear it unhelped by any other human creature.

At last he turned and from a distance could no longer be distinguished from the growing grain. Kneeling, he burrowed through the corn-tunnel he'd used many times to give his friend Joey the slip.

But it was no game today—no Joey was chasing, no laughter was welling up inside. Today he sought the consolation of seclusion. He crawled on hands and knees until he reached a roomy area some five-feet square where failing cornstalks had fallen, leaving a matted-down carpet in the middle of the huge field about which no one but he knew.

Here he could relax. Sometimes he came here to read, even sleep, and no one would discover his presence. This was his place of quiet, of identity, of security—and sometimes of escape.

Today, however, his cornfield was called on to witness a singular new stage in the young boy's progress toward adulthood, and to do what it could to soothe.

He stretched out on his stomach, curled himself up as if asleep, laid his face on his forearm, and—knowing no one could hear—sobbed in the anguish of loneliness.

The sudden blare of a horn jolted Jackson back to the present. In his reverie he had wandered over the center line slightly, dangerously close to a passing car on the left. He swung the steering wheel quickly to the right and once again settled into the monotonous drive as his introspection closed in upon him.

He didn't want to be isolated, cut off from the rest of the world. Intellectually, of course, he knew he wasn't. Nevertheless, he *felt* so desolate. Was this what orphans went through—the sense of abandonment, of being forsaken in the cold with nothing? The comparison was ridiculous, of course! His folks had given him everything—love, affection, a healthy feeling about himself.

But an ingredient remained missing, something they could never supply. The blood line, the sense at the bottom of his soul of being able to say, "This is who I am. This is where I came from. This is the rock from which I was hewn!"

Was the answer to his "Who am I?" only to be found on the physical plane? As a Christian was not his heavenly Father supposed to be his all in all? If he had been reborn into God's family, did earthly roots matter?

Jackson reached over and pulled a tissue from the car's Kleenex dispenser and wiped his nose.

No, he thought. Heresy though it may be, a relationship with God wasn't enough to fulfill that primal need.

By the time he arrived in Quincy several hours later, the rain had stopped and he had recovered his equilibrium. He was ready for the holiday.

Fred and Ellen Maxwell had never conceived children of their own. They had tried, both before and after Jackson. But he was destined to be their only son. Now in their sixties, with no grandchildren and no prospects on the horizon, their lives were gradually winding down. Jackson's visits always provided a special highlight but were short and too far between.

They loved Jackson, in possibly a deeper way than had he come from their own bodies and continued to long for the opportunity to pour more of themselves into him. But he was a boy no longer and was out to discover his own manhood and destiny. His move to Wheaton had been hard on them. But the blow was severe when he wrote during his final year to inform them he had accepted a position with the *News with a Vision* staff in Chicago. The handwriting had been on the wall years before. But somehow Fred and Ellen had convinced themselves Jackson would eventually return to Quincy, settle down with wife and family, and take up the operation of the farm, thus carrying forward the family tradition of the last three generations of Maxwells.

Though cordial enough on the surface, Jackson's visits since had been accompanied by a strained undercurrent. In his mother's subtle remarks about marriage and observations on the carrying on of the Maxwell name and in his father's muttered expostulations about selling the farm, Jackson sensed a subliminal resentment of his journalistic profession. He wondered how they could reconcile his desire to grow into significance as a Christian communicator with what they perceived as a slap in the face to the heritage they had tried to give him. He tried never to allow the discussion to center for long on his job.

Fourteen years earlier, during Jackson's second year away from home, Fred had arisen early one morning and driven his tractor to a distant field intending to clear away some fallen logs from a portion of ground that was to be sold. Ordinarily it was a job he would have enlisted Jackson's help with. But on this particular day Fred was feeling unusually independent despite his sixty years and fickle back. Ellen had admonished him to wait.

"Nonsense," he had replied. "I'm as good as I was at thirty."

The job progressed well enough, and he was three-quarters through when the partially loaded tractor hung up on a chunk of rotted stump. Leaving the engine running, Fred took the tractor out of gear and, grabbing up his shovel, jumped down and began hacking away at the disintegrating wood to free a path for the tire. He'd been careless and in the need of the moment hadn't considered the danger.

Either from the resultant jarring or from the jerky idle he'd been meaning to fix, somehow the gear engaged, and the tractor suddenly lurched forward. Nearly in front of its gigantic tire, Fred threw himself aside, wrenching his back terribly in the process.

The sudden movement dislodged the logs that had been perched precariously about eight feet above the ground on the tractor's twin forklift prongs. Though he'd barely escaped the driverless machine, Fred was now lying immobile on the ground from a severe spinal spasm. As he attempted to crawl backward and sideways up the slight incline, the falling logs made a direct hit, two of them smashing his ankle and pinning his left leg in a vise-like grip. The tractor quickly encountered the remainder of the logs, bounced to a stop, and stalled.

It took Fred nearly two hours to free himself and then crawl the twenty feet to the tractor. Then he had to haul himself up into the seat. Miraculously he was able to drive the tractor home where he stopped the engine, climbed down and fell in the front yard senseless from pain. Ellen ran out of the house hysterically, saw the bleeding leg, hurried back inside for some hasty, makeshift bandages, half-dragged, half-carried her agonizing husband to the car and then drove to the hospital with an abandonment of caution she had scarcely known. Both had been courageous and had made gallant efforts. But it was too late and the injury too severe. Both the foot and shinbone were crushed beyond repair, blood had been lost, and infection had already set in. The leg had to be amputated just below the left knee.

Since that time, they'd sold increasing portions of the land in order to pay for help for those things Fred could no longer do himself. Though he managed adequately with his partial wooden leg, his mobility, not to mention his spirit for farming, was severely diminished.

Every visit since Fred's accident provided an opportunity for Jackson to work side by side on the farm with his dad, in perhaps more of a man-to-man role than had been possible when he was younger and Fred more independent. Now by necessity they were forced to work together, and the experience had served to strengthen the bond between them.

The Christmas holiday was enjoyable. Ellen always managed the magnificent sort of spread only a farmer's wife can—sweet potatoes topped with a teasing of molasses, freshmade dressing, turkey (or ham if a hog had recently been butchered), marvelous fruit salad, and a full complement of pies. After every such meal, Jackson regularly resolved to get back into serious training.

He remained for nine days, helped Fred with some of the two-man chores he'd been putting off, read two books, visited old friends, and sat for a whole day in front of the TV watching the Orange, Rose, and Cotton Bowls.

17

By January 2, Jackson was prepared to head back into the gritty air of Chicago and all—known and unknown—that awaited him there. He'd typed not a word for almost three weeks, and his fingers itched for a story.

He entered his darkened apartment at eight-thirty that evening. He wasn't hungry; Ellen had packed several sandwiches, which he'd devoured en route. He turned on the heat, then picked up his mail from the floor.

His advance copy of *Christian World* lay at the top of the stack. There was something different about reading one's own work once it was actually in print. It was a regular ritual he followed: detaching himself from having written a piece and placing himself in the position of a reader encountering the story for the first time.

Jackson sat down, kicked off his shoes, opened the magazine, and leisurely read the second of his articles.

Two months ago, in the opening article of this series, the subject of contributing to Christian ministries was raised in relation to two fictional women, each who gave, for her own private reasons, to a well-known multinational organization whose avowed purpose is to further the cause of Christ. Now we propose to extend that inquiry further and to promote discussion regarding what has in our time become a normal and accepted method of financing the spread of the gospel in the twentieth century.

In its simplest terms, such an inquiry reduces to two very distinct positions the way one can look at the parable of the widow at the Temple treasury. The two views capsulize the debate that has circulated for thirty years over the integrity of Christian fund-raising, and indeed the propriety and financial foundation of the whole Christian enterprise.

Do we look at the Temple widow as a servant of the Lord, whose sacrificial willingness to give provides the strength and backbone of a vital, functioning church of God that effectively and life-changingly furthers the gospel? Or do we view her as one being fleeced by the Temple Pharisees, both of that day and this—kept bound in her poverty in order that they might wear gold-trimmed robes of white and enjoy the fat of the land?

The question is not an easy one. Which perspective Jesus had in mind as He spoke to His disciples is not readily apparent.

Surely the deeper import of Jesus' teaching drives us to prayerfully consider God's work within the widow's heart and to ask Him to likewise humble us in our daily circumstances that we too might give with such a pure heart of devotion.

Yet what of the larger issues raised? How do we interpolate His observation to gain wisdom in attempting to come to grips with present-day realities? Where along the line of interpretation do we discover God's truth in the matter of Christian finances?

The foundational query is this: Is there scriptural justification for the long-established tradition whereby working men and women dig into their own pockets to support churches and ministers, priests and preachers? Does precedent exist in the New Testament for the modus operandi of today's church? What do we make of the teaching "the laborer is worthy of his hire"? How do we view those millions of individuals who give out of their poverty, filling present-day temple coffers of huge organizations and ministries and schools and agencies? Is the financial cornerstone upon which contemporary Christendom is built and by which it maintains itself scriptural? It *may* be. Yet is it not time we find out? It is too easy to take for granted that what has always been is indeed right, when in actuality there may exist today many "traditions of the elders" that perhaps need to be reexamined.

How might the gospel enterprise differ today were it to heed the recommendation of the nineteenth-century Scottish preacher who gave the following counsel:

> *The great evil in the church has always been the presence ence in it of persons unsuited for the work required of them there. One very simple sifting rule would be that no one should be admitted to the clergy who had not first proved himself capable of making a better living in some other calling. What a foundation would be the experience in life he would gather by having to do so. Behind the counter or the plough, or in the workshop, he would come to know men and their struggles and their thoughts. I would have no one ordained till after forty. By that time he would know whether he had any real call or only a temptation to the church from the hope of an easy living. I suggest that though the laborer is worthy of his hire, not every man*

is worthy of the labor. I would see a man earn bread by the sweat of his brow—with his hands feed his body, and with his head and brain feed the hearts of his brothers and sisters. It is one of the lowest articles in the social creed of our country that a man is not a gentleman who works with his hands. He who would be a better gentleman than the Carpenter of Nazareth is not worthy of Him.

Posed yet another way, Does God still require of the ministers of His gospel that they make tents by the labor of their hands to sustain themselves and their apostleship? Or are our modern-day Pauls and Timothys somehow absolved from the standards that guided the steps of their first-century predecessors and forebears? Have we reached the point as a body of God's people where we invalidate such scriptural precedents by explaining them away in light of "changing modern times"?

When donations were requested by Paul, was it not for some specific purpose? Did not money from the hands of believers throughout the Mediterranean region go directly into the hands of those in direct need in Jerusalem, not into the hands of church leaders? Though Paul and Peter and Timothy and Luke and Apollos and the rest were engaged in the greatest missionary undertaking the world has ever seen, never that we can determine was an organization built during their lifetime, never were funds used to construct buildings and purchase land and equipment or to establish a first-century bureaucratic Christian structure to "manage" the outgoing of the Word of God. And surely no money donated by those early believers piled up in first-century banks. Throughout those times the leaders of that glorious movement remained primarily its servants, owning little beyond the clothes on their backs—working with their own hands, sacrificing, giving, chipping in, pulling their weight, helping do what had to be done so that the whole community of believers might mutually support and nourish one another. Their example was their Lord and Master, who neither accumulated for Himself nor sponged off His followers but always served and gave of all He had and was. *He* washed *their* feet, not they His.

Can the example of Jesus and Paul, preeminent among Christian leaders, be applied today? It is a difficult and multidimensional question. The purpose here is not to raise doubts regarding specific ministries according to some scale of relative validity. Nor is the purpose to point fingers or sow suspicion but rather to promote prayer and inquiry and healthy discussion—and chiefly to address the larger issue: What do we make of today's financial foundation of Christian organization—a structure built on millions upon millions of small donations from people like you and me, from the Ada Windenberrys and Edna Howdens of this world, who make up the grass roots ranks of Christendom—donations asked for and received in abundance by ministers of the gospel, ranging from Catholic priests to Protestant preachers to fundamental tent-meeting evangelists to the leaders and fund-raisers of a multitude of parachurch groups spread throughout the world?

Throughout the entire spectrum the pattern is similar—give your money, the masses are told, that the church and its incumbent ministries may flourish, that the clergy might be provided for, and that God's blessings may come to rest upon you for your generosity. Such is the message broadcast by television and radio personalities. Such is the message of an avalanche of fund-raising mailings entering American homes daily with urgent requests for financial help. And such is the message spoken weekly by thousands of clergymen—ministers of the gospel who no longer make tents and earn their *own* bread but who are amply provided for out of the offering plates over which they so seriously pray every Sunday.

Is this spectacle the purpose behind God's institution of the tithe? Is this why He tells us to give that we might receive out of His abundance? Or might there exist a deeper principle somewhere behind His injunction to give of the firstfruits of our labor? Do we give to support a massive Christian superstructure—or do we give to God Himself?

It is vital that Christians today—both leaders and followers, spanning the breadth from the seemingly most insignificant to the most well-known of personalities—earnestly examine these questions for one very simple and yet profound reason: The world is watching.

In the eyes of the world, there are many for whom the huge finances of modern evangelical ministry indicate a secularization and commercialization of the gospel. It is hardly a secret that in today's world economy, vast sums *are* required—to take God's Word into the world as well as to accomplish anything else. Thus do church treasurers and the wielders of the purse strings of various large organizations justify their unending pleas for money and aid. Yet these same petitions cause a skeptical, watching world to question the legitimacy of what appears little more than temple-treasury padding by modern-day Pharisees. The Christian body has for years been divided over this sensitive issue. Many wonder at the impression of wealthy evangelists, well-dressed and standing in the midst of expensive television production studios continually begging from a gullible public.

The world is watching. And the world wonders at such things. Within the church, our concern must be the application of scriptural truth to find the appropriate balance. But in the world's eyes, the question becomes one of integrity, honesty, and morality.

What might become of the gospel enterprise if its leaders and ministers and preachers and evangelists and priests and apostles and missionaries become its servants, working with their own hands to serve their people—if they lived as its servants rather than the recipients of its benefactions and handouts? Would Christianity collapse without the service of its smooth-handed ecclesiastics standing behind their polished oak pulpits preaching to their well-fed and contented congregations? Or, with those same ministers out in the forefront of service with sleeves rolled up and hands dirty, might the gospel not go forth into all the world with a power never seen since that indeed *was* the case during the first century? What might become of the gospel in our hands and issuing from our mouths if we lived lives consistent with the Master, who is the foundation of the mighty church? We can only hope and pray that one day we will witness the answer to that conundrum.

In light of such questions there has arisen a legitimate concern among investors in many gospel endeavors that contributors know for what purpose their money is actually being spent. It is an old story—out of $100 given, $55 goes for administrative purposes, $20 for additional fund-raising, $10 to local bureaucracy, $5 is lost to waste, with the result that only $10 ever finds its way into actual food to feed hungry children. Do concerned participants have the right to expect that their $100 gift (in response to a plea to help feed the world) actually be used to buy *food*?

When Paul told the churches of Corinth and Galatia and Macedonia of the need for financial assistance by the church in Jerusalem, he took special care throughout the entire process to keep everyone informed as to what he was doing. His progress and thoughts can be tracked from 1 Corinthians 16 to 2 Corinthians 8 and 9 to Romans 15. He diligently placed himself squarely in the middle of accountability for the collected funds, desiring to take the funds to Jerusalem and there personally present them to the saints—and in full. In other words, without Paul and his company's skimming off the top for their expenses, the apostle delivered every coin himself into the hands of those in need.

Similarly, do Christians have a right, even a duty, to expect that their gifts be used for the purposes to which they intend them?

In the next article of this series, we will examine some of these specific questions more closely. Might a more direct accounting be appropriate in the fiscal realm of Christian endeavor—a tighter link between given dollars and final expenditure? Is such realistic? Is it practical?

We must reiterate that the intent is in no way to assess the specific validity of widely varying ministries but to call the Christian community to the prayerful self-examination necessary to frame a response upon which a greater foundation of integrity and accountability can be based.

PART 3

Sondra DeQue

18

"We've got to talk," said Jaeger.

"Hamilton, I thought all that was settled. Surely you don't mean to start bringing up—"

"It's got nothing to do with us. Purely business. Can you be at the office in thirty minutes?"

"I'm barely awake!" she said with an edge in her voice. "Your phone call woke me. Can't it wait an hour?"

"I'll give you forty-five minutes. That should be plenty of time."

"OK, OK, I'll be there!" she said, irritated.

Sondra DeQue walked to her closet, slipped off the faded pink terry cloth robe she had hastily grabbed to put over her silk pajamas, kicked off the heel-trodden slippers, and quickly searched for something to wear.

Hamilton always had a way of insisting things be done his way, on his timetable. He rarely concerned himself with the schedules and priorities of others. When something came up, he demanded action. Sometimes Sondra could handle it. More often, however, his insistence irked her. She did not mind the hour. She had long before grown accustomed to early calls. It went with the responsibility of her position. But an occasional word of appreciation for her dedication would be nice.

The floor was cold. She chose a blue suit, dressed hastily, and hurried into the tiny kitchenette to boil water for coffee. The small, three-room apartment was inviting and comfortable. Sondra knew it was a far cry from the chic apartments featured in the glossy career women's magazines. Still it was a place she loved to come home to every evening to sink into one of her chairs or the cushions of the big overstuffed sofa that had given the movers so much trouble when she had brought it here from her parents' home in Quebec.

She'd had it recovered since then in floral shades of brown, yellow, and tan and had picked up two small armchairs to flank it from the want ads. They were growing a little threadbare but were still marvelously comfortable. On the far side of the living room stood an oak rocker, now probably valuable as an antique, in which she had rocked and daydreamed as a child and about which she was nostalgically sentimental. The room was highlighted by a rolltop desk against the windowless wall, now closed and rarely used except to write occasional letters, noticeably out of place with everything but the rocker. Sondra had impulsively bought it at an antique show during a fit of longing for "the simpler days of times past."

In thirty minutes, after coffee, an English muffin, and a quick makeup session before the mirror, Sondra DeQue was driving toward the office. She disliked having to hurry before work. She couldn't feel ready for the day lacking the full complement of her morning toilette. Hamilton had better have a good reason for this.

When she arrived in Hamilton's sixth floor suite, he and Jacob Michaels were waiting.

"I presume you've each seen the article," Hamilton began without delay.

"What article?" asked Sondra.

"In *Christian World*. Here's a copy," he said, handing her the magazine.

Not recognizing the cover, Sondra was confused. "You mean the piece about the two elderly ladies? I thought we decided to just let that matter drop."

"No, no! An entirely new article and much more damaging!"

Sondra flipped to the appropriate page and hurriedly scanned the piece.

"Really, Hamilton," said Michaels, speaking for the first time, "I still fail to see what the difficulty is. The first article itself was actually quite positive. After that interview with him we could have come out far worse. And now this—not even mentioning our name. I just don't see the problem."

"But that's the whole point! Don't you see? Under the guise of being complimentary this clever young man has taken a direct shot at our soft underbelly. He's out to do us no good, I tell you. He's taken aim at our credibility in the public eye."

"I think you are imagining it," insisted Michaels.

"He leaked the Greenville location, after my express constraint. And now this! His insinuous line of questioning now all becomes clear. He has some deceitful objective, I tell you."

"Hamilton, when I was informed of this second article—only last week, and not by you I might add—I discovered from my secretary that the young man had attempted to talk to us further. He may have wanted to discuss it in a reasonable manner. But what should I learn but that you scuttled his efforts. It seems, Hamilton, that if anyone is responsible it is you."

"I simply felt further interviews would be counterproductive, that he would probe further into areas we would rather keep private."

"That may be true, but then we must suffer the consequences of his article if we're not willing to see him."

"But there we are again at his motives," said Jaeger. "And I most firmly feel that we have to shut down anything further along this line by this no-account Maxwell."

"How?" asked Michaels.

"There are ways. I know people near *NWV.*"

"It seems the best thing would be to talk to the young man."

"No good. He'd turn an interview to his own advantage."

"Really, Hamilton! Don't come unhinged. Maxwell's not the enemy. His first article, as I told you at the time, could actually enlarge our number of donors. And now this one, as ticklish as might be some of the issues raised, is just not going to hurt us if we lie low and don't get drawn into defensiveness."

"But don't you see the suspicion it subtly casts on our spending? Just look at the inferences he clearly hopes his readers draw. All that talk about the poor widows and the Pharisees. There can be little doubt who he means. Criticizing you for not working with your hands—why the whole premise of his article is absurd! As if you can apply such obscure Scriptures as somebody's tentmaking to an organization like ETW! It's so farfetched as to be laughable. Yet he could damage us with such insinuations. There are people who take those words literally. And the point is, Jacob, underlying the entire article is the implication that we are supporting ourselves from the gifts of unsuspecting old ladies. It's lethal! He has, with that syrupy beginning about the two women, now succeeded in very skillfully sowing doubt on the financial integrity of the whole organization. It's the little things like an article such as this that can be the loose thread. Pull on it, insignificant as it seems, and everything unravels!"

"Nonsense, Hamilton!"

"Jacob, I'm afraid I must insist that—"

"Listen to me, Hamilton," interrupted Michaels. "I know you mean well. Your instincts are usually sound. And I understand that we must tread carefully until the people in Texas are comfortable with our presence. But about these articles, I emphasize again that there's no danger to us in the public mind. The more you try to douse the enthusiasm of someone like this reporter, the more new suspicions you'll arouse about your own intentions. Now, he's told the world about Greenville. We wouldn't have ourselves. But it's done. OK. Let's deal with it in a gracious and diplomatic manner. I don't want to hear any more paranoia about Maxwell's vendetta against ETW. If he wants to talk, I want to give him an interview. We'll be courteous and nip any problems in the bud. You and Sondra can work out our official response to the article. I imagine the press will be about the building today."

He rose and left the room.

Sondra looked up to Jaeger, standing, and sighed as if to say, "Well, . . . he's the boss."

Jaeger walked slowly toward the large picture window and gazed out into the distance where his eyes were diverted by clouds of vapor rising into the cold air above the warmer water of Lake Michigan.

The silence continued a moment. Though the financial district below was now in full swing, no one else was present on the sixth floor because of the early hour.

"Ironic isn't it, Sondra," he mused, "all over this city people are scurrying about to buy and invest and spend. Where will it all be in a hundred years? But this work of ours is so different; we're involved in eternal things, Sondra. People depend on us for their faith. We have a sacred spiritual calling. We mustn't let this one article stand in the path of its fulfillment. Do you know what I'm getting at?"

"I'm not sure. Mr. Michaels seemed pretty clear that—"

"They give to us," he continued, not heeding her response, "and it not only furthers the ministry, it builds their faith. We can't let one ambitious reporter take that away from them."

His words trailed off as he became lost in thought, reasoning with himself, trying to balance the instructions of his head with his personal goals. Then as if his mind was finally made up, he turned quickly and addressed his female counterpart.

"Sondra," he said, "here's what we're going to do. You can use my typewriter there. We're going to come up with a straight-forward plan to deal with this thing, nip it in the bud, just like Jacob said."

Sondra rose, walked to the large maple-topped desk, sat down behind the typewriter, and typed as Jaeger—still gazing distantly out the window—dictated: first a press release, then a series of responses to what he was certain would be the reporters' predictable questions.

19

Two hours later, Sondra DeQue emerged from Hamilton Jaeger's office and promptly made the public announcement that a brief press conference would be convened that afternoon at four o'clock in the Colonade Room of the Luxor Towers. Sometimes she wondered why she went through the motions of presenting herself as such a knowledgeable spokesperson for ETW. As she stood before reporters, speaking for a vast network of ministries and agencies, speaking in fact as the mouthpiece of Jacob Michaels himself, she oftentimes felt she knew less than anyone in the building about what was really going on inside the organization. But that was her job. Put on a pleasant face, smile, and if necessary double-talk her way around thorny questions that probed a bit too deeply.

She drove the six-mile distance back to her apartment, took a shower, enjoyed a relaxing brunch, and dressed—this time more meticulously—for the afternoon at the office.

The private session with Hamilton had set Sondra's mental wheels in motion. It wasn't that she was actually forced to compromise values or beliefs as such. And though not profound, Sondra DeQue did have beliefs. Her "walk with the Lord" could not be termed personal as she knew many would describe theirs. Nevertheless, she maintained convictions which, to whatever degree, were important to her. But her position frequently demanded "discretion," as Hamilton was so fond of putting it. She questioned what part honest communication, on the other hand, played.

Meanwhile she carried out her assignments dutifully, trying to convince herself that, as Hamilton had reminded her, theirs was a sacred calling.

Is Hamilton grating on me? she wondered. Maybe it wasn't the job at all. Why did past closeness so frequently yield to this petty sort of annoyance? She couldn't still love him—she was beginning to doubt she ever had. Her reflective mood carried her back . . .

It had been a dozen years before when she had first landed the job of part-time secretary to Henry Michaels's son, Jacob. She was twenty-two, away from home in Quebec for the first time, and Chicago had proved a virile and exciting world for the beautiful and naive young Canadian. Jacob's mystique had been too much, and his young secretary had fallen blissfully in love. The delight of being near him gave a life devoid of outside social involvement a thrill of meaning.

She worshiped him in silence for more than a year, cherishing those evenings in his office, working late, just the two of them. Jacob Michaels was no one's fool in such matters and guessed her feelings quite accurately. Nor was he immune to the blandishments of her charm and the drawing force of her attraction to him. Sondra dressed exquisitely, always wore captivating fragrances, and was certainly more than ordinarily good-looking. Her thin, five-foot, ten-inch body, natural shyness, and bewitchingly innocent smile were enough to bedevil any man's imagination. To what extent Jacob may have subtly encouraged her even he could not have known.

But he kept himself in check and did not go too far, knowing that his rise to a more conspicuous position upon his father's retirement was imminent. He'd learned his lesson and had matured over the years, cared about the ministry, loved his wife, and was not prepared to sacrifice all for a brief moment of madness, fond as he was of Sondra.

Their "affaire de coeur," which was never to be, dramatically began and ended one evening when they were forced to work late preparing the final galley proofs of his second book. They'd broken off about five-thirty, gone for dinner together nearby, and had returned to the office. Everyone else was gone. The floor was deserted. As he turned back into the office after closing the door behind him, not realizing how close Sondra was still standing, he bumped into her, nearly knocking her down. He reached to support her, their eyes met, and then suddenly she embraced him and kissed him without pretense or reserve. He was caught so off guard that for a moment he began to respond. Then, thinking better of himself, gently took her shoulders and eased her back.

Though his words had been tender, his unmistakable message was clear: there could be no deeper involvement. Sondra was shattered, mortified at what she had done in the heat of the moment, embarrassed at her lack of inhibition.

Nothing was ever said about the incident. No one else ever knew, and Sondra eventually recovered, if not a great deal older, certainly more wary. The hope in her heart did not fade overnight. Still she watched for signals that might have indicated in Jacob a change in the weather. But she was disappointed, and relieved therefore when some three months later she was transferred to the public relations sector as part of its full-time staff.

Still smarting inside, Sondra's emotional defenses were off their guard when Hamilton Jaeger began to make subtle advances toward her. At first it had been strictly business. He needed her help with this, a bit of extra typing, could she go to lunch to discuss such-and-such. But when he had unexpectedly shown up at her apartment one Saturday evening there could be no mistaking his intentions. Common sense warned Sondra against deeper involvement. Inside she guessed she wasn't in love with Jaeger. A year earlier she had known what love meant—she thought—as well as the intolerable anguish of loss. And the difference between Jacob and Hamilton was like night and day.

Yet there was a sense in which his warmth and obvious feeling toward her obscured more practical matters. On the one hand she knew in the end it would probably mean breaking, . . . parting, . . . heartache. Yet on the other, he cared, and that touched a deep feminine longing.

Thus Sondra DeQue and Hamilton Jaeger became an item within the walls of ETW. Their meetings were clandestine at first, contrived by Hamilton in the most cunning of ways, taking on the pattern of a game of chess—Hamilton carefully protecting his would-be untarnished reputation, but fooling no one. Sondra was less careful; after all they were both unmarried. Eventually there came to be something legitimately resembling love in Sondra's heart for the man, although it was far more pragmatic than the phrase "being in love" would imply. For that reason, she never considered herself in love with Hamilton Jaeger. She enjoyed his attention and relished being made to feel like a woman. And though she reminded herself of the unlikelihood of anything permanent, still the image persisted—daydreams circumventing reason—of his softly whispered words, "I need you, Sondra."

Two years with Hamilton Jaeger, however, taught Sondra that love must mean something more. There was a void inside, and she knew it. She had bounced into the eager arms of Hamilton Jaeger on the rebound from a deep hurt. It was no basis for the most meaningful of relationships. Now she saw that her deeper self wanted permanence, communication, and shared emotions far more than simply another human being to keep one warm.

She determined to talk to Hamilton, to share her innermost thoughts. She could bottle it up no longer.

It was seven-thirty when he arrived that night at Sondra's apartment and settled himself into one of the two deep armchairs and stretched his feet up on a footstool.

"This is one of the coziest places I know," he said.

Sondra was busy in the kitchen. He watched her thoughtfully. As she returned to the living room, he found himself admiring her beauty and gracefulness. There was a rhythm about each of her movements.

"Sondra," he said, "you're an astonishing girl."

"In what way?" she asked.

"Well," he went on, "even in a simple dress like you're wearing you've got to be one of the best-looking women I've ever seen."

He stood up and kissed her. After a moment she eased herself gently free and turned away.

"Hamilton," she said, "this just isn't any good."

"Any good, Sondra? I don't understand."

"I think you know—between us."

"We have a good thing going here. We're free to live our own lives, yet we have each other when we need—"

"I don't think that's enough for me any longer," Sondra had burst out. She wanted love, she thought. Her body, her heart, ached for it.

"So it's marriage you want, is it?" asked Jaeger.

"No, of course not. You know me better than that. Not that I've anything against marriage. But that's hardly the point. There's just got to be something deeper to a relationship."

"I could try to kid you," Hamilton said slowly, "with a bunch of phony words, Sondra. But we're both grown-ups. I thought that was understood."

"I don't want to be kidded," she answered. "But I don't want to be just a bag of desirable bones to you, either. There ought to be something more."

"Of course there's more—"

"Is there?"

"If you're honest with yourself," he responded harshly, "sometimes maybe there isn't any more."

Sondra's eyes filled with tears. She took out a Kleenex and wiped them. *What's happening to me?* she asked herself. *The self-reliant Sondra DeQue, crying like a baby! Why can't I take this in stride like I've done before?*

Something changed for Sondra DeQue that night. Hamilton was an insensitive man, and as she later reflected on it, she knew that her earlier resolve had indeed reflected her true desires. She had tried to express them, but Hamilton had been incapable of hearing. But if he wouldn't listen, if he didn't care enough about her as a person to penetrate the veil of her emotions, then their relationship was meaningless anyway. She would not continue to play a game, even if—as Hamilton had said—for some people there sometimes wasn't any more.

For her there had to be. That she was certain of.

It was not long afterward that Sondra had volunteered to be a crusade counselor. Her incentive was ostensibly to see the crusade from the inside, to gain a fresh perspective of how things operated. But in her heart of hearts, this was Sondra's way of responding to the urgings toward life's deeper meaning. There had been sporadic moments in her life when Sondra had sensed instincts within her yearning for the personal religious faith she'd heard talked about but had never experienced. Oddly enough, it was the bitter episode with Jaeger that opened the door to it.

At the meeting Jacob Michaels had declared, "You tonight who are lonely, feeling an indescribable void down inside, won't you please come forward now, down here to the front, and accept Jesus into your heart? He can give your life meaning." Sondra had risen from her seat and had gone to help pass out literature to those who came. But inside her soul she had made a decision of her own. She had prayed, "God help me be something better. Show me the way—I want to be more than I am." The prayer was less intense than many. But it was sincere and motivated from a heart recognizing its need and convicted of its own inadequacy.

From that moment, life began gradually to look up for Sondra DeQue. Revelations did not come quickly. But she began to participate semi-regularly in more of the spiritual life of ETW, attended staff prayer meetings, read some of Michaels's books, and attended the crusade meetings with greater frequency and listened with deeper personal interest.

She never again went out with Hamilton Jaeger. He did not for some time give up trying to reason with her, seeing no inconsistency in her maintaining newfound convictions while carrying on with him as before. On several future occasions Sondra attempted to discuss with him what she sensed had to be part of a meaningful relationship. But, though paying lip service to her notions, Hamilton was unable to grasp the reality she was searching for. Their relationship cooled, and eventually the businesslike demeanor between them resumed.

Now Sondra, at thirty-four, found herself much more confident as a person and far less tolerant of one such as Hamilton. She had grown. But not only did it seem he hadn't, he appeared oblivious to the maturing taking place within her and continued to address her as if she were the same naive youngster of a decade before. The years had deepened Sondra, while they had only aged Hamilton.

She still worked around him daily, found him increasingly annoying, and couldn't help wondering if he didn't upon occasion choose her assignments and speak to her in his most conciliatory manner with the intention of subtly knifing her for the hurt he perceived she had dealt him.

20

Sondra DeQue walked briskly toward the center of the platform. She wore a tailored brown suit with a light cream silk blouse that complemented her fashionable tan glasses and rich auburn hair. The room of twelve to fifteen reporters quieted. *Newsweek, Time, The Washington Post,* the *New York Times,* and the *Chicago Tribune* were all represented. The remainder were all from Christian magazines, most notably *Moody Monthly* and *Christianity Today.* She adjusted the microphone and immediately began to read the prepared statement on the sheet before her; no advance copies had been distributed.

"Ladies and gentlemen," she began, "a brief article appeared two months ago in the *Christian World* concerning Evangelize the World, Inc., followed by a second article yesterday. Since it appears that the magazine intends to run a series focusing on our organization, Mr. Michaels felt some response would be appropriate.

"First of all we want to thank the *World* for its interest in our upcoming meetings in the Chicago area. It's a shame," and here she hesitated, looked out toward the small roomful of reporters, glanced around momentarily, and then continued, ". . . it's a shame Mr. Maxwell couldn't be present today for Mr. Michaels wanted me to express his personal thanks for the first article which he feels will provide a positive contribution to preparations. We do, however, have a concern, especially after yesterday's article, for what may look to some like a disregard for attempting to faithfully balance the charts, as it were, in each specific area of endeavor. There were a number of very pointed questions raised. And we do want—"

In mid-sentence, she momentarily paused as the door to the rear of the room opened quietly and about half of those present turned in their seats to witness Jackson Maxwell's attempt to slip in unceremoniously. He smiled greetings to those few nearby and sat down while Ms. DeQue attempted to continue as if no interruption had occurred.

"—as I said, we do want to be certain it is clear in the minds of our faithful supporters that each and every dime they contribute is spent on the Lord's work. Great effort is made to correlate specified gifts with those ministries for which each is pinpointed. And that, ladies and gentlemen, is the primary purpose of this statement today—to let our followers know that nothing has changed in the manner in which their contributions are administered and to assure everyone of the financial integrity of ETW. Now if there are any questions on that, I have time to take a few."

Several hands shot in the air.

"Yes, Mr. McPherson."

"Ms. DeQue, can you tell us exactly what Mr. Michaels is concerned about? I really see nothing in the first article to arouse your following. And yesterday's release never even mentioned ETW. Are your people defensive? If so, I see no reason for it."

"You're right. There is no anxiety in that regard whatsoever. We're not 'concerned,' Mr. McPherson. That is perhaps too strong a characterization—"

"Concerned enough to call a press conference, I would say."

"That may be true. I concede your point, Mr. McPherson. Let me just reiterate that Mr. Michaels wants it clear to our faithful patrons that they should continue viewing their gifts to ETW as always, that nothing has changed in our approach to—"

"Keep the money coming, and don't ask any questions, is that it?" shouted a voice from the back. The speaker, one Harold Adams, was noted for his attempts to disrupt the calmest of settings, delighting in flustering spokesmen whenever he could find the opportunity. His writing was free-lance, not the best, and he was viewed, if not with contempt, yet with definite reserve. Rarely were his questions even addressed; to do so usually resulted in derailing an informative press session. Today, however, Sondra—ordinarily even-tempered and in control—fell victim to his bait. He had pushed the right button.

"That's not it at all!" she lashed back. "Mr. Adams, you should be ashamed for even thinking Mr. Michaels would mean such a thing!"

"Then what, may I ask," continued Adams, now on his feet and eager to pursue it finding himself so suddenly cast onto center stage, "do you mean? You expressed your 'concern.' To me it sounds like you are worried the gifts will stop coming because of the financial indelicacies hinted at in the Maxwell article."

"Indelicacies!" she said indignantly.

"Come now, Ms. DeQue," protested Adams, "spare us all the carefully worded enigmatic baloney, and tell us what we came to find out—what's the big deal about those two articles?"

"Mr. Adams," she said bitterly, "do you dare cast suspicion on the financial integrity of either Mr. Michaels or ETW? If so I can tell you—"

"Excuse me, Ms. DeQue—" The voice came from Jackson Maxwell, now on his feet. "If I may just have a brief word. I know I'm out of order, but I feel I must say—to Mr. Adams—that such was never my intent. There is not the least ground for his insinuations, and nothing I have written can be regarded as substantiating what he has implied."

He resumed his seat. Sondra, relieved, cooled a little. Adams, however, was not willing to let go so easily. He stood once again, but before he could voice another question a second hand shot up, and DeQue promptly recognized it.

"Aren't we really missing the key element of revelation in Maxwell's article?" The speaker this time was Doug Cochran of the *Post.* "Despite the fact that it was this second article yesterday that really began to pull the scabs off the sore spot of Christian financing, it's really Maxwell's first article that contains the biggest of what we might call *news.* It seems we ought to be focusing our attention on the mention of a new Michaels complex outside Dallas. What's the nature of this new center, Ms. DeQue—what's it going to be for?"

"The article called it a Christian outreach center, and that's what it will be, no more, no less."

"Surely you could be a little more definitive?"

"I'm sorry, I really can't be at this time."

"Ms. DeQue," interjected a young woman from *Christianity Today*, "we've all taken time out of our day to come here. And we want to give you good reports in our magazines and papers. After all, we're on the same side. But if you're going to hold out on us in secrecy like this, we're hard-pressed to put a positive image on what we write."

"I'm not being secretive. You've heard of diplomacy, haven't you?" she said, heating up once more.

"What's there to be diplomatic about?" put in another reporter. "The land's there, you're going to build. Why can't you tell us—"

"Negotiations, Mr. Harper. Certainly you can appreciate that in an organization of the size of ETW—"

"Negotiations with whom?"

This was really going too far! Sondra knew she was dangerously close to losing it. She could feel Hamilton's eyes burning on the back of her neck from the foyer nearby. He would be infuriated. She had to get out of this interview! It had not gone well. The very concerns Hamilton had been trying to allay were intensifying.

"Negotiations, Mr. Harper, that are delicate in nature. I just cannot reveal further details without—"

"With whom?"

"There are other organizations in the area whose ministries and goals we must be sensitive toward."

"What organizations? Could you be a little less abstract?"

"I'm sorry," said Sondra glancing up at the clock. "I see our time is up. I won't be able to take any further questions. Thank you all for coming."

She hurried from the room, noticeably flustered.

21

Jackson rose slowly from his seat and wandered out of the building toward the parking lot.

"Buy you coffee, Maxwell?" The question came from *Moody Monthly*'s Jeremy Harper.

"Thanks, Harper, not today."

"Why were you late, especially with your articles on the line?"

"I didn't find out about the session until 3:30," said Jackson, "and then by accident. I was clear across town."

"They didn't call you?"

"No," said Jackson puzzled. "You?"

"Sure. They're really good about posting us on things like that."

Jackson looked up quizzically but said nothing.

He wasn't anxious to return to the office—not yet. He drove to the park, walked to a bench, and slowly munched on an apple left over from lunch. Why was Ms. DeQue—and therefore, he assumed, Jacob Michaels—so agitated over reaction to his first story? He'd said nothing objectionable. If they were disturbed the best posture would have been to low profile it. Though he had questions about ETW, he'd been careful not to let them show through in his story. If they were going to be upset, he'd certainly brought up plenty to raise their hackles in the second story. But the first? It had been positively innocuous. Why the concern?

It was chilly. Not many people out now. Even the ducks waddling up in search of some crumbs of bread looked cold.

It reminded him of the interview involving Hamilton Jaeger some months back. Their paranoid approach was all so absurd if they had nothing to hide. But DeQue's angry outbursts and refusal to deal straightforwardly with legitimate questions only insured there would be more flap after the press conference.

Why the press conference at all? Why hadn't they informed him? How could an otherwise topflight PR staff allow themselves to blunder into an awkward session like that?

His thoughts trailed off.

The deep reverie was interrupted several minutes later by the sound of approaching footsteps. He hadn't seen her in a month, but knew the footfall anywhere. He looked up; there was Diana.

"Jackson—you're lost in thought."

"Stumped on a story I'm working on."

"Can I help?"

"Not unless you have an inside line on the Jacob Michaels organization."

Diana gave him a singular look of questioning but said nothing.

"I just returned from a press conference," Jackson continued, "called to alleviate some misgivings about finances but which raised more than anyone had in the first place."

"Doubts about Jacob Michaels's finances—I had no idea."

"No, I wouldn't go so far as to say there actually *are* any serious suspicions. But I do know there's bound to be negative press fallout for ETW after today."

"That's too bad."

"If there are improprieties the public ought to be aware of them. But it's too soon to know that. The whole thing may be just a misunderstanding—one I'm responsible for."

"You're feeling guilty?" asked Diana.

"No. My article was sound—but I'm keeping you from your run!"

"Too cold! I was about done anyway."

"Well, I've got to get back to the office too," said Jackson. "But I did promise myself that the next time I saw you I'd get your phone number so we wouldn't have to depend on chance meetings in the park once a week, or once a month—whenever we happened to run into each other. Is that allowable information for a newspaperman like me to have?"

"Sure," she laughed. "I have no deep dark secrets from the press."

"Glad to hear it. Maybe I'm just getting skittish myself—occupational hazard, I suppose."

"You love it though, don't you? The questions, digging for answers?"

"You've found me out! Yeah, you're right. I guess I do. I want to make sure things are told like they are. Anyway, how about lunch sometime? How full are your days?"

"I'm flexible. But I'm at school most of the time. Why don't you let me call you—at your office—when I can make it? Tuesdays and Thursdays are best. I'm off from twelve to three."

"Next Tuesday?" asked Jackson.

"I'll call you," said Diana and ran off with a wave.

Jackson's eye followed her, thinking it curious—*Most girls don't want to do the calling.* Then he realized—he still didn't have her phone number.

22

Leaving the Colonade Room, Sondra DeQue hurried to the ladies' lounge where she remained several minutes. She had to cool the red from her cheeks and veins before encountering Hamilton. How she wished she had time to change her blouse and apply some fresh deodorant! She could feel the dripping emotional perspiration. Oh, to be home right now, standing in the shower—this day had already been several hours too long. When she emerged from the restroom, Hamilton was not around. She rode the elevator to the fifth floor, where he was predictably waiting in her office.

He wasted no time getting straight to the point.

"Sondra," be began, "that was a disaster! Surely you could have controlled your anger."

She was in no mood, however, to have the entire blame shoved her way.

"Look, Hamilton," she said, the heat rising once more, "I read your statement, and I handled the questions just as you told me to. How was I to know—"

"Just like I told you to!" he laughed huskily. "I hardly suggested you allow a term like 'financial indelicacy' to come up!"

"That was not my fault!"

"But you hardly helped matters, Sondra—lashing out, taking the defensive. Our stance must be one of composure and confidence."

"That's fine for you to say!" snapped Sondra angrily. "How often have you had to stand up to the cross fire and take the heat?"

"That's your job. You've always relished it before."

"Maybe I don't like your insinuation that my blunders are going to take us all under."

"Nothing's going under!" he shouted. "I don't want to hear that sort of thing from you again, do you understand?"

"Maybe I can't take the pressure of your expectations, Hamilton. Maybe it's time you found someone else to do your bidding with the press."

"No need to get upset, it's just that—"

"Look, I do what you tell me. I skirt around issues. I lead the press on wild goose chases for you. I select my words to keep everyone's images untainted. Well maybe I can't do it anymore! You called that stupid press conference. It was a bad idea, and I'm not responsible. If there's anyone to blame—it's you!"

Without giving him the chance to say another word, Sondra spun around and ran from the office. After another ten minutes in the lounge, she hoped he'd be gone. She returned to her office, speaking to no one, and was relieved to find it empty. She locked the door and sat down.

Not that it'll do any good, she thought. *Hamilton's still got the key and never hesitates to go wherever he wants around here.* But she doubted he'd be back this afternoon.

She breathed deeply and stared out the window.

There has to be a change. I can't take this much longer.

23

The following morning, Jackson Maxwell walked into the building at six-thirty. He needed time to think.

The motives spinning in his head were mixed. As a Christian, he felt it his duty to interpret everything in the most favorable light for all concerned. He wanted to faithfully represent ETW and Jacob Michaels. Yet on the other hand, as a reporter, his nose detected something adrift here, and how could he not pursue it? Maybe he'd stumbled unknowingly into more than he realized by what he'd just written.

When his editor arrived shortly after seven, Jackson recounted the events of the previous day.

"That really steams me they didn't call," McClanahan said. "It had to be intentional!"

"But why single me out if the whole idea was to discuss my articles?" rejoined Jackson, irritated himself, yet voicing a measured response, "It doesn't make sense." Since his interview with Michaels and Jaeger his anger toward them had cooled.

"If they were doubtful about the impact of your stories—"

"Which doesn't figure," interrupted Jackson.

"Granted," resumed McClanahan, "but *if* they were, what better way to undermine your credibility and provide you no line of defense than to make sure you weren't present."

"But I was there—and you heard what happened. They didn't come down on me, or even the second article at all. They were the ones who looked bad."

"Serves them right," said McClanahan with a wry smile.

"So what do I do now, Ed? Go to work on the next article as if nothing happened?"

"Maybe I've been a newspaperman for too long. I was in the news business long before I was a Christian. I like to think my motives are good and that my ethics come ahead of my reporter's instinct. But when there's a potential story somewhere, containing no clear-cut requirement that would compromise a Christian, my first inclination is always to go for it—dig—find out what's going on. I don't ponder every literal word I write ahead of time."

"You consider that sound—I mean, is that a Christian's proper response?"

"God made me a newsman—and a good one, I think. I enjoy unearthing news. So I go after news. I feel I am honoring Him—honoring what He has made of me—by being the best, most skillful reporter I can."

"If I get your drift, you're saying we should look into this thing a little deeper?"

"What I'm saying, Jackson, is that if you don't follow up on it, I'll assign someone else."

"And if I run into rough water?"

"If the Lord wants us off the story, or to move in another direction, we have to trust that He'll make it clear. That's one of the foundational assumptions. We have to listen for His voice, then move confidently forward. There's no other way to get anything done in this world. You'll be on life's sidelines forever if you wait for some kind of 'leading' before every step you take."

"I do know that principle," said Jackson thoughtfully.

"Look, Jackson," said Ed, "it was your curiosity that started the whole thing. But I'll respect your decision if ethically you feel you shouldn't—"

"It's not ethics so much. But now I wonder whether I'm imagining the whole thing, making more of it than really exists. If there's a story, believe me I want to be part of it. But I don't want to be guilty of—"

"This is a switch," said McClanahan, "you questioning yourself! Usually you're so busy getting the lowdown on everyone else you don't stop long enough to ask if your approach is right. Why so hesitant?"

Jackson paused. "I suppose it is out of character for me, isn't it?" he said with a laugh. "I guess lately I've been thinking a little more about my own motives."

"That's good too," said the editor, "as long as you don't let it grind your work to a halt. But believe me, you're not making this up, Jackson. I've been around long enough to sense double-talk when I hear it. And usually that Ms. DeQue is pretty good at it. But yesterday she lost herself. I don't know why. But it means something. It's our duty, as newspapermen, as reporters—and God's

120

reporters—to find out just what it does mean. Why the conference? Why was she on edge? Did she eat green onions for breakfast, have a fight with her boyfriend—or did they put her up there for a smoke screen to hide something they are worried about? What raw nerve did you touch? Why did they try to keep you away? Most important of all—who's pulling the strings behind Ms. DeQue? Michaels himself? If so, why is he so defensive? Is Ms. DeQue acting on her own? What stake does she have in it? There's your story!"

"You make it sound as though there's a room full of dark secrets. We don't want to overreact."

"You're right. We mustn't be guilty of the slightest impropriety. I'm not suggesting you *print* those questions. I'm just saying your reporter's nose must wonder about them. If all is well at ETW, we'll find out, and it'll make the next article that much stronger. We're not looking for wrong—we're looking for truth. But to find it you have to probe. Along the way you ask a lot of questions, even if there proves to be no substance to your doubts. That's how the truth becomes known."

"I see your point," said Jackson slowly.

"You raised good, tough issues in your second article. You pointed no fingers. Their reaction tells me they're worried, and that has implications. We have to find out what they are."

He paused. Neither spoke for a moment. The room was gradually filling with the rest of the staff. Here and there a computer's keys could be heard. The gurgling of the coffee maker sent a pleasant aroma around the floor.

"OK," Jackson said at length, "where do I go from here—what next?"

"Be a reporter! Talk to people—investigate. The two key Ws, Jackson. Surely you haven't forgotten them this soon—who and why? Find out who and why, and you're ninety percent home."

"You think Michaels would see me again?"

"Why not? Worth a try. If he won't, try someone lower down on the staff. There was a guy we had here last year—only with us a couple months. He went over to ETW, the publishing end, I think. If you can't get anyone to talk to you, I could probably set up an interview with him. I imagine he'd at least be able to tell you who to talk to. I'll get his phone number later today."

Jackson walked to his desk, filled his typewriter with a fresh sheet of paper, and typed out the questions that had been cluttering his mind since the press conference. Then he spent the next hour and a half organizing his thoughts into a plan on how to proceed.

It was nine forty-five before he was ready to make his first call. He started right at the top.

"Good morning," the voice at the end of the line answered. "This is Evangelize the World, International."

"Good morning," replied Jackson. "I would like to speak with Jacob Michaels."

"Just a moment, sir, I'll connect you with his office."

There was a pause while the extension phone rang.

"Mr. Michaels's office," another secretary answered.

"Hello—is Mr. Michaels in? I'd like a word with him."

"May I ask who is calling, sir?"

"My name's Jackson Maxwell. I've spoken with him before."

"One moment."

A longer delay. Then Jackson heard another extension line ringing.

"Hello, Mr. Maxwell—Hamilton Jaeger here. I'm sorry, Mr. Michaels is unavailable today. Might I help you?"

Jackson's fist tightened and quietly pounded, as if in slow motion, on his desk. The frustration was immediately visible on his face. *I'll never get through,* thought Jackson. *This guy's going to cut me off at every turn.*

"Well," he said, working hard to retain his composure, "I was hoping to make an appointment to meet him again. I'm going to be working on another article."

"I'm sorry. That'll probably not be possible just now. We've a pretty heavy schedule between now and the crusade—a book deadline and another compact disc will be released. There just isn't time."

"But," replied Jackson, "he assured me if I needed any help on these articles I had only to call and—"

"Certainly, young man," soothed Jaeger in a condescending tone, "Mr. Michaels does want to cooperate with you and give you every possible assistance. Tell you what, I'll talk to the public relations department and set something up for you, an interview with someone in their section. They ought to be able to give you everything you need."

"I really don't want to go that route," insisted Jackson, feeling the temper again that Jaeger had triggered in him before, "I need—"

"I'm sorry, Maxwell, my secretary's buzzing me. If you'll excuse me, I'll have someone give you a call within the next few days."

Jackson replaced the receiver, exasperated. His recent more positive thoughts toward Michaels and his people were rapidly evaporating. Why did Jaeger unleash such hostility in him?

It didn't take much experience to recognize the runaround when you'd been the victim of one. Jackson stared at the paper before him, full of his random thoughts of an hour ago. His vision blurred, and he found it difficult to read them.

"OK, if that's how he wants it," he said to himself at length, giving in to his anger, "two can play that game! If you want hardball, Jaeger, I'll jump in the game with you!"

He'd get to Michaels one way or the other!

The call had enraged him. Yes, he'd talk to the fellow Ed had mentioned—and soon. He'd get a lead inside ETW.

That smug attitude! he thought. *That closedness!*

He went to see McClanahan. From him to personnel, then back to his desk to make several phone calls. His adrenaline was still flowing when three hours later he sat down to lunch opposite twenty-six-year-old Cooper Graves of the book publishing division of ETW, formerly an employee of *NWV.*

24

"I appreciate your seeing me," Jackson began. "I realize I'm probably not the most popular at ETW right now."

"I heard about your articles," said Graves.

"No doubt!" Jackson laughed.

"But the press conference caused more talk around the building than anything you wrote. The fallout from your statements would've had a short half-life if it hadn't been for DeQue's floundering in front of the press."

"It's being laid on her?"

"Yesterday's blunder? Yes, I suppose it is. Down in publishing we don't hear much though. Sometimes it's like we're an independent printing agency."

"But surely there's scuttlebutt that floats in and out?" asked Jackson.

"Of course—that can't be helped."

"So what's being said—who ordered the press conference, and why?"

"I assumed it was—like Sondra said—to alleviate concerns your articles may have raised. And Greenville's something of a sore spot, I've been told," said Graves.

"But that was an insignificant detail, not even central to the point I was making."

"Maybe so, but there's something different about it."

"How so?" Jackson asked.

"It's not talked about on staff. All we know is that it exists, and if it goes through, we may all be shipped down there eventually, but—"

"The whole organization headquartered there?"

"I don't know. Everyone's pretty tight-lipped."

"But why? The land acquisitions are public record. No secrets there."

"They don't want to say anything till it's more definite. No sense working people up over a change that might never happen and is years away in any case."

"That's standard precaution," said Jackson. "But Jaeger is irrationally defensive and cryptic about it."

"Greenville's more his baby than anyone's. Michaels is involved, of course, but I think it's Jaeger who's carried the vision from the beginning."

"The vision—of what?" asked Jackson.

"Of a kind of conglomerate of Christian ministries, a central headquarters."

The interview was certainly going differently than he'd planned. Graves seemed to trust him to a certain extent. But Jackson couldn't seem pushy or too eager. He'd come to talk about the articles and the press conference, but here they were back on the subject of the center. Why did all roads lead to Greenville?

"Michaels—or maybe Jaeger—intends to centralize ETW's structure there and add radio and TV broadcasting, training, probably a college, that sort of thing?"

"I've said too much already," said Graves, hesitating for the first time. "I don't like to speculate when I have no basis of knowing for sure."

"I understand," said Jackson cautiously. "But do you think Jaeger himself is the force behind it?"

"I've gathered so. I heard two fairly high-up secretaries from the sixth floor talking in the snack bar the other day. I wasn't intentionally eavesdropping, but I was alone and could hardly help overhearing. One of them said something about Michaels not knowing all the details, and then there was something about Jaeger and his talk about the common good. I assumed they were talking about Greenville."

"And Greenville's going to entail more than a simple change of locations?"

"Why else would the plot be so extensive? Sounds to me like a whole self-contained little country, you know. It could house fifty ETWs. But I've got to be careful. It's all conjecture anyway. Probably I've said more than I should have as it is. I trust you won't use this or quote me until there's an official release on it?"

"I'll be discreet," said Jackson. "Oh—one other thing I meant to ask. Do you suppose you could find out Mr. Michaels's secretary's name for me?"

"That's easy. Her name's Liz Layne. There's something of a

joke about comparing her with Lois Lane and Michaels with Superman. Not in very good taste, is it?" Graves laughed. "Lunchroom talk, you know."

"I was also considering talking with Sondra DeQue. Do you know her? What do you think my chances are of meeting her, in private—off the record?"

"I don't know. She's practically as inaccessible as Michaels himself. A bit of an enigma around the building. No one knows her that well, what she does, who she's close to. I gather she's a loner. She's been coming to the staff Bible studies lately, but usually alone. I don't really know anything about her."

"Know anyone who does?"

"Not really."

Graves paused, thinking. "You know," he went on after a moment, "come to think of it there *is* someone you ought to talk to. I don't know how well he knows Sondra, but he's pretty involved in the Bible study group, and from what I understand he used to be close to Michaels."

"Who is it?"

"Name's Robert Means. A real interesting guy. Soft-spoken, doesn't always say much. But one look in his eyes, and you can see there's a lot going on down inside. He's in the correspondence section."

"And you think he might know DeQue?"

"I would think, though I can't say for sure. How well, it's hard to say. Might be that no one is going to have the chance to know her either."

"Why do you say that?"

"Just this morning I heard there's a possibility she might be demoted from her spokeswoman's position. Jaeger was livid about her performance yesterday—hey, I've got to be getting back—time slipped away from me. Thanks for lunch."

"Don't mention it. Thank you, Cooper."

"And remember—off the record."

25

It was admittedly a cloak-and-dagger scenario. But Jackson had to know about the relationships behind the doors that were closed to him. He'd arrived at seven-thirty that morning and parked across the street.

At eight forty-seven Sondra DeQue entered the Luxor Towers. He jumped out of his car, dashed cross the street and into the lobby, just in time to see the elevator doors close behind her. He tore up the flights of stairs to the fifth floor where ETW's public relations section was located. Chest heaving from the ascent, he cautiously opened the door into the hall. He heard the elevator close and start up once more. He emerged slowly and glanced up and down the corridor, then spotted what he recognized as Ms. DeQue's coat disappearing through the public relations door.

That was all he wanted to know. She was in!

Her impending potential ouster was of little consequence to him at this moment.

Jackson turned and began to make his way slowly back down the hall. As he opened the door to the stairway, his steps were arrested by sight of a man exiting a nearby office and walking along the corridor toward him. In the midst of his hasty intrigue, the man's serenity caught his attention, and as he offered Jackson a smile and "good morning" as he passed, the two men's eyes met for the briefest of instants.

As the stranger continued on down the length of the corridor, Jackson glanced back at the door through which he had come. The small sign on it read "Correspondence."

"I wonder if that was the man Graves mentioned," mused Jackson to himself as he continued on through the door and on his way.

Jackson walked back down to the ground floor, out of sight from curious ETW eyes, located a phone booth across the street, and quickly dialed the number he'd scribbled on a notepad before leaving home.

"Public relations, please," he said to the receptionist who

answered.

Then after a moment came the greeting he'd been waiting for.

"Sondra DeQue please," said Jackson.

"May I ask who's calling?"

"Jackson Maxwell."

"One moment."

He'd been harboring a hunch. He'd soon know if he'd been reading between the lines correctly.

After about a minute—longer, he knew, than would have been required to buzz DeQue's office—a voice came on the line, one Jackson knew instantly.

"Hello, Mr. Maxwell, this is Hamilton Jaeger. I'm sorry, Ms. DeQue isn't in at the moment. Is there anything I could help you with?"

So Jaeger held a lock on receptionists and secretaries too! He had been on the right track.

"No, not really," Jackson answered icily. "I wanted to speak with Ms. DeQue."

"What about, if I may ask?" queried Jaeger.

"I just wanted to follow up on some of the points raised at the press conference the other day."

"Yes, well, she's going to be out quite a lot in the next month. I'll certainly tell her you called, and I'm sure she'll get back to you as soon as she is able."

"Maybe you can tell me, Mr. Jaeger," Jackson said. "I've heard a rumor that Ms. DeQue has been demoted because of her handling of the press conference. Is that true?"

"I can't imagine how you heard such a thing!" answered Jaeger quickly, his congenial manner shifting.

"Is it true?" Jackson asked pointedly.

"Mr. Maxwell, there are certain things we prefer to keep out of the papers until we have them resolved. I simply cannot comment further."

You hardly need to, thought Jackson. Then to Jaeger, he suggested with a wry tone, "And Ms. DeQue's not available for comment?"

"As I said, Ms. DeQue will not be in her office regularly for some time, and nothing with regard to her future is certain at this moment. Now, Mr. Maxwell, if you'll excuse me."

Jackson let the receiver down slowly. Jaeger's position—or was it a stranglehold he held on things?—in ETW grew more and more intriguing.

He had to penetrate the Jaeger security net. He must get to Michaels—alone!—and DeQue. Away from Jaeger's interference!

Late that same afternoon, Jackson once more resumed his watch across from the Luxor Towers. Five o'clock came, five-fifteen, then five-thirty.

This was a stupid idea, he thought. He'd give it another fifteen minutes.

At five forty-one, out of the building walked his prey. She was accompanied by two others. Jackson cautiously slipped out of the car and followed on foot to the parking lot where first one, then the other of her companions went to their cars.

At last she was alone. He seized the opportunity; it might be his last.

"Miss Layne?" said Jackson approaching hurriedly.

"Actually, it's Mrs.," she answered, "but yes, I'm Liz Layne."

"My name's Jackson Maxwell. I'm a reporter, a writer with *News with a Vision.*"

"Ah, yes, Mr. Maxwell, I remember you now."

"I'm sorry to do this—in the parking lot and all—but I really need an opportunity to talk to Mr. Michaels again."

"You called yesterday. Wasn't Hamilton—Mr. Jaeger, that is—wasn't he able to help you?"

"It isn't Jaeger I want to see."

"Mr. Michaels is very busy. Surely you must understand. That's why Mr. Jaeger has given me strict instructions to intercept as many calls as possible and send them his way, so that Mr. Michaels won't be interrupted every few minutes. He specifically told me if you called—I remember your name—that I was to alert him immediately."

"Well, that certainly explains why I haven't been able to get through."

"It's all for Mr. Michaels's good. Don't you see, Hamilton's job is to shield him from the details."

"I understand," said Jackson, the frustration in his voice showing through. "But Jaeger is determined to shut off my attempts to interview anyone. It simply isn't possible to do a story thoroughly under such conditions."

"I'm sure he has his reasons."

"No doubt. But could I just ask you one favor? Please at least hear me out, and consider it."

"I can do that much. But you have to understand my position too. Hamilton was insistent that you not be given an interview. He claims you are a disruptive influence."

"Please, you've got to understand that I'm just trying to get at the truth here, not to disrupt or undermine anyone's ministry. Won't you please just tell Mr. Michaels—in private, not when Jaeger is around—that I've been trying to see him. I have to talk to him if this story's going to be possible. I want him to know. Then, if he doesn't want to grant me an interview, I'll respect that. But it's only fair of me to expect it to be his decision, not Jaeger's."

He stopped. She said nothing for a moment.

"I don't know—" she said at length.

"All I'm asking is that you tell him I've been trying and can't get through. You can reach me at the *World*."

"OK," she said after another pause, "I'll tell him."

"Thank you," said Jackson. "You won't regret it."

He half-ran back to his car, jubilant at the small bit of success. Adrenaline still flowing, he decided to follow up on his one other idea.

Remarkably enough, her name and address were in the telephone book. Jackson grabbed a hasty deli sandwich, drove to the Beverly Gardens apartment and condominium complex, parked his car, and walked to the directory. It was seven-twenty. How he hoped she'd be alone!

He ran his finger down the list. There she was—Sondra DeQue, Apartment 25 C.

26

The door opened, and there stood Sondra DeQue.

She seemed taller than Jackson had remembered her and had clearly expected no visitors. Though still wearing the day's brown suit, her stockinged feet were bare, the top of her blouse was casually unfastened, and her shoulder-length hair showed traces of rumpling. As she stared at Jackson her first look was blank, but almost instantaneously, a trace of recognition crossed her face. Her brow clouded slightly.

Jackson seized the offensive immediately. "Hello, Ms. DeQue. I'm Jackson Maxwell. I'm terribly sorry to infringe on your evening like this, but I need a few words with you."

"Mr. Maxwell, the man of the troublesome articles," she said with a half-sarcastic smile.

"Honestly, I didn't mean to cause all this commotion."

She laughed cynically. "Well, it certainly did me no good. If it had only dropped after your November piece. Hamilton was mad then, but content to let it go. But after the second, he hit the roof. With your article and the press conference, to tell you the truth, I'll be lucky to have a job by next week. Well, you're here now. Might as well come in."

She opened the door wider and led him into the small living room where he sat down.

"I'd just finished my dinner and was planning to have a cup of coffee—care to join me?"

"No, thanks."

"Anything else? I've some orange juice in the refrigerator."

"That sounds good—thank you."

If only she could see him as a flesh-and-blood person, thought Jackson as she went to the kitchen and poured his glass of juice. He had to get the conversation past the usual journalistic animosity that flared up when opposite sides squared off.

She returned with the juice and coffee and sat down across from him.

"I'm afraid I can't give you any information," she began. "I

131

am, after all, the press representative for ETW, and I'm obligated to work through channels. How could I justify—either to other newspersons or to my superiors—giving you an exclusive interview just because you showed up on my doorstep?"

"Let's not think of it as an interview," said Jackson. "Let's just have a discussion to clarify some unclear points."

"You poised there with your pen and tablet—and you want me to differentiate between an interview and a discussion. Come on, Mr. Maxwell, what do you take me for?"

"OK, OK. We'll make this whole thing off the record if you'd like. Look—no pen, no notebook." He held up his empty hands in a gesture aimed to say, "I've nothing to hide.'

She looked at him thoughtfully.

"All I want is to understand this situation a little better. I'm not even after a story. If I'm going to write about ETW I need to make sure my attitudes are straight. Maybe I need to know people like you, not as 'official representatives' of ETW but just as individuals. Does that make sense?"

"I suppose it does," she said slowly. "But why me? I'm just one person in ETW."

"I've been trying to get an interview with Mr. Michaels too. He seemed positively inclined after my first conversation with him, given the initial facade which I suppose is standard for one in his position. But at every turn I've been stymied. My calls haven't gotten through to him, or to you. Finally I just decided to see you however I could. I was running out of options."

"You called me—when?"

"Today—this morning."

"And what were you told?"

"Jaeger answered the phone and told me you were out."

Sondra was silent a moment, staring into her half-empty cup.

"Hmm," she mused, "that's interesting. And when you called Jacob—Mr. Michaels? What then?"

"Same thing. I wound up speaking with Jaeger. I later spoke with Mrs. Layne who told me she'd been directed to refer all my calls to Jaeger."

"Well, I never gave any such order," she said. "Although if I'd been informed of your call I still might have refused to take it, notwithstanding your attempt to come to my aid the other day with Mr. Adams, for which, by the way, I do thank you."

"Not at all. He was clearly trying to make more of my words than I intended. I couldn't stand by and allow that."

"Anyway, thank you. But of course by that time I was losing control myself, and—it was an ugly session. At least insofar as my future's concerned."

"How so?"

"They're worried that because of the press conference, your articles, questions raised about our finances, and so on, the whole thing's going to escalate and cause even more trouble."

"But no one seriously suspects ETW's finances. The article never implied that. I was just using the little fictional scenario provided by my first article as a springboard to explore something, with no intent to tie it specifically to ETW."

"Maybe so, but the fears are real enough, rational or not."

"I have to admit to some doubts about Jaeger and his motives. I'm finding myself downright fed up with him in fact. But when I wrote the article I tried hard to keep those feelings out of it and to project a positive viewpoint. Mentioning Greenville—that I felt was something I was bound to tell by virtue of my obligation to the public as a reporter."

"Well, if it hadn't been for your mentioning Greenville in the first one, it all might have escaped notice. But because of that, Hamilton was set up to overreact to the second."

"But except for your press conference, the first article would have had positive repercussions regardless, just as I wrote it, whatever anyone thought of the second."

"You may be right. Anyhow, I didn't call the session."

"Jaeger?"

She nodded.

"And he's the one putting heat on now?"

She nodded again.

It had started to rain, and the sounds of the first drops could be heard on the windows. It was going well, Jackson thought. She was opening up. He might as well probe a little deeper. Such an opportunity might not come again soon.

"What about Jaeger?" he began again. "Why is he worried about everything? He's so jumpy, apprehensive, as if I'm the enemy."

"Hamilton's, well, highly motivated. He's different. He doesn't take things casually as they come. He's used to setting the tone, determining the outcome of what he's involved with."

"But why so suspicious? Does he suspect everyone's out to get him?"

A flash of emotion surged through Sondra's memory. Once more the pain surfaced—and with it confusion. If, as she now suspected, she hadn't loved him at all, then why was there still pain?

As she began once more to be aware of the present, Sondra could hear Jackson's voice still asking about him.

"Is he married?"

"No," she said, voice faltering.

"Is there anyone at ETW really close to him—as a person?"

This was really too much, she thought. She didn't need old, hurtful memories stirred up, not now.

"Not really," she said. "I don't know—of course everyone has friends. Sure. I imagine he's close to people. He and Jacob have been friends for years."

It was difficult to talk about Hamilton. Especially with someone she herself hardly knew. What did she owe this Jackson Maxwell anyway? She was hardly obligated to divulge inside gossip about ETW.

"How about you?" Jackson asked. "You've worked side by side with Jaegar . . . how well do you know him?"

"Look, Mr. Maxwell," said Sondra, aggravation finally surfacing. "I don't feel I can talk about Hamilton's personal life. He is part of our organization, and I know that Mr. Michaels trusts him completely."

"I'm trying to do the man no harm," said Jackson, sensing the change in Sondra's voice. "I'm just attempting to get to the bottom of what's going on."

"Nothing's going on!" she snapped. "I can see it was a mistake to talk to you."

"I'm sorry," said Jackson. "I never meant—"

"Mr. Maxwell," she said rising, "I think you'd better go."

"Please don't be upset. I only wanted—"

"I'm not upset! I just can't talk about it anymore now. Please, just leave me alone!"

He walked slowly toward the door. As he turned the knob, he glanced back. She was looking his way, face flushed, in a confusion of anger and hurt, emotions visibly throbbing.

He opened the door and stepped into the wintry night.

He had no umbrella or raincoat. Therefore, reaching the end of the roofed-over corridor, he stepped onto the terrace and ran across to the parking lot.

Just as he reached his car he heard his name.

He glanced back. There was Sondra, standing in her open doorway, shouting to him through the wind and rain.

"Jackson, please come back!"

He turned and sprinted across the wet terrace again. It was coming down hard now, and the top portion of his slacks were wet. He reached the overhang and ran all the way back to 25 C where Sondra was still waiting, holding the door open.

"Jackson," she said, struggling to speak, "I behaved badly. Please, come back in."

Without a word he reentered the warm apartment, discarded his wet sport coat and stood for a moment beside the heater.

She said nothing for a minute, blew her nose twice, and busied herself in the kitchen temporarily. Jackson looked at her quietly. She had regained herself remarkably fast.

"I have some cookies here," she said reentering the living room. "I made them yesterday." She offered him the plate.

"Ms. DeQue," he said, "I really don't want to impose any further. I know this isn't the best time, and—"

"It's OK," she interrupted. "I'll be fine now. And I want you to call me Sondra. Now, please, have a cookie."

Jackson consented, took two, and began immediately munching on one. "Very good!" he said.

"Thank you," she said. "I hear chewing settles the stomach."

He laughed.

"I'm sorry, Jackson. I do apologize. I wasn't angry with you."

"I understand," he said. "No offense taken."

"It's just that it's been . . . well, a rough last couple of days. I imagine I was on the edge, lying in wait for someone to take it out on. You came along at the wrong time and got caught in the middle."

Jackson said nothing. He'd let her determine where the conversation went from here.

"You've probably guessed the problem's with Hamilton. He

and I've been . . . close, in the past. Too much so. Once we began talking about him my emotions became ensnarled in it. The personal element jolted my perspective out of whack."

Jackson still said nothing, judging it best to listen and wait for an invitation.

"He's dedicated to the cause and all that. But you put your finger on it. He *is* paranoid. He was foolish to call that press conference. And then to blame *me* for all the flack. He has no right! Now there's talk of my being transferred. And all the while his reputation will remain untarnished. He's so blasted condescending lately! I'm sick of his coming down on me for everything. I'm sorry for taking my frustrations and anger out on you. The article really has nothing to do with it."

"Would you be offended by my asking what *does* have something to do with it?" asked Jackson.

"Hamilton has his own interests," she said, then stopped and seemed reminiscent for a moment. "I must admit," she went on, "that I have mixed feelings about talking to you. Hamilton has me so programmed to suspect the press of all manner of self-seeking motives and tear-down tactics."

"That's all right. Don't feel pressured to say anything you're uncomfortable with. No story, no interview. If we can be friends, I'd like to be yours."

"Thank you," said Sondra, then turned her head away. Tears once more rushed to her eyes. Had anyone ever said those words to her? Composure vanished once more. Emotions had been bottled up too long; it felt good to cry.

Jackson rose, walked slowly to her chair, and laid his hand gently on her shoulder. She broke down and wept. He felt the moisture of sweat beneath her blouse as her body trembled. He sat down beside her, stroked her back and shoulders, but said nothing. In a few moments she collected herself, and he resumed his former chair.

"Thank you, again," she said at length. "I'm not used to crying, you can probably tell. I'm a self-sufficient career girl, you know." She laughed and looked at him—her eyes puffy and red, but a smile beneath them. This was a different Sondra DeQue than he'd encountered an hour earlier.

"I haven't really been close to anyone since I left Quebec, except Hamilton. I guess I just hadn't realized how sequestered he'd kept me until recently."

"What happened recently?" asked Jackson.

"I don't know. Nothing specific. There's just been an isolation. I've been reading more, going to some Bible studies. Maybe that's sparked a dissatisfaction with the rut of the job. But since the Greenville thing came up about nine months ago, it seems it's just been Hamilton and me—writing press releases, devising a PR campaign, trying to move plans forward while keeping a lid on it. Half the time it doesn't seem Jacob has anything to do with it. Every now and then, some aspect of it comes along that doesn't feel right to me. Everything is so secret. Maybe it's all those long hours with Hamilton. I suppose I was ready to crack. I needed to get these things off my chest."

"Why is Greenville such a sore point? Jaeger's whole attitude seems to rise and fall around that piece of ground."

"Again, personal interests. As far as I can see there's nothing so different than many other acquisitions we've handled. But *he's* different—edgy, defensive. That's why I'm sure he has something at stake."

"No ideas?"

"As fond as Hamilton is of putting my efforts to work to serve his interests, he's never been one to confide in me. I'm not sure he confides in anyone. And—to answer your earlier question—no, he's not married. Or maybe he is, to his career, to the organization, to his vision of Greenville."

"His vision? Is it financial?"

"Hamilton's not after money. At least that's never been my perception. He talks a lot about unity, about Christians and churches and ministries coming together to function as one. It's a noble concept. I don't think his ambition is primarily selfish. He truly considers Jacob Michaels God's salvation to the modern world. And he's willing to pay any price, make any sacrifice, to advance the cause of his leader. He forgets where to draw the line, becoming so intoxicated with the notion of Michaels's prestige and clout that he ceases to be objective. Then at that point, the end justifies the means. It's a common enough flaw in top assistants to powerful men."

She stopped and stared straight ahead for a moment, deep in

thought, then continued: "—not that I would for a moment suspect him of any dishonesty. It would be all 'for the good of mankind,' for the good of America, for the salvation of us all. He feels anything he does to advance Jacob Michaels is God's work, God's will, and therefore allowed."

"Well, whatever his motives," said Jackson, "I don't want to rush headlong into any false conclusions. We have to give the man the benefit of the doubt. At least that's what part of me keeps saying. The other part—my old self, I suppose—wants to nail him. But I don't intend to print anything along this line. Not yet anyway."

"I'm in an awkward position myself," said Sondra. "He monitors my every step. After all, I work for him. And to a certain extent I still respect his leadership and diligence. I doubt Jacob Michaels would be where he is today without the help of Hamilton Jaeger."

"Do you suppose you might get me a name or two—other people I might contact to shed light on this? If we're in error here, if I'm wrong in thinking there's something to uncover, I want to know, so I don't mistakenly slander his motives. By the same token, if there is something going on, I want to know."

"I don't know. I'll try. At least I'll keep my ears open."

"Thanks—but it's late! We've both got to get to work in the morning."

"And Hamilton's an early riser! Here, have another cookie for the road."

"Thanks, Sondra. That's an offer I'd never refuse."

27

It was several days later. Jackson and Diana were seated together in a sandwich shop two blocks from the *NWV* building.

It was only the second time Jackson had seen Diana in other than jogging garb. On this occasion, as during the pancake breakfast, she was simply dressed in faded blue jeans and a blue sweatshirt embroidered with a butterfly. *The perfect stereotype of the university culture,* thought Jackson, *hardly blending in with my tie and sport coat.*

He ordered roast beef on a French roll, she an avocado and cream cheese with sprouts on whole wheat.

"I'm glad you called," said Jackson. "I needed to get out of the office."

"You were hard to track down. Our meetings in the park have been so secretive. I didn't even know your last name."

"Likewise. I don't know yours either."

"We'll have to work on that one of these days. Anyway, when I called I felt silly asking if there were any Jacksons working there."

"But you found me."

"Yes. And I didn't know you were a genuine feature writer— *the* Jackson Maxwell! I'm impressed. I've read some of your articles. And I heard about the two on ETW. Quite a stir I understand."

"Nothing but internal organizational strife if you ask me. And actually there was only *one* article on ETW! The second was intended as completely general. How the two articles may dovetail together—*that* may be the operative question."

"So what is the writer Jackson Maxwell working on now?" asked Diana. "More daring exposés of Christian organizations?"

"Hardly. I don't know what my status is exactly. It all hit the fan—and the reaction was so surprising."

"Jacob Michaels?" asked Diana, eyebrow lifted.

"One of his lieutenants."

"Who's that?"

"I'd rather not say—yet. I have nothing definite."

"Hamilton Jaeger?" suggested Diana.

"How'd you know?"

A strange look passed quickly over Diana's face. "Let's just say I'm not altogether unfamiliar with the Michaels organization. I know about a few of the personalities he has under him."

"And what do you know of Hamilton Jaeger?"

"Now it's my turn to take the fifth."

"Fair enough. But I didn't come here to talk about my frustrations. Tell me about your singing—I'm still looking for your name in lights."

"Not for a while, I'm afraid," said Diana. "There is a group we're trying to get off the ground."

"How do you find time to run so often, with going to school and launching a new musical group?"

"You may have noticed," said Diana unashamedly, "that I'm not exactly what you'd call thin."

Jackson hadn't noticed. But as he looked at her now he could see how she might think such to be the case. Her short, five-foot, two-inch frame would certainly not be termed petite. But neither would Jackson consider her overweight in the least.

"Believe it or not," Diana continued, "I used to be quite heavy, genuinely fat! Nearly one hundred sixty pounds. I suppose eating was my refuge from school pressures. I've never been one of the 'beautiful people' like my mom and dad are—"

She stopped and looked at Jackson, then went on.

"Maybe eating was an escape . . . maybe it was my subconscious reaction against what they symbolized—like my affinity for casual dress still is, I suppose." She laughed and gestured toward her jeans and shirt.

"Looks fine to me," said Jackson. "If I could get away with it, I'd do the same."

"Anyway," continued Diana, "eventually I realized that if I was going to amount to anything I had to start somewhere, especially if I intended to stand in front of people and sing. So I started running to get my weight down."

"Must have worked pretty well."

"Yeah, I've lost thirty pounds. But my dad still hates these clothes, called me a hippie once—and he was serious. But I keep wearing them—true to the bohemian musician image, you know."

"So is the group actually started? Maybe I can do a story on it—might give you the boost you need."

"If we want a story, you'll be the first I'll call. But I don't think now's the time."

She stopped. "Possibly after next week I'll know more," she went on, almost to herself, then grew silent.

"Why? What's happening next week?" he asked.

"Oh, nothing," she said. "Sorry, I was just thinking out loud. It's just a busy time, and I get sidetracked thinking about it sometimes and lose concentration."

"Come on—a concert, an audition—what's going on?"

"Always the reporter," said Diana smiling. "Nothing's going on, I tell you. Let's walk back, Jackson. I have a two-thirty class and have to get going."

Jackson glanced at his watch. It was barely one-thirty. There was certainly no hurry, and her sudden shift in mood was bewildering. She had grown noticeably uncommunicative.

Before leaving he asked, "OK, if you won't tell me what's up, at least tell me the name of your group. I want to follow your career rise to the top."

Diana laughed. "That'll be the day! Still, I don't suppose there'd be any harm. We call ourselves God's Country."

"Catchy name. I'll be looking for your first million seller."

Diana smiled but said nothing, then turned with a wave and headed down the street. Jackson watched her momentarily, then turned and headed back to work. "I wonder if her group's done anything that'd be on file?" he speculated.

28

Jackson's thoughts were a good deal occupied with Diana in the coming days. He neither saw her nor heard from her, however.

A week and a half later, on Friday afternoon, Jerry Ziegler approached his desk where he sat typing.

"Jackson," he said, "I think you might be interested in this."

"What do you have?" asked Jackson.

"You know that girl you were telling me about, with the singing group? I checked around like you asked, but couldn't find a thing on her or the group. No one had ever heard of them. Nothing on file anywhere. I'd all but given up. Then just a few minutes ago this bulletin came across my desk about the LeCroix happening tonight."

"Harmon LeCroix?"

"Yeah, he's having a big concert tonight at the Muni Auditorium. I received this news bulletin about it, routine stuff. But on the bottom was this."

He laid the paper on Jackson's desk, finger pointing to the lines in question: *"Appearing with Harmon LeCroix tonight on stage in Chicago will be 'God's Country,' featuring the vocal debut of Diana Michaels."*

Jackson read it over a second time, pondering the implication.

He glanced up at Ziegler with a questioning look. "Is this all you know?" he asked.

Jerry shrugged. "That's it."

"Do you realize what this might mean?"

"I know," said Jerry.

"If it's true, why didn't she tell me?"

"Must've wanted to keep her identity from you."

"Man, I've got to get to that concert!" said Jackson.

"No way—it's been sold out for months."

"Surely my press card'd get me in?"

"Security's tight. Only specified reporters are cleared."

"We have anyone covering it?"

"Andrews, I think. But he's gone for the day."

"I've *gotta* get in. I'll call him."

Jackson jumped from his seat and hurried to the directory to get Andrews's home number.

No answer. Jackson returned to his desk, but regaining any authorial momentum was impossible considering the jumbled state of his mind. He'd get no more work done today.

He tried the number again. This time Andrews's wife answered. No, Bill wasn't home. She expected him about six. But only for an hour. He was covering a concert tonight.

Jackson thanked her, hung up, and decided to head for home, have an early dinner, and then try Andrews again. If nothing worked out with him, he'd go to the concert anyway and hope something turned up.

At ten minutes after six he dialed the Andrews home again. Bill was home.

"Bill, it's Jackson Maxwell—from the office. Say, something's come up, and I really need to get into that concert tonight. I understand you're covering it. Any chance you can get me in?"

"I don't know, Jackson, they're watching it pretty tight."

"It's urgent, Bill. Is there anything we could do?"

"Be at my house at seven. We'll think of something."

29

Jackson was still a frenzied mixture of emotions when he left home at six-thirty.

He liked Diana—had even thought the feeling was mutual, that something might come of it. Why would she do this? She knew of his interest in ETW . . . in Jacob Michaels. Was she playing a game with him? Stringing him along?

Maybe he was worked up about nothing. Michaels was a common enough name. There could easily be no connection whatsoever. But something in his gut kept saying it wouldn't be explained so conveniently. And there was the matter of her evasiveness . . . her refusal to divulge her last name . . . her intentionally keeping news of the concert from him. He'd asked specifically, and she had warded off his questions one after the other.

He *had* to get into that auditorium! He had to know.

Jackson parked in front of Bill Andrews's home at ten till seven. He rang the bell; Andrews answered.

"Come on in, Jackson," he said, "I think I have an idea."

Jackson obeyed.

"Here," went on Andrews, shoving a duffle bag into his arms, "take these." He handed him a camera and several telephoto lenses in their cases. "You're going to be my photographer tonight."

Jackson laughed. "Me, a photographer?"

"I've seen stranger things," said Andrews. "You have your press card?"

Jackson nodded.

"OK, let's go. We'll bluff our way through. They know me at the door. I'll vouch for you. Just act like you know your way around with that equipment."

The concert was scheduled to begin at eight. Traffic was congested as Bill and Jackson parked at seven-thirty in a nearby city lot and walked the three blocks to the Muni hall.

Bill led the way through the official side-door. A guard was stationed validating entries by press and concert personnel. Bill flashed his press card and pink concert pass, and they moved quickly through the door.

"Nothing to it," said Andrews.

"Bill, thanks a lot. I appreciate your help. I owe you one."

"You going home with me?"

"Listen—I'm not sure what's going to happen. If I'm not back at the car after the show, go on without me. I'll take good care of the equipment and bring it to the office tomorrow."

"You might even take some pictures. After all, you're a photographer for tonight!"

"I'll do it!" said Jackson and walked off to find a spot to wait for the concert to begin.

The hall filled quickly. The seats were completely sold out, and 275 SRO tickets had been sold for $5.50 each as well. Even the foyers would be packed. To get anywhere near the stage would mean he'd definitely have to look like a bona fide photographer.

He held up the camera with its 200 mm lens and peered through it to focus on the stage. He could see everything clearly from the rear of the hall. Maybe he wouldn't need to get close at all—the camera's lens would serve as binoculars.

The buzz of anticipation gradually increased to a low roar. By ten till eight all the seats were filled. Jackson stood in back, toward the exit, on the side of the aisle.

His palms were wet. With everything magnified now in his mind he hadn't realized the extent to which he cared about Diana. Now suddenly he could think of nothing but her name.

Settle down, Jackson, he kept saying to himself. *Surely you're mature enough to handle it.*

He couldn't stand still! The anticipation was killing him. He turned and wove his way through the bodies crowding to find their seats, hardly seeing the faces. He found a drinking fountain, took a drink, then walked aimlessly to a window looking over the landscaped front of the building. Hands in pockets, equipment slung over his shoulder, he stared blankly out into the night. He turned, walked back to the drinking fountain. He wasn't thirsty but took another drink and slowly made his way back to the hall. He'd better secure a position where he'd have a decent vantage point.

There it was again, that irrational preoccupation in his own psyche with names . . . belonging . . . roots.

Maybe he'd been comfortable with Diana as long as she had

no name—like him.

Maxwell was a convenient label, a word to give him an identity to the world, to make life palatable. But he was no Maxwell—he was nobody. He *had* no name. What right had *she* to one? Especially *that* name!

At two minutes past eight the emcee walked onstage. The crowd grew silent. "Ladies and gentlemen," he began, "we know you've all come tonight to hear Harmon LeCroix, and you won't be disappointed. But before he comes, we have an added treat for you. Making their debut here in Chicago, let me introduce you to God's Country, led by the daughter of Jacob Michaels, Diana Michaels!"

The crowd applauded, the stage light flashed to the accompaniment of the band's introduction. As the applause died away the multicolored spotlights zeroed in on Diana, who began to sing.

Jackson stood numb.

He turned and stumbled into the crowded foyer, toward the men's room. There at least he could be alone. He doused his face with cold water, dried it slowly, and tried to regain his composure.

Back in the lobby he made a vain attempt to look the pressman he was as he inched his way toward the door he hoped might lead around the circumference of the hall toward the dressing rooms in the rear. A second song began. If only he could get to her dressing room ahead of the finale.

Jackson encountered no opposition. Here and there a security guard was posted, but they hardly noticed as he passed. By the applause of the second number he was backstage. Another was beginning, probably the last. He asked directions of a stagehand, who directed him to an unmarked door. He tested the knob. It was open. He let himself in, then sat down to wait.

He tried to calm himself. After all, he reasoned, she has every right to do as she pleases. She was under no obligation to tell him every detail of her life. They hardly knew one another.

But though his intellect could form plausible enough explanations, on the deeper level of his emotions he could not come to terms with himself. Was his perplexity over Diana's identity a reaction to the insecurity he felt over his own?

He hardly had time to pose the question, however, before the applause began again. He waited, and presently the sounds of shuffling feet and voices gradually filled the backstage area. A hand turned the knob, and in walked "God's Country"—laughing, joking, high on the success of their first appearance. Diana entered third, among the others. She was well inside before she spotted Jackson sitting toward the back of the small room. Their eyes met, hers dropped instantly and turned away. By now the others had become aware they were not alone.

"Please," said Diana, "this man's a friend of mine, and we have something to discuss. Would you mind leaving us alone for a few minutes?"

They complied and filed out.

Then Diana looked up at Jackson.

"I guess you're surprised," she said meekly.

"That's a mild way of putting it! I—"

"I'm sorry, Jackson," she said, "I didn't realize you'd be here. It just never seemed like the right time."

"Sorry!" he burst out. "That hardly explains it."

Diana looked to the floor in silence.

"Diana—why? I asked you about your singing, your group, and you said nothing. You knew I was involved with your father and you let me talk without so much as a hint. I just don't understand all the secrecy!"

"I don't know, Jackson. I didn't plan it. I guess maybe you were different. Maybe I cared about what you thought too much. I didn't want to color your impression of me by telling you he was my father."

"You imagined I would think differently of you. Is that it?"

"Possibly."

Jackson sighed heavily and looked away in frustration, then began, "But how can you—"

"Wherever I go I'm Jacob Michaels's daughter. You don't know what it's like. Especially since I don't fit with that image. I'm not beautiful, I didn't inherit his charm. I'm just cut from a different mold altogether."

"But what about me? How do you think I feel?"

"I'm sorry. What more can I say? There was never a suitable time to bring it up. Then after we'd met a few times—well, it just became more and more awkward."

"Awkward!" exclaimed Jackson. "I'll tell you about awkward. I feel like an idiot—being played along like this, kept in the dark."

"Honestly, Jackson," said Diana, "I never intended—"

"But it happened regardless!"

"You're making more out of this than is there."

"Am I? Am I making up that for months you've kept your identity from me? That hardly seems an insignificant matter!"

"But now that it's out, why can't we just put these last months behind us?"

"How can I put it behind me that you didn't trust me enough to—"

"Didn't trust you!" exclaimed Diana, growing more agitated. "Jackson, it's hardly a matter of that. I just had to have my space, that's all. It's got nothing to do with not trusting you."

"How can you say that?"

"Jackson, this is ridiculous. It's not worth all this hostility. Why can't we resolve it calmly?"

"I see," he returned sarcastically. "My feelings aren't worth it."

"That's not what I said, and you know it," she said.

There was silence in the small room for a moment. Neither looked at the other. Then Jackson rose.

"I guess I'd better go. You have things to do."

He walked past her to the door. She sat still. "Jackson," she said softly, "please don't go like this. I don't want to ruin—" She hesitated, then looked up at him.

He paused, hand on the doorknob. "I'm sorry," he said with emotion, then opened the door and left. She started to her feet and looked out the door after him, but said nothing, only watched until he was out of sight.

Diana slowly reentered the dressing room, shut the door behind her, had a quiet cry, stood up, pressed a cold moist towel onto her red face, dried it, and opened the door to greet her group along with other well wishers who had gathered in the meantime.

The following day at *NWV* Jackson spent an unproductive morning at his desk. Over and over he relived the events of the previous evening. Though the cab ride home had settled him somewhat, he had slept little.

Just before eleven Andrews approached his desk.

"Thought you might want to see this," he said. "It's the start

148

of my piece on last night. You missed a great concert!"

Jackson nodded without a word, then took the sheet to read Andrew's opening:

> Last night's Harmon LeCroix concert at Chicago's Municipal Auditorium was packed. And none of the 15,000 plus attending were let down as LeCroix—one of gospel music's leading and most innovative personalities—kept them clapping, singing, and even worshiping for well more than an hour and a half.
>
> But perhaps most surprising of all was the debut of 'God's Country,' featuring lead singer Diana Michaels. After the concert the dimunitive but lively Miss Michaels praised the others of the group for the obvious warm reception. But it was clearly Diana herself who makes the group destined to become contemporary gospel music's brightest new entry of the year. Plans are already underway for a compact disc to be released later this fall, and a Midwestern concert tour has been scheduled for late May.

Jackson handed the paper back to Andrews with no comment.

"You and this Michaels girl have something going?" asked Andrews.

Jackson shrugged. "We might have," he said, then stopped.

Andrews looked at him, as if expecting more, then slowly turned and walked back to his own desk.

Jackson returned his stare to his cluttered desk.

A few minutes later, the mail boy brought him a small envelope. It had only his name on it—no stamp, no address. It must've been slipped under the outside door early in the morning.

He opened it and read the words:

> *I'm sorry. I simply wanted you to appreciate me for who I was. For once I didn't want to be someone's daughter—I just wanted to be me. I'm sorry you got hurt in the process.*

It was simply signed, *Diana.*

Jackson rose, still clutching the note, and walked to the men's restroom. It was empty. He chose a stall, lowered the lid, sat down on the makeshift stool and read Diana's words again, then covered his face with his hands and remained alone with his thoughts for the next forty minutes.

PART 4

Hamilton Jaeger

30

The 727 droned along at thirty-two thousand feet. Hamilton Jaeger eased his seat into a reclining position, laid his head back, and closed his eyes. There was much to do, so little time. If there was one thing he didn't need right now it was that confounded fellow Maxwell stirring the pot and directing more curiosity toward ETW's acquisitions. He was also growing unsure of Sondra's dependability.

"Another drink, sir?" asked the first-class stewardess, interrupting his reverie.

"Yes, thank you," replied Jaeger, glancing up, then settling back again.

No doubt about it, he thought. *Time is of the essence. I'm the one who's got to make it happen. It's been too long in the planning to let it slip through our fingers now. Too much is at stake.*

He opened his eyes and looked out the window. What a time to get away, he mused. Chicago's first major snowstorm of the winter—an uncharacteristically late one. The warmth would feel good.

The stewardess brought his drink and Jaeger sat up, lowered his tray, and pulled out his notebook to review his upcoming appointments. Sebastian Elliot would be first, tomorrow morning. The realtor, he hoped, would confirm acceptance of his offer on the ranch and they'd be able to get the ball rolling there. Then lunch was scheduled with Carson Mitchell of Sonburst Ministries. He'd talked to him by phone just yesterday. Mitchell, fortunately, hadn't yet been aware of the inquisitiveness of the press. If an arrangement could be firmed up quickly, he hoped a negative effect could be averted.

In the afternoon he'd drive over to the SCWE headquarters for a casual and friendly visit. The favorable reception of his plan by Anthony Powers, president of Students Committed to World Evangelism, was the capstone of his scheme. Thus far Powers, founder of the worldwide student mission organization, had been cordial and receptive but noncommittal. Jaeger hoped to bring him all the way in soon, if not on this trip, certainly within the month.

He'd been laying the groundwork for some time with friendly overtures and visits, and even modest financial assistance. He was confident that if Sonburst and SCWE could catch his vision then others would quickly come along. Among those he was also wooing were Evangelism Radio in Houston, Word of God Publishers in Austin, the Jericho Recording Company, and the powerful Exodus Community located right in Dallas. All were not only respected Christian organizations, each was a pioneer and leader in its particular field. Word of God and Jericho had both established themselves in the top five Christian businesses in the country and were growing steadily.

Evangelism Radio now sent its twenty-four-hour programming worldwide on more than 175 stations. And Exodus Community, begun just eleven years before as an experiment in creative lifestyle, had exploded. Christian spokesmen, recording artists, authors, families, and pastors had been joining its movement in droves. Now the facilities were cramped and, Jaeger was certain, its leaders— thus far positively inclined toward ETW—would look favorably upon some kind of a joining of forces for the mutual good.

It was professedly a far-reaching dream, and concessions would have to be made of course. He'd have to dole out power to the various single-star generals. Just so long as he and Jacob Michaels retained the precious 51 percent.

And certainly there could be but one man with five stars on his shoulder. "Where there is no leader, the people perish." That's how the Scripture went, was it not? And who else could it be but Jacob Michaels, respected the world over as the spokesman for organized Christianity. Bits of autonomy here and there, but over the whole there could be but one head. And over him . . .

I should say "beside" him, Jaeger reflected, but did not bother to complete the sentence.

What potential!

What magnificence! Radio and TV, publishing and recording, right there. What possibilities for mass communication to impact the world—so much vaster than CBN or the Moral Majority and all such organizations begun in the seventies and eighties ever dreamed of. The nineties would be the decade! He had been preparing his whole life for this! If he could just manage to scuttle that reporter Maxwell!

His soaring thoughts were cut short by the sound of the captain over the plane's intercom: "Ladies and gentlemen, we'll be landing in Dallas/Fort Worth in approximately twenty minutes. The weather there is fair, temperature is seventy-two degrees. We hope you've enjoyed your flight. Now if you'll please tighten up those seat belts I'll wish you a good day. And thank you for joining us."

Jaeger gulped down the remainder of his drink, snapped up his tray, cinched his belt, and readied himself for the day that lay ahead.

31

"You want to drive out to Greenville to look the house over again?"

"I've seen all I need to, Seb," answered Jaeger. "How often do we have to keep going over it? All I want is to find out if my offer's been accepted."

"I understand that," said Elliot, "but there's a hitch—nothing we can't work through if—"

"What kind of hitch?" snapped Jaeger.

"The people—Mr. and Mrs. Haley. They're older, retiring, moving to a condo in Dallas—"

"Yes, I know. What of it?"

"They're concerned about the place, want to know it's going to be put into the right hands."

"Are they questioning *me*? I thought you gave them my references, my financial papers?"

"I did, Hamilton. Don't worry. We can iron it out. It's just that they're cautious about how the old homestead, as they put it, is going to be used. They know about the land being bought up all around. They've heard rumors and don't want to see their ranch torn down for some industrial complex."

"But surely you told them—"

"I told them you're with Jacob Michaels. And that settled them down some. But when they asked if the property would be purchased by ETW, I had to answer no. After all, it is your name, not the organization's, on the legal documents."

"What's wrong with that?"

"They want to make sure their house stays as it is and is put to a peaceful use. They want a family there—gives it a sense of permanence they say."

"And you told them I'll be living there."

"Yes, but your being a bachelor is disquieting to them. 'What could a single man possibly want with a ranch house so large?' Mrs. Haley kept asking."

"I thought they wanted to sell," said Jaeger, nettled by the annoyance of the petty whims of an old farmer and his wife. "I've offered to meet their price."

"They're a queer old couple, and we just have to wait them out."

"Maybe I should meet them myself."

"I don't think so, Hamilton. It's best if I handle it. But they don't like my being vague about your intentions. They're sure some kind of industry is moving in and will swallow their land in time. It would help if I could tell them a bit more."

"All right," said Jaeger. "I suppose they can't do us much harm now. We're close and I need that piece of land. OK, tell them— but urge on them the requirement for discretion, secrecy—that the surrounding land is being bought by Jacob Michaels. They are churchgoers, aren't they? Didn't you tell me that?"

"Yes, nominally so. They respect Michaels."

"Good. OK, tell them that ETW's buying the land for the purpose of Christian work. Don't get more detailed if you can help it. Simply assure them no industry's coming in. Then tell them I'm buying their place for my private home, from which I'll be involved in the Michaels organization's work, that their land won't become part of the ETW complex."

"That should satisfy them," said Elliot.

"I should hope so. We're running a risk saying that much. I'm not happy disclosing my purchase of this land. It could jeopardize my negotiations with the other ministries."

"I don't see why. Through all this I've never understood your intense desire for secrecy."

"Seb, do you have any idea what people would think if they knew I was buying an eighty-acre ranch adjacent to the acquisitions? They'd holler about self-interests. Even Jacob won't have his own private piece of land there."

"It does put you in a rather central position in the whole scheme of things doesn't it?" said Elliot with a cunning smile.

"Isn't that the point?" Jaeger shot back, failing to perceive the humor in his friend's tone. "If we're to do what we hope, there has to be a command post, a central heartbeat from which things originate."

"I know, Hamilton. I'm with you. I was only—"

"And you're not coming out so badly either, my friend," added Jaeger. "Your commissions have amounted to a tidy sum, I'll wager. We've both been working on this too long and have too much at stake to see it falter now."

"Yes, yes, Hamilton, and I'm appreciative. I'll make the deal with the Haleys. Have patience."

"I've been patient! But the timing's crucial, Seb. That's why I'm here. To see that things are all tied up as closely to the same moment as possible. If any links are missing, the momentum could shift. I'm seeing Mitchell for lunch, and Powers later today. If those two come in, we're on the way. With their endorsements, the others should be much easier to persuade. I tell you, it's rolling, and we have to jump on before any of the parts grind to a halt."

"I really don't see what the Haley parcel has to do with that end of it. I'd think a little wait might even be best. Then once the physical presence of Evangelism Worldwide becomes a reality, then your buying a home here wouldn't seem the least bit suspicious."

Jaeger cast him a steely glare. "I thought we agreed not to use that term—not yet!"

"We did. But it's getting so close. It just popped out."

"Make sure it doesn't again!"

"The point remains—what harm would a little patience do where the Haleys are concerned?"

"It's the timing I tell you, Seb," insisted Jaeger. "Don't you feel it? Things are starting to click. It's taken years, fitting the pieces together, setting it up, getting you situated here, Jacob's gradual rise to prominence, waiting for the right parcels of land, Jake's growing influence in D.C."

"How is Jake's end going?"

"It's coming on all sides. He thinks another two, three, four years at the most ought to do it. Once we have four or five ratifying signatures, we can begin to build. Others will join in, Jake can start more actively. From that point it can go public. That's why I need that ranch house. I need to be in a position to feel the pulse of it, to direct where we want it to go."

"I thought it was going to be all three of us? That's how it began, you know. We all three shared a vision."

"Yes, of course, Seb, it *is* the three of us. You and Jake and me—it'll be like we planned. But I'm *there*. I'm his right-hand man. I'm in a focal position, with Jacob's trust and with a public image to get things done. I've got the leverage to make it happen. But of course, it's *our* vision, together. You'll be right with me. We each have our distinct responsibilities in this thing."

Sebastian Elliot was pensive a moment, thinking back quietly to that day ten years ago when the three of them had launched this dream. Now, suddenly it seemed, they were on the brink of reaching for the final rung they'd so wistfully discussed back then. Lots of water under the bridge. He'd had to mortgage his family, compromise ideals, even integrity at times, and cater to Hamilton's insatiable thirst for more. Had it been worth it? Sometimes he wondered. Still, if they *did* pull it off, he would be one of the most influential men in the country. And what price wasn't worth that?

Hamilton's voice brought him back to the present. "You'll talk to the Haleys again?"

"Yes, I'll call them today."

"I'll check with you tomorrow, Seb. I'll be in town about three days. Have good news for me! Maybe we can get together for dinner tomorrow night and celebrate your victory—and mine!"

Elliot nodded as Jaeger rose to leave the office. Then he closed the door behind him, returned to his desk, and sat down once more to think.

32

Sonburst Ministries was not a nationally known entity among Christian groups. It was only two and a half years old and was still concentrating its efforts primarily in the South. The principal thrust of its activities consisted of training eager young people—who were required to pay their own way to Dallas and to support themselves during the first six months of their tenure—who were then sent out to serve in various capacities. They employed several teams in the inner cities of Houston, Fort Worth, El Paso, Oklahoma City, and Atlanta. Others carried on street evangelism. Still others participated in money-making activities and businesses that helped support the ministry. They were gradually exploring the fields of tract publication and recording.

But Jaeger's attention was focused on Sonburst because of the stature of its leader, Carson Mitchell, one of the Christian community's most valuable leaders throughout the past six years. His book on the end times, *The Sensational Future for God's People,* had been the biggest-selling mass-market Christian publication in more than a decade, eclipsing Lindsey's and Peretti's figures, and had overnight catapulted him into the prophetic spotlight along with names like Livingstone, McKeever, and Joyner. He followed it up with several books—commercially successful but nothing like the first—and made the regular rounds of the Christian television talk shows, magazine interviews, and celebrity functions.

When he had begun Sonburst Ministries just under three years ago, Jaeger recognized immediately that he provided a logical starting point and determined to talk to him. If Mitchell could be drawn in, his magnetism would attract others in turn.

Mitchell had been congenial; he had little to lose organizationally, and much to gain. Jaeger ensnared him slowly, and now, at last, was ready to pluck the fruit and secure the deal.

They met in one of Dallas's posh restaurants for lunch. After a few moments of small talk, Hamilton, never one to avoid the issues at hand, jumped directly into the subject of their meeting.

"Carson, as you know," he began, "plans are progressing

rapidly for our center. The time's approaching when I'm going to need a definite word from you."

"I understand," said Mitchell. "I feel good about it. But I have to be sure about a few final details."

"Specifically?" asked Jaeger.

"The site for one thing. That's always been a little vague. I need to be sure we'll be able to construct a facility for our needs."

"To be sure," replied Jaeger. "Our draftsmen and contractors are waiting for my go-ahead, and your direction, to put together a facility that will meet your needs perfectly. Once you come on board we'll have our planners meeting with you before the month is out, with arrangements, as well, for your personal office and headquarters."

"The building to be financed by ETW?"

"Of course, once the merger takes place. The finances will be cooperatively shared, the bulk certainly born by ETW since we will be underwriting the lion's share of the project initially. Then those involved in the merger will be able to select a certain number, which has yet to be determined, from among them to serve on the new board of directors. And, Carson, your prominence in this thing, I would think—of course, it's not up to me personally—but nevertheless I would think you might be a logical choice for such leadership. I would certainly put my influence behind such a recommendation."

"Well, thank you," said Mitchell. "Yes, I can see how that might be a possibility."

"From that vantagepoint, I think your potential for ministry would benefit greatly. You would be able to maintain your present activities, yet with an expanded facility which would be immediately tied into a worldwide communications network. Not to mention your own personal prestige occupying so focal a role, what they would do to bolster your book sales. It seems, Carson, that it represents quite an opportunity for you—and for Sonburst Ministries."

"Yes, I can really see the advantages," said Mitchell thoughtfully, hardly immune to the intoxication of Jaeger's blandishments. "It's just that it's such a big step."

"It's the future, Carson. You wrote about unity in your book. You said that unity was destined to be the hallmark of the church of the future, that unity is what the Lord is looking for before He returns. Just think, Carson, this is the opportunity we've all been waiting for . . . the chance to put that truth into practice, to take a visible stand for unity. What better way to say to the world that we take these truths seriously? I must say, I don't think it's by accident that you are potentially the first to make the commitment. Providence has brought us together."

"I see what you mean. And I suppose down inside I am convinced. It really has to be, doesn't it? We *have* to quit talking about unity and begin *doing* it."

"If you are ready. Of course, I would never want to rush you, but if you are, I do have some documents here I'd like you to sign." Jaeger pulled from his coat pocket a sheaf of papers.

"These," he went on, "merely state your intent to unite Sonburst Ministries with ETW. Though these are not the actual merger papers as such, they will serve to get the ball rolling. We'll be able to get underway planning your offices and buildings, and then our attorneys will conclude the final arrangements at some later date."

Mitchell glanced over the documents briefly, seemed to hesitate momentarily, then said, "Yes, . . . yes, this seems fine. I suppose we have covered it all."

He turned to the back page and signed his name.

Jaeger quickly refolded the papers and stuffed them back inside his coat.

"Now that that's settled," he said, "let's enjoy this lunch!"

33

Hamilton Jaeger was elated!

Mitchell had signed! The first domino had fallen. If only he could prove equally persuasive with Powers. He would clearly be a tougher cookie, with far more at stake.

Not that gaining Mitchell's support wasn't a major success. It was! Vital for his plan. Financial union with Mitchell could prove the backbone of the whole thing. Royalties from a Mitchell bestseller would easily amount to millions—all the more once his present contracts expired, and Word of God could begin handling his work. Mitchell's following was enormous. Mitchell's endorsement of Jacob Michaels would indeed create a dynamic duo!

Yet Anthony Powers was perhaps even more influential, but in a less public way. His organization was vaster. Bringing in Powers would not only generate additional celebrity appeal but the strength of a worldwide organization. That's where the solidity of a coup with Powers would be felt. It would greatly enhance the reach of ETW's arm into areas heretofore untapped.

He hoped to pull it off. Powers had been receptive up to now, even warm and inviting. Yet there remained an undefinable distance. Jaeger couldn't quite pinpoint his hesitation. If he could discover the basis for his uncertainty, the rest should be easy.

The drive into the countryside south of Dallas was beautiful. All the more when he reflected on the snow blanketing Chicago. He was glad the rented Seville had air conditioning. The Chicago winter had hardly accustomed him for this unseasonable heat. The appointment was scheduled for three-thirty.

Anthony Powers was a charismatic man, tall, lean, handsome, well-dressed, and confident. He strode into the foyer where Jaeger was waiting, greeted him with outstretched hand and smile, and warmly invited him into his adjoining private office. Though seldom cowed by anyone, even Hamilton Jaeger felt the powerful sway of Powers's personal charm and magnetism.

Fifteen minutes of light discussion ensued—the state of SCWE, new countries opening up, upcoming ETW crusades. Powers was the first to bring the meeting toward its inevitable head.

"I must say, Hamilton," he began, "I've been speaking with some of my associates on the board of directors of SCWE and in general they appear amiable to the notion of working more closely with you."

"I'm glad to hear that," replied Jaeger with a good-natured smile. "It cannot, as I've said before, prove anything but a significant boost to the cause of evangelism worldwide. With both our organizations committed to the cause of Matthew twenty-eight, nineteen through twenty—especially when the dedication of your youthful task force is combined with the impact of Jacob Michaels's name—we can expect to witness revival encompassing a much broader cross section than either organization could hope to penetrate single-handedly."

"That would certainly be our hope. Evangelism throughout the world—the great commission in the twentieth century—that's always been our goal."

"And ours!" said Jaeger. "I can assure you that Mr. Michaels views your willingness to participate in this as a highly significant link in the fulfillment of that charge the Lord gave us. He has nothing but the highest regard for what you have achieved for the cause of Christ."

"I'm flattered," returned Powers.

"And," Jaeger went on, sensing the tide turning in his direction, "he has mentioned his strong feeling that you would be a likely candidate for the board of directors when it is selected. And I would just add, Anthony—although of course it won't be up to me personally—but I would say I think your being on the board would not only be likely but necessary. For you would enhance it with a great deal of experience and impact. We would all find ourselves heavily dependent upon you for the direction the new organization would take."

"Well—I would certainly be willing to serve in any capacity where I could be useful," said Powers, defenses faltering under the compelling seduction of Jaeger's complimentary arguments.

"And I think we've hit upon the very essence of why this move is so necessary," Jaeger went on, sensing the quarry entering his grasp. "We've all dedicated our lives to reaching the lost. Yet we experience frustration in the process, the assignment seems too huge. We long for unity within the Christian body. Now at last we face this unparalleled opportunity to achieve both dreams in a single stroke. In the practical step of unity we take, the vision of worldwide evangelism suddenly draws within our reach. Together, I firmly believe, we *can* take the gospel to every creature."

"It *is* exciting," said Powers, shifting in his chair. "We certainly share that dream. Still, we have concerns."

"Possibly if we could discuss them. What explicitly is on your mind?"

"Some of my people," began Powers slowly, "are reluctant—to say it aloud makes it seem so trivial—nevertheless, they are hesitant to give up the influence—even, if I can use the term, the power we now have—if I may use these words in a spiritual context. They fear we will somehow lose the identity we've acquired as an organization, as a ministry."

"Let me respond in two ways," said Jaeger, clearly prepared with a well thought-out rebuttal. "First, if we're going to put earthly power above our heavenly calling, then we really have nothing to achieve in this thing. This is a major new step for all of us—for all of Christendom. Nothing like it has ever taken place. We're *all* concerned about what you've mentioned. We're *all* going to have to give up much in the way of our former organizational status."

"I understand that," responded Powers. "And I do see the necessity for laying down one kind of power for something greater."

"Potentially *far* greater," broke in Jaeger. "We're on the brink of one of the greatest tests of spirituality of all time. God has put this opportunity into our hands—yours and mine and a handful of others. He has given us the chance to chart a new heading for the church—a direction that will lead God's people into the future. Just think of it!"

There was silence for a moment in the small room. Both men contemplated, in their own way, the ramifications of the words.

"And as for organizational identity," Jaeger went on at length, "I would be the first to admit that, yes, there will be a sense in which all of us will lose some. Maybe 'lose' is an inappropriate word. Let's say it will change. But change for the better, improve, be enhanced. There will be no sacrifice involved. It will instead signify the gradual acquiring of a new and more significant identity. That's the very nature of unity. A new identity, yes. But a greater, not a lesser."

"I see your point," said Powers thoughtfully. "From that standpoint it does make a great deal of sense."

"I have to tell you, Anthony," said Jaeger excitedly, "it thrills me—if we can actually *do* this thing, whatever sacrifices it will mean to each of us personally. Just think what it will mean to the body of Christ at large—the example we'll be setting. If we can overcome our big-fish-in-a-small-pond mentality and convey the larger picture. I tell you, Anthony, I think we're on the brink of something which can usher in true unity."

Another silence followed. Jaeger had indeed been eloquent on behalf of his cause; he knew he'd struck nerves and sensed he'd said enough.

After another moment, Powers spoke once more. "Well, you certainly present a convincing case, Hamilton!" He laughed. "And I must say, I see the points you've made. It's an awesome step, even frightening, . . . charting a new course. No one's ever been there before. Yet, . . . maybe it's time we were."

Jaeger said nothing. He'd done his part. Now it was time to wait.

"Yes," Powers mused again, "Maybe it is time." Then standing, he changed his tone, "Listen, I've got a meeting to get to. I'll discuss your thoughts once more with my people. We'll try to come to a decision and have an answer for you within the week."

They shook hands, and Jaeger left the office.

He'd carried it off well, Hamilton thought. He'd drive out to Exodus tomorrow and would tonight call the heads of both Word of God and Jericho Recording. With the positive reports he could deliver from Mitchell and Powers he had no doubt the others would listen with considerable attentiveness. Their organizational prestige could only be heightened by any association with those names.

If circumstances warranted he'd even fly down to Houston and Austin. Any commitment he could firm up now would solidify his position that much more. He remained confident of Evangelism Radio, particularly after the purchase of the Phoenix transmittal station. ER's shaky finances of late would immediately dissolve with an infusion of ETW cash, and the Phoenix site sweetened the pot that much more.

34

Five days later Hamilton Jaeger was seated once more in the first class cabin of a 727. He hardly relished the thought of sub-freezing temperatures and eighteen-inch snowbanks, but for the present the Dallas warmth remained with him.

It had been a good trip!

Circumstances were ripe, and the success of his foray into the South was invigorating. He could taste the final victory.

Carson Mitchell and Jerome McGrath of Word of God Publishers had each signed letters of intent. McGrath's had been unexpected and had totally repaid the extra day spent flying to Austin. And he'd received a firm verbal agreement to the same effect from the directors of Evangelism Radio. They'd have the signed papers in return mail, they said, moments after they received them.

Jericho Recording was leaning his direction too, he thought. A little more time, a little more momentum . . . they'd come. Having a leading publisher and radio station would undoubtedly sway some of Jericho's undecided votes. The radio network would greatly enhance their record sales.

Exodus Community he wasn't sure of. Their reception had been cool. Not a closed door by any means, but it would take some persuasion. The thing *could* fly without Exodus. It was, after all, still a fairly local ministry. He could wait. If the other crucial ministries came in, Exodus could be viewed as optional.

Anthony Powers and SCWE remained the kingpin. If they came along—with the papers of intent and following legal requirements of a full-scale corporate merger—then it was done!

Jaeger grinned at the mere thought of it. With Mitchell, Word of God, ER, and positive responses from Powers and perhaps one more, then they could go public, make the announcement, begin the ground breaking. From that point it would simply entail standing back to watch Evangelism Worldwide mushroom. From then on they'd have to carefully select whom they *let* join, so many groups and ministries from all over the nation would scramble to be part of it.

It had all along been such a seemingly unattainable dream—dare he at last think of it as a reality?—the bringing together within one vast complex, a Christian—what? An organization? He could find no appropriate word to capsulize the magnitude of his vision—a city . . . a culture all its own! Could he hope he was now on the brink of pulling it off? With these highly regarded Texas-based groups poised behind him, there was no limit to what they could accomplish!

He had to get the thing with the house settled. Those foot-dragging Haleys had to be persuaded—and soon. Whatever Seb said about patience, all the pieces had to culminate as closely together as possible. Otherwise, if one backed out, an unhealthy trend could ensue. Everything had to be cocked so that the moment the announcement was made, a fresh rush of snowballing momentum would result. The ball had to keep rolling forward.

The interview with Powers had been magnificent!

Days later he couldn't help feeling a surge of satisfaction. He had indeed waxed eloquent. The persuasive words had flowed from his tongue almost in spite of himself—unity, a major new step for Christendom, one of the greatest tests of spiritual unity for all time, a new course for God's people!

He had done what he came to do.

Now he had to wait. The pieces would fall into place by themselves. He simply had to keep from interfering, from making any mistakes. He was on the side of destiny. Fate had placed him here, at Jacob Michaels's right hand. He was fulfilling a divine calling. It would all happen—it *had* to. The progress of history, unity, God's will, *destiny* could not be averted. And he—Hamilton B. Jaeger—stood directing its path!

True, he'd had to imply major concessions. What man in a powerful position, even a man of God, would willingly choose to have his wings clipped? He'd had to make promises, giving men such as Mitchell, Powers, and McGrath to believe they would share authority on a level compatible with his own, even Jacob's. Of course he'd never actually *said* such, but he knew the notion had been implicit in his words. And though the documents of intent left specifics undisclosed, he'd drawn them up to heavily imply that a high level of autonomy would be left in the hands of each ministry.

But he'd leave it to his own capable lawyers to make sure the actual merger contracts were favorable for ETW. At the moment no one need know that he planned a board of directors composed of five members—himself and Jacob as permanent and the other three chairs chosen yearly from among the various organizations and ministries involved, one of the three to always come from ETW. It was only fair, he thought. After all, ETW would be staking by far the largest claim in the organization, and its finances would initially underwrite most of the construction. Why shouldn't they retain controlling dominance?

Under cover as well must remain the financial arrangements he was in the process of having his own attorneys write into the final contracts. There would be an initial financial incentive for joining ministries, such as ER, who would immediately see their own hopes and visions flourish with the infusion of ETW capital. But down the road, the finer print, couched in the most incomprehensible of legalese, would detail more specifically the nature in which ETW and its solid grip of the majority position (no matter how many groups ultimately became part of Evangelism Worldwide) ultimately profited from the many incomes being thus generated.

And there was his own position to reflect on. He would quite naturally come to occupy, with properly ethical subcommittees, of course, the top financial position in the new multifaceted organization. This would evolve spontaneously out of his current status with ETW. He would gather around him "advisers" from all the other ministries to make certain their funds were wisely administered. But he himself would occupy that focal position from which his dreams could be launched.

If Hamilton Jaeger could not help an occasional twinge of compunction for the relative independence he led others to believe would be inherent in the new structure, it was accompanied by no corresponding twinge of conscience. The vision was the thing. The end was what mattered. If it took some clever negotiating to prevail upon minds smaller than his, so be it. His motives were pure. Like them all, he wanted to see the world evangelized. If their sight was limited by the ruts of their plebian mentalities, he had to force them into the bigger picture. They would ultimately see the light and be glad they were part of it. They'd thank him many times over.

He settled back into his seat. Chicago was an hour away. There, phase two awaited him. It was time to bring Jacob Michaels himself into the game plan. If not fully just yet, nevertheless another giant step closer.

35

How many times this office had been used for this very purpose, Jaeger reflected. High level ETW discussions and decisions. And now, today, they were facing new direction of a magnitude unprecedented. For the past thirty minutes he had been laying out his masterful plans to Jacob Michaels. The sketches and drawings lay on Michaels's desk. Behind it, staring out over Chicago, stood Michaels, contemplating what he had been hearing.

Michaels had been part of the concept of Greenville from the beginning. But not until today had Jaeger actually spelled out in concrete terms what he envisioned. For Michaels it had always been a hazy dream—a training center, a radio station, some ambiguous "coordination" with other ministries. But in the midst of always more pressing affairs he had at each step left the details in the capable hands of his trusted assistant, Hamilton Jaeger. He had given him a free hand to explore the possibilities—within certain guidelines, he thought. Now he realized Jaeger's notion of those boundaries were substantially more liberal than his own.

Yet the concept was alluring! Could genuine Christian unity happen? Could organizations and ministries really lay down their differences and join in a common goal? What a grand experiment! Maybe Hamilton's vision outdistanced them all. Was his the perspective of the future?

He turned, opened his mouth to speak. But then he thought better of it and slowly returned his gaze to the city below.

He did have reservations. Who wouldn't? Was he leery of giving up a portion of the stature ETW had built? According to Hamilton there would be no sacrifices, only gain—in potential ministry, in financial capabilities.

It must be Hamilton's hunger that gnawed at him. He'd seen the seeds of it before but never so blatantly. He was grasping high. He was clearly a man driven to reach ambitious goals. He had dedicated motives to be sure. Maybe he did care about unity, about the lost. But as he'd listened to Hamilton caught up in the glorious concept of an undivided church marching as one into the corners of the earth, of witnessing revival never seen before, while he spoke of the appointed time and of us—the appointed servants whose charge it was to make it happen—Jacob sensed something in Hamilton's grandiose perceptions was out of balance.

Again he turned. This time the words came.

"It's—it's awesome, Hamilton, far-reaching—" He stopped, turned to the window again.

What to do? His thoughts were twisted. He had to make the right decision about how to proceed.

Jaeger sat quietly waiting. The momentum was his. He sensed destiny's hand on him now.

"—magnificent," Michaels picked up again. "Still, Hamilton," he went on, voicing at last the reservations that had been bubbling to the surface, "I can't help but wonder why it's all been so secretive. Why did you wait till now to fill me in?"

"I merely assumed you wanted me to take care of the specifics," replied Jaeger, "as you usually do. We'd discussed the broad concepts of the plan. I felt you were thinking along the same lines."

"But you've made some rather audacious moves—on your own. Going directly to Carson and Powers, so much as asking them to give us their people, their facilities, their bank accounts. I mean, Hamilton, you've been playing a risky game!"

"I've been cautious. And besides, the proof of the pudding, you know. They're coming along," said Jaeger smiling confidently.

"The point is, Hamilton," said Michaels with growing sharpness, "I think this time you went too far. What if one of these men had called me to discuss it?"

"I took measures to insure—"

"You took measures into your own hands!" snapped Michaels.

"I apologize," said Jaeger, with no small touch of sarcasm in his voice. "It has always been my impression that my job was to shield you whenever possible from the daily detailed aspects of decision making."

"I'll not debate that point. But this hardly falls under the classification of a minor detail! You have to know when you've gone far enough. I have a reputation to uphold."

"We're all too well aware of that," said Jaeger, losing his patience and his smile all at once.

"Look, Hamilton, I'm not going to argue with you about this. I like the idea. I'm all for unity. And I'm one hundred percent committed to our plans for Greenville. But I think it's time we backed off just a little, take another look at the master plan. I need some time to consider all you've told me today. You did say the documents you have at present are merely statements of intent?"

Jaeger nodded.

"Well, I want to review it further. I'm just not totally comfortable with an all-out merger situation with—"

"Excuse me, Mr. Michaels," the intercom interrupted with the voice of Liz Layne, "there's a long distance call for Mr. Jaeger. Should I have it transferred to your office?"

Michaels glanced at Jaeger, who nodded his assent.

"That'll be fine, Liz."

Jaeger picked up the receiver. The call was brief, punctuated only occasionally with nods and responses in the affirmative.

"That's great news," he said at length. Then nodding again, "That's just fine . . . yes . . . our lawyers will be in touch with you . . . yes, you should have some additional documents to look over within a couple weeks . . . yes, fine. Thank you for calling. We'll be in touch."

He set down the receiver, obviously pleased.

Michaels, however, continued as if the interruption had never taken place. "As I said, Hamilton, I'd like us to withdraw ourselves from the active role of trying to rush this through. I want to review it—put it on hold temporarily."

"I'm sorry, Jacob—that's just not going to be possible." Jaeger's tone was now deadly serious.

"What? I don't believe what I'm hearing! Are you telling me you're determined to proceed on your own, without my authorization?"

"I wouldn't exactly phrase it like that, Jacob," said Jaeger, with bite in his voice.

"What would you call it, then?" Michaels's temperature was steadily rising.

"That call was from Neil Pierce, president of Jericho Recording. They've decided to join the merger. Their letters of intent are in the mail."

"That's just it, Hamilton. Don't you see? This thing is mushrooming, and we've got to slow it down before it gets out of hand. I tell you, we need time to mull it over and decide where we want to go with it."

"All that's *been* decided," pressed Jaeger intently. "The momentum is moving, and there's no way to stop it. Now's the time. If we back off we might never regain it!"

"That's a chance we may have to take."

"That, Jacob, is a chance I am not prepared to take! I tell you, it's not possible to jump off the train now. It's gaining speed!"

"Confound you, Hamilton! Who works for whom around here?"

"That's clear enough!" said Hamilton with a smile that could have been taken for a sneer. "But this is something I've put a lot of myself into, and I won't see it derailed—not even by you!"

"If I make a public statement that so much as hints at my own personal reevaluation, that would be enough to send everyone running back to their own camps for cover."

"But you won't."

"What makes you so sure?"

"Jacob, let's not kid ourselves. You are the clear winner in all this. Whenever there is a joining of this magnitude, the powerful parties emerge all the stronger. This merger will do nothing but elevate ETW's prominence and yours along with it. I've got it set up so you are the uncontested head. You will be the single man at the top. You wouldn't jeopardize that."

Michaels was silent. Jaeger was touching deep nerves.

"And," he went on, "I needn't remind you that there are skeletons in everyone's closet—even yours."

"You wouldn't dare turn on me like that!" said Michaels, spinning on his colleague with muted wrath. He felt the immediate tightening of Hamilton's net around him.

Jaeger shot him a quick, shrewd glance.

172

"My friend," he said with a voice uncharacteristically cool given the heat of his inner passion, "I would dare nearly anything for the cause of Greenville."

"My reputation's the foundation-stone of your very career, of your plans, of your Greenville dream. Take me down, and you lose everything! Two can play the game of threats just as well as one!"

"That may be true," said Jaeger. "But I don't think you'd make that sacrifice to keep me from going ahead. In your heart of hearts, you know I'm right about this anyway."

Michaels was silent.

"You may hold the key to my future," Jaeger went on. "But I in turn may hold the key to yours—just as I do the key to your past. That door's locked, and as far as I'm concerned the key's thrown away. I simply bring it up to remind you of the resolve with which I'm determined to move ahead with this, with or without you for the present. You'll be right there with smiling face and waving hands and soul-stirring messages in time. I know you well, Jacob. You enjoy the adulation and public esteem just as much as I crave being able to see my goals brought into reality. Greenville suits us both to a T."

Michaels said nothing, merely began moving restlessly about his office, finding himself once again in front of the large window. When he turned, after a minute, he was alone in the office.

Hamilton was right, Jacob knew. He would not challenge him. When he dug in, he was an impossible man to cross.

36

Jackson's fist slammed down on the table in frustration.

He flipped off the electric typewriter, rose, walked to the window, and stared out blankly. "I just can't do it," he said aloud.

For two days Jackson had been attempting to get a handle on his third ETW article. As was often his custom when a particular piece of writing was due, he spent the afternoons in the quiet of his apartment. Tackling a rough draft was easier at home, even if the number of trips to the kitchen for a glass of water per reporter-hour far outweighed the known bodily need for fluids. He found the office fine for rewrites, editing, or busywork. But to unleash any form of creativity, Jackson required solitude.

Locking himself up with his typewriter, however, wasn't doing the trick today. Nor did his countless excursions to the kitchen and picture window help in the least. After numerous false starts and crumpled first pages he continued to bog down. The fingers rested on the keys; the flow simply wasn't there.

Jackson stood for perhaps five minutes. Then he sighed, paced the room, and returned his gaze outside. *It's no use,* he said to himself at length. *I might as well go back to the office.*

Riding the elevator to the third floor, he hoped to sneak through quietly to his desk. But McClanahan was filling his coffee cup near the door when the elevator stopped and Jackson emerged.

"Maxwell," he called. "Haven't seen you around much the last couple days. That third piece should be about ready for me."

"I'm stalled, Ed," returned Jackson with a sigh. "I'm wondering whether I'm even going to be able to get going on it."

"Start-up block?"

"No, it's more than that. I've got the ideas. I thought I knew where I wanted to go with it. But the juices aren't flowing."

"You should know by now that writing's a matter of guts. Sometimes you just have to crank it out."

"I know, but my whole attitude toward the thing's shifted."

"How so?" asked the editor.

"When I started I was generally positive. But the more I got into it, the more negativity I found creeping into all my impressions. I just have the distinct feeling that some of my second-article questions may apply more directly to ETW than any of us thought. And I can't seem to avoid them finding their way onto the page."

"You think you're too critical?"

"I don't know. The more people I talk to and as I reflect on it, the more I really suspect something isn't as it should be in the Michaels camp. I no longer think it's just my own reaction. Then I find myself concocting ways to 'uncover the truth' at ETW."

"What's wrong with that? You're a reporter," said McClanahan.

"My objectivity seems to be slipping. I'm torn two ways. I want to be fair. I don't want to do anyone a hatchet job." He paused. "Yet, on the other hand," he went on, "I think something's amiss. There are just too many indications."

The editor waited for him to continue.

"I guess at first I was annoyed, and that made me want to get them. But as my irritation cooled, I realized such couldn't be my motive. As my attitudes softened I determined to follow up the first story with two more that were genuinely positive. Yet, the more I look into it, the more I think something is wrong, even if my initial reaction to Jaeger's smugness and Michaels's patronizing tone wasn't right either. And even you wouldn't deny that there *was* an undercurrent of doubt in my second article. Maybe their reaction was justified, and I was hinting at things I had no right to hint at?"

He stopped, obviously struggling between the two motives. "But what if I'm wrong? I could do them a great injustice."

"But what if you're right?" asked Ed.

"That's the dilemma! I have to look at my own pride. Am I trying to 'get' somebody? That can't be my focus. It's not the foundation of my job I'm questioning. I believe in investigative reporting as a valid pursuit for a Christian writer. But if my pride *is* in any way involved, then my conclusions would necessarily be suspect. I'm not sure this article is the place for all these thoughts. Like I said, my perceptions could be wrong. And at this point, anything I write seems colored with a negative cast. Maybe someone else should write it."

"Kind of late for that," said the editor. "Are you sure it's the article? What about the girl you've been seeing? Could it have anything to do with her?"

175

"It has everything to do with her! When I learned she was Michaels's daughter I made a first-class idiot of myself. I've been afraid to see her since. I reacted like an eight year old. But don't you see, it's all tied together. She was so secretive with me, withholding her name, keeping the concert from me. She's just like Jaeger and Michaels—part of the organization—secure behind locked doors where no one intrudes."

"Do I detect a note of bitterness?"

"Probably. But, Ed, it's almost as if they're baiting me to look behind those doors."

"So? Why don't you take the bait?"

"I don't know. Part of me relishes the idea of a full-scale investigation. What writer doesn't dream of it? Yet another part of me cringes at the thought of finding myself misled by my own assumptions and misrepresenting a legitimate man of God."

"Mixed motives—death to solid writing," said McClanahan, half to himself. "OK, tell you what. I'll see if Ziegler can do the last story. You and he can get together, and you can fill him in on where you were going with it. Then he can pull in some stuff from the files and ought to be able to finish it."

"That would sure take the pressure off." Jackson sighed.

"I'd still rather have your slant on it. You have a lot of thought invested. But I can respect where you are, and we'll have to live with it. We'll put you on routine work for a week or two. Let things settle down. Then—Michaels is doing a three-day engagement in Detroit in two weeks. Why don't you drive over for a day or two? Fill in your perspective, see it from another angle. Forget Greenville, the first article, Jaeger. Get your head together and see where you wind up. If you come up with a piece on the Detroit meetings, fine—we'll use it somewhere."

"That sounds good. Thanks."

"Don't sell yourself short, Jackson. You're a sharp reporter. Something might be up. This burr under your saddle might be one you're supposed to follow. If there's a scoop to be had, I want you there, not off moping somewhere about confused priorities and a lost romance."

Jackson laughed.

"OK, OK, I'll get my head screwed back on. Then I'll dig in . . . whichever side of the fence I land on."

37

Jackson had opted to drive the three hundred miles to Detroit rather than fly. Five or six uninterrupted hours of solitude was just what he needed.

The previous two weeks had brought him no further toward a resolve on how to proceed—or even whether to proceed—in any sort of investigation of ETW and Jacob Michaels. Actually most of his thoughts had been occupied with Diana. Her simple note had at last sunk in. He realized she was struggling with her bloodline too—in a different way than he, but that made it none the less painful for her. She had a name; he in a sense had none. Yet whereas his mental skirmish was to obtain a heritage, an ancestry, hers was just the opposite—to break free from the lot that had been forced on her by virtue of heredity.

They were each fighting a similar battle but in different directions. Knowing her roots all too well, Diana was seeking to frame an identity in spite of them. Knowing nothing of his, Jackson was seeking the identity only his roots could bring.

Meanwhile, the miles sailed by. The first meeting—tonight's— was scheduled for seven-thirty. Jackson arrived in Detroit at four-twenty. He checked into his room, took a shower, and went out for a light dinner in a nearby restaurant. He headed for the auditorium at seven.

Walking into the spacious hall at seven-fifteen Jackson saw that many thousands were already in their seats. At one end of the building an immense choir was rehearsing. Numerous TV cameras stood in readiness, particularly surrounding the central raised platform where speakers and singers would gather. Jackson noticed the press table down front where reporters and communications technicians from around the world were seated along with camera equipment from a half dozen countries. The low roar of preparatory confusion, children scrambling around in search of seats or parents or friends, the constant blinking of strobe lights—the atmosphere was one of near pandemonium, a fact millions of television viewers would never be aware of.

Jackson headed for a seat as high and close to the front as he could find. Tonight he would be a spectator, an "ordinary" Christian, not a writer. He wore no press card. He simply wanted to open himself to the spirit and tone of the place, to hear Jacob Michaels's message in a fresh way.

Twenty minutes after he had slipped into his seat, a small group of men and women emerged from a side entrance and made their way to the central platform, Jacob Michaels among them.

The meeting went pretty much as Jackson had anticipated. He made a concerted attempt to enter into the worshipful spirit he sensed on the faces around him. Try as he would, however, he could not undo his awareness of the technical side—the cameras and lights, the hubbub of behind-the-scenes activity programmed to make it all *look* so right. Certainly, he tried to reason with himself, in order to telecast a major gathering such as this there was a technical aspect to be considered. Of course total spontanaeity could never exist in such an environment. That was the price of reaching into homes across the continent.

But other doubts began to assail him as well. Everything was so carefully orchestrated toward appearance—hundreds of dollars in plants and flowers for the podium, expensive suits and tuxedos for everyone on the platform, the ultimate in sound equipment. Is this how Jesus would have evangelized the world? he wondered.

As he glanced around, the faces of his fellow listeners all seemed satisfied and content, so well fed, all dressed in fashionable clothes, most carrying Bibles. Not only did most appear well off, the majority seemed to be Christians as well.

If we're all Christians, he thought, *what are we doing here listening to an evangelistic message? If our professed purpose is to reach the lost, then why is ninety-five percent of this audience made up of middle-class, well-dressed, comfortable Christians?*

Jackson's mind drifted back in time. What a contrast it all seemed to the methods Jesus used. He held few meetings but instead sought out the people where they were. He went into the streets and bars and skid rows of His time—leper colonies, tax offices, harbors, and markets. He spent His time with the most despised of men and women—prostitutes, drunks, the immoral, the poor, the sick, the unemployed, the lame, the lazy, beggars, outcasts.

Speculating further, Jackson put the question to himself: Would Jesus be here?

It was a sobering thought and jolted him like a shot of ice water in the face. Would Jesus wear a $600 suit and submit to the ministrations of a makeup artist to go before a TV camera? Is *this* how Jesus would take His good news to the world if He were on the earth today?

Might He not more likely at this moment be found out in a run-down section with the city's homeless, involved in some barroom discussion, helping some minority family whose food supply had just run out, sitting with a group of old and lonely widows through the cold, dark hours of the night, or ministering healing in a hospital or psychiatric ward?

Michaels was winding down his message and had begun his impassioned appeal. "We're going to sing 'What a Friend We Have in Jesus,'" he was saying, "and I'm going to ask those of you who desire to make public your decision to accept Jesus into your life tonight to get up out of your seats and come down here—right down here in front of the podium. I know it might seem difficult, but come. The Lord will give you strength. You will not be alone. I sense in my heart that there are many of you out there tonight . . . possibly thousands of you. So don't be fearful. Come . . . as others come. You will see that many share that need you feel deep in your heart. Come . . . as we sing . . ."

The choir began softly, and the entire congregation had soon joined in.

Immediately from every corner, dozens—even hundreds—rose and began making their way to the front. All around Jackson saw them leaving their seats and heading for the aisles. But as he looked more closely he began to see that all the forward-marching troops came from the same well-dressed and prosperous cross section of the crowd. He saw no tears, no heartache, no apparent emotions of decision or conflict.

"They're carrying Bibles," he said to himself in disbelief. "Most going forward are Christians."

Suddenly it all seemed so superficial—the programming of the counselors to walk down at the same moment, giving the appearance of a huge response, the goats leading the hesitant sheep, all orchestrated beforehand for the benefit of the TV cameras, to prod the reluctant, the swelling of the ranks of converts so the meeting—and Jacob Michaels!—looked successful.

Something within Jackson snapped.

He quickly rose, followed the steady stream to the ground floor and there made a right turn rather than left and walked briskly out of the auditorium. A gray-haired gentleman in a suit poised at the exit interrupted his flight. "Excuse me, sir," he said, "but if you'd like to talk—if you have a need . . ."

Jackson just shook his head and continued out the door.

38

The night chill felt refreshing on Jackson's face.

He was hot, angry, confused—disillusioned with what he had seen. He had to walk, settle himself down, gather his thoughts.

In the distance he could hear the late-night sounds of the city—sirens, train horns, traffic, an occasional yell or screech of tires. He walked on and on, past desolate parking lots, imposing apartment buildings, darkened industrial warehouses. An occasional car zoomed by. One, a convertible full of teenagers yelling coarsely, careened along. Jackson's mood was too withdrawn to mind.

I love God's people, he thought. *They're my spiritual family. Yet something seems so wrong!* He walked on, thoughts suspended temporarily.

Are we really telling the world about Jesus? he pondered. *How can the gospel impact the lost when we primarily promote gatherings where Christians preach to each other? Aren't we just talking to ourselves?*

What about the parts of the world where urgent hunger and spiritual darkness exist? How are our meetings and sermons and television broadcasts reaching out to those people when we're speaking the language of middle-class America? We're just bound up in our own little Christian subculture, speaking our own jargon, carrying our expensive Bibles, building our lavish churches. We could feed the hungry, lonely, afraid, angry, immoral, cold, confused people of this very inner city. We could help! We could clothe them, teach them, bear their burdens, share life with them. But instead we're sitting huddled together in our own complacency.

Jackson walked on. His thoughts gradually shifted to the man who had drawn him to this city in the first place. He could hardly imagine Jacob Michaels in jeans with shirt sleeves rolled up helping some elderly lady get her toilet unclogged because she couldn't afford a plumber and then sitting down to tell her about God's love. Or out feeding a homeless child from his own hand. But isn't that the sort of thing Jesus might do?

His mind went back to the meeting he had just left and the Hollywood atmosphere of it all. The whole spectacle of Christian entertainment—huge concerts, mass media publicity, videos, magazine reviews, autograph parties, best-sellers, even televised church services—what was it but another form of show business!

Is this the lifestyle Jesus came to demonstrate?

In the confusion of his thoughts, Jackson knew his indictment fell upon himself as well. *Who am I to criticize?* he thought. *How much better do I do? I'm not involved in the gutters of life either. What am I giving anyone? Am I any more dedicated to a Christ-like lifestyle than Jacob Michaels?*

Jackson walked past several bars. He could hear yelling and laughing. A police car rushed past him, stopped in the next block, and two officers hurried inside. Three minutes later they exited half-dragging a handcuffed man, shoved him in the back seat, and sped away. A small crowd had gathered. As he approached to walk past, a scant-shirted, heavily perfumed girl—hardly more than eighteen and looking for a score—sauntered toward him.

"Hey, baby," she purred, "how about it?"

Jackson kept slowly on. "Not tonight," he said.

"Come on man, what's wrong—I'll make you a good deal."

Jackson shook his head, held on, and was once more alone.

Lord, he thought, *what do those poor people know of You? What would You do if You were here right now? How am I to model my life after You?*

Jackson turned up a side street, thinking about heading back to find where he'd left his car. But he'd try a different route. He was in no mood to encounter Vaunette and her friends again.

Lord, he said again, thoughts and prayers mingling freely, *give me a right attitude toward my fellow Christians—toward ministry—toward Jacob Michaels. I love Your people . . . I've dedicated my life to them in what I do through my writing. Keep me from wrong judgments. Give me Your wisdom in the midst of these questions and confused motives. Show me Your mind in this—show me the truth!''*

He continued on, the thoughts stilled for a time. He glanced at his watch. It was past midnight. The meeting would be long since over. He'd been walking for more than two hours. He must've covered miles! The auditorium loomed several blocks away. His car was in a lot on the other side—probably the only one left by now. He hoped the lot hadn't been locked.

Lord, are my impressions valid . . . or am I way off base? I know there's a place for much of what we do. Yet at the same time there seems such a contrast between that meeting, with its paunchy men in nice suits carrying soft-leather Bibles and its fashionable women in tailored dresses—such a contrast between them and helpless, straying Vaunette who is so lost she doesn't know up from down . . .

I don't want to be cynical, Lord. How can those two pictures be brought into focus? Has tonight been a respresentative picture of the evangelical Christian body?

What do I do, Lord? Do I write about these things? Does anyone want to hear it? Does anyone want to be confronted with the sham that I see? Or am I even seeing it correctly?

Lord, should I continue with these stories on Michaels? Perhaps I'm as biased in my own way as all the rest! I'm sunk in my own patch of prejudices too. Jesus condemned both *Pharisaism and self-righteousness. And if Michaels is the former, who knows but what I'm the latter! Is truth knowing about Jesus—or doing what Jesus said?*

He stopped on the sidewalk. He had found his car. The last words jolted him momentarily. As his thoughts had rambled, they had struck many nerves in his own awareness. Jackson realized he was confronting major questions—about what faith entailed and where he was to go from here.

Do I, he thought at last, *do I—Jackson Maxwell—want to be challenged to do what Jesus said? How willing am I,* myself, *to know the truth and then to follow it? For that's really the bottom line after all.*

For the moment, he could give himself no answer. But at least he knew he'd arrived at the critical question.

He unlocked his car and slowly drove back to the motel.

PART 5

Diana Michaels

39

The train sped along, rhythmic clacking of the tracks producing a dreary nostalgia. She gazed out the window at the passing industrial complex that would soon become Gary. To the right were the shores of Lake Michigan in the distance, whitecaps churning its surface; another storm was due in tonight. She was glad she'd be home before then.

Diana had tried with all her might to twist her father's arm to come with her by train. What were a few extra hours?

But he'd declined despite all her wiles. Singing together in Detroit, jointly receiving a standing ovation—he had to have felt the gratification. Togetherness had been rare enough between them. Standing on the podium as father and daughter, it had been special. In the absence of a closer relationship, a welcome substitute.

If only he'd have come on the train! How nice to spend an afternoon together, just the two of them. Diana knew you could never go back to recapture the past. Still, why couldn't they go forward—toward the mature adult relationship that had eluded them all these years? She wanted—as does any son, any daughter—nothing more than a few memories of closeness.

But time is a commodity too precious to be squandered on empty sitting, riding, looking out windows. So Jacob had flown—"an important meeting with Hamilton and the board of directors," he'd said. Disappointed, Diana stuck to her guns and rode the train anyway—alone. The day by herself would do her good.

It was always something. If it hadn't been an important meeting there would have been another reason. They weren't excuses. Her father loved and cared for her. But he was caught in the inexorable pull of career, business, urgencies, and a hectic schedule. Like millions of mothers and fathers, he was simply too hurried, too busy, too preoccupied to take part in the insignificant tiny moments of interaction in which a relationship is made. Days slipped by, weeks, months. Now Diana was twenty-seven and hadn't really spoken to her father, *really spoken* about things that mattered for, what was it? Ten years? Fifteen? Maybe twenty. Had she been close to him since becoming a teenager—ever?

Certainly the crowd in Detroit would have said, "How wonderful—father and daughter so close, ministering together." But it was superficial at best. She supposed she loved her father. But not since high school had she been able to muster a genuine respect for him.

Not that she had rebelled as such. She had simply grown in her own way, and it had been difficult for Jacob to accept. Her younger brother Richard, now twenty-five, *had* rebelled vigorously against what he considered the sham of religiosity. He'd nearly dropped out of high school and only agreed to see it through until graduation when Jacob enticed him with a sporty green Audi 4000.

The gesture only deepened what he perceived as hypocrisy in his father. After two years of traveling he enrolled in college, not with a particular goal in mind but because college represented the perfect environment to extend his self-indulgent, socializing lifestyle. He was now in his fifth year, and no graduation looked promising in the near future. The name Dick Michaels was one that symbolized on campus the free-wheeling fraternity life of wine, women, and song, and in the Michaels home one that brought silence to the discussion and usually a tear or two to Elizabeth's eye. Diana had not even seen her brother for three years.

She admired, loved her father. But respect? That was a more difficult commodity to come by. Certainly her career wouldn't be hindered by the fact that she was the daughter of *the* most distinguished name in the Christian world. In just a month since her group's debut there was already talk of tours, promotions, records, contracts—why, they'd barely begun! As much as she wanted to believe it was because of their talent, in her heart of hearts she knew a large part of it was the commercial potential the promoters spotted in the Michaels-Michaels connection. Just last week she had a call from *Christian Women Today* magazine with a request for an interview. They wanted to make her the cover story for their upcoming publication.

Was it all going to fall in their laps? What about the years struggling young artists, singers, and writers toil in obscurity, honing their skills, developing patience, strength of character, and virtue? But God's Country had her and her father's name, an instant ticket straight to the top!

The thrill of success was intoxicating. How could she say no to it all? Still, there was something disquieting about having it handed to you. Especially since she hardly felt her father was worthy of the incredible public adulation. Maybe if she had a deep spiritual regard for him, if she saw evidence of his attempt to maintain a relationship with her, if she'd seen in him a desire to understand Richard—

If, if, if! If . . so many things!

Could she see in her father, in his solitude, behind the doors of their home, an image consistent with the public perception, then flying into the limelight on his coattails might be easier to swallow. But to her, Jacob Michaels remained a public image—and sadly, little more.

She and Elizabeth were reasonably close—mothers and daughters usually were. On one level at least. But Diana even wondered if Elizabeth really knew her father. Diana had perceived a deepening loneliness in her mother. She held up her end in public, attending most of the crusades, singing, smiling, retaining faith in the prophetic nature of her husband's ministry. But inside Diana could tell she longed for something more permanent.

How was it, she thought, that a family like theirs could grow so apart, could diverge so entirely in four separate directions, and yet maintain the outward signs of relational health and vitality? What a contrast between the public image and the private reality!

Would it perhaps have been easier if she had rebelled more forcefully in ways that more visibly asserted her independence? As it was, enmity toward her father grew unseen, eating away at their relationship silently, she seeking ways to vent her individuality, he quietly resisting the impact of her friends, her clothes, the groups and protest marches she joined, the social involvement she insisted on pursuing, even down to the backpack she always carried with the prominent Greenpeace patch sewn on.

Why couldn't he see that she had to find a life of her own? If she was going to discover a faith in God and a means for expressing it that were hers and hers alone, she had to test life's waters. If it took some experimentation and some time, what was the harm?

But he could never see it from that perspective. When he walked into her room and saw for the first time her wall posters of Kathryn Hepburn, Amy Grant, Jimmy Carter, and Mother Theresa, he had merely muttered a few words of disgust. But nowhere in his consciousness could he perceive that his daughter was searching for standards of meaning and reality, role models from which she could fashion a place in life to stand.

As she had matured, tempered her social involvement, and come gradually into a more traditional brand of self-expression as a Christian, his objections to her patched jeans and bumper stickers grew less vocal. And now that she had broken into the spotlight with him, looking so thoroughly the part of middle-class Christendom, she knew in his mind the resolution of her youthful "wayward" ways was complete. She had at last come around.

But had anything in their relationship really changed?

She was now walking as a Christian in a closer way than ever. But was it possible for her father to grasp what being a Christian meant to her? Could he ever understand what Hepburn, Carter, Grant, and Mother Theresa symbolized in her faith?

Suddenly the phantom of Hamilton Jaeger filled Diana's mind. *Hamilton,* she thought, *he's as much a part of our family as any of us . . . a permanent fixture.*

For as long as she could remember, Hamilton had been there. Her earliest recollections of her father and grandfather included Hamilton. When they'd come home from church every Sunday—she must've been only four or five—Hamilton would regularly join them for Sunday afternoon dinner. It had been a tradition. Grandma, Grandpa, Uncle Lance, and Hamilton—every Sunday.

That was before the stardom had suspended the steady flow of their life as a family. She at least had known her mother and father for a short while in something resembling a private manner. By the time Richard was six or eight, however, and should have been playing catch with his dad, Jacob was caught up in the schedule that was daily claiming more and more of him.

Father and son had but rare moments together. She, not his father, had taught six-year-old Richard to ride his first bike. Grandpa Henry, involved as he was, had rummaged through the attic, located an old footlocker, and had dug down to find an already aging baseball mitt—the very one belonging to Jacob as a child—which he presented to eight-year-old Richard, whom he then taught to use it.

Jacob was experiencing the thrill of the climb to success. And he was too busy. And there was Hamilton right beside him, pushing, pulling, straining, always grasping for something more, something beyond.

Diana had been fortunate to be a girl. Girls needed just as large doses of parental love. But maybe they could get more of what was required from their mothers. Possibly they didn't need their fathers in quite the same way. She had had her mother to cut out paper dolls with and to teach her to make cookies. She recalled her first batch of chocolate chip cookies—so hard you had to chisel them apart!

Everyone had eaten several and lauded their merits. She smiled. Even Hamilton had eaten two! What a pack of liars they all were!

But Richard had suffered. When high school came it was no wonder he chose a different road with a different set of friends. No wonder he could hardly have cared about the church youth group. Jacob had felt the pain, but he remained oblivious to the true source of it. Otherwise, he'd have begun to make amends. But his rise continued, and the distance between father and son widened. Henry retired, and suddenly Jacob was propelled to his status as nationwide spokesman for evangelicalism. He had never looked back.

What parent, Diana reflected, ever knows what is going on in children's minds or is aware of the hurts they suffer through parental selfishness or lack of thought? She recalled Richard's tumultuous high school years—what agony he went through then, as a sensitive fifteen year old.

She had seen the look in Henry's eyes that told her he knew. He'd been years on the top. He'd drifted away from his own wife. He'd known the effect on his own son of an overly extended father, a spiritual man unknowingly on the road to losing one of the relationships that matters most, the bond between father and child. And now Henry could see his own grandson suffering at the end of the line. His was the heartache of witnessing still another generation of father and son growing distant from one another.

But Henry was aging. It was too late for him to make the changes he wished he'd made years before. He had to weep silently inside for the concealed turmoil within the family of his son, looked up to by so much of America as their model.

Diana sighed and wiped her eyes.

Was this the price God's people in high places and positions of influence had to pay for ministry? Was it inevitable that these public figures had to sacrifice private relationships to carry out the tasks God had given them?

She looked outside. Chicago wasn't far now.

Another sigh. A family in upheaval. Yet there they were on the podium together just last night. What a dichotomy!

It would be good to see her mother again. Right now she longed simply to hug her and feel the answering pressure of her mother's embrace. She wanted the security of that love. Elizabeth had missed two crusades in a row.

Maybe they each needed one another—right now in a greater way than ever.

40

"Mother, it's good to see you!" The two embraced, Diana longer than for a routine hug.

"I haven't had a squeeze like that since you left for college," said Elizabeth.

"I guess I'm feeling more affectionate than usual."

"Anything troubling you?" asked her mother.

"No," replied Diana. "I enjoyed a quiet ride home on the train and had the chance to do a lot of thinking. I guess I realized how much I cared about you."

"Thank you, that's . . . that's nice of you to say," said Elizabeth, taken a little off her guard.

"I mean it, Mother."

"I hear you were quite a hit in Detroit. Of course, I'm not surprised."

"How'd you hear that?"

"Your father stopped by. He arrived about noon and was home to shower and change before going back to the office. Why didn't the two of you travel together?"

"I tried persuading him to come on the train with me, but you know Dad," Diana said with a sigh.

Elizabeth sensed more to her daughter's words than was apparent on the surface. Yet it had been so long since she had occupied the role of motherly comforter and Diana was now so much older that she hardly knew what to do. Besides, she herself had been the victim recently of too many similar moments, saying lighthearted words but feeling their sting much deeper.

She awkwardly stepped forward, placed her hands on Diana's shoulders, facing her back. She wanted to offer a word of encouragement. How she yearned to turn Diana toward her and give her the deep-felt embrace she longed to feel. But her touch was tentative. Diana continued to stare out the window.

Discovering a deeper expression to the bond they shared would take time. Each uncertain, they groped cautiously toward relationship, having to discover anew the complex personality each held deep inside.

Then, patting her daughter's shoulders, trying to change the subject, Elizabeth said, "There's been a young man calling for you—quite insistently."

Diana stepped away, turned, and sat down. "I don't think I'm up to talking to anyone for a while . . . probably something to do with the group."

"Now that you're a celebrity," said Elizabeth with a smile, "your time's not going to be your own. Believe me, I know!"

"If I'm going to be hounded at all hours, maybe I should move back into an apartment."

"Nonsense! We love having you here."

Diana smiled. "*You* love having me here, don't you mean? Dad's never home long enough to notice."

Elizabeth sighed and nodded. "Still," she said, "I do enjoy it. It used to be so dreary sometimes, when you were away at college. I'm glad you wanted to be here when you enrolled at Cosmopolitan."

"It does make life easier in a way. Not having to worry about the place—roommates, and all that. Besides, I'm older. The apartment life just isn't me anymore. I actually don't fit in that well anywhere at the school. At Berkeley maybe I would, but hardly at Cosmopolitan. But they've got the courses I need."

"You're suddenly a star—you probably won't have to worry about staying single for long. You'll have men beating a path to your door!"

"I worry about it though, Mother. I didn't want to marry right after school, like so many of my friends. There was so much I wanted to do—wrongs to be righted, ideals that needed living, societies to change. But now here I am in the thick of the establishment, embarking on a career. It hardly seems real. And I wonder if that resolve to wait a while has doomed my prospects forever."

"No chance of that, my dear," said Elizabeth. "You're a talented young woman on your way to the top."

Diana shrugged noncommitally.

"That young man who's been calling this past week—he sounded like more than a passing acquaintance," suggested Elizabeth, "as if his interest might have been more on the personal than the professional side."

"Did he leave his name?"

"Yes, let's see—where'd I put that note? Oh yes, here it is, I knew I wrote it down . . . Maxwell."

41

"I thought about writing you," said Jackson, when he at last found Diana at home.

"And why didn't you?"

"I felt I owed you an explanation—in person."

"I'm glad you came," said Diana.

Jackson looked down, fumbling in his mind for the right words. "I . . . I don't know. I guess I just have to apologize for what happened and leave it at that."

"Apology accepted," returned Diana.

"I feel so foolish. That little note you sent cut me to the quick. I hadn't stopped to consider your motives and feelings. I am sorry."

"Forget it," said Diana. "I knew something must've been on your mind."

Jackson nodded but said nothing.

"Like to talk about it?"

Jackson hesitated. "Yes, of course I'd like to share it with you, but I don't want to hurt you again. It does involve you in a way— your father actually."

"Ah, so that's the rub," Diana replied. "You had something going on the side you weren't telling me either."

"Now wait a minute, I didn't—"

"You were just as secretive about your background as a writer as I was about my singing."

"But at least you knew who I was."

"That's a minor point," insisted Diana. "You never gave me the least indication of what you were doing. We both admitted we had our reasons for keeping to ourselves. And it was you who over-reacted and got angry, not me. At least now my background and identity's out in the open. But, Jackson, you still haven't leveled with me about your investigation of my father."

Jackson looked up, but said nothing.

"Surprised I knew?"

Jackson shrugged.

"I've done a little homework these last three weeks, Jackson.

The library's been most informative—as have some of the people down at ETW. Some of the people there don't have much good to say about what you've been up to."

"Now wait a minute," said Jackson. "I tried to write a perfectly sympathetic article. The first time anyway. I gave your father every advantage. Can I help it if their reaction was—"

"I won't argue any of that," Diana interrupted. "I know what Hamilton's like. I grew up with him. And my father is closed much of the time too. My point is, you weren't open to me either."

Jackson opened his mouth to respond, then thought better of it. He settled quietly back into his seat.

She was right of course. Whatever she'd done, he'd done the same.

"The whole thing's still too recent," he said after a moment. "My reactions sometimes get in the way of reason. What happened with you the other night had more to do with my own hangups about my identity than with yours. I've always tried to be open as a reporter. Then I discover lurking deep inside me unknown personality twists that pop to the surface when I least expect them. Even though some of my perceptions of evangelicalism may be relatively accurate, I'm now wondering if I'm not doing exactly what Jesus described, seeing the sliver and ignoring my own mote?"

"Any final conclusions?"

"No, I've been wondering if I should take a leave, at least from this series of articles—remove myself from an environment where I'm forced to write about these things. I'm questioning whether I'm mature enough to draw any conclusions."

"But how will that maturity and wisdom come if you throw in the towel?"

"Who knows? Right now I'm really discouraged. I've been wondering about the very basis of my writing. Maybe it's all just a clever bit of self-delusion. Perhaps I don't possess as much insight as I think. I'm only thirty-one—young, opinionated. Am I just making up the importance of my incisive words to God's people, is it my own private little ego trip?"

"But, Jackson," said Diana, "no proud and self-glorifying person would question his motives as uncompromisingly as you do. The very things you're asking demonstrate your thoughtfulness as a Christian—and as a writer."

"I would like to believe that," said Jackson without enthusiasm, "but I can't help but wonder about my negativity."

"Sometimes God places a divine discontent in certain of His people to keep the rest of us on our toes. That's a needed role, a stirring of the pot."

"I want to believe what you say. But I'm the one who has to live with myself. And when I'm in the doldrums like this, I'm gun-shy about writing something that might not be true."

"Do you really think God would allow you to deceive His people?"

Jackson shrugged.

"He's guiding you, Jackson, whether or not you feel His direct inspirational control every time you sit down to the typewriter."

"Still, I don't know where to go from here. I can't envision cranking up for more writing at the moment."

"What's the status of your series?" asked Diana.

"Boy, you have been getting the lowdown on me!" said Jackson.

Diana laughed.

"I asked my editor last week to assign someone else to the final article. I couldn't face it feeling as sardonic as I do." Jackson was pensive. "Then you think," he began, "that I *should* continue to look into things that concern me—like ETW and your father and Jaeger and Greenville?"

"I don't see how you can't."

"Even though you're on the other side of the fence so to speak?"

"But I'm not—don't you see? Truth is truth. It *has* to come out. Besides, I don't talk to my father like this. If I had to land on one side of the fence or the other, I'm not sure I wouldn't wind up on yours. Not that I wish my father any harm. But if something's not right, it has to be rectified."

"I would never want to be part of something that would alienate you from your father. Maybe it's because there's something about that relationship I can never share that makes me leery of upsetting it."

"I don't follow you . . . aren't you close to your dad?" asked Diana.

"Yes, I love him dearly. And we are close. But, . . . well, he's not my real father—"

"Jackson, I had no idea."

"I was adopted at birth and have always loved my folks. It's just that since I was a teenager I've wondered if there was anything special about genuine 'blood' relation. It's always been there—a nagging question. Lately, it's been playing havoc with my mind. I guess I'm going through the midthirties identity crisis. That's probably part of why my writing's stalled too, why I just feel out of kilter all the way around. I just somehow don't feel—I don't know— *whole,* I suppose. There's something missing that won't be right until . . . maybe until I look my *real* father in the eye, shake his hand, and feel his arm around me."

He stopped abruptly. "I'm sorry," he went on in a moment, "I didn't intend to get into that. It's been on my mind a lot."

"I can't vouch for the fatherly relationship personally," said Diana. "My father and I aren't close in the least. I'd like to be, but that's one of the unfortunate things about his position."

"Nevertheless, there's still something about it. At least you know who you *really* are. That's why I could never intentionally undermine that relationship. If I pursued this, there'd be no telling where it might go."

"But, Jackson, you have a duty to follow the threads of this wherever they lead. People are sometimes hurt by the truth. But if they are open, it will lead them to maturity."

Jackson sighed.

"Have you ever thought," said Diana, changing the subject, "about looking into your past—trying to locate your biological parents?"

"Sure. When I found out—I was thirteen when my folks told me—it really hit me hard. I guess I blocked it out of my mind, maybe until recently. I have been thinking about it in the last few months. I don't know why now all of a sudden it's come back out of my subconscious. Sometimes it's almost an obsession with me, wanting to *know.* But I haven't done anything to follow up on it. I don't even know what I could do. And I'm afraid of hurting my folks—my adopted folks. Seems like stirring up the muddy water could only injure them."

"But if you have to know for your own peace of mind?"

"And tracking back like that is nearly impossible. All the personalities stay well hidden."

"It can be done much easier than most people think," said

Diana. "I have a friend at school. She was from an orphanage but only recently discovered she'd been taken there by living parents. She managed to locate them in just a few months. There are agencies who'll help. We're living in a liberated era, you know. No more sacred cows. Everything's out in the open."

"Hmm . . . maybe I should talk to her," said Jackson pondering her words. "But I've got to get back to the office. You've given me enough to think about for at least a month!"

"I'm out of time too. I have a class in twenty minutes."

42

Throughout the days of Jackson's soul-searching as to whether he should continue to probe into the affairs of ETW, a name continued to rummage through his subconscious—the name mentioned by Cooper Graves.

He decided before coming to any conclusions that he at least ought to make an attempt to talk to the man. What could it hurt? He needed a different perspective on ETW, and maybe the man Means could provide it. He'd already forgotten that the first mention of the name was in reference to Sondra DeQue. Now he found himself curious about the man for his own sake.

After the talk with Diana, therefore, he decided to drive over to ETW headquarters and see if he just might be able to see the man. If Diana was right and he should plow through his doubts and get on with his job as a reporter whose duty it was to get to the bottom of the truth, then perhaps he needed some little nudge, a word from someone else confirming that to be the right direction. He didn't even know Means; yet, as he'd said to himself before, what could it hurt? He didn't want to leave any stone unturned through which the Lord might be able to speak to him.

He took the stairs instead of the elevator to the fifth floor of the Luxor Towers, hoping to avoid being seen. Emerging from the stairwell, he turned in the opposite direction from Sondra's office and headed straight for the door labeled "Correspondence."

A moderate-sized outer office was empty. It showed signs of secretarial occupation—two desks, a couple of phones, several file cabinets, a large table with papers and files and books and other material on top of it, and several chairs scattered around. Despite the lived-in look, no one was home. From an inner office, whose door was open, Jackson heard the sound of a man's voice. As he waited, it was impossible not to pick up the man's half of the telephone conversation.

"Yes . . . I understand . . . I appreciate your keeping me updated on his condition, Mrs. Bloom . . . yes, of course I will be praying . . ."

A long silence followed. Jackson could not help feeling like an intruder. He busied himself looking around the outer office but was, after another moment, drawn again into the role of an eavesdropper.

"—I was just rereading your letter a few days ago," the man went on. "I had planned to write you again, so I'm happy you called . . . right . . . we have been praying for you both in our prayer group here . . ."

Another pause.

"Oh, I am so sorry to hear that . . . yes . . . I understand . . ."

Again the voice on the other end of the line spoke for some time, with brief sounds of encouragement and responses from time to time on the part of the man from ETW.

"Let's pray together now, shall we," the man said at length. "Yes . . . that would be fine . . . yes . . . I'd be happy to. Father," the man went on in a softer voice, "I'm so grateful for my sister, and that she called today and that we have been able to fellowship together on the phone. I lift her up to You, Lord God, and ask that You would fill her with the encouragement and love of Your presence. And for her son, Lord, I ask that You would comfort and heal and . . ."

The praying voice grew so quiet that Jackson could no longer make out the words. He felt as though he was intruding upon a solemn moment of privacy where he had no right to be. He sat down in one of the chairs and waited quietly.

In a few minutes he heard the conversation come to an end

and the phone being hung up. The next moment a man emerged from the inner office. It was the same man he had seen in the hallway outside the day he had been following Sondra.

He came forward with outstretched hand and a smile.

"I'm sorry to keep you waiting," he said. "I'm Bob Means— what can I do for you?"

"It's I who should apologize to you," replied Jackson. "I didn't mean to intrude—it sounded like a rather personal phone call."

"It was—they are all personal. Somehow the Lord sends people my way who are in need. But as for your intrusion, no—I knew you were here. It was personal, but not private. Kingdom business involves us all. For all I knew, you might have been out here joining me in prayer for the dear lady."

"I suppose I didn't think of that," responded Jackson a little sheepishly.

"No matter. Our Father has dear Mrs. Bloom in His hands. Now—how may I be of service to you?"

"My name is Jackson Maxwell," said Jackson, then waited for what he anticipated would be a reply of recognition.

"Happy to meet you," replied Means.

"I'm a reporter."

Means nodded, but still showed no sign of recognition.

"Perhaps you're aware of the stir I've caused around here?"

"Sorry . . . no."

"Well, actually that's a relief!" Jackson laughed. "I figured everybody in ETW had me on their don't-talk-to list by now."

"I'm not really in what you would call the mainstream of ETW," replied Means with a smile. "So you'll have to forgive me if I'm not aware of all that's going on."

"Believe me, I don't mind at all! But how can that be? I take it you're the man in charge of communications for ETW."

Now it was Means's turn to laugh.

"Don't let the sign on the door fool you. This office is probably the single lowest rung on the proverbial corporate ladder! *Important* correspondence and communications, media contracts, TV, radio, international stuff—that's all handled elsewhere. What the name on the door means is that we handle personal communications from individuals, the kind of thing not considered important enough by anyone else in ETW to do. Phone calls asking for prayer, handwritten notes by elderly ladies and children, asking a question or requesting a book, all kinds of things. The volume of mail and contacts is unending, and it's usually the kind of thing no one wants to bother with when so many more so-called important things are going on."

"You don't seem to mind it?"

"Mind it! Mr. Maxwell, I wouldn't be any place else!"

He paused, and a smile of reflection passed across his face. "You wouldn't know this, but at one time I used to be pretty high up in ETW."

"You've been here a long time, I take it?"

"More than twenty years. Jacob and I practically grew up together. But whereas most people move 'up' in an organization through the years, I've followed a downward path. Most people would be bitter at such a development in their so-called careers. And I have to admit that I used to wonder and pray a little about it, and had to work to keep my flesh in check. But now I realize what a great blessing it has in fact been."

"How so?" asked Jackson.

"I haven't been demoted at all," Means went on. "In God's economy things are often upside down from the world's perceptions. And over the years I've come to see that it's been *me* whom God has blessed with the greatest role within ETW of all! I wouldn't trade places with anyone. Right here, in this little office, hidden from view, doing what a man like Hamilton Jaeger might shun as meaningless, I have the unparalleled opportunity every day of touching men and women, individual lives. And not just randomly—I mean lives that God has specifically sent to me. I tell you, it's such a profound ministry! I get to touch the daily, living, breathing body of Christ, feel its pulse. As I pray for him, sometimes I actually feel sorry for poor Jacob in my heart, sorry that out there in the glare of the public spotlight he doesn't have the opportunity to see what I see, hear what I hear, read the letters I read. Half of them are addressed to him. But it's me the Lord has put in the position to answer them. And I tell you, it's a mission field so ripe with opportunity. Truly, the Lord answers my heart's prayer daily to be involved in the real grass roots of ministry and evangelism."

He paused.

"I'm sorry for carrying on so," he went on with a slight laugh. "I just am so blessed by this position the Lord's put me in that I tend to run on and on about it."

"I'm intrigued," replied Jackson. "I'd like to hear more about it."

"Well, take that woman you just heard me praying with—Mrs. Bloom. A sweet lady from Minneapolis. She's in her mid-eighties, one of God's dear ones. She wrote me a year ago—wrote to Jacob actually, but I answered her letter. Since then we've struck up a lively correspondence. She writes or calls about once a month. To tell you the truth, I think she considers me one of her true personal friends. She shares her thoughts and problems and hurts and anxieties with me, and we pray together. It's like the Lord led her into my life to give her a lifeline. She lives alone in a little apartment, can't get out much, no family nearby. I really feel I'm doing a little good in her life. Just now we were praying for her son and for her burden for him."

"That really is a different sort of ministry from the public one," said Jackson. "I see what you mean."

"And it's not only that I might be helping her. She blesses me too, and I know she prays for me—and Jacob—every single day. And I've managed to put her in touch with several other elderly shut-ins who now correspond with one another and talk on the phone and share prayer. It's really quite wonderful. A whole new dimension has been added to their lives, not because of me, but because of what the Lord allowed to happen because He has me here. It's truly a ministry of expanding the borders of the kingdom for some of these people and I wouldn't be anywhere else. They are, I guess you'd say, sort of my congregation."

"And a lot of people contact you?"

"As I said, they don't think they're contacting me personally. They just write or call in, and I happen to be the one at ETW that they get—all accidental from their perspective. But not from mine! I pray daily for *every* contact I will have, from whatever source. So every one of the many thousands of people I have written to or spoken with over the years—I consider every one of them a very distinct and personal answer to prayer. Why, in the same way I prayed for *you* early this morning too, Jackson Maxwell. I prayed that there would be no chance encounters during my day, and that every person I met would be sent me by the Lord for a specific purpose."

"Hmm . . . well, I hope I don't disappoint you," said Jackson.

"No chance of that," replied Means. "Whatever your reason for coming to see me, God's hand is in it. I consider you 'sent' to me, however you happen to view me. So . . . what *is* your purpose? How can I be of assistance to you?"

"Your name was given me as one I might be able to talk to for some perspective on ETW as a whole, and on Jacob Michaels," said Jackson. "I've been working on a story for my magazine, *The Christian World*."

"I see. And you think I may be able to help?"

"You already have given me a whole new slant on some of the behind the scenes workings of ETW that I'd never considered. What could you tell me about Mr. Michaels, and about I guess what you'd call the more public direction of ETW?"

A cloud passed over Means's face. It was the first truly sober expression Jackson had seen on an otherwise exuberant face. A look of pain seemed to accompany it, and he did not reply for a long minute. When he did, it was not what Jackson had expected.

"I believe God is at work in ETW," he said at length. "If He were not, I would not be here. As I said, in my little corner of it, I couldn't be more excited about what God is doing."

He paused a moment, reflecting. "Yet in another way," he went on, "I do have to tell you, I am very concerned for what you call the public direction of this ministry. To tell you the truth, I'm not really sure what that direction is. And I find myself wondering at times if it is a direction that the Lord is setting . . . or if it's instead a direction being laid out by men—by men perhaps not seeking God for what He would have them do. In other words, there are things going on inside ETW that I am unsure about. My heart has been heavy lately with a great burden for the future of this organization, and for Jacob himself. He needs our prayers, Mr. Maxwell. He needs them greatly. I sense that there are hard times and severe trials ahead for him. He is going to need all the strength he can call upon God to give him."

"My own struggle has been whether to continue my investigating and my writing with respect to ETW," said Jackson.

"Seek the Lord's direction, young man," said Means. "If you're trying to grind your own personal axes, then I would caution you to move slowly and warily. But if it's truth you're trying to find, hold nothing back."

"It wouldn't bother you to know that I was 'investigating' your old friend?"

"Of course not. Truth must come out. As long as your motives are pure, then you will only serve as an instrument in the hand of God to do His work. I will pray for you now, that such is the case. But as to my reluctance as to what you might do, as far as I'm concerned, in God's kingdom, the wider open we throw the doors of light, the better. I would see nothing hidden."

"And if ETW's reputation suffers as a result?"

"I owe no allegiance to an organization, least of all this one. I may be employed by ETW, so to speak. But my allegiance is to One higher. I owe Jacob a servant's heart—and my prayers. But if there are things that are not as they should be, the Lord will reveal them—whether through you or through another. And they *should* be revealed. As I have said, there are things I wonder about, and I'm praying for the opportunity to relay my concerns to Jacob."

"Would you care to be specific about your concerns?" queried Jackson.

Means laughed lightly. "No . . . no, Mr. Maxwell. Though I am concerned, and prayerful, neither do I owe *you* my allegiance. I will do nothing to further your ends—to help your story—any more than I would try to help the cause of *any* mere man. My advice to you is this—be in prayer, be cautious, walk slowly, but as God leads, be bold to walk forward. You are a reporter, a writer— then ask your questions, probe, think, question, and trust God to lead you into truth."

Jackson did not reply immediately. He drew in a slow breath, then exhaled with a smile.

"I must say, you have invigorated my mind in some new directions. I am very grateful for your time, Mr. Means," he said at length.

"My time is the Lord's, Mr. Maxwell, as I told you. No accidental encounters, remember?"

"Yes, I believe you did say that."

"I am very pleased to have met you. You strike me as a young man intent on truth beyond a mere story. That is probably why

I felt such a freedom to open up to you as I did. Usually I am able to read people pretty well."

"You don't give interviews like this as a rule?"

"Interviews!" laughed Means. "You're the first person from the media I've spoken with in fifteen years or more."

"Then I'm honored."

"In any case, I hope circumstances may permit us to meet again one day. When the Lord sends someone into my life—whether you, or Mrs. Bloom's phone call, or a handwritten note asking for prayer—I know He always has a reason. I'll be looking forward to discovering the reason for His opening the way for *your* visit today."

"I hope you're right and that we may meet again, Mr. Means."

"We will—I'm sure of that. And when we do, you must call me Bob. We're brothers now, no longer strangers."

"Agreed," said Jackson.

43

The day was warm and humid.

Jackson had been out on his bike for two hours and was sweating profusely. It felt refreshing. His mind was full, and he had needed a break from the mental pressure.

The interview with Means had been on his mind constantly in the last forty-eight hours. It couldn't even be legitimately called an interview, though it was certainly one of the most interesting encounters he had ever had. It hadn't contained the normal question-and-answer elements, the flow of interaction Jackson had come to expect. Rather, it had been a conversation of unexpected openness that had set his brain to working in new and previously unexplored directions.

A few days ago he'd not been able to imagine any further

work on the third article. Now suddenly this fellow Means had put everything in a brand-new light—both raising the same kinds of questions Jackson had been feeling, while at the same time encouraging Jackson to move forward. Yet in his words, too, was the unmistakable exhortation to proceed with integrity and prayer, two ingredients perhaps Jackson hadn't emphasized enough lately.

So Jackson *had* been praying and asking God what he should do, rather than trying to figure out every detail that would go into a rational decision. At the same time his mind continued to work overtime, weighing all the elements involved.

Then Sondra had called.

She had some information for his investigation he might be interested in, she said.

He wasn't conducting an "investigation," the still-reluctant side of Jackson's ambivalent nature had replied.

Nevertheless, she thought he'd want to know what she had. Could he come over tonight?

He'd agreed and had taken off early. After the hard miles on his bike, a cold shower, and a sandwich during the six o'clock news, he had hoped he'd be able to put some of his conflicting thoughts and emotions on hold for a while and respond rationally to what Sondra had to tell him. If he was to move forward with the story, he had to do so, as Means had stressed, on the basis of clearheaded thought and God's leading, not on the basis of emotional ups and downs.

"Jackson—come in."

"It's good to see you again."

"I baked some cookies—oatmeal-raisin this time."

Jackson laughed. "My weak spot penetrated once more."

Sondra brought out a tray and set it on the coffee table. Her mood was noticeably more relaxed than the last time they'd met, Jackson observed.

"I'm puzzled," she began, "by what you said on the phone about not being on the story any longer. Last time you seemed so bent on finding the bottom line. What happened?"

"It's a long story. Let's just say I've been going through a personal crisis of my own as a result of this thing."

"Last time it was me."

"I don't know what it is about ETW, but it seems to bring conflict to whomever gets close to the inner workings."

"Well, according to that theory," said Sondra, "my life should begin to straighten out any time."

"How's that?"

"You could no longer say I'm close to the inner workings."

"You've been moved?" Jackson asked.

"Not formally. I'm still in PR . . . still have my office . . . for how long, who knows? But my role and daily functions are more and more taking on a mundane characteristic. No more meetings with the brass . . . no more speeches . . . no more press conferences—the subtle isolation of one who has said too much."

"I'm sorry you've had to suffer for something I started."

"It's hardly your doing. The disease lies solely with ETW . . . like a cancer, slowly and quietly eating away at the internal health of the whole organization."

"Pretty serious," replied Jackson, thinking about the concerns Bob Means had stressed to him. "Don't you think you might be exaggerating just a bit?"

"I don't even know. Sometimes it all looks rosy enough. Then at others it seems it's all about to topple over. I finally decided I had to do something. That's why I wanted to talk to you. I think I have a lead you can use."

"Sondra, I'm no Watergate detective," spoke up Jackson's reticent side.

"But, Jackson, don't you see how important this is? It *has* to be brought to the surface. I love Jacob Michaels. I believe in him, in his message. But I tell you, Hamilton is going to undermine the good if something isn't done."

"Why me?"

"Because you've done the groundwork. You've talked to them—you're the one who first publicly broke the news about Greenville. You're a natural to see it through."

"But I'm not sure enough of my own motives."

"You have questions and doubts," said Sondra seriously. "Who doesn't? But you have an obligation to make the truth known."

"Hmm . . . that's the third time I've heard that in the last week," mused Jackson almost to himself.

Sondra was pensive. Neither spoke for several minutes.

"OK," said Jackson at length, "tell me what you've got. I guess I owe you that."

"I went out on a limb talking to some people," said Sondra. "If Hamilton finds out what I've been doing—especially that I've been talking to *you* about *him*—I tell you it's my head! That's why you've got to go through with this. Your lethargic attitude is hardly just reward for what I've done."

"Sorry."

"Well, I've taken it as far as I intend to. I like working for Jacob Michaels, and I want to stay there. I believe in the man too much to see him ruined by one such as Hamilton."

"OK, what do you have?"

"Nothing in the way of concrete information," said Sondra. "That part of it is going to be up to you. I've kept my eyes and ears open, and I discovered two people who might know things—and they may be willing to talk. I didn't approach them, and I don't want my name used at all. You're on your own."

Jackson nodded.

"One of them, Harriet Steadman by name, works in the finance department. I've heard things that are interesting. She and Hamilton have been, shall we say, *close* recently, and it wouldn't surprise me if she's doing some of his 'under-the-table' financial arrangements for him."

"You're not suggesting outright corruption?"

"I doubt he's breaking the law, if that's what you mean. But I have gathered there is money somewhere in ETW that's just floating. Whether you'd term it a 'secret fund' . . . that's the sort of thing reporters dream up. All I know is that there is money someplace not specifically designated for use. And I have the feeling Hamilton's fingers are pretty heavily attached to it."

Jackson pondered her words.

"Then the other is a young man who's no longer with ETW. Name's Jerome Bullinger. He came to work for Hamilton a couple years back. He was sharp—a hard worker, intelligent . . . and ambitious! At first we thought Hamilton was grooming him to follow in his footsteps, training his own personal protégé, as it were. It turned out young Bullinger was more grasping than Hamilton had bargained for. They were both headstrong and zealous, but the pushy young lieutenant proved too enterprising for Hamilton. It came to a head, and suddenly Jerome was no longer with ETW. The scuttlebutt was that he had learned too much—both about Hamilton's past, and even Jacob's—and was trying to use it to his own advantage as a lever over them. There was talk of something they were both involved in years ago. But knowing Jerome as we did—he was really an avaricious guy, no one really trusted him—no one took any of his talk seriously. We figured he was making it up to protect his own position. As it turned out, he'd bitten off more than he could chew. Hamilton got rid of him, and he never caused any further trouble. Hamilton probably had him over some barrel of his own. Hamilton's not one to tangle with lightly. He usually comes out on top."

"So you're flinging me to the wolf?" said Jackson with a smile.

"What harm could he do you? You don't even work for ETW."

"If Jaeger is as cunning as you imply," said Jackson, "I'm sure he'd find a way."

"Just watch your step."

44

Jackson closed the door of his refrigerator, poured a tall glass three-fourths full of orange juice, then filled the remainder with grape. He walked over to his overstuffed chair, kicked off his shoes, and sat down with one leg draped over the chair's arm, the other on a footstool.

The scent of a good story lured him. Especially one so fraught with potential intrigue—schemes . . . hidden money . . . secret plans.

Yet this was no pulpy detective novel. This was real life. People could be hurt, careers damaged, a worldwide evangelism effort undermined. How he carried himself would have profound implications. The stakes were high.

If he proceeded and in fact discovered impropriety in ETW near the top, what would become of the untold good being done by the organization? How was he to weigh the exposing of some relatively minor ethical slips with the feeding of starving children and the evangelizing of lost nations?

The question could hardly be considered on a mere one-dimensional level. There was much to consider. He undeniably saw but tiny pieces of a huge puzzle. Yet he had to formulate a decision on the basis of the little he could see.

Truth—what was it—really?

Was it intellectual? Or did it primarily have to do with behavior? Was truth a function of belief—or of conduct?

He—Jackson Maxwell, reporter—was a Christian. He believed certain things about God, life, Jesus, the Bible. In that sense, he felt he possessed the "truth." Yet these beliefs were clearly intellectual—any philosopher would make the same claims about his academic conclusions.

If he, then, proceeded to live in an unprincipled manner, ignoring the instructions of Jesus—while still maintaining belief in those cognitive precepts—would he be living the truth? Would his life reflect truth?

He raised his glass to his mouth and downed half its contents in two satisfying gulps.

On the other hand, he mused, if another man held the view that his spiritual viewpoints were completely mistaken and yet in the way in which he lived his daily life and related to people was actually in harmony with the teachings of Jesus—would that man be living the truth?

Clearly, in both instances something would be missing. Elements of truth might be present to be sure. But in neither case could the claim be substantiated that truth was being fully demonstrated.

Both an intellectual assertion to God's Word as postulative truth *and* a daily living of its principles seemed to be called for—behavior consistent with mental belief. Both elements had to unite for genuine truth to be evident.

How then to apply that to his present predicament?

He finished the glass of juice and went for a refill.

Evangelize the World was obviously doing "good" things—

people were hearing the gospel. Wasn't that the clear command of the Lord to His followers—go into the world and tell the good news? And there were those in ETW he respected, like Bob Means and Sondra DeQue, and probably hundreds like them, who were good people doing their best to fulfill what they perceived God wanted of them. Who could argue with the very clear spiritual basis of what Bob Means was doing?

But what if, on the other hand, within that organization—at its crowning point—were one or two key persons who were *not* carrying themselves in an ethical manner? Would that nullify the corresponding good being done?

Certainly not. The good was still valid. Yet it hardly justified the continuation of questionable behavior on the part of the organization's leaders. Weren't trustworthiness and conscientious moral fiber the very basis for a God-ordained ministry?

How did the two balance?

Jackson closed his eyes and laid back his head. The questions were not easy ones.

From the hazy distance he suddenly became aware of the sound of a car engine turning over—without success. He stood up and walked to the window—in time to see one of his neighboring tenants coming out of his car in obvious disgust. Jackson watched as he looked around, reached in to release the brake, then began laboriously to push his car toward a nearby hill.

Jackson ran downstairs and outside.

"Looks like you could use a hand," he said laughing as he began pushing on the stalled car's back bumper.

"Hey, thanks—it should start fine once I get rolling down this hill."

After a minute, Jackson called out, "Hop in—I think we're rolling now. I can push you from here!"

Ten minutes later, Jackson was once again sitting in his apartment, cooling off from the exertion. After two false starts, the engine had cranked over and started.

He fell to thinking once more.

Lord, how much does living the truth matter? To what extent are Your people obligated to live the truth?

He faltered. No more words of silent prayer would come.

He then reflected on what had just happened. *Who would have ever known, he thought, if I hadn't gone down to help with that car? I was alone. What difference did it make whether I went or not? No one was watching.*

Yet what of mere obedience? A life of integrity demands allegiance to something higher than my own comforts. And after all, isn't integrity what you do when no one is watching? Doesn't a life of truth boil down to obeying with integrity the sort of life Jesus told us to live?

Again his thoughts were silent.

He sat still. The evening was now late.

"Lord," he said again, "show me what to do—what to think. Help me see Your perspective. How *do* You want Your people to live?"

His head rolled back, his eyes closed, and his mingled thoughts and prayers strayed far afield.

Suddenly, after what seemed a long time, Jackson started forward in his chair. A thought jolted him wide awake.

The message drove itself deep into his brain, solidifying all his previous questions and mental ramblings. *Of course,* he said to himself. *It's so clear! Certainly truth matters! Integrity matters! Whether anyone's watching or not. God's people* have *to live lives consistent with His principles—not perfectly, but consistently.*

His active mind once more pursued the verdict that in his confusion had eluded him earlier. *We'll stumble,* he thought. *And He'll forgive us. Then we'll stumble again! But we can't do just anything that suits us. We're under orders to obey His ways. We* have *to order our lives with virtue—by doing as Jesus said. We have to make every effort to live the truth!*

That means me . . . and Hamilton Jaeger . . . and even Jacob Michaels. However influential a writer I may one day become, I still have to live honorably in the tiny, unseen corners of my life. Whatever good ETW may be doing, those men still have an obligation to carry themselves with integrity.

And so do I! I have to push toward the truth . . . in my life, in my writing—and in this story!

Means's words came back to him, "Truth must come out . . . you will serve as an instrument in the hand of God . . . the wider we throw open the doors of light the better . . . ask, probe, question, and trust God to lead you into truth." First from Diana, then from Means, finally from Sondra—they had *all* encouraged him to go ahead. The direction was finally unmistakable!

Then as if his resolve was finally determined, Jackson thought, *God help me . . . I have to move forward . . . integrity demands it. I* must *pursue it!*

45

Well, the die was cast. He'd made his decision.

Later today he'd try to talk to Harriet Steadman. He wondered, was she a Ms. or a Miss? Sondra had informed him that Jaeger was leaving town overnight. This would be his best opportunity. He'd go to her home, present himself as cordially as possible, and hope for the best.

At 7:18 that evening, Jackson knocked on the door of Harriet Steadman's home on Viewcrest Drive. It was a nice neighborhood and a larger home than he'd expected for a working single woman. To his surprise the door was opened by a man.

Faltering, Jackson began, "Hello, I'm Jackson Maxwell. I'm a reporter . . . is Harriet at home?"

Hesitating a moment, the man turned inside. "Honey—it's for you," he called into the kitchen, "—it's a reporter."

A moment later Mrs. Steadman appeared, drying her hands on a dish towel.

"Hi," Jackson began again, regaining his composure. "I'm with *Christian World Magazine.* We're doing some stories on ETW, and I wondered if I might talk to you for a few minutes?"

"Uh . . . well, sure—I guess," she said, then looked at her husband, who merely shrugged his shoulders noncommittally. "Come in."

They showed him into the living room. "Have a seat," said Mr. Steadman, then turning to his wife, "Harriet, give me that towel—I'll finish up the dishes while you two are talking."

His wife said nothing, handed him the towel, and sat down.

"What I really wanted to ask you about," began Jackson, "is Hamilton Jaeger. I understand you work rather closely with him?"

Mrs. Steadman cast a nervous glance toward the kitchen, looked toward the floor briefly, then said, "Well, yes, I do work in the finance department, and Hamilton, that is . . . Mr. Jaeger, is head of that part of ETW."

Jackson saw the flush of her cheeks and knew he had to tread with care.

"I've spoken with both Mr. Jaeger and Mr. Michaels," he said, "and during the interview for my first article we talked quite a bit about finances. I was hoping to follow up that interview with some additional information—from other sources. We're trying to learn more about the finances of ETW so as to present our facts more accurately—"

"I really think you need to be talking to Ham—Mr. Jaeger," she said nervously. "He's the one with the best grasp of the information you need."

"As I said," resumed Jackson, "I have spoken with him, but I want to get another slant on it. You were mentioned to me as someone who might clarify for me a perspective which I couldn't obtain from the press releases."

Harriet fidgeted uneasily with the frayed edge of the couch's armrest.

"What I've been trying to nail down," said Jackson, "is more or less how specific money donated to ETW is put to use. I've been laying the groundwork by following a given donation from inception to use. I felt that would give our readers a valuable sense of their pledges being used in a significant way."

Mrs. Steadman nodded her approval.

"Now I'm to the point of needing some specific insight about actual funds in ETW that are used in various ways. In my discussion with Mr. Michaels and Mr. Jaeger, we talked about the extra money that occasionally accumulates for one reason or another . . . money donated over and above actual expenditures in the area for which it was given."

He paused, waiting for some reaction.

She looked up, then merely said, "Yes . . . ?" waiting for him to continue.

"What I'm trying to get a handle on," Jackson went on, "is

how such funds are used. In my previous inteview, we didn't really have the time to get that far, but it is my understanding that there is a certain fund into which that money is placed." He was probing, watching her carefully to detect any trace of a clue that might tell him which direction to pursue. "Is that correct?"

"That's right,' said Harriet without hesitation.

Jackson continued, "And then how is it spent?"

"I don't know that it *is* spent," she replied, beginning to loosen.

"It just accumulates?"

"I suppose. I've been with ETW in the finance department—as a bookkeeper—for four and a half years, and it's been there all the time I can remember. I don't recall ever seeing a check drawn on that account."

"It must be quite large by now?" asked Jackson.

"I don't really know. Mr. Jaeger is in charge of it himself."

"How is that money actually handled?"

"At the end of every outreach or project, there is a certain sum that is designated for the "Aggregate Reserve" account. Hamilton takes that sum and invests it in some kind of notes or funds."

"Then he retains the control over it from then on?"

"I suppose—I've never really thought about it. I tell you, he's the one you should be asking about all this. I'm just a bookkeeper. I don't really know that much about the higher finances."

"You're doing fine. I appreciate it," said Jackson. "This is a big help. Now earlier you implied there was a cash account—of some size—that checks could possibly be drawn on. Then you said he invested in notes and funds?"

"That's true," she said thoughtfully. "I never stopped to think about it before. Maybe there are two accounts—or possibly some of the Aggregate is held in cash, and the rest invested."

"Well, let me ask, then, if you know what these funds—either as cash or investments—are intended for . . . are they being held for a purpose?"

"An emergency, I guess, or a special project . . . I don't know."

"Like Greenville?" Jackson suggested.

"No, the money for Greenville comes from other accounts. That's all clearly spelled out. We do have a building and expansion account—"

She stopped abruptly.

"—but we're not supposed to talk to the press about Greenville. I'm sorry. I forgot myself. I really can't say any more."

"OK, then what about the reserve account? You say it's not for things like Greenville—but other things . . . of an even greater magnitude?"

"I'm sorry. I really shouldn't say more. I may get into trouble as it is for bringing up Greenville. Say—does Hamilton know you're here? Did you clear this interviw with him?"

"No," said Jackson, losing the initiative, "but he's out of town."

"Then I shouldn't be speaking with you."

"Please," insisted Jackson, "just another question or two—what sort of special project would that reserve account be earmarked for?"

"I don't know. I just can't answer any more questions."

"A project . . . possibly something political?" suggested Jackson, guessing.

Harriet looked down.

Then after a moment's pause she said, "What if that were the case? Certainly Hamilton and Mr. Michaels have the right to use that money as they see fit. It's the Lord's money, and they are its stewards."

"Does Jaeger have in mind a renewal of something like the Moral Majority, perhaps?" asked Jackson pointedly.

"I tell you," she snapped, "I don't know what his specific plans are!"

"But he does have political ends in mind?" Jackson said, daring one last attempt.

"Yes! But I'm going to say nothing—I really think you ought to leave, Mr. Maxwell. Talk to Hamilton if you want more information."

Driving home, Jackson's thoughts were spinning. Political lobbying—it wouldn't be the first time. But if Jaeger pulled it off it could certainly be the most successful, with the money they had— apparently substantial.

There were other leads he had to follow up on quickly—Jerome Bullinger especially. And he had to find the time to meet with that friend of Diana's at Cosmopolitan too.

46

Three days later, Jackson saw Linda in the lobby as he entered after lunch.

"Linda!" he called.

She turned.

"I haven't seen you for a while."

"I've been out several days—a 'Chicago cold.' "

"We've got to get together for a visit."

"Oh, Jackson, my work's really piled up on me."

"Mine too—hey, I have an idea. Could you come in early, say tomorrow? We'll have a talk before the day gets under way."

"Sure—I'll call you when I get in."

The next morning at seven-twenty the phone rang at Jackson's desk. It was Linda. In a few minutes, they were both seated in one of the empty conference rooms on the fourth floor, where most of the executive offices were located.

"I need your perspective," said Jackson. "I've got so many things coming at me at once, I can hardly keep them straight."

"What besides the Michaels stories?"

"My own past for one thing. I talked to a girl who thought she was an orphan, discovered otherwise, and searched into it. She found her biological parents in a matter of just a few months. Something inside me has been in turmoil lately, it's as if I *have* to get this thing with my identity settled before I can do anything else."

"How did she do it?"

"There's an agency—privately funded—called 'Distressed Persons Anonymous.' They help all kinds of people with a variety of needs. One of the things they do occasionally—and discreetly—is help with adoption cases, and sometimes help an adoptee find his blood parents."

"I've heard of them," said Linda. "Matter of fact, seems like I remember someone here doing a little piece on them for the paper a year or two ago."

"They certainly helped this girl I talked to—aided her in establishing contacts with other agencies. I talked to the people at DPA yesterday. They said especially if everything occurred in Illinois—which may or may not be the case, I have no way of knowing at this point; Quincy's close to the border, but my folks have always lived there—that there would be records of everything . . . somewhere. It's just a question of getting them."

"Do your adoptive parents know what you're doing?" asked Linda.

"Not yet. I'll tell them—when the time is right. But I may never find a thing. I have no intention—whatever happens—of letting this change my relationship with them. I'll always love them as if they were my blood parents. But I know it's a sore spot, especially with Mom. I don't want to get her worked up over nothing."

"Do you think they know the identity of your real father and mother?"

Jackson was silent. "Funny," he said at length, "at times it gets rather academic, like I'm searching for statistics in some archives storage vault. But just then, when you said 'your father and mother,' something leaped inside me—brought me back to the reality that we're talking about *people*—two human beings who loved one another. And because of that love—"

He stopped, and turned away, fighting back emotion.

Linda reached across the table and gently laid her hand on his arm.

"My *father* and *mother,* something about those words . . . just hearing them."

He reached for a Kleenex, blew his nose, and went on. "It calls into being emotions I never even knew I had."

The room was quiet. Jackson regained himself, then said, "To answer your question, no . . . I doubt they know. I think I would have noticed subtle things. But there's never been so much as a trace."

He sighed deeply.

"Is it hard?" asked Linda, attempting to feel the moment with him in her sensitive way.

He rocked back and let out a long breath. "It's something I've learned to live with all these years—not knowing my pedigree the way other people do. You learn to block it out. But, yes, there's an incompleteness. And suddenly it all surfaces and I begin to wonder, 'Is it *really* possible I will someday *know*?' Yes, I find myself struck with these pensive moments more often lately . . . sure, it's hard."

He paused. "Especially when it comes right in the midst of this Michaels thing. I can't figure out why the Lord would allow me to be bombarded by both bewildering situations at the same time. One of them I may have been able to handle. Together, they've got me in a complete mental jumble!"

"Are you still pursuing it—still planning to write more stories?"

"Tentatively, yes."

"Where are you going with it now?"

"One step at a time. I've been trying to contact a fellow who used to work closely with Jaeger, then left after a minor power struggle. But so far I haven't been able to locate—"

Just then McClanahan's head popped in.

"I heard you might be here . . . Maxwell, I've got to see you upstairs, in the vice president's office. Five minutes—OK?"

"Sure, Ed, what's up?"

"Five minutes," said McClanahan, and closed the door.

Jackson turned back to Linda, shrugged, and they rose to leave.

"Thanks," said Jackson. "It always feels good to talk to you."

"We've got to start getting together regularly," said Linda.

47

A few minutes later, Jackson and McClanahan were seated in the plush office of the executive vice president of *News with a Vision*. Mr. Dillow, balding, in a conservative gray suit, sat behind his desk wearing a solemn expression. Jackson had met him but once formally. He was not the most popular of the "upstairs executives," having acquired the reputation of being *NWV*'s most rigid and straitlaced personality. This made him a capable administrator but totally inept when he tried to insert himself into the daily give-and-take so necessary on the lower level of the hierarchy where the work was accomplished. McClanahan spoke first.

"Jackson," he began, "Mr. Dillow here has received a very sour phone call about you . . . from the head of PR over at Evangelize the World. Seems Jacob Michaels is really agitated. You've been interviewing some of their people in what they claim is an imprudent way."

There was silence as the other two eyed him, waiting for a response.

"And you believe them?" Jackson asked at last.

"Mr. Maxwell," said Dillow, "it isn't so much whether we believe them or not. Ed here has vouched for you in a most determined fashion. It's just that ETW and Jacob Michaels are extremely influential. We have to remain in their good graces."

"Jackson," said McClanahan, "you have to understand how serious this is. They want your job—they want you fired!"

"Fired!" exclaimed Jackson. "Surely you wouldn't consider—"

"They can hurt us if we don't comply, if we don't make some sort of amends—an apology, that kind of thing."

"What about the story?" insisted Jackson.

"Jackson," said Dillow, "no story's worth raising the ire of Jacob Michaels. One negative word dropped from him and our circulation could drop fifty percent."

"But surely you wouldn't sacrifice principle—you wouldn't submit to that sort of pressure? Why, it's blackmail."

"A strong word, Mr. Maxwell."

"Mr. Dillow, with all due respect, I've been completely courteous to everyone I've interviewed. Certainly I've raised some gutsy subjects. That's a reporter's job. Ed and I discussed this thoroughly before I began. But the lack of discretion . . . the lack of openness and trust lies entirely on their side. They have railroaded me on this thing. I'm being made a scapegoat for whatever it is they are trying to hide."

"Again, Mr. Maxwell, your choice of words is graphic. It may reveal your true bias in this matter. And as I said, no story's worth the potential damage this could do."

"But what of finding the truth . . . isn't that what news reporting is all about? What of our obligation to our readers?"

"Jackson," said Ed once more, "look, I've gone to bat for you already. I've tried to convince Mr. Dillow here that you're a good man, that you're important to us. But you're not making it any easier on yourself. You've just got to give—bend a little."

"Ed, I don't understand this. You were the one who encouraged me to go ahead. You said if there was a story we had to probe— bring it to light. Now you're telling me to sacrifice those very principles because a little pressure's coming to bear."

McClanahan said nothing. Jackson's words revealed the awkwardness of his mediating position between the two extremes.

"I would interpret it differently," said Dillow, rescuing McClanahan from having to attempt a response. "I would say you need to be adaptable. You don't have to make a headstrong stand for every little matter of principle that comes along."

"Certainly not," said Jackson, "but the important ones."

"And there's my point, Jackson," said Dillow. "You have to choose your issues with care."

"I consider that this *is* a crucial issue. Most Christians are so pliable it doesn't take much to convince them that 'in this particular case' they can relax the standards and settle for second best. Adaptability is fine; bending with the wind is not. Standing on principle is important to me. I can't do otherwise."

"And neither can we, I'm afraid, Mr. Maxwell," said Dillow firmly. "For us too this is a matter of principle, the principle of this organization. We are *News with a VISION,* not News with an Obsession. I won't see our vision undermined by a headstrong young reporter, no matter how good he may be. If you are going to continue on the staff of this organization, I must insist that you withdraw from this fixation you seem to have with Jacob Michaels."

Jackson glanced at McClanahan, who hadn't said a word for several minutes. He was obviously torn by the direction of the interview.

"I was assigned to do three articles—" said Jackson.

"I'm afraid that's the end of it, Mr. Maxwell. You're off the story, is that clear?"

"Very clear, sir," said Jackson coolly. "And if you're going to hold to those kind of archaic methods and values, then I will have to cast my lot elsewhere."

"Jackson," said McClanahan rising from his chair, "you don't mean that. Give yourself a chance to settle down."

"Ed, I'm afraid I do mean it. I'm sorry to let you down like this. But this timid—this cowardly—stance that our superiors seem determined to take is one I can't believe in. I'll clean out my desk and be out by this afternoon."

"I regret that you feel this way, Mr. Maxwell," said Dillow. "We will hate to see you go and will miss your services. Unfortunately, the position of the paper and the magazine is firm."

McClanahan sat silent in his chair, unable to devise a way to reopen the negotiations.

"One final thing, sir," said Jackson, rising to go. "Would you mind doing me the courtesy of telling me who it was from ETW who called to deliver this surprisingly uncharitable message from our Christian leader Mr. Jacob Michaels?"

"It was Ms. DeQue . . . Sondra DeQue."

48

"Sondra DeQue, please," Jackson said, trying to disguise his voice lest his call be rerouted to Jaeger.

After about a forty-second wait, Sondra answered.

"This is Jackson. We need to talk."

"I'll call you back," said Sondra hurriedly in a low voice and instantly followed a click and the line was dead.

Jackson slowly replaced the receiver and began to sort through his desk. In about ten minutes his phone rang.

"I'm at a pay phone now," she said. "I couldn't talk in the office. Hamilton's been on me like a hawk, and I've got to be back soon so I'm not missed."

"I need to see you," said Jackson "What's the deal on your call to Dillow?"

"I'm sorry about that," said Sondra. "I had no choice. Listen— I'm free tonight."

"May I come over to your place?"

"No—there's a little cafe a couple of blocks away at the corner of Prospect and North. It's called the Blue Ox. I'll be there at eight."

Jackson seated himself in a corner booth of the Blue Ox a few minutes before eight. In fifteen minutes he nervously glanced at his watch and reread the menu. Sondra didn't arrive until eight-forty.

"I'm sorry, Jackson," she said. "There was a car parked outside my building, and I just wasn't sure. Like I said, Hamilton has been all over me. My every move is watched. It's spooky. I've even suspected he has someone following me. I'm sure he thinks I'm in league with you. Probably figures I'm trying to get back at him."

"Is that what the call to Dillow was about?"

"Hamilton handed me a typed script to read, with specific instructions about whom to call and to say the message was from Jacob Michaels—which I seriously doubt. I hated to do it, but I had no choice. It was either make the call and do his dirty work, or else openly tell him I wouldn't speak against you. I hoped nothing serious would come of it and that Dillow would just regard it as the sort of constant banter that goes on between the press and the public."

Jackson smiled. "Well, it had ramifications a bit wider than that."

"Why? What happened?"

"They gave me an ultimatum—lay off ETW, withdraw from the story and any more interviews."

"And you agreed?"

"Hardly! A week ago I might have. But once I felt I was supposed to go forward with it . . . Jaeger is no stooge—he surely knew who to call!"

"So, what happened?"

"I said I couldn't agree. Dillow wouldn't budge. So I quit."

"You're kidding— Jackson, I'm sorry—really! I had no idea it would come to this."

"It's all right, it's not your fault, Sondra."

"But in a way, that's exactly what it is."

"It's OK. I'll have the freedom I need. I have some savings— I'll be fine for a few months."

"Still, I feel terrible. It makes me furious with Hamilton! That was so like him to make me do that—rubbing salt in the wound. He can be so cruel. He's had his own way too long. He needs to be brought down a notch or two."

"I've no intention of trying to bring him down," said Jackson. "At first that's what I wanted. But now I realize my priority has to only be to find the truth. If that truth topples him from his high horse—so be it."

"It doesn't surprise me," Sondra continued, thinking further about Jaeger. "Hamilton was livid when he learned you went to Harriet's—white with rage. Of course she told him every detail. This was his way of getting revenge on us both."

"I hope seeing me doesn't jeopardize your position," said Jackson.

"My days are already numbered," said Sondra. "As soon as it's expedient, no doubt Hamilton will have my head."

"I did learn some interesting things from Mrs. Steadman, though," said Jackson. "And by the way, I didn't know she was married."

"Hamilton's equally comfortable with single or married

women—the man has no scruples about that. As long as he calls the shots, and the lady complies," said Sondra cynically. "What about Bullinger?"

"I haven't located him yet. He dropped out of sight after leaving ETW."

"I'll see what I can dig up in personnel."

"That would be helpful. Anyone else I might talk to?"

"You're persona non grata around ETW right now. I doubt if anyone would give you the time of day, especially if you started probing. They'd fear for their jobs. Hamilton has ears everywhere. I seriously doubt he's finished with you yet. I wouldn't be surprised to see some damaging piece published before long discrediting you. He has contacts all over the country . . . in high and low places. If there's something he wants—it gets done."

"Sounds serious," said Jackson with a laugh.

"It is, Jackson," said Sondra. "I'd watch my step. Hamilton's not used to being bucked. You're a threat—and he can be nasty when challenged."

"I'll heed your warning."

"Be careful," said Sondra. She rose to leave the cafe by the back door.

Jackson waited ten minutes, then left alone.

49

It was time to see Diana. Somehow it was only fitting to meet her again in the park.

Jackson laughed to himself. He didn't even know her name when they'd first met, hadn't yet written the infamous article, and God's Country's first public appearance still lay on the drawing board.

Water under the bridge. As the search into ETW had grown more complex, Jackson had become increasingly uncertain about how to regard Diana—now standing smack in the middle of it.

Becoming attached would be all too easy. Yet he was apprehensive—of hurting her with his investigation, of being hurt himself because he cared too much.

With such an array of blurred thoughts skipping through his mind, Jackson moved cautiously forward, desiring a deeper level of trust between them, yet conscious of the risks such trust would entail as he probed the integrity of ETW to which her life was so intrinsically bound.

Meanwhile Diana's mind had not been vacant with regard to the young reporter. For years she had painfully realized the uniqueness of her position. The moment her father's identity became known, Diana could immediately detect a change in nearly all of her relationships.

At first she tried to ignore it. She dated in college—was nearly engaged once. Yet she could never be totally certain she was appreciated just for who she was. The impact of the influence of her surname was an unknown that plagued her.

Who was she—Diana Michaels?

What was she really like, what did God think about her, what did God's love functionally mean in her life? Was she merely an extension of her father . . . did she have a personhood of her own?

Of course, intellectually she could spout off ready answers to such questions. But on the emotional level, God's love, her father's love, a sense of personal identity—they all remained remote.

There were times she had experienced surges of warmth she

associated with God's hand upon her. She felt confident about her faith in the Lord. But it was not something that gave her exuberant feelings of great joy. The father image remained too distant.

Thus, into every relationship Diana dragged an accumulation of emotional baggage that ultimately kept her from entering into a mutual exchange of love. She could neither accept love—not being well trained in the practice of doing so—nor adequately give it. She had not experienced true godly love herself—as a child or a grown woman—from the heart of her father, the only image of God's love she had been provided.

But then, from out of nowhere, had come Jackson Maxwell, seeming to care for her, knowing nothing about her. It had been refreshing at first, knowing that he didn't know who she was. And though they'd practically come to blows over the disclosure, in the familial knowledge he'd become even more special—for if anything, to Jackson, Diana's father was a liability.

Thus she found herself more and more preoccupied with the thought of Jackson, yet remaining skeptical of giving more of her trust to one she knew so little.

A light mist was falling, hardly more than a heavy fog. It felt good. Jackson entered the park; Diana was already sitting on the bench where they'd agreed to meet.

She rose as he approached. "Shall we walk?" he asked. She said nothing, and they turned toward the lake.

"It looks like things may get more tangled in this before they get better," said Jackson at last.

"How so?" asked Diana.

"New directions of inquiry are presenting themselves—and it keeps leading toward Jaeger. He thinks I'm after him."

"Are you after him?" asked Diana looking up into Jackson's face.

"No!" he burst out, then calmed. "I'm not *after* anyone. I guess what I'm after is that the truth comes out, that's all. Is that so difficult to understand . . . is that such a wrong thing to want?"

"Of course not," said Diana softly.

"Then why are my motives so misunderstood? Why do I make people angry?"

"It's *you*, Jackson. You are a—well, a different sort of person. You're the kind of person people either love or hate. Your motives may be pure, but you come across with . . I don't know, an intensity that is sometimes hard to swallow. Especially for someone standing on the other side of the fence."

She paused, then added, "But everyone can't be easygoing. Sometimes the world needs people like you."

Silence fell upon them. The mist was heavier now. They walked along the lake, side by side. The drizzle increased. No one else was left in the park. Their thoughts went no further than the realization that here was another with whom to share the moment in a special way.

Finally Jackson said, "I quit the magazine today."

"Jackson . . . why?" asked Diana, turning toward him.

"That pressure I told you Jaeger was putting on me . . . they called our vice president who told me to lay off, or else. I said I couldn't compromise my principles—and that was that."

Diana had no words to offer, just looked at him with an expression that conveyed, "I understand—and I'm behind you."

They walked around the lake as the descending drizzle picked up and the darkness gradually enfolded them, talking occasionally, laughing, and sharing the silence. But the subject of Hamilton Jaeger or Jackson's writing did not come up again.

PART 6

Jacob Michaels

50

Though the meeting was serendipitous, it was by no means unexpected. Robert Means had been praying daily and earnestly for an opportunity to visit with his old friend. Thus their chance encounter outside ETW's conference room did not come as a complete surprise to Bob. Nor did Jacob's spur-of-the-moment invitation to lunch.

An hour later the two sipped coffee at a private table in the Luxor's penthouse restaurant, while waiting for their order of two chef salads.

"It's really been far too long, Bob," Michaels said after the waitress left them. "And I apologize—I should never have let so much time pass."

"Think nothing of it," said Means with a smile.

Michaels sighed, then went on almost wistfully. "But good friends are hard to find, Bob," he said. "Especially now . . ." He paused a second or two, a distant look coming into his eyes. Then just as quickly he seemed to come back to the present and added, "And I regret that we've drifted apart."

"It's never too late to pick up friendships that are true, Jacob."

Again Michaels sighed. *He looks tired,* Means thought.

"Too late . . ." Michaels repeated thoughtfully. "Sometimes I wonder if it's already gone too far," he went on softly, as if speaking to himself.

Means said nothing. Inside he silently prayed for the right words to speak when the time came.

"But I didn't want to get together with you to bring you into my troubles," said Michaels, attempting to sound upbeat once more. "So tell me, Bob, how are things down where you are? What have you been working on?"

"Oh, much the same as usual—answering letters, handling phone calls, sending out information. I find it very challenging.

Every day it seems the Lord brings someone my way who's in genuine need. I find that little office of mine full of opportunities for personal ministry, praying with someone on the phone, sending out letters of encouragement."

A strange look passed across Michaels's face, almost a look of envy mixed with regret.

"That's interesting," he said with a wan smile. "Here I am supposedly the leader of this huge enterprise of ministry, and yet I wonder if you don't have more to do with the hands-on nuts and bolts of people's lives than I do."

"You don't feel ETW is doing the work of ministry?" asked Bob.

"Oh, I suppose it is. But the organization is so big, so far-reaching—it's as though it has a life of its own that's destined to go on, with or without me. Sometimes I wonder what difference I make."

"You're the one people look to," said Means, praying inside. This was just the opportunity he had been asking God for. *Open his heart to really share, Lord,* he said silently.

"That's just it, don't you see! They look to me, but what am I really *doing* in anyone's life to make a difference? I mean personally, Bob, like you do when you talk to somebody who calls in? Do you know what my day's made up of?"

He looked at his friend, giving his words time to sink in.

"Schedules, meetings, goals, finances, grandiose plans," he went on after a moment. "But no people! There's no flesh and blood to it, Bob. It's all ministry in the abstract."

"Why don't you make a change then?" asked Means with sincerity in his tone. "Surely you could if you really felt you ought to."

Michaels sighed again. "I doubt it would be that easy," he said at length. "These things have a momentum of their own. I tell you, lately I've been wondering if . . ."

"If what?" probed Means.

"I don't know, Bob . . . I guess I've just been thinking recently . . . reflecting on the two roads you and I took, wondering if your work isn't more significant than mine. Sometimes I really regret not keeping you beside me. We had some things we really wanted to do back then, remember?"

Means nodded.

"But now . . . so many years have passed . . . and I find myself wondering if things might have been different."

"In God's economy, it's never too late," suggested Means.

A long pause ensued. Means could tell his friend was struggling with unseen frustrations, but how far to probe he wasn't sure. He prayed silently, and waited. But then suddenly the opening into the inner chamber of Michaels's heart seemed to shut. When he next spoke, his voice had again resumed the polish of a professional preacher.

"In another way," Michaels finally went on, "things couldn't be better. Exciting things are happening, Bob! New outreaches, new opportunities for unity with other Christian organizations. A lot of what we used to dream of is finally happening." By his tone, Michaels seemed suddenly to have gotten himself back onto the corporate wavelength.

Michaels went on to talk in glowing terms about many of the things he was at that moment involved in. His friend listened with interest, posing here and there a probing question. But as the great man spoke, Means could not escape sensing the undercurrent of frustration that had partially revealed itself during their first minutes together at the table. However, though the conversation flowed freely, never again, as they ate their salads, did that frustrated, hungering part of Jacob Michaels surface.

As they prepared to go, Means made one more attempt.

"Jacob," he said, with deep sincerity in his tone, "I sense in my spirit that there are some things right now you are unsettled about. I don't know the details . . . I don't need to—the Lord knows them, and that is enough. But I would like to pray with you about whatever the frustration is that is on your heart. We could just pray right here, just for a few moments."

Michaels glanced nervously at his watch.

"I'm, uh . . I'm a little pressed right now, Bob," he said. "We'll get together again—real soon! I promise. We'll find some time to pray together then." He rose from the table.

Means nodded, hiding his disappointment. "Jacob," he said, "you call on me *any time*—day or night . . . if there is *anything* I can do to be of service to you."

"I will, Bob. Thank you," replied Michaels.

The two left the restaurant together, then parted—Michaels to an afternoon with Hamilton Jaeger that left him unsettled and with a headache, Means to an afternoon of intermittent prayer for his titular boss and friend.

51

"Hi—I'm looking for a Jerome Bullinger. Is there by any chance someone there by that name? Or do you know him?"

"No on both counts," said the voice at the other end.

Jackson hung up his phone slowly.

"Well, there's that idea shot down," he muttered to himself. There were only a half-dozen Bullingers in the Chicago telephone directory, and he'd struck out with the final one.

"I know," he said aloud, "I'll just call up good ol' Hamilton and ask him what happened to Jerome!" He laughed. "Working alone in my apartment is turning me into a fruitcake!"

He picked up the phone again and dialed his old office number.

"Advertising, please," he said.

He soon had Linda on the line.

"Hello, remember me?" he asked.

"Jackson—how are you? I just heard yesterday."

"You once warned me about getting too involved in controversial stuff. You said I might get demoted like you. Now look what happened? I went and got myself fired."

"Fired? The word around here is that you quit in a huff."

"That's not exactly what happened. They gave me an ultimatum I felt was unprincipled. I had no choice but to leave or compromise what I consider being a writer is about."

"Compromise—that's a dirty word for people like us."

"You know how it is, eventually you get tired of it. You walk into a bakery whose storefront boasts 'Fresh daily' and wind up with a stale roll. Have you ever tried to actually *get* one hour service from a one-hour cleaners? And potato chips—they're the worst of all! Every bag is only half full! I don't buy that song and dance about the 'settling of contents'—it's compromise pure and simple. The same thing you encounter with auto garages, plumbers charging for four hours when they worked three-and-a-quarter, and having to wait in line needlessly every time you go to some 'official' agency. People blind their eyes, get used to it, and accept compromising for second best as a way of life. But I think there comes a time when you've got to take a stand."

"Well, you told me you were after something you could sink your teeth into—something that fought back. I guess you got your wish!"

Jackson laughed. "Yeah, I'd forgotten about that—Scuffy the Tugboat, huh?"

"Well, if there's anything I can do," said Linda.

After Jackson hung up he walked over to his kitchen table. Spread over it were clipped copies from magazines and newspapers—anything he could find pertaining to ETW, Hamilton Jaeger, Jacob Michaels, or the Greenville site. He circled the table, walked to the window and looked out, then returned to the table.

I can't stall forever, he thought. *I've made my phone calls. I've wandered over every square inch of this place today . . . might as well sit down and read through them again.*

He'd spent four days gathering data. He'd drawn heavily on articles out of *Christian Organizations and Ministries,* hoping to outline the financial structure and growth of ETW over the past six or eight years. He had collected articles on infinitely varying facets of the ETW organization.

Now he had to piece it together.

Particularly interesting were brief notices in the Dallas papers he'd found on microfilm at the library. He'd searched the classifieds and other sections to learn as much as possible about the Greenville acquisitions. He was especially curious about the realtors handling the various sales. If he could just contact a person—some flesh-and-blood individual out from under the protective wing of Jaeger—he might discover something that would shed light on motive.

It had been hard work.

But a picture of the Greenville property was at last coming into focus. On a large plot map of the area he'd obtained through a friend in the assessor's office, he had outlined all those properties in the area surrrounding Greenville that had changed hands within the last three years, and the puzzle looked to be fitting into place. He as yet had been unable to learn the actual names of the purchasing parties. But he detected a pattern. Many adjacent properties to the northwest of town had been sold, and together they formed an enormous chunk of united acreage that totalled what appeared to be more than forty-five hundred acres. Once plotted out, this huge expanse caught the eye because it interconnected completely.

And to the extent he'd been able to determine, it was all sold through the same land office—Western States Development. He'd called and hadn't been able to learn the name of the agent, or agents, who'd handled the sales. But if he could get to those persons, he had no doubt the next course of action would become readily evident.

Clearly, out of work though he was—and expensive as the fare would be—a trip to Greenville was next on the agenda.

52

1986

"I'm so glad you came, George."

"It has been a good summer, hasn't it? If you hadn't twisted my arm I'd probably never have seen Europe."

"I knew you'd like it. Dad's handled things fine without you."

"Won't be long now. Hard to believe we've only been here three months—seems like years!"

"We've seen a lot," said Marsha. "I wonder why the plane's stopping."

Her brother peered through the tiny window into the pre-dawn mist. "I don't know," he said. "We were right to the end of the runway. I thought we were ready to take off."

Suddenly the door just beyond the first class section burst open with a crash. Almost simultaneously a voice in the rear of the plane shouted harshly, "Nobody move! Stay where you are and no one will be hurt!"

Then through the front door emerged two jeans-and-sweat-shirt clad men, automatic rifles in hand, stocking caps over their faces. "This is a hijack!" one shouted. "I don't want to hear a sound—understand!"

Gunfire . . . wild screaming . . . passengers hunched down in their seats as best they could. Windows shattered, blood splattered as the terrorists fell . . . bullets ricocheted . . one of the policemen yelled in pain and sank to the floor grabbing his chest.

Then it was over, as quickly as it had begun.

53

The warm March sun felt good. The huge downtown Dallas highrise was imposing, but a thirty-four-floor elevator ride could hardly terrify a Chicagoan.

Adjusting his tie one final time in the ground floor window, Jackson began the ascent to the Western States Development Company. He'd always been proud to be a reporter. But today he was glad he could truthfully allege himself free from the least connection with the press. The flash of a presscard usually brought the initial reaction of silence. Today he needed information.

As he emerged a few moments later, the Western States door stood straight ahead. A secretary greeted him.

"I'm interested in the deals you've been putting together out in Greenville," he said. "Have those been handled by one or several of your agents?"

"Mr. Elliot's been in charge of most of those," she said, "he's in Suite D, down the hall to the left."

Jackson thanked her and turned in the direction she had pointed. He found Suite D without difficulty; the door was ajar and he heard voices.

". . . very lucrative, of course, Seb. I agree. The company appreciates your success there."

"Then how can you ask me to pull off?"

"You said yourself there's only one, maybe two, more deals to be secured—that your friend had nearly all the properties he's been after."

"True, but those last holdouts are hardly a cinch. And if I can put together others, he may be interested."

"All that notwithstanding, Seb, I'm going to need you in other areas before long. We can't expect something like this—as good as it's been for us—to go on indefinitely."

The door opened and out walked one of the speakers, nodded to Jackson, who poked his head through the door while knocking tentatively.

"Mr. Elliot?" he queried.

"Yes—come in."

"I hope I'm not disturbing you. Your secretary sent me down. I'm interested in the parcels you've been putting together for ETW up in Greenville."

"Yes," said Elliot, half muttering to himself, "seems everyone's interested in that today." Then turning more directly to Jackson, "Why—how did you know those acquisitions were made for ETW?"

"I'm from Chicago," said Jackson, set to test the phrase he'd been rehearsing all the way down. He hoped it would—without actually revealing the full nature of his position—get him past the barricade of secrecy he'd run smack into everywhere he turned. "I've been in touch with some of the Michaels people with regard to this thing and have flown down to get a firsthand look at how the plans are progressing."

Elliot paused, seemed to ponder his words, then said, "Yes . . . well, things are moving along well I would say . . ."

Jackson silently let out a sigh of relief.

". . . very nicely in fact. There's just one major holdout left. Actually the main section of the plot is intact, and most of the properties have closed—the others are in escrow proceedings."

"And that last property," asked Jackson, probing gently, "is it a critical one?"

"Not on the first level," said Elliot. "Mr. Jaeger is interested in it, but I don't think anything highly significant actually hinges on it—are you a friend of Hamilton's?"

Jackson hesitated. "No, not really what you'd call a friend," he said. "Acquaintance might be more accurate. We've spoken together but that's about it. I take it you and he are close?" he then asked, thrusting the conversation away from his shaky relationship with Jaeger.

"Hamilton and I go back a number of years."

"You've been working on these acquisitions a long time?"

"Hamilton, Jake, and I've been dreaming about this center for years," he said. "Seeing it about to happen is like a long-awaited vision come true. Well, young man, what's your interest in this thing? I do have some work to do, so we should probably get to the point. Actually," he went on in a lower tone, confiding in Jackson momentarily, "my superiors want me on to other things. They think

241

I've been wrapped up in this Greenville situation with Hamilton too long. You can see I must get busy."

"Certainly," said Jackson, "and I don't want to detain you. My interest, I guess," Jackson was thinking fast on his feet, trying to prolong the interview hoping something useful might pop up, "deals primarily with that final holdout you spoke of. I wondered if you might give me their name and the location of the property in question?"

Elliot hesitated. "I don't know," he said, "the negotiations are rather delicate at this stage. I wouldn't want to do anything to upset the balance. Mr. and Mrs. Haley still have some major reservations. I don't think I'd better say more."

"Well, if you think that's best," said Jackson, "it's just that the people in Chicago—"

"When Hamilton was down here last month I wouldn't let him go out to talk to them either. These people are very uncertain at this point. Too much pressure could send them over the edge against us."

Jackson nodded knowingly.

"I mean," went on Elliot, "if Hamilton wants a place for personal use adjacent to the center, that's fine with me. He's an important cog in the Michaels machine and may need a command post for all I know. But the Haleys . . . well, they're dubious."

Jackson sat still, nodding at the appropriate times.

"I've assured them of Mr. Michaels's plans for Christian facilities and all the good it'll do. But they're holding out. Not that it will hinder plans for the center much, but Hamilton wants that home badly. But I don't think I'd better divulge any more."

"That's fine, Mr. Elliot," said Jackson. "I understand the delicacy of your position . . . I guess I do have to be going. I may drive out to look at some of the other sites."

"If there's anything more I can do, let me know."

54

Indefinite though it was, Jackson had come away from the interview with several new directions for his thoughts—the Haleys, Elliot's long friendship with Jaeger, a personal headquarters . . . and Jake?

He consulted his plot map of the area and isolated two or three apparent properties that hindered a smooth, uniform block of land. Following a visit to the assessor's office, Jackson located the Haley farm—seventy-eight prime acres of the southwest corner of what would be the ETW center . . . eight miles from Greenville with convenient access to the freeway into Dallas forty miles away. As Jackson approached the home in his rented Escort, he could instantly appreciate Jaeger's enthusiasm for it.

George Haley had come to Greenville immediately after his discharge from the service following the Korean War. Land had been cheap, and he'd begun with ten acres and a dream. He'd built their home himself, married his wife, Sarah, shortly thereafter, and over the next twelve years the two of them had enlarged both the home and the acreage.

Their children—son, George, Jr., and daughter, Marsha—had been the pride of their lives. No farming couple could have wished for more. From earliest recollection both children loved the agrarian life—the soil, the animals, the crops, the harvest, the seasons. By thirteen, George, Jr., was already sharing a major hand in the farm's operation, and—joy to George and Sarah, by his own choice—it had become an accepted tenet of the Haley family that he would gradually assume the operation of the farm and continue throughout his life what his father and mother had built.

By 1970, George had added their final purchase, bringing the total to seventy-eight acres. Since that time, inflation had driven real estate prices through the roof—prohibiting further expansion yet at the same time putting them in a position to emerge handsomely should they ever opt to sell any portion of the farm.

Such a thought would, of course, never have occurred to them had not a tragic turn of events forever altered the course of the

Haleys' lives, making the beloved farm seem at once pallid and lifeless.

After graduating from the University of Iowa in agriculture and putting in a three-year stint with the Peace Corps in Kenya, George Haley, Jr., was ready to return to the farm for good. His dad was now sixty-seven, he'd received his education and had seen some of the world, and the time to solidify his roots seemed right.

Marsha, having just completed her third year of economics at Texas State, planned to spend a summer in Europe—traveling in a rented Volkswagon and visiting two friends from school. She begged her brother to accompany her, and it probably being his last such opportunity, he agreed. The farm could wait until September.

In a dire twist of fate, Marsha and George happened to be aboard a plane targeted for a hijacking by Belgian terrorists trying to bargain freedom for imprisoned PLO compatriots. As hijackings go, this one had ended rather quickly and had been overpowered while still on the ground by the authorities and a crack S.W.A.T. team. Out of nearly two hundred passenger hostages, only six had been killed in the gunfire that began and ended so quickly. All four of the terrorists involved lost their lives. It had been a heavy price, said the world's newscasters. Still, it could have been much worse, and, all in all, there was great praise for the police and airport officials who had contained the incident.

George and Sarah Haley, however, could hardly consider themselves lucky. Marsha would never teach economics at Greenville High School, as had been her dream. Nor would an enthusiastic young George take over his dad's farm under the watchful and loving eye of his proud father.

It was simply not to be.

Only then had they first considered the idea of selling the place. Jaeger had from the start been willing to meet their price. But at this stage of their lives money was not the primary consideration. They would have plenty to retire on. Of greater concern was their desire to see their home and land put to a use they could be proud of.

The land had been their life, their sweat, their love, their tears, their dreams. Now—suddenly—it was gone. There was nothing to live for, nothing to keep the land for. But if George, Jr., could not till the beloved soil, someone could. The son might be dead . . . but the dream could never end.

Jackson wondered what tack to take with the Haleys. What business did he even have being there? Better to lay all the cards on the table, he thought. If he learned something, fine. If not . . . well, that was the chance he'd have to take.

The door opened to his knock by a short, gray-haired woman he judged to be in her mid sixties. Though she smiled when she saw him, Jackson could not help detecting a shadow of sadness in the gentle face. Her sleeves were rolled up, and her hands showed traces of flour.

"Mrs. Haley?" asked Jackson.

"Yes."

"My name's Jackson Maxwell. I'm a writer. I'd been working on a story regarding ETW and their land acquisitions . . ."

Jackson paused, hoping for some opening on Mrs. Haley's part.

She merely nodded, kept silent as she stood holding the wood-framed squeaky screen door open, and waited for him to continue.

". . . and, I understand many of your neighbors have sold their land to ETW and that you have been considering doing so. I was hoping to talk to you and your husband briefly—to gain your perspective on this whole matter."

"We haven't come to any decision about selling," said Mrs. Haley.

"I understand that," said Jackson. "And I'm in no way trying to influence you. I've nothing to do with ETW myself. As I said I'm just trying to get an overall look at what's been happening."

"I see," she said thoughtfully. "Well . . . I'll have to talk to my husband a moment. Excuse me."

She closed the door, and Jackson was left alone on the porch. He turned and scanned the expansive fields in every direction. There was a peacefulness here. The sweet scent from the rippling grain fields filled his nostrils . . . every now and then the pungent aroma from the barn assaulted him—offensive to the city-dweller, wondrous to the lover of cattle. He could see why the Haleys would be reluctant to see it destroyed. This was a heritage.

After a few minutes, the door opened again, and Mrs. Haley reappeared. "Won't you come in, Mr. Maxwell?"

She led him into a farmhouse-style kitchen where Mr. Haley

was standing on a wooden chair in the midst of a minor repair job on the screen door leading to the backyard.

Following her through the living room, Jackson saw obvious signs of arthritis in her stooped back and slow, hobbling walk.

"I'm in the middle of baking some bread," she said wearily. "I hope you don't mind if I keep kneading while we talk?"

"Not at all," said Jackson.

She introduced her husband, and then the old man spoke, "My wife tells me you're a writer," he called from his high perch. "I doubt there's anything we can tell you. We haven't decided to sell to that man Jaeger yet." His voice was lively, in marked contrast to his wife's.

"Jaeger is the one who's been handling all the acquisitions here, I take it?" asked Jackson.

"His name is on the offer we received."

"He's made a firm offer then?"

"Oh yes—for the full price."

"But you're uncomfortable with it?"

"The money and terms are fine," broke in Mrs. Haley, "But they're secondary. What we really care about is how this place is used. We've worked hard. We'd always intended . . ." She stopped, wiped her eyes with a dishtowel, then said, "Excuse me . . . I'm sorry."

"I understand," said Jackson. "I can see that you love the place. It's beautiful."

"Sarah and I practically built it with our own hands, inch by inch. It was hard enough thirty years ago."

"You've worked the land yourself?"

"At first . . . but our son—he really loved the place. He helped a lot too . . . we always intended, that is, all of us had planned on his one day taking over."

"But that's not going to happen now?" asked Jackson. "His plans have changed?'"

"Not exactly, Mr. Maxwell," said Mr. Haley sobering. "Our son is dead."

"Oh . . . I'm sorry."

"It's all right. It's been several years now. But whenever we get to talking about the farm and what to do with it, well, it makes it difficult . . ." He stopped.

246

Mrs. Haley sat down, eyes filling with tears. She blew her nose, stood up with a deep breath, and said, "So now we know it's time to get a place where we won't have the concerns of such a large ranch . . . and where the memories won't be quite so painful."

"Age does take its toll, Mr. Maxwell," said Mr. Haley. "We hate to do it. But in a way we're looking forward to moving into town."

"But we still care about the old place," interjected Mrs. Haley.

"I can tell that," said Jackson, "I think your motives are very understandable."

"We know we have to move. Our life here is past. If young George had lived, things would have been different. But things happen, and life must go on, as they say."

"So when we learned about all the land being bought up around here, well—we just didn't know. At first it sounded like some industrial complex coming in."

"But you discovered otherwise?"

"Our realtor—actually, the man who approached us—Mr. Elliot—"

"He first approached you—you hadn't placed your property on the market?" asked Jackson.

"We'd thought about selling occasionally," said Mrs. Haley. "But only vaguely. We'd thought how wonderful it would be if we could find some young man, with a family, maybe, who loved the land like our son and daughter did, someone who would carry on the tradition—if not our name . . . someone who would love this place as we have—"

"Things have been rough, Mr. Maxwell," said her husband. "Times change. Not many young people today are looking for this sort of thing . . . and no one has the money. This is an expensive chunk of ground. We let the word be known that we were looking for someone . . . and were prepared to give the right person a good buy on it—we really care about the land more than the money."

"But no nibbles."

"No . . . nothing."

"Then one day this Mr. Elliot turns up on our doorstep saying he has a client who'd been considering our property."

"Interesting," said Jackson.

"We asked about the person, and he was very vague. But of course we couldn't help but think about it more and more seriously."

"And what finally convinced you to sell?"

The two looked at one another. Neither spoke for a moment.

Finally Mrs. Haley said, "Nothing really *convinced* us. Mr. Elliot kept calling on us, said his client was very interested and would probably pay nearly anything within reason. We just moved into it slowly."

"But there was something we were uneasy about," said Mr. Haley. "The fellow who wants to buy it—Jaeger—isn't married, isn't interested in farming, and isn't even from around here. Mr. Elliot assures us he wants the place strictly as a private residence and that no industry is coming in. Still . . ."

"He's told you about the plans for the other land that's been sold? The Michaels training center and so on?"

"Yes, but he insists our place would not be included, that nothing would be torn down."

"Mr. Maxwell," broke in Mrs. Haley, "probably most people don't care what happens to their home and land after they sell and leave—but we do!"

"You want someone here who's going to continue to work the land, keep up the house?"

"Yes," said Mr. Haley. "Being from Texas, I've seen a lot of shysters come and go. And something about this whole deal doesn't feel right."

"But now that we've made the decision," said his wife, "we're ready to sell. This is the only offer we've had. It's a good offer—"

"Cash no less!" said Mr. Haley.

"And who knows when—or if—we'll find another so favorable if we turn this one down."

"I see your dilemma," said Jackson.

"Mr. Maxwell," said Mrs. Haley, "we'd be pleased if you'd join us for a cup of coffee, or tea. We don't get many visitors."

"I'd enjoy that," said Jackson. "Tea would be fine."

"Here are some blueberry muffins I made this morning too—have one."

"Thank you," said Jackson. "You remind me of my own mother. I was raised on a farm much like this one."

"Oh, do tell us about it," said Mrs. Haley, sitting down once she had put the water on the stove to boil.

A lively conversation followed.

When George and Sarah Haley walked him to his car, some two hours later, Jackson felt like he was leaving old friends. And he noticed that the gloom seemed lifted from Sarah's face, for the moment at least.

Driving back into Dallas, Jackson reflected on the Haleys. They were quite a couple. Excruciating as the years since George and Marsha's deaths had been, they nevertheless were still able to muster great pride in their place. They'd shown him the additions they'd built onto the house over the years—the barn, some of the nearby crops, the huge garden. Obviously they'd done well enough not to require a garden to live on. But he could sense they enjoyed being part of the earth—fingering the sensitive roots, carefully plucking the ripe fruit. Suddenly he found himself much more sympathetic to his *own* parents' desire for him to feel a greater interest in *their* farm. It was something he would have to give more thought to than he had previously.

His thoughts moved northward to Hamilton Jaeger. How greatly he would differ from them. Would he tend a garden, lovingly inspect the blossoms on the fruit trees, sift the moist dirt through his fingers when uprooting a heavily laden potato plant? Would he take visitors to the barn, climb into the loft, look around with pleasure, filling his lungs with the rich smell of hay, and then walk over to gently pat his cow on its pink, wet nose along with a few tender words?

No, thought Jackson. Hamilton Jaeger was of an altogether different breed from George Haley.

How out of place Jaeger would seem in the midst of this peaceful environment. What a shame it would be to see this unpolluted lifestyle severed from the land so that Jaeger could bring his own ambitions to fruition.

There would be no more smell of hay . . . no more soil to tend . . . no more pink roses. Jaeger would probably slab over the garden with concrete and tear down the barn.

55

"Mr. Maxwell," said Sebastian Elliot with outstretched hand the following morning. "Nice to see you again."

"Thank you," said Jackson. "I had a few more things I wanted to discuss. I hope you don't mind."

"Not at all."

"For openers," said Jackson, "I should tell you that I'm a writer."

"You didn't mention that the other day," said Elliot, tensing slightly.

"I didn't want to prejudice you against me. People have a way of clamming up the minute you divulge you're a reporter," he said laughing.

"You're a reporter?"

"Strictly free-lance. I'm on no staff. And I've no specific plans to write about Greenville in the near future. As I said, I'm in touch with some of the people in Chicago. Maybe when the time is right, but now it's primarily background."

"Well . . ." said Elliot slowly, "we pretty much covered those things I would be at liberty to discuss."

"What I was interested in," said Jackson, "and again I want to stress that this is not for use in any story as such—off the record—I found myself intrigued yesterday about what was said about you and Hamilton and another man—Jake, I believe it was— that you three had been working on this for years?"

Elliot shifted his weight in his chair, thought for a moment, then simply nodded.

"And who is Jake?" asked Jackson.

"An old friend—" said Elliot, then broke off.

"And the three of you have been working for some time to put this land purchase together for Mr. Michaels?"

"In a manner of speaking . . . well not really *for* Michaels. It was Hamilton's idea all along."

"And then you and Jake . . ." Jackson began, hoping the realtor would complete the sentence for him.

"We were all so close back then," he said, looking up at the ceiling, beginning to reminisce. "We shared a dream of Christians coming together—unity, brotherhood. We felt the Lord had given us a mission and that we could do something significant to make it happen. There was the feeling, as Ted White used to say, that we could make events march in the direction we pointed, if only we could point clearly enough. Time will tell."

"And has the vision continued—been fulfilled in any way?"

"Sure, it's continued. Hamilton and Jake have it mapped out on their end. It's come along, I suppose. Jake was in the state assembly then, and he's certainly come a long way. Then Hamilton arranged for me to be situated down here. One by one things have fallen into place. Jake made it to Washington, I've located the land parcel by parcel . . . yes, I'm sure Hamilton finds gratification in it all."

"You sound as though you've lost some of your enthusiasm?" suggested Jackson.

Elliot was silent a moment, still looking upward, feet on his desk. At last he sighed. "Enthusiasm? . . . Yes, I suppose I am drained of that. The dream was so real. We were all so alive back then. Life was before us! Yet somehow, the reality of it, the enthusiasm does fade. I imagine you're right."

"You wonder if it's been worth it?"

Another deep sigh. "Yes—I left friends and a job I was happy with. My wife and kids haven't enjoyed it here. I hardly see them, I've been so embroiled in trying to hold the parcels together. I've had to skirt around the truth occasionally in my dealings with the people up in Greenville. Otherwise, I'd never have been able to complete a package exactly as Hamilton wanted it. But I wonder if it's been worth it. I really question that."

Neither man spoke for a moment. Jackson sensed the conversation had come to a close. He rose to go.

"Thank you very much for your time. Again I appreciate your candor, Mr. Elliot."

The realtor simply nodded.

"I'll look you up next time I'm in Dallas. I hope all goes well with you."

56

Jackson walked into his apartment a little after 7:00 P.M. He promptly made himself a sandwich, glanced through his mail, then flipped on his telephone answering machine. There were two messages.

The first was: "Mr. Maxwell—this is Sylvia over at Distressed Persons. I have something for you. Call me when you can."

He then went on to the second recording. It was terse: "Jackson . . . Sondra. Blue Ox, the sixth—midnight."

Just then the phone rang.

Maybe that's her calling again, he thought picking up the receiver.

"Mr. Maxwell?"

He vaguely recognized the male voice but couldn't place it immediately.

"Yes."

"I'm sorry to call you at home . . . this is Jacob Michaels."

"Hello, Mr. Michaels," said Jackson with far more composure than he felt inside. It took a moment to place his spinning brain back in order. "Nice to hear from you."

"My secretary, Mrs. Layne, has relayed your message to me, and I wanted to get in touch with you to say I'm sorry your attempts to see me have been unsuccessful."

Jackson had nearly forgotten his talk with Liz Layne. He'd hardly expected much to come of it.

"Thank you, sir. I appreciate your taking a personal interest. And yes, I did want to talk with you again. There was quite a stir in your organization from my article."

Michaels laughed. "Yes, I'm aware of that. Nothing too serious though."

"I'm afraid Mr. Jaeger might disagree with you there. He seemed to think it was quite serious indeed."

"Hamilton does have a tendency to get rather flustered about things," said Michaels. "Still he's invaluable to me, so I take the good with the bad . . . anyway, Jackson, do you still want an interview? I would be happy to arrange it."

"Yes, of course, although in a way it's too late. I'm off the story series I was doing."

"I'm sorry to hear that. I thought your treatment was good. I enjoyed your piece. Why did you decide not to continue?"

"It was decided for me, after the negative fallout from the first one."

"I didn't think it was that malicious," said Michaels.

"Jaeger felt I was trying to tear you down."

"Don't you think that's an overstatement?"

"Hardly. He's the reason I'm permanently off the series—or so I must assume after talking to you."

"What do you mean?" asked Michaels.

"After a call to my magazine's vice president from your organization, I was 'relieved' of my position."

"You were fired?"

"Not in so many words, but it amounted to nearly that."

"And who from ETW called your vice president?"

"Sondra DeQue actually made the call, but it came on direct orders from Hamilton Jaeger. And the statement read as if it had originated with you."

"This is the first I've heard of it."

"That doesn't surprise me," said Jackson. "But it's the sort of thing Jaeger has been doing ever since my article appeared."

"Mr. Maxwell, I offer my apologies. I'm certain there must be a misunderstanding of some kind. Hamilton may be overzealous from time to time, but he's a first-rate, loyal man whom I trust implicitly."

"Could you answer just one question for me," asked Jackson, "while I've got you here on the phone—what do you know of a floating fund in ETW, a reserve account that's added to but never drawn from?"

"I leave the finances to Hamilton," said Michaels. "I can hardly keep in touch with bookkeeping details."

"But this fund itself you're unfamiliar with?"

"I don't know about the various accounts as far as the specifics are concerned."

"This particular fund, it has been said, may be earmarked for some political use. Is that anything you're aware of?" asked Jackson.

253

"Well, of course we do from time to time make small political contributions when a Christian man is running for office or when there is an issue on the ballot we feel is of particular relevance."

"I think this fund is intended for something sizably larger than that, sir. It's a rather significant amount."

"Well, as I said, I'm unfamiliar with the details. But if you'd want to pursue this, why don't you talk to Hamilton? I'm sure he'd—"

"Mr. Michaels," interrupted Jackson, "every call I've made to your office building has been thwarted one way or another by Jaeger. He has given me the runaround, kept me from talking to you, and now has cost me my job. Do you really think he's going to open up and give me straight answers?"

"Ah yes . . you think he has some aversion to you. I guess from your standpoint then—I can see now an interview with Hamilton would look to be out of the question."

"I'm not making this up, Mr. Michaels," insisted Jackson. "With all due respect to your position, I tell you there are things going on in ETW that Jaeger is intentionally trying to keep from the public. And for all I know, he may be trying to keep them from you too."

"Strong words, Jackson," said Michaels. "Strong words indeed. But I will look into it. I'll see if there isn't something I can do to patch it up with your former employer."

"If you do that, how will you explain the previous message— purportedly from you—insisting that I be taken off the story?"

Michaels was silent a moment. "I see your point. It could be awkward, couldn't it?"

"Jaeger has us backed up to a wall," said Jackson cynically.

"Be that as it may," said Michaels, "I will look into this whole situation. I'll promise you that. And I will inform my secretary that you will be calling and instruct her to set up that official interview with you."

Jackson thoughtfully put down the receiver. It had been a peculiar phone call. He hadn't been braced for Michaels to be understanding and tolerant. Was he sincere? He seemed to care about doing the right thing. Yet he defended Jaeger at every turn. Was his congenial demeanor a smoke screen to cloud him from digging deeper?

He walked to his couch and sat down. His mind was swirling with random thoughts, nagging doubts, and the conviction that important matters were converging and that he—without knowing it—held the key that would unlock them. He sighed deeply and tried to assess some order in his brain.

What did he know?

Fact One: Greenville was a reality. The land had been purchased.

Fact Two: Jaeger had kept the whole thing secret.

Question One: How much did Jacob Michaels know? If he knew more than he was letting on, he concealed his feelings well, for Jackson could not escape the notion that he wanted to do right.

Fact Three: Jaeger was edgy, defensive, even revengeful. It was clear by this time that to him a great deal was at stake.

Question Two: What was Jaeger hiding?

That was the crux of it! And if Michaels wanted to do right—as it seemed—then why didn't he do something? Or were his hands tied?

Where is *the true source of muscle behind the walls of ETW?* Jackson wondered.

57

The next morning, Jackson drove to the DPA office. He had no appointment and therefore had to wait twenty minutes until Sylvia could see him.

"I got your message last night," he said as he sat down beside her desk.

As he eyed the woman he'd only met once before, it struck him what great hopes he was placing on her shoulders. Whether or not it was even possible she'd be able to deliver he couldn't tell. She was wearing a loose-fitting white blouse, which was not tucked into her drab green skirt. A large woman, she would have seemed more at home in the inefficient surroundings of a governmental agency. Her oily black hair was short-cropped, held back from her eyes by a tasteless bobby pin. Her half-rimmed glasses, sliding halfway down her nose and fastened in back with a gold chain which went round her neck, completed the picture.

"I have good news and bad news," said Sylvia.

"Give me the bad news first."

"It's not that easy, they're both part of the same package."

"OK . . . out with it then."

"I've been tracing through the leads we had—talking to people I know. I've telephoned a number of agencies and have come up with nothing but dead ends. I have a friend down in Springfield who works for an agency by the name of Adoptions, Limited. They're one of the country's largest, privately funded. They've recently gone completely over to computer and have access to information all over the nation. The profile parents, potential adoptees . . . everything. It's amazing—they can access computer banks wherever information is on file—and here's the interesting part!—both concerning new adoptions *and* any adoption that's taken place over the last forty or fifty years . . . *if* there's any scrap of information recorded."

"So—on with it!" said Jackson excitedly.

"We fed in your name, your folks' names, their address, your birthdate—everything."

"And . . . ?"

"Nothing. Not so much as one word of printout in response."

"Nothing?"

"I'm sorry, Jackson."

"So where does that leave us? Is that the end of the line?"

"In one way, yes. But it does tell us something, so we now have a better idea where to concentrate our efforts. It tells us the records of your adoption were either lost or destroyed. If that's the case, then I'm afraid we're up against a dead end with no place else to go."

"And if that's not the case?"

"Then that would tell us your adoption was handled privately—between two parties themselves. No agency involved at all."

"Is that so unusual?" asked Jackson.

"It's a bit rare," said Sylvia, "though not unheard of. But if no agency was involved we're in a whole new ball game."

"How so?"

"If it was a private agreement, so to speak," she went on, "that would undoubtedly mean your folks were in on it—they must know something."

"You think they could know who my real parents are?"

"No, I doubt that. But they would at least have been part of the transaction. They would probably have dealt with a middleman. But it leaves your folks as our only remaining lead."

Jackson drove home slowly. His mood was pensive, even somber. Too much was assailing him all at once. As he drove his spirits ran still further. A resurgence of grief swept over him. With anguish he wished himself a child again. Now in the privacy of his moving car, his lips moved silently in a bewildering disarray of prayers, thoughts, and memories.

What was the purpose? What was he doing it all for anyway? What could come of his search into his past but hurt—to himself, to his folks? And why this wild goose chase involving Michaels? What had it accomplished? He'd lost his job, his enthusiasm for writing, his vision of Christian unity. What had he become? Wasn't he failing in the only real calling the Lord had given him?

Confused and tired, he parked his car and walked up to his apartment. No job, bank account running out, no purpose, no motivation to begin writing again. The only thing that had kept him going in recent weeks was his—was it an *obsession* as Dillow had suggested?—with Hamilton Jaeger.

He opened the door and walked in. It was silent—cold—unappealing. How lonely and isolated he felt. Who was he anyway . . . Jackson Maxwell? To whom did he belong?

His thoughts turned to Fred and Ellen. How he loved them. But he could not escape the nagging question—did they in fact know more of his past than they'd told him? Something about the mere suggestion made him feel more cut off than ever. He was *alone.* His biological parents hadn't wanted him . . . the magazine didn't want him . . . Jaeger was out to destroy his credibility.

Why was he taking his talk with Sylvia so hard? What was so unsettling about being adopted privately rather than through an agency?

Was it the inescapable sense of being shuffled about, a helpless infant in nothing but a blanket, an unwanted bag of goods handed person to person under cloak of darkness? Outcast baggage, not even worth adoption through a bona fide agency, auctioned off to the highest bidder in some backroom of a warehouse—helpless Fred and Ellen Maxwell forced to negotiate with a shadowy "middle-man," probably led in blindfolded, handed their new "purchase," then ushered out and sworn to secrecy forever.

Jackson's fantasies only heightened his distress of mind. He felt tears filling his eyes again.

"God . . . !" he said but could go no further.

He sank down onto the couch emotionally spent, laid his head on his arm . . . and quietly wept.

58

It was 11:45 P.M. The Blue Ox was open until 2:00 every morning. The place was nearly empty. He chose a booth toward the rear and away from the windows, sat down, and ordered a cup of tea. In about five minutes Sondra sat down across from him.

"You don't look too good," she said. "Tired?"

"Yeah—rough day."

"Anything I can do?"

"No, I've just got to work some things out."

"I've found something on Jerome Bullinger. Don't ask how. I called in about every favor I had lined up in the building. But I managed to get an address."

She handed him a slip of paper:

3216 Wayfarer Lane #3
Kankakee, Illinois

"That's where he was after leaving ETW."

"Looks like an apartment."

"And it's two years old, no guarantees. Might be a dead end. But it's all I could come up with."

"Thanks—I'll check into it."

"Jackson, are you OK? You seem really down."

"I am. But like I said, I have to work it through myself. I guess everyone has times of upheaval . . ." He stopped for a moment, thinking, then went on. "Six months ago I was in a place of confidence. I felt the Lord guiding me . . . steadying me. I knew if there was something He wanted me to do or write about, He would show me. I had confidence in Him, and in myself as a result. But now I'm not the least aware of Him in my life, haven't felt His leading for months—in anything—and have just about run dry on any self-confidence I ever had."

"I'm sorry, Jackson," said Sondra and reached over to place a hand on his arm. "For me it's been just the opposite. Months ago I was disoriented. But since meeting you, there's been, I guess you could say, a purpose to getting up every day. Even if a lot of it's been negative—looking at Hamilton's motives in a new light—still, something has changed. I don't feel isolated anymore. I suppose, in a big way, I have you to thank for it."

"I'm glad for that," said Jackson with a smile. "The Lord does move in mysterious ways, doesn't He?"

"How long I'm going to be feeling good about life I don't know," Sondra went on.

"What happened?"

"Nothing yet. There've just been clues about Hamilton's lining things up so I'll be the one to take the fall. He's not through with you either."

"What more could he do to me?"

"He's writing an article for the ETW quarterly newsletter. It goes out to over a quarter of a million leaders—the cream of the crop of the Christian world. He's going to succinctly point the finger at 'certain forces in the Christian press' who are utilizing cruel and vicious techniques to undermine the ministry of Jacob Michaels. The unnamed target of his remarks will be unmistakable. Once that newsletter is printed, your byline won't amount to much—especially if he gets Jacob's imprint on the thing."

"I doubt he'll try that," said Jackson, musing on his call from Michaels.

"Maybe not. But he'll couch it in the most deferential of tones so his own bias doesn't surface. Half the time Jacob doesn't know what goes in that newsletter anyway."

"What can one more thing hurt? My reputation's about as tarnished as it could be."

"The point is, it's all untrue!"

"I know," said Jackson wearily. "But there comes a point past which you just can't fight the powers that be. Remember *Chariots of Fire*? I'll never forget Abrahams's classic statement: 'Those who stalk the corridors of power guard them with a venom and jealousy.' That's just as true in Christian circles as political. Once you're 'out'—you're there to stay."

"Don't throw in the towel so easily, Jackson. You're on the side of right—truth will win . . it has to!"

"Does it? I'm not so sure anymore."

"I'm not giving up. And I'm about to be axed, in favor of

some new lackey for Hamilton."

"Sondra—I didn't know it would come to this" said Jackson.

"Don't worry. We're in it together. And remember," she said with a laugh, "things always look darkest just before they go completely black. It'll come right in the end, you'll see . . . but, it's late, I have to be getting home."

"I'll drive you back. It's nearly one."

"Thanks."

"Thank you—for the lead. I owe you one."

59

It was a rare moment in the Michaels household—a late brunch together. Elizabeth had fried the sizzling sausage, scrambled the eggs, and then warmed breakfast rolls in the oven. Jacob scanned the day's newspaper as she added the finishing touches to the table. Diana, slouched sideways on an easy chair, glanced through the ETW newsletter sent out the day before. Her picture was included, along with a brief article about the group. Jacob's spring and summer schedule of activities and speaking engagements was listed as well.

"Daddy," said Diana, "there's a short article here without a name about the negative press ETW's getting. Who wrote it?"

"What's that?" asked Jacob, trying to keep his mind on the paper before him, "I don't know, dear."

"It's pretty pointed."

"I saw that too," said Elizabeth, removing the rolls from the oven and placing them on the table. "And I saw that Sondra had left. I didn't know that."

"Hamilton said it was her choice," said Jacob disinterestedly. "I regret seeing her go . . . time to move on, I suppose."

"But what about this article?" asked Diana once more. "It refers to 'critical elements in the Christian press.' Is this a reference to the article Jackson Maxwell wrote some time back?"

"Everything is ready!" announced Elizabeth, not to be deterred from her goal. This was wonderful, all three of them together!

"To tell you the truth," said Jacob, "I hadn't seen that article before today. Hamilton merely told me he wanted to say something about the obligation Christians have to uphold one another—an example being things that are said in the Christian media concerning various ministries."

"Well, he certainly did that!" said Diana. "And the article he's referring to was hardly as vicious as suggested here."

"Maybe Hamilton overreacted a bit," admitted Jacob.

"A bit!" said Diana sitting up straight and now on the edge of her chair. "This is quite a distorted picture. Maxwell will be lucky ever to find his writing accepted anyplace after this."

"I doubt it's that perilous, my dear."

"How can you be so indifferent?" she exclaimed. "A man's career is on the line, and you don't think it's serious."

"Come on, you two," interrupted Elizabeth, "here are the rolls, the eggs are just right, the sausage hot. Stop talking long enough to eat."

Diana and Jacob walked to the table and sat down. Neither spoke for a few moments, passing the plates around. Elizabeth was obviously pleased. Now they could settle down, enjoy the breakfast, and visit—like other families.

"Diana," said Jacob at length, "I spoke with Maxwell himself just last week, and I've told him I intend to speak with Hamilton about their differences."

"Little good that's going to do after this newsletter goes out. Every influential Christian in the country will see this."

"What makes you so interested in him all of a sudden?" asked Jacob. "Do you know Maxwell?"

"Yes, we've met a few times. I like him. I don't want to see him hurt."

"So, I've a spy from the press in my home!" said Jacob with a laugh.

"It's hardly funny," said Diana with exasperation. "I'm sure if Hamilton knew he'd turn on me."

"Diana!" said Jacob, losing his composure. "Those are harsh words. I couldn't get along without him."

"But surely you could find someone equally suited to the job whose Christian principles were a little more active in his life?"

"Diana," said her mother, "that's uncalled for. Hamilton's a fine man."

"How well do you know him, Mother?" said Diana spinning around to face her.

Elizabeth said nothing.

"Hamilton has been with the family since my Uncle Lance brought him in still green from the service. He served Lance and my father faithfully, got me out of a scrape or two when I was young and foolish. I owe him plenty."

"But can't you see he's too influential? I sometimes think he's in charge and not you."

"That's enough!" said Jacob, voice rising. "We've discussed Hamilton all we're going to."

"I see," said Diana, growing angry at her father's refusal to listen to her words. "You're determined to preserve the image, the spiritual aura, no matter what goes on, is that it?"

"Diana!" shouted Jacob. "That is enough! Leave this table, do you hear me?"

"Please . . . Jacob," begged Elizabeth imploringly, "just let it drop. Diana . . . please—"

"I'm not your little girl anymore," said Diana rising. "You can't order me about. If I'm no longer welcome in your home, then you may ask me to leave. But I'm a grown woman, and you cannot send me from the table as if I were a mere schoolgirl! Maybe if you spent a little less time with Hamilton and had paid a little more attention to your own children as they grew from childhood into adults you'd be able to hear me now—and understand me. And it certainly wouldn't have done Richard any harm either!"

She turned and ran from the kitchen.

Elizabeth silently wept. The eggs had long since grown cold.

Jacob was silent, then rose and paced the room. In a couple minutes they heard the back door close, and it was followed shortly by the sputtering yet insistent sound of Diana's ancient Volkswagen driving off.

60

Elizabeth's tears eventually dried. She'd been at the table thirty or forty minutes, she supposed. Jacob had left the house without a word. She was alone.

The pain had been there before. No doubt it would come again. Her mother's heart—full of love—was so vulnerable. The image of Richard suddenly was in her mind, and the tears filled her eyes once more. Poor Diana! She longed to hold her close.

Oh Jacob, she thought. *You are such a great man to so many. Why must you remain so distant from we who love you the most?*

She was suddenly seized by the impulse to flee. She paced the floor uncertainly, then in an uncharacteristic moment of recklessness, grabbed her coat and hastened out the door. *I can't stand it in there any longer,* she said to herself.

An icy blast of the chill wintry wind was not even enough to bring her hot face to its senses. She kept walking . . . toward what she had no idea. She'd been left alone many times before. And it would undoubtedly happen again. She recalled the first time Jacob had ditched her—during a Cubs game the summer before they were married. The game had been unusually long, and a thriller. But he'd left long before Ernie Banks's eleventh inning game-winning triple. Handing her five dollars he had said, "You can take a cab to Dad's when the game is over. I've got to make that meeting with Uncle Lance in fifteen minutes." A swift peck on the cheek, and he was gone.

The Michaels's home was in suburban Chicago—an elite section that bordered one of the aging downtown districts. In the forty minutes it took to walk to the corner of Claymore and Winston, Elizabeth relived many of the hurts from the days of their marriage. But the happy memories filtered into her consciousness too, like unconnected fragments of a disjointed dream.

Her mind drifted back through the years to the evening Diana had been born—bringing with her such promise of joys to come.

"She's beautiful, darling." She could still hear Jacob's tender voice whispering in her ear, "She looks just like you."

The radiant new mother looked up and simply smiled. Her proud husband knelt beside her and planted a gentle kiss on her forehead.

First-time parents wore a special glow during those days and weeks following a successful birth of their son or daughter. It was always such a cheerful time, full of optimism and hope, bright with the promise of life.

"Oh, Jacob . . . I'm so happy. I'm glad you could be here to share it with me," she'd said.

Parenting . . . such a complex assignment. Yet at the moment they become fathers and mothers, few are thinking ahead. Diapers and tantrums, tricycles and careers, teenagers and priorities, college and communication—those are not usually thought of in advance. In the exhilaration of creating life and giving birth, all other concerns fade into the distance. The bouyancy of the moment carries on its crest the dream notion that absolutely nothing could derail a new family's momentum toward ultimate happiness and fulfillment. Other families have problems . . . but we will stay close . . . we will communicate . . . we will demonstrate the reality of harmonious daily living—we will succeed!

Jubilant young parents can be so starry-eyed!

"Where else would I be? This is my family too, you know. I'm as thrilled about this as you are," Jacob teased.

"Are you, Jacob? It makes me so glad to hear you say it. I guess I thought you might be like other men—you know, try to maintain a tough exterior, not let your emotions show."

"Nonsense. We're in this together. And this is only the start."

"Oh, I can see it now! A houseful of six children—"

"One step at a time, Elizabeth. Let's get this young woman on her way and healthy first. Then we'll have a son—"

"To carry on the family," said his wife.

"One for you and one for me," said Jacob laughing.

"A boy for you to romp with and play ball with and a girl for me to play dolls with and teach to sew and cook."

"Then we'll see about increasing the litter."

"Oh, Jacob we're going to be so happy—this family of ours."

"If you were any happier right now, I think you'd pop."

"Look, darling—she's asleep."

"And still she looks like you."

"I love you, Jacob."

Oh, Jacob where did we go wrong? Elizabeth thought. *It was all in front of us then. But look at us now.*

The compounded anguish seemed unbearable. If only there was some way to undo the damage . . . make up for all the years they'd lost—start afresh.

Suddenly Elizabeth looked up. She'd walked for miles, heedless of direction. Looming in front of her was the Mystique Club—a singles bar—flashing neon lights casting a psychedelic shadow across her face. Music blared from inside. An aroma of stale beer hung in the air.

From behind her a voice spoke softly. "It's not as bad as it looks, you know."

Elizabeth turned quickly to face a tall, thin man, his jet black hair streaked with gray. His rumpled slacks could only be outdone in tackiness by the threadbare sport coat, which could only have looked at home on a Salvation Army discard rack, but never on his frail frame.

"I . . . I was just passing—" Elizabeth faltered. Then the realization came that she owed no explanations. She turned and walked on briskly.

"I'm sorry if I alarmed you," he said. The man was at her side in a moment walking with her. "I don't often speak to women who are alone. I meant no harm."

Despite his looks, his tone seemed sincere.

"I'm not a masher," he went on. "It's just that you looked like a nice lady. We don't see many like you around here. And it's been so long since I had someone to talk to."

He stopped and let her walk on.

Her pace slowed, then stopped. Elizabeth felt a slight breeze and shivered momentarily. She glanced back. He was standing regarding her. It suddenly dawned on her that he was a lonely man, struggling—maybe like her—to grasp whatever thread of relationship offered itself.

She tried to speak again, each word was a struggle. "I don't come here—I was just out for a walk. I . . ."

The words caught in her mouth. Her heart was racing.

"Would you like to go in—have some lunch with me?" he asked. "It's really not such a bad place."

Elizabeth stood like a statue, crumbling inside under the weight of his words. Was this really happening . . . a stranger? Could this man whom she had never seen before take the loneliness away? Elizabeth Michaels in a singles bar! Yet something drove her to say yes . . . to try to forget . . . to escape the marriage that at this moment seemed so hollow.

The stranger approached her slowly.

Something inside impelled her to throw caution to the wind, to do the unthinkable. But the words that finally came could not agree.

"I'm sorry. I've got to leave . . it's a mistake. I can't . . . I really must go."

She turned and walked quickly away, toward home, praying almost aloud, "Lord, please don't allow me to turn back." She strained to hear pursuing footsteps, but none came.

At home Elizabeth walked into the empty house, locked the door behind her, and fell breathless on the couch. *Oh, God,* she thought, *how close I came!*

After a few moments she rose slowly, walked into the kitchen where the remnants of the morning's events still sat. She began clearing away the half-finished breakfast. "Lord," she sighed, "we need You now more than ever."

61

Jacob had quietly walked into the den, picked up his brief-case and coat, and slipped quickly out of the house while Elizabeth sat alone in the kitchen. He'd always considered it the best policy at such times to say nothing, allowing her to work her way out of emotional difficulties alone. He never dreamed that what she craved more than anything at that moment was the touch of his hand, a tender caress on her cheek, anything to simply say, "I care . . . I understand . . . I love you."

But Jacob was oblivious to the side of a woman's nature that needed such tokens of reassurance sprinkled throughout the day. He expected his wife to react like a man—because that was the only response he'd ever given himself—exactly as he would do.

But today he might have unusual difficulty making that policy work. Diana's words had stung him. The troubled uneasiness refused to go away.

Ordinarily the drive to the office invigorated him. And two free morning hours to work on his latest manuscript would customarily have provided a delightful highlight of the day. But this time the drive was unsettling. The prospect of offering any helpful gems of wisdom on the subject of communication with the body of Christ seemed an impossibility.

Did Diana's words bite so deep because of the gnawing suspicion that possibly she was right? Hamilton was an asset, that could not be denied. And certainly he owed his very reputation to his shrewd handling of that delicate matter so many years ago.

But in his more lucid moments didn't he know, as Diana had blurted out, that Hamilton cared more for the prestige of his position than living the principles ETW stood for?

Communication in the body of Christ, he thought. *It's a joke! I'm writing a book on the subject that will probably be a best-seller. Yet I can't even manage to communicate in my own home . . . or in my organziation.*

Jacob Michaels was struggling with issues he'd not faced in many a year. Alone in his office he sat with head in hand. Faces flooded his memory. The face of that reporter Maxwell . . . *confound the fellow*, he thought. *He's the one who started all this!* . . . Then Sondra DeQue, now leaving ETW. What did he know of her—as a person? Why was she leaving? Then Diana—running out of the kitchen in tears, his own daughter—he loved her!—saying he didn't care, didn't understand. The phantoms swirled through his brain, shouting their accusations, leering at him.

Suddenly the face of Richard loomed in his memory—an unwelcome intrusion. Tears came to his eyes, as they hadn't for decades.

Maybe he didn't understand. His spiritual calling as a man of God certainly hadn't accomplished much in the way of Richard's salvation! He could not remember so much as one time when he and his son had really laughed together—just the two of them.

"Hey, Dad," he could hear him say, "how about a game of hide-and-seek in the yard?"

"Sorry, Dick," he'd answered, "I've still got on my slacks from church. Can't today."

"OK, Dad . . . how about—?"

"Sorry, son. I've got a meeting this afternoon back at the church. I'm going to have to leave pretty soon."

Then in the father's memory was the poignant picture of the son turning dejectedly back toward the house and walking slowly inside to spend the rest of the afternoon watching pointless reruns and cartoons on TV.

Jacob reached for a Kleenex, dabbed his eyes, and blew his nose.

Had he missed his destiny as a man of God? He didn't know . . . such questions were new.

Maybe he needed a break, a trip with Elizabeth—no books, no schedules, no Jaeger.

But he was caught in something larger than himself—America's man of the hour couldn't extricate himself that easily. There were commitments practically daily for the next six months.

It had been that way for years. Plans were going forward in Greenville. The impetus of Hamilton's plan was in full force now. Even if he chose to stop it, what could he do? He wondered about his power over Jaeger to achieve much of anything.

Maybe he could ease back, schedule fewer commitments. In a few months, in a year perhaps—the pace would slacken. Then he'd have more time for Elizabeth, for things he'd neglected too long. Or was it a dream to hope for a change?

The intercom sounded.

"Mr. Michaels," Liz said, "Mr. Maxwell is here to schedule an appointment. I wanted to confirm next Tuesday afternoon with you . . . will that be OK? Your slate is clean."

"Maxwell is here now?" asked Jacob, clearing his throat, "in your office?"

"Yes, sir."

Jacob paused a moment. No, he thought, he couldn't let Hamilton dominate every phase of his life. Then he said, "See if he'll come in now, Liz."

"Right now?"

"Yes, that is if he's free."

After another pause, she said, "He said that would be fine, Mr. Michaels. Shall I send him in?"

"Please do. And, Liz, see that we're not disturbed. If Hamilton comes looking for me, tell him I'm out."

In a moment Jackson walked into the expansive office for the second time, not a little surprised to suddenly find himself there once again.

"I hope you don't mind an impromptu visit," said Jacob, greeting him warmly.

"No—not at all," faltered Jackson.

"I'm afraid I've been thinking about some things this morning that I've overlooked too long. And, frankly—aside from the fact that you've been in my thoughts as well—I just need someone to chat with. You happened by, and well . . . here you are. Are you agreeable with that?"

"Yes, sir . . . certainly," said Jackson.

"But," said Jacob, "no interview. This is 'off the record'—just friends."

"Agreed," said Jackson.

When Jackson Maxwell emerged from Jacob Michaels's office seventy-five minutes later his impression of the head of ETW was considerably altered. At the same time, Jacob had set in motion several avenues of thought that would permanently affect a good many of his attitudes for years to come.

62

"Hamilton . . . Seb. I thought I ought to call you immediately."

"What's up?"

"I just got a call from George Haley. They've—reluctantly—agreed to the terms of your offer."

"Good work, Seb."

"Well, it wasn't me actually."

"How so?"

"I had a visit a while back from a friend of yours . . . young fellow who said he worked there and did some free-lance writing—fellow by the name of Maxwell."

"Maxwell!" exploded Jaeger. "What was he doing there?"

"He was quite inquisitive—asked me about you, your plans, about our background together."

"And you told him nothing?" said Jaeger, furious.

"Nothing much, we just talked, seemed like a nice enough kid. I saw no harm—"

"No harm!" interrupted Jaeger in a rage. "He's out to undo everything we've worked for."

"I wouldn't say that," said Elliot. "He went out to see the Haleys after leaving me—"

"Why the nerve!—that vile—"

"Hamilton," interrupted Elliot before his friend could complete the imprecation of his lips, "take it easy! It was after his visit that the Haleys made their decision to accept your offer. I couldn't get them to tell me anything—if he'd said something, or what. All I know is that they were quite taken with him and that his visit somehow sparked a decision on their part."

"Well—" said Hamilton, the rumpled feathers of his passion

settling back into place.

"I was angry at first too. I had specifically told him not to go out there. But all's well that end's well I always say."

"Naturally—I'm delighted," said Jaeger, nearly composed once more. "And I just received word from Tony Powers—he's in. I'm planning a public announcement in a couple of weeks. All the escrows should be closed by then, shouldn't they?"

"All except the Haley one. Of course cash will help speed it up, but it could still run two-and-a-half, three weeks."

"That disturbs me about Maxwell," said Jaeger, thinking aloud. "I've got to find a way to scuttle that obstinate young reporter once and for all."

"Any word from Jake?" asked Elliot.

"I'm flying there next week."

63

An hour later Hamilton Jaeger walked into Jacob Michaels's office unannounced. "Jacob," he said, "I have some good news!"

Jacob looked up from his desk. "Yes—what is it, Hamilton?"

"You sound rather glum, Jacob."

"I'm in the middle of something and—well, get on with it," he said, annoyed with Hamilton's intrusion.

"I had a call from Tony Powers yesterday evening . . . of SCWE in Dallas. He's decided to join with us."

Jacob said nothing.

"—and naturally, this clinches major public acceptance of the proposal. Major national ministries fully consolidating their efforts with our own . . . and with the world-renowned ministry of Jacob Michaels—"

He paused, grinning, tongue in cheek. Jacob eyed him with something akin to cynicism.

"Well, I need hardly tell you what that means."

"Tell me, Hamilton," said Jacob coolly, "what does it mean?"

"It means we are on the verge of launching the greatest Christian effort the world has ever seen. With Greenville as our launch site, as it were, the potential is limitless. Other organizations will trip over themselves to join the movement. There will be potency unheard of before—to change lives, to change society, to change history!"

Jacob had seen that gleam in Hamilton's eyes before. The words sounded right, but the lustful glow frightened him. Alarms were ringing in his brain, yet he himself was caught in the inexorable flow of events.

"I take it there have been all the proper legal signings and that you are planning some sort of ceremonial public announcement designed to maximize PR value?" Jacob asked matter-of-factly.

"Your tone is one of less than elation," said Hamilton. "I would think it would be otherwise, considering you will be the chairman of the board and the reigning monarch over this new empire." There was detectable sarcasm in his voice. "But yes, you're right, everything's legally documented and yes—I do have a press conference scheduled for next week. Carson, Tony, Jerome, Neil Pierce, and Jeff from ER will all be on hand. It should be quite a media coup. And needless to say—you, Jacob, will be behind the podium to make the announcement yourself."

Jacob nodded. "Naturally," he said. "And you, the mastermind, will be nowhere to be seen—waiting in the wings, as it were?"

"Where else would a dedicated servant like myself be?" he asked.

"And should I continue between now and then to harbor some of the doubts I expressed earlier, I presume there would be nothing I could do to stop this from taking place, is that correct?"

"That's exactly right, Jacob," said Jaeger looking him full in the face. "The documents that I've had drawn up are binding on all parties. It is in the works, and nothing can stop it."

"I have given you considerable power around here, haven't I?" said Jacob.

"You've given me the authority to sign on your behalf," said Jaeger slowly, "—to relieve you from the pressure of your position . . to make decisions for you . . . and to carry the vision the Lord had given us—both of us! It's been a two-way street all the way, my friend. You've given me nothing you didn't want to give."

"I see, then," Jacob said at length, exhaling a long sigh, "that you've essentially left me no choice but to comply—to go along with your plan."

"I think you grasp the situation correctly, Jacob," replied Hamilton. "And in the meantime, I'd be giving some thought to your announcement. The eyes of America will be on you."

Jacob turned his chair toward the window, and Jaeger left the room as he had come.

Thirty minutes later, Jacob still sat motionless. His thoughts during that time had been exploring much unfamiliar territory deep within his own being. He now realized he could no longer continue his inner quandary alone.

At length he turned, rose and walked slowly to his desk, picked up his phone, spoke briefly to his secretary, then waited.

"Bob," he said the moment his call was answered, "it's Jacob. Do you have some time you could spare me? I need your help. I think it's finally time I need to ask you to pray with me."

64

"I hardly even know what to say, Bob," said Jacob, once the two men were comfortably seated in two chairs on the opposite side of Michaels's expansive office from his desk. "Here we have hardly seen one another in years, and suddenly since the last time we spoke, I find myself realizing how much I've missed you."

He gazed into Means's face earnestly, yet had difficulty looking him in the eye. "I'm embarrassed to have to say that," he added.

"I told you before, Jacob," replied Means, "think nothing of it." His own eyes, swimming in liquid, were full of love for his friend.

"It's just that I find myself caught in the midst of so many circumstances pulling at me, and suddenly I realize I've got no one to turn to. No one, Bob . . no one I'm close to, that I can confide in . . . no one to really trust—like a *friend*."

His voice contained none of the calm and dignity and self-assurance that it unfailingly presented to the public from a podium or in front of a television camera, none of the poise, none of the confidence that came across in his recorded songs or his written words. The polish and prestige and celebrated image were gone. In their place were eyes of confusion, a voice groping, probing, struggling for words he had never spoken, hoping in desperation that here was someone to whom he could pour out the uncertainties and questions that had been silently building for months.

"Tell me whatever you like, Jacob," said Means gently. "Nothing you say will leave this room, I promise you that."

"I appreciate that, Bob . . . more than you know."

"You are my friend."

"I know that—I know it *now*. I regret it has taken me so long to realize it . . . again. In so many ways, I've been a fool, Bob— yet I'm only now seeing it. Now—after all these years . . . when it seems too late!"

His voice was full of anguish and regret.

"It is never too late, my friend. In God's economy nothing is ever wasted—especially time."

A pause came, during which Michaels seemed by his expression to doubt his friend's words.

"God never wastes time," Means continued. "Time often passes. Sometimes our earthbound eyes cannot see anything fruitful being accomplished. But in the realm of the spirit, God is ever at work—tilling and preparing soil for the growing of His fruit in His time."

"I would like to think you're right." Jacob sighed. "But look at me, Bob. I'm over fifty, my kids are grown, my wife and I hardly know one another anymore. Look at me, for heaven's sake! I'm a world-renowned Christian personality, yet in my heart suddenly I wake up to the fact that inside my own soul . . . I'm empty. I'm the head of this huge organization, and sometimes I don't even know half the things we're doing—or why we're doing them."

He stopped, glanced hastily around the room as if looking for something that would help him express the inexpressible.

"I . . . I don't know, Bob . . . I can't imagine how all these years could have gone by. It's like two decades passed in a flash and I was asleep. It seems only yesterday Diana and Richard were born and you and I were talking of things we hoped to accomplish as Christians . . . and now all of a sudden, twenty years have gone by. The kids are adults, I have no relationship with them, they don't respect me, you and I haven't talked in twelve—what is it, fifteen years? Elizabeth and I . . ."

He faltered, obviously overcome with emotion.

"Too late, Bob," he finally said, repeating the words softly. "I have to admit, from where I stand right now, it *does* seem too late—like I'm waking up after a twenty-year sleep, to find that everything I used to care about has passed me by."

A few moments of silence fell in the office. In the distance the sounds of the city could be heard. But the two men were oblivious to them.

"No, Jacob, there is no such thing as *too late* for God. He yet has something in mind for you. Something wonderful—though it may be quite different from what you have imagined. And I think this day is perhaps the beginning."

"What could He possibly have for me to do that I haven't already done?" asked Jacob, half sarcastically. "I've already *done* everything for God, don't you know—at least that's what people say."

"I didn't say He had something for you to *do*. That's the most damaging mistake so-called Christian workers make—thinking that God's great purposes have to do with what we accomplish in His name. No, Jacob, God is not nearly so much concerned with what we do as with what we *are*. He is not in the business of building empires but of making people—people of a certain sort, people that are like His Son—like Him *inside*, not by virtue of external achievements."

"That's not something you hear very often," replied Jacob sadly, "especially from *my* lips. I'm not sure I've ever heard it put just like that."

"God's great intent, Jacob, is not what He wants to do *through* you . . . but *in* you. In your heart—not especially through your hands—is where His most vital activity takes place. You are His son, and His desire is to remake you, to transform your heart and mine, and those of all His people who will listen to His voice—He wants to transform us into His image, so that we reflect His being and nature. *That* is His great work on this earth—not missions, not the building of churches, not even the externals of evangelism. His great work is the transformation of hearts . . . and *that* is how true evangelism will ultimately take place."

"I've never heard you talk like this before, Bob."

"I've been through some ups and downs and much learning at the Lord's hand these last twenty years myself. He's had a great deal to do in *my* heart too, in order to reveal some of these things to me."

"If what you say is true, it sort of throws everything we're about here into a new light doesn't it?"

Means laughed. "A *very* different light!"

"Why have you stayed with ETW all this time then, if you feel our efforts are fruitless?" asked Michaels. His question was a sincere one, containing no hint of hidden meaning or cynicism.

"Did I use the word 'fruitless'?" Means asked with a smile.

"No, I suppose you didn't say that exactly. I only thought . . ."

"Evangelism remains the calling to which I feel God has led me," Means replied. "Evangelizing the world, as our name says, is still my dream. It is just that my view of the process has changed rather dramatically over the years. Hearts are brought into the kingdom one at a time. There is no saving the world en masse, so to speak. We can't preach salvation to vast throngs. We can't beam salvation to the world via satellite. We can't sing or write salvation into hearts with songs and books. The phrase you and many of your evangelist colleagues are fond of using when giving a call when you talk about the 'hundreds and thousands who will now come'—that phrase has become a misnomer for me. Hundreds and thousands are not saved in one fell swoop. The kingdom of God is entered one at a time, soul by soul. Whether it's at a crusade or through a book or a song or a television program or a tract—it still happens one at a time, in the quiet individual heart of every man, woman, or child who gives his heart to God. And that's why I couldn't feel more blessed than to be exactly where I am, down in that little office of mine, with the unparalleled opportunity of responding to letters and phone calls. I tell you, Jacob, the work I do down there fills me with purpose! Everyday the Lord lets me be part of individual lives and hearts that are struggling toward the kingdom each in own personal way. I can't imagine being more in the heart of what evangelism is about!"

Michaels shook his head slowly, then sighed deeply. "I just . . . never imagined," he said at length. "Here all this time I've been out in the forefront, the man everyone looks to and admires, preaching and singing and writing *about* evangelizing the world, and yet down there in that little office of yours, unseen by anyone, hidden away out of view, who knows but what you haven't been doing a more significant work than I have. All this is mind-boggling, Bob! I have to tell you, my head is spinning. It's . . . it's such a new perspective—on everything!"

Means did not reply.

"Which brings me back to what I said a while back," Jacob went on after a moment. "It seems that so much time has passed—for me, I mean . . . so much water under the bridge, so many years wasted. Yet you say it is never too late . . . that with God time is never wasted. I just don't see how that can help in my case. Suddenly, I feel my life has been foolishly spent going in all the wrong directions."

A peculiar smile came over Means's face.

"There is one other reason I've remained all these years," he said, "in addition to the involvement and ministry with those people the Lord sends my way."

"And that is?"

"To pray," Means replied. "You are not only my friend but also the leader of this organization. Many years ago when He began to show me some of these things I have been sharing, He also put on my heart the burden to pray for you. I came to feel that to be one of my most important functions here at ETW—simply upholding you in prayer daily, asking God to accomplish His purpose in and through you. So you see, I believe all these things work together in God's timing and in His purpose. I truly believe He has been all this time preparing the ground of your spirit for some great work—not a great work in the world, as I said, but a great work in your heart.

"I don't know everything you are facing, but lately I have felt an increasingly heavy burden to pray diligently for you. I have sensed that the Lord is stirring things up inside you, that He is preparing to move forward in your life in ways perhaps you never

278

dreamed of. You see, Jacob, I believe God's timing is perfect and that this divine discontent you are feeling is His calling to you deep in your heart. He wants you to seek Him in new and deeper ways. Too late? Not at all—now is His *perfect* time for the carrying out of things that will perhaps impact the kingdom in greater ways— though perhaps far different—than ever before in your life."

Jacob sighed deeply. "Everything you say is . . . is just so new! I don't even know what to say, how to thank you for . . . for everything—your concern, your prayers. I know I haven't demonstrated it, but I see so clearly now that you are one of the few true friends I have ever had."

"God is getting you ready, Jacob—ready for new directions, possibly new relationships, new ways of being involved in people's lives. I have sensed this for some time as I've prayed. I do not know what circumstances are coming to bear upon you, but I do know that God will send other of His messengers, and I know that His truth and His purpose will come to bear upon your life."

Michaels was silent a long while. Means hardly could realize the importance of his words. Jacob reflected on all the changes that had been infiltrating his life recently—problems at home, all the turmoil with Texas, a souring of his attitude toward Jaeger, the reporter Maxwell, and now suddenly Bob's coming back into his life and all these new questions in his soul. Could it all be part of a divine plan, as Bob said? Was God really trying to speak to him through all this?

Truth . . .

The word Bob had just spoken slammed into his brain with sudden force. Did the beginning of whatever "new directions" God had for him in the future, perhaps lie in the past? Was coming face to face—perhaps for the first time in his life—with the *truth,* the necessary starting point? Was his present turmoil rooted in a past he had been trying to submerge all these years? If his life had been a sham, an empty shell, a mere public facade, was it perhaps not too late to begin anew, to try to right past wrongs, to become whole, to see if there was anything God could do with him yet, even though so many years had slipped rapidly by?

He closed his eyes. He could feel himself perspiring. It was as though his life were flashing before his eyes, and he was disgusted with everything he saw.

It had to end! The duplicity could not go on! He had to somehow become a real person. He had to become a man—not just a shell. He had to face the truth of what he had been . . . and what he was.

He opened his eyes. Bob still sat opposite him, still gazing upon him with a look he could only describe as the love of a true friend. He drew in a deep breath, weighing one last time whether to plunge in and tell Bob everything that was swirling within his heart and brain, yet knowing he had been brought to this point and that he had little choice.

At last, with a look of both hopelessness and resolve on his face, he launched forward into what for Jacob Michaels was unchartered territory—that of unburdening the depths of his soul.

"I've lived a double life in many ways," he began. "The public and the private. For all these years I managed to squelch the one side of me, and put on the public face—all for the good of the cause. I suppose until today I'm not even sure I myself was aware there were two sides. The inner part of my being was so empty, so devoid of real personhood, even *I* thought the public image was the real me. Now suddenly I see the facade for what it has been all this time. Here I've written and sung and spoken all the right and proper evangelical words and let myself be acclaimed and praised and lauded, and yet I suddenly wake to wondering within myself if I've even got a spiritual life of my own."

He took a deep breath. His voice was trembling.

"God help me—it's all been wrong, Bob! My eyes are opening to what Hamilton's been doing . . . to my failure with my family . . . to my failure to friends—like you. And my eyes are opening to *myself* . . . and I don't like what I am seeing."

He stopped again, then struggled to continue.

"I suppose the deception began many years ago," he said, "and it's continued on all this time, though I've tried to hide it even from myself . . ."

He went on, sharing openly things he had never before told another soul, unburdening himself of more than twenty years of regrets and emotions and heartaches suddenly come to life. Robert Means listened with compassion, praying silently as he did, praying for the healing and restorative powers of God's Spirit to descend upon his friend during his time of need.

Forty minutes later, both men as in one accord, slipped to their knees. Jacob's reservoir had been thoroughly spent, and his eyes were wet with the tears that had remained unwept far too long.

"Oh, God, our loving Father," prayed Bob, "You have heard the heart cries of this humble child of Yours. Take his weakened soul, O Lord, into Your care. Remake and rebuild him. Now that he is ready to submit to Your re-creative hand, fashion him according to Your image. Now that he has humbled his heart, fill him with Yourself, Your own Spirit, and restore him to strength. Place within him the manhood You have ordained him to attain. Let him be an example to Your people, not by his words or his deeds, but by the humility and quality of his character, by his reflection of the image of Your Son. Let me serve him by my continued prayers. Accomplish Your purposes in his life, and in mine, our Father. Bring the circumstances and people into our lives that point us toward Your will. Open our hearts to hear Your voice in all that comes to us. And God, we pray for this organization that has been established. Whatever its past we now pray for what You will for this organization to become in the future . . . and for Jacob as its leader."

He stopped. Again the room was silent.

A quiet "Amen" followed from the lips of Jacob, and that was all.

In a moment both men rose to their feet. As they gazed into one another's eyes, the look was one of anticipation and new beginnings.

They embraced, and held each other tight for a long moment. Friends and comrades they were again—though on a level more profound than even during their youth.

Then Means turned and left the office leaving Jacob at the window where he had been two hours earlier as Hamilton Jaeger had exited.

How different indeed were the two partings!

Jacob sucked in a huge breath of air. He felt like smiling again. For the first time in memory, his heart was filled with hope.

65

Jackson's phone rang. It was Sondra.

"Can you talk?" he asked.

"No problem," she said, "I'm calling from home. Yesterday was my last day with ETW."

"Finally happened, huh?"

"The newsletter carried the story about my moving on from ETW. Hamilton's sinister motives will never be suspected."

"What was it you were telling me about things always getting better?" asked Jackson with a laugh.

"I guess I'm still smarting from the pain of his words."

"Why? What did he say?"

"He called me into his office and then with mock concern had the nerve to say, 'Sondra, I know you've not really been yourself here lately. You have so much to offer that we feel you might be better off elsewhere where your talents might be put to better use— we don't want to stand in the way of your advancement. So we've decided to replace you as ETW's press secretary. It's for your own good to think of moving beyond ETW in your career.' Why it was a snow job, start to finish!"

"At least it's over."

"I'll admit, it does feel good not to face the daily pressure."

"What now?" asked Jackson.

"I'm going to sit tight . . . wait to see how it works out. Then I'll decide—which reminds me. That's why I called, I have something for you. Just a couple of days before I left I caught wind of a trip Hamilton's taking next week. He's low-profiling it, keeping his plans under wraps, which made me think something might be up. I nosed around and made an interesting discovery. He's flying to Washington—going to meet with the Senator."

"What senator?"

"Montgomery. They are old friends."

"If they're old friends, what's the big deal?" asked Jackson.

"I peeked at his appointment log, and all that's written down is lunch. But I'm sure it's more than a social call."

"I don't see how that does me any good? To be a fly on the wall of his private office—now *that* would do me some good. But otherwise . . ."

"I'm not through, hear me out. Hamilton and I used to—well, I've told you that. We flew to Washington several times. While he and the Senator were meeting, I became fairly well acquainted with his aide—a fellow named Sydney Wilson. He liked me and trusted me. I think he'd help us, as a favor to me."

"So—what can he do? Surely they'd never allow Sydney to take notes, much less let him share them with me."

"Maybe not. But if anyone would know what is up, Sydney would. It may not lead you anywhere. But then we have to see, don't we?"

"But Sydney would never reveal anything confidential to me."

"I learned early in this business that favors for favors is all part of the commerce of journalism and good PR work. Hamilton trained me well. I scratched Sydney's back a few times. I think he'd help. Besides, if it's confidential, Sydney won't know of it. If he *does* know anything, it's fair game because everyone has access to it. That's how the information game is played in Washington. All you'll be doing is probing for public access information."

"You have something in mind?"

"Well, here comes the bold part of my plan, if you can call it that. I thought I would call Sydney . . . tell him about you by phone—sort of introduce you—tell him you and I work closely together and say we're working on a very important project and that you need to know what that meeting is about."

"You wouldn't tell him you were no longer with Hamilton?"

"That would spoil everything."

"What about the mailing?"

"I went to the mailroom and took the liberty of pulling the newsletter addressed to the Senator's office. I'll see that it's mailed as soon as you've met with Sydney."

"You've thought of everything it seems," said Jackson.

"I don't think Sydney will worry if you assure him your conversation is off the record. It would obviously have nothing to do with any of the Senator's delicate political negotiations. Things like this go on day and night between the press and politicians in Washington. Like I said, if information hasn't been specifically put under wraps, it's fair public game. You have as much right to that information as anyone."

"Hmm . . ." said Jackson, "it is a daring proposal."

"What do you think?" asked Sondra.

"It's a tight line we're on. We're trying to discover if there are unethical dealings going on in ETW. We can hardly be unethical ourselves in the process. Yet sometimes I'm just not sure where the balance between the two is."

"I won't do it if you tell me not to," said Sondra.

"I know you're just trying to help," said Jackson. "Listen—we'll tentatively consider it. But you have to be sure not to actually mislead Sydney when you talk to him. We'll let the Lord direct us by Sydney's response. If he agrees, I'll do it. If he's hesitant, we'll forget it."

"I understand. I'll call him this afternoon."

"Wait before you call him. Let me think about it a little more. I want to be sure that's the right move first."

"I'll wait to hear from you. By the way, have you got anything on Jerome Bullinger?"

"Not yet. I'm driving down to Kankakee this afternoon."

66

Jackson eased forward slowly, straining to see the numbers. That was the trouble with apartment houses—sometimes you could hardly tell how the sequences went. Finding Wayfarer Lane hadn't been difficult. Driving in Chicago had made any town of less than 100,000 seem a breeze. One stop at a service station to consult a city map had been all he'd needed.

Unfortunately, the numbers weren't all labeled. He'd been back and forth several times and had passed right by 3216 each time.

There was a large apartment building, looked to contain twelve to sixteen units. That could be it. He parked the car and walked over. Sure enough . . . on a wooden engraved sign—not visible from the street—was the number 3216.

Jackson walked to the front door and scanned the list of occupants. There were fifteen units, arranged on three floors. However, none of the mailboxes was labeled with anything like Jerome Bullinger. Number 3 showed the name Smith; number 12 was unlabeled.

He decided to try the office.

A middle-aged, rather grumpy woman opened to his knock. She was on the plump side, her unkempt hair was about half-gray, and she wore a smock-type orange floral housedress. A daytime television soap blared from inside, and she clearly didn't appreciate being taken from it.

"Excuse me," said Jackson, "I was looking for a Jerome Bullinger—I understood he lived in Number 3."

"No one by that name here," said the woman. "Didn't you read the mailboxes? . . . Smith lives in three."

On a hunch, Jackson asked, "Is Mr. Smith by any chance about my age?"

She laughed. "Hardly, son. Mr. Smith's past seventy. That's why we had to put him down on the first floor."

"And how about Apartment 12?" asked Jackson. "Mr. Bullinger wouldn't by any chance live there?"

"I already told you," she said sharply. "Didn't you read the mailboxes—twelve's vacant."

"I'm sorry. It's just that I've driven all the way down from Chicago and it's rather important I locate Mr. Bullinger. This was the last address we have."

"Well, there's no Bullinger here, and I don't know of any," she said.

"He hasn't been here?"

"I tell you—I don't know the name."

"So you wouldn't have a forwarding address or anything?" suggested Jackson.

"How many times do I have to tell you? I've got nothing!" The door closed—not gently.

So much for that, thought Jackson. All this way for a dead-end.

He turned and slowly walked back to his car. He'd hoped Bullinger would be able to unlock the mystery.

"Hey . . . young man!" he heard behind him.

He turned. The apartment woman was waving to him. He ran back to the office.

"My husband was listening while you were at the door. He says Bullinger was here for a while. I was in the hospital—kidney stones—at the time . . . that's why I didn't know."

"That's all right," said Jackson. "Does your husband know anything about where he went?"

"No, he left us no address. But one of the other tenants told him he moved up to Janesville—supposed to be taking a job doing something with computers."

"Thank you," said Jackson. "That's something to go on. I appreciate it."

Jackson returned to his car and began the drive north.

It gave him some time to think. He must get to Quincy as soon as he could. He had to talk to his folks. If they knew more about his adoption than they'd told him, he prayed they'd understand his desire to know.

Then there was the matter of Sondra's friend in Washington. That was sticky too. It was a complex dilemma. He played devil's advocate with himself all the way home.

No clear-cut answers.

The further Jackson was absorbed the more of his decisions he found he simply had to make on his own, trusting as best he could his judgment, discretion, and spiritual values. Pray as he would, no effervescent "leading"—no special delivery telegrams from on high—came to him. He simply had to plow ahead doing what he judged right.

When he returned to his apartment, he called Sondra.

"Sondra," he said when she answered, "call your friend in Washington . . . I'll meet with him—*if* he's agreeable."

67

The following Wednesday, March 18, promptly at 11:50, Hamilton Jaeger strode confidently into the office of the senior Illinois senator, the honorable Jefferson Montgomery. The congressman had been expecting him.

"I thought we'd lunch here, Hamilton," he said shaking the hand of his visitor firmly. "That way we can have more privacy—oh, Sydney," he said, turning to his aide busy with some paperwork in the outer office, "you may take the rest of the afternoon off. I'm going to be tied up with Mr. Jaeger for some time."

When the young man had left, and they were alone, the Senator poured two cups of coffee and, motioning Jaeger toward a tray of sandwiches, hors d'oeuvres, and fruit salad, said, "Have there been any favorable developments?"

"On a grand scale, I believe," answered his companion.

"How's Seb?"

"He's worked hard putting the property together—and I think his end of it has worn him out."

"Doubts about whether it's been worth it?"

"That's part of it," said Jaeger. "But he's held up his end. He can have his doubts now. That's behind us. He can relax. Now it's our turn to move to the forefront and carry out the next phase."

"And the merger?"

"Progressing nicely . . . five major organizations are in—

besides us. The movement is growing. I've arranged a press conference for next week. Jacob will make the announcement of course."

"And your position in the new order?—any complications?"

"None I can't work through. I've employed the shrewdest lawyers I could find," said Jaeger with a cunning smile. "So, yes to answer your question, I'll hold a high position once the dust settles. Jacob and I have an unspoken understanding. It's his face people want to see, but I am the one who can grind the wheels of action into motion. Much as he hates to admit this very pragmatic state of affairs between us, I think he grasps the nature of the situation."

"Does he know yet?"

"No, he's proving a bit resistant. He still naively assumes we'll be somehow sharing the soil but not the rest. He isn't fully cognizant of the totality of the merger idea."

"Are any of the others either?"

"I suppose not. They still think they'll be free to function independently. To a degree, of course, that's true. But as I take a more direct interest in the daily affairs of their organizations as time progresses, they'll come to see things as we do. I'm confident of that. What we envision will increase the opportunities for ministry in their selective fields."

"But what if they don't see it that way?"

"They have to. Once they've merged, they've pretty much given us the authority to do as we like."

"They'd run like jackrabbits to hear you say so!"

"They won't. Sure, even Jacob is scared—now. But this is the future! This is the march of progress of the Christian enterprise. Visionaries like you and I have to take the bull by the horns and make it happen. Jacob . . . the others—they have to be led, that's all . . . spoon-fed the vision. I'm just leading them where they really want to go but are too weak-kneed to move on their own."

"So Michaels still doesn't know what we intend to originate from Greenville?"

"No, I doubt he's thought about politics in his life."

"A public figure like him, it must have occurred to him."

"Maybe. But not seriously," said Jaeger.

"You think there'll be any trouble persuading him—once the

time is right?"

"By then, the media potential of Greenville—do you realize what we'll have there, Jake? Publishing, recording, radio, TV, the country's top author, students . . . why it staggers the imagination—and that's my point. By then the sheer media impact will be so enormous we'll be able to launch a movement to draft him that won't even need his endorsement in the early stages. By the time his OK is necessary—we'll be halfway there. I wouldn't be surprised if we could even mount a write-in campaign."

"That may be so," said Montgomery seriously, "but I've been around this game long enough to know we'll never get anywhere without a sense of personal enthusiasm from the candidate himself. People feel that in a man."

"Don't worry, my friend," said Jaeger. "Believe me, once Jacob feels the public adulation, he'll come along."

"I still think the Senate's the place to begin, Hamilton. I know you've had higher ambitions, but we must build a base."

"Maybe you're right, Jake. But only for two years. I tell you, Greenville's literally going to explode onto the national map. Look what the Moral Majority accomplished. That's kindergarten stuff compared to the resources we'll have. We have a man known and respected the world over."

"I agree, Hamilton. I think he can win. But I'm the politician here. You handle the merger, and let me handle the campaigns. I know this business, and it can get nasty. No election's a cinch. It'll be a tough fight even with all your organizational wizardry. And I tell you we'll have to have Michaels all the way in with us—*all* the way! If he's not, there's no way this thing can fly."

"Give me time, Jake, I'm bringing him along on my own timetable. Don't rush it. I've an ace up my sleeve that'll turn the tide in our favor. He's much too conscious of what people think of him to risk scandal of any sort. I think we can count on his support."

"When are you thinking of?"

"The sooner the better," said Jaeger.

"I've been thinking next year might be an appropriate jumping off point. There are a number of states with weak races. I'm certain he could get residency in any of a half-dozen. He already has homes in three. But we have to get it soon."

"You select the most advantageous race, I'll woo Jacob and lead him along. After the press conference we'll begin construction in mid-May. You think a run for it all is conceivable two years after that?"

"Three years is a long time from now, Hamilton. We'll have to handle one race at a time . . . watch the polls. What about your 'command post,' as you enjoy calling it?"

"Seb wrapped up the deal last week. It was a tough one," said Jaeger. "The perfect setting from which to run a Christian empire," he added with a laugh.

"Or a country," added Jake.

Jaeger nodded. "You'll be there with me, don't forget, Jake. This whole thing won't do your political career any harm either. You could be in line for the vice presidency if you play your cards right."

Neither man spoke for a moment.

"Heady times, Hamilton . . . heady times," said Jake at length. "Who would ever have thought we'd come this far with our dream?"

"Don't tell me you doubted it?" asked Jaeger. "It was in the cards all along. The time was right. Destiny was with us."

The senator merely shrugged and reached for another sandwich.

68

It was Thursday evening. Jackson peered through the dusty venetian blinds of his motel window, then glanced at his watch. It was 7:35—Sydney was supposed to be there between 7:00 and 7:20.

He sat down, tried to read a newspaper, stood again, paced the room, opened the door, and walked onto the balcony. Just then a car drove into the lot, parked, and out jumped a man Jackson judged to be about thirty-eight or forty, wearing bow tie and glasses.

"Mr. Maxwell . . . ?" he called to Jackson from below.

"Yes."

"I'm Sydney Wilson. Sorry I'm late. Got tied up with some last minute work at the office."

"No problem," said Jackson, leaning over the rail. "I've no place to go. Come on up."

In another minute the two were seated in his room.

"Sondra says you can help me," said Jackson.

"That depends on what you want," said Wilson, "but I'll do what I can. Any friend of Sondra's, you know."

"I'm grateful," said Jackson. "Tell me, do you know Hamilton Jaeger?"

"No. I've seen him a couple times. Usually when he visits, I'm sent off."

"He and Sondra have worked very closely together in the past, as you know."

"Yes. A few times Sondra's come to Washington with him. When the senator and Jaeger met, it was my job to entertain her."

"Showed her the town?" asked Jackson with a laugh.

"You bet!"

Jackson could scarcely imagine it. Five-foot five inches, balding Sydney Wilson hardly seemed Sondra's type.

"What we need," Jackson resumed, "is some information on Hamilton's meeting with the senator yesterday."

"Why don't you just ask him?" asked Sydney.

Jackson inhaled an invisible sigh, readying himself for another of his carefully worded phrases. "It's got to do with something Sondra and I are working on between ourselves. I understood Sondra had discussed it with you on the phone?"

"We talked—and I agreed. Just so long as you're not a reporter going to print something . . ."

"Not a word," assured Jackson, "I promise. Before anything would go to print, Hamilton—and the senator—would be made fully aware of everything Sondra and I are doing."

"In that case," said Wilson, "I suppose I may be able to help you."

"Is there any way you can find out what they discussed?" asked Jackson. "Would the senator confide in you?"

"Probably not. But that's no obstacle."

"How so? You weren't there were you?"

"Recorders didn't leave the capital after Watergate, Mr. Maxwell," he said. "I do the senator's transcribing when he needs it for something. I have complete access to the equipment."

"The meeting was recorded?"

"Without a doubt."

"But surely you can't give out secrets? Aren't you bound to some kind of confidentiality? I mean I don't want to cost you your job," said Jackson.

"No. Nothing like that. This is no secret stuff. When there's a strict veil of secrecy to be observed, he informs me, and I'm quiet as a mouse. Otherwise . . . the circulation-of-information game is what oils the machinery of Washington . . . everyone plays it . . . it's one of the givens of politics. I have reporters and newsmen on me from morning till night. The senator knows that. You have as much right to ask me questions as anyone. Believe me, if he'd told me it was confidential, you'd get nothing from me."

"If you're sure . . ."

"I can't give you anything written. You'll have to settle for word of mouth."

"Fine," said Jackson.

"You spending the night here?" asked Wilson.

Jackson nodded.

"I'll be back tomorrow. Better keep the room for another night. I might not be able to get away during the day. I'll go back to the office tonight and will see you tomorrow evening. It may be late.

But whatever they discussed yesterday, you'll know something about it—whatever I can give you—in twenty-four hours."

When Jackson and Wilson parted the next evening, Jackson at last began to realize the extent to which he had stumbled into far more than he had bargained for when he decided so long ago to take Linda up on her words and seek out an interview with Jacob Michaels. Things had all at once taken a decidedly more serious turn.

69

"Mom, you have to understand," said Jackson, "this has nothing to do with you and Dad. It won't make me care about you any less."

"I just don't see why—"

"Ellen," interrupted Fred, "Jackson's a man now. He has to live his own life. We can't do it for him."

Jackson's mother touched a handkerchief to her eyes once again and was silent.

Jackson rose and walked to where she sat, placed his hand on her shoulder, and said tenderly, "Mom, I love you. Nothing will take that away. Nothing could make me less thankful for all you've done. You've loved me *more* than my blood parents, I know that."

He stopped. Ellen cried softly. Jackson returned to his chair.

"But," he went on, "there's something in a man that has to know himself. I'm compelled to learn as much as I can about the person I am. I didn't plan this. Events have just rolled in upon me. I have no choice but to follow where they lead. I'm so grateful for the part of me that's come from you—but that's not all there is. I have to explore the other areas of my life that contribute to the person God has made me. Don't you see—I *have* to."

"We understand, son," said Fred. "It's just painful for us."

"I know, Dad," said Jackson. "It's painful for me too. I don't want to put you through this either."

Ellen nodded as if to say, "It's OK. I understand." But she couldn't speak.

"But, son," said Fred, "even if we wanted to, I'm not sure we could help. We never met the people—never heard any names, where anyone was from, where you were born. It was all very secretive. It always is, you know, in those kinds of arrangements."

"You must have had contact with someone. There had to have been papers?"

"Of course we had contacts. But there was no agency and all the paperwork that would have gone along with it."

"How could it have been carried out so confidentially? I thought there were regulations?" asked Jackson.

"There are—but they get bent a good deal—every case is so different," answered Fred.

"We were anxious, son," broke in Ellen in a faltering voice. "I suppose it was wrong of us, but we were tired of waiting. We'd had our name on a list with several agencies for years. But we were poor and couldn't afford the adoption costs that were so often required."

"Our name kept being passed up," said Fred, standing and hobbling to his wife's chair where he placed his hand on her shoulder. "We began to see our dream of raising a son of our own evaporating."

He stopped, obviously feeling great emotion from the memory. He turned away and fought the rising tears. The room fell silent once more.

"Son," said Ellen at length, slowly regaining her composure, "you have no idea how badly we wanted you. We dreamed about you, thought about you, prayed for you—for years—before you actually joined our family. That's why it's so hard—"

She began to break down again.

"—so hard to let go of you now."

"You don't have to let go, Mom," insisted Jackson.

"I know . . . I know," said Ellen in a faint voice. "Still it is difficult."

Jackson nodded.

Fred now spoke again. "There was a woman, who was I guess what you'd call a 'broker.' It sounds so fly-by-night now, to talk about it. But in those days, so much was done that way—private agreements you know. And we were desperate. We just couldn't let go of our dream of a son. So one day we called her, and she came to visit. We told her what we'd been through with the agencies and about our money problems. She was nice, decently dressed— not a smoke-filled room, barroom sort. And she ran a bona fide business—had contacts with several governmental and private agencies. But she wasn't limited like they were, she said. Sometimes she had contacts with people who didn't want to use an agency for one reason or another. She said she thought she could help and that she'd do what she could for us."

"And . . . ?" said Jackson, moving toward the edge of his seat.

"We didn't hear a peep for over two months," said Ellen. "We began to think this was one more dead end like all the rest."

"Then one day, up the drive she came in her big old brown Chrysler," said Fred, "dust flying behind her, chickens running for their lives in all directions. She had news, she said. 'A possibility.' A man had contacted her about the placement of a child—a boy. Couldn't go through official channels—had to be a private arrangement. The baby's father was somebody who had to remain anonymous. Money was no object, simply a placement fee for her was all that was necessary, she said. And the man had said he'd even pay that if need be. His only concern was that the child be placed in a Christian home with solid parents, preferably in some small community, a farming family would be perfect, and that the parents be avowed to secrecy. She'd thought of us immediately."

"And that was it? That was all you ever knew?" asked Jackson. "She never divulged anything else about the baby's background?"

"No, that was it. Of course we signed papers. But there was never a word about the child's parents. Sybil handled everything, and that end of it never came up. Of course we never expected to know . . . never even wanted to know."

"That was the lady's name—Sybil?"

"Sybil Macon."

"Is she still around? Still handling adoptions?" Jackson asked.

"I don't know. Last I'd heard she'd had some problems with the law—licensing or something. I think they shut her down."

"I heard she moved down to St. Louis," said Ellen, "several years back. I don't know for sure."

No one spoke for a minute. Then Jackson said, "And this Sybil never mentioned any other names—never a word about the man who had come to her?"

"Nothing."

Another silence.

"I do remember one curious thing," said Ellen after a moment. "When we were all done signing the papers and paying our half of the fee—that's how it wound up, we each paid half. Otherwise we might not have been able to afford it. Times were really rough there for a while. It got better though—you brought us luck, Jackson! Anyhow, like I was saying, we were all done, the check was made out and everything, and suddenly Sybil snapped her fingers and said, 'I forgot about the fee to get these papers registered.' She'd said it almost under her breath. Then she muttered, even softer, half to herself, 'Oh, that's OK—Bruce'll take care of it.' Then she closed her satchel, stood up, shook our hands, and left. That was the end of it, no more mention of the extra fee. That was the only other name I ever heard. Course I've no idea in what way this Bruce was connected. Could have just been someone who worked for her for all I know."

She paused. Jackson was silent.

There were no more questions to be asked for the time being. He'd put his folks through enough for one day.

70

It was admittedly a long shot. But better that than a wasted drive down to St. Louis. The Quincy library was not of national renown, but it did stock the country's major metropolitan telephone directories, and for the moment that was all Jackson needed.

He thumbed through the yellow pages' "Adoption Agencies," then ran his finger quickly down to the M's. No Macon was to be found. Neither was she listed in the white pages—another dead end.

Jackson closed the book slowly and sat down.

Suddenly he jumped back to this feet. What about another name? Who knows what she'd call it. Hurriedly he opened the bulky book again to the same page, this time beginning with the A's. He carefully read the entire list, eye peeled for any recognizable clue.

His face lit up when he reached the S's. There it was—right below the St. Louis Agency . . . "Sybil Macon, Adoptions."

He ran from the library, jumped in his car, and headed for the nearest service station. A two-or-three-hour drive to St. Louis might pay worthwhile dividends after all.

Later that afternoon, his knock was answered by a tall, slender woman, mid sixties Jackson surmised. The residue of stateliness was present, but she had clearly seen difficult times as the hard lines in her face and the hollowness of her deep black eyes revealed. She silently invited him into a sparsely furnished office, rundown and hardly tidy. The building itself was old, and most of the other offices—real estate agencies, insurance brokers—clearly did not occupy upper-echelon positions in their respective fields.

"I'm looking for Sybil Macon," Jackson began.

"You've found her," said the woman in a raspy voice. "You interested in adopting?"

"No," said Jackson, "I'm not even married. I'm curious about an adoption you arranged some years back."

"I can't divulge private information from my files—you ought to know that."

"This is a matter of some consequence. Besides, I'm here with the consent of those involved."

"It's always of some 'consequence'!" she said with irony. "What case was it anyway?"

"The Maxwells . . . over in Quincy. They adopted a son. Would have been thirty-one years ago."

"Thirty-one years! Sonny! What kind of files do you think I keep, anyway?" she said with a hearty laugh.

"I merely assumed—"

"Look," she said, "I've moved around a lot in the last thirty years. The state's seen to that . . . shut me down twice . . . had my files confiscated a time or two. I managed to get most of my records back and to stay on my feet. But I doubt I have much left from the old days."

"But is there some possibility?" insisted Jackson. "It's really of some gravity. I could pay you for your time—and for the information."

She laughed.

"Maxwell, huh?" she said, then fell to thinking, "I remember them—farm couple, no money."

Jackson nodded expectantly.

"They were a nice man and woman—got them a son."

"There was a fellow named Bruce involved too," Jackson said—gambling.

"Yes—Bruce came to me with the child . . . his boss's nephew's little misbegot . . . got into trouble . . . everything had to be kept very hush-hush. Well-known names were involved."

Probing deeper, Jackson asked, "This Bruce contacted you initially?"

"Yes—he'd heard I was in a position to make discreet arrangements."

"But you never knew anything about the child's background?"

"I suppose there were other names on the documents Bruce and I drew up. After all, Bruce himself was just a go-between, not the custodian of the child himself. But I can recall nothing about anyone but him. That Bruce was the sort that sticks in your mind, a strange character. To him the child was just a piece of merchandise to be disposed of."

Jackson winced.

298

"Such a contrast with that Maxwell couple. You should have seen the joy on their faces."

I have, Jackson thought silently.

"Do you think you might be able to look for those records?" asked Jackson.

"I really doubt I have anything," insisted Sybil, "but I'll look—when I get the chance. Can't today—probably in storage someplace. Call me in a few days."

"OK," said Jackson, disappointed. "But be sure to look. I will definitely be calling."

"Say," said Sybil, thoughtfully eyeing Jackson for the first time, "that child would probably have been about your age by now . . ."

"Probably just about," said Jackson and turned to leave. "Thank you very much. I'll be in touch."

She watched him go, then sat down quietly and looked around her cluttered but empty office. *I really should clean this place up,* she thought.

71

Jackson headed for the interstate. He'd drive directly back to Chicago instead of stopping by Quincy. He'd rather not talk to his folks again for a while. They needed a chance to accustom themselves to his resolve, and he needed more information. *If Sybil finds the papers,* he thought . . .

But no use speculating. In any case he doubted there were any means to track down the shadowy character, Bruce.

But there was plenty to think about. It was time to see Jacob Michaels again. It had only been two days since he'd left Washington . . . seemed like two weeks! Somehow he had to divulge to Michaels what Jaeger had planned. From what Sydney had said—and from what he'd gathered on his own—Michaels himself knew very little and was but a pawn—granted, a significant pawn!—in

Jaeger's daring gambit to thrust himself into a position of great power.

If Michaels chose to throw in with them, that was his business. But he had to be told. Jackson had an obligation, on the basis of decency and honesty, to inform him. Even though the information he possessed had been gained surreptitiously, Michaels nevertheless had a right to know of the forces swirling around within the inner circles of his organization.

Since his second talk with Sydney, Jackson had struggled with what to do. He'd hardly slept a continuous hour for the last two nights. How far did his responsibility for confidentiality go? If he held a secret against Jaeger, to what extent did he owe Jaeger anything insofar as how he put that knowledge to use?

Yet to say nothing would be irresponsible—even untruthful toward Michaels.

There could be no other reasonable course of action but to tell him.

He'd do so tomorrow evening. It would be best to go to his home. He couldn't risk an office meeting with Jaeger listening in. He'd call Diana, stress the importance of seeing her father, and ask her to find out when he'd be home . . . without visitors.

PART 7

Henry Michaels

72

The late March sun shone through the kitchen window. It was nice, Elizabeth thought, when the days began to lengthen once again. The evenings were so long and dreary during the winter.

She stirred the soup on the stove, finished setting the table, and set some rolls from the freezer into the microwave to warm.

"Anything I can do, Mother?" asked Diana cheerfully as she walked into the room and planted a kiss on Elizabeth's cheek.

"You could mix up some orange juice. Then I think we'll be about ready. When did you tell him to be here?"

"Six—he'll be on time, you can count on it."

Just before the hour a car approached on the gravel driveway. A few minutes later the doorbell sounded. Diana bounded up and opened it quickly. There stood Jackson. She took his hand and led him into the kitchen. She was wearing a skirt and peasant blouse and appeared at home in the feminine attire.

"Mother," she said, "this is Jackson Maxwell."

"Mr. Maxwell," she said, "I'm glad you could join us for dinner. I've heard so much about you."

"I appreciate the invitation," he replied. "When I called Diana yesterday to ask about speaking with your husband, I had no idea this would be the result."

"Sit down, Jackson," said Diana, "we're all ready."

"Thank you—will your father be here too?"

"He'll be late this evening," said Elizabeth. "He often is. Usually I wait and have dinner with him while Diana fends for herself. But today—with such a special guest—I wanted to be part of it. Please, Jackson, have some soup."

"I'm glad to have the opportunity to meet you. Diana's told me a lot about you—both of you."

A good deal of lighthearted dinner talk followed and continued into the living room until seven-thirty, when another car rolled up and stopped.

"There's Jacob now," said Elizabeth rising.

She greeted him at the door. "We have a visitor, Jacob," she said. "I believe you already know Mr. Maxwell."

"Why, yes—Maxwell, nice to see you again," said Jacob, somewhat taken by surprise.

"Thank you, sir," said Jackson. "I'd actually come to see you, but your wife and daughter have been kind enough to feed and entertain me."

"You wanted to see me?" said Jacob, puzzled.

"Yes," replied Jackson. "I have something I believe is rather important—if not urgent—to discuss with you. But of course I wouldn't want to upset you before dinner."

"Sounds serious," said Michaels. "I had a sandwich late in the afternoon. I'm not really hungry. Let's get right to it, Maxwell, shall we?"

Jacob led the young reporter into the den. Though their last meeting had done much to dissolve the previous walls between them, Jackson nevertheless felt some of the old apprehension in his stomach as the door closed behind them. Was he imagining it, or did he detect annoyance in Michaels's countenance at his presumption in calling at home?

It had been nearly a week since Michaels had met and prayed with Robert Means, and his resolve to see things in a new light had temporarily taken a backseat again to the press of business concerns. Knowing this, and feeling a little guilty from it, served to put Michaels slightly on edge.

"I wondered, sir," said Jackson, "whether you might not want to have your wife present . . and maybe Diana too. What I say may be the sort of thing you as a family would want to discuss."

"Jackson!" said Michaels. "You're getting more evasive all the time. Now you want to drag my family into it. What's it all about?"

"Hamilton Jaeger, Mr. Michaels."

"What about him!" said Jacob, temper and headache beginning to get the better of him. It didn't help that he'd been arguing with Jaeger all afternoon and was feeling beaten down by his assistant already.

"Well, that's the point where I thought you might like your wife present. It's not going to be pleasant, and it just seems . . . well, I thought you'd want her in on it with you."

"Confound you, man!" exploded Michaels. "Out with it or I'll throw you from the house. How dare you come here and presume to tell me how I should run my family—or my organization! What business is it of yours what my wife and I discuss, or what my assistant Mr. Jaeger does?" Even as he spoke, Michaels regretted his words.

"I'm sorry," said Jackson, disturbed at the turn things seemed to be taking. Michaels had apparently all but forgotten their previous talk. He'd confided in him then. But today, his mood was drastically altered. Jackson began to think his coming had been a mistake. "It's just that I—"

"What gives you the right to intrude upon my affairs?"

Summoning his courage in one final attempt, Jackson said, "The truth gives me the right, sir."

"The truth! I'll have none of your impudent reporter's rhetoric!"

"I'm sorry," said Jackson, "I intended none. I'm trying to conduct myself with integrity, to do right by you, to do for you as I would hope you would do for me under similar circumstances."

"We'll have to send out for a halo for my saintly friend here," said Jacob sarcastically.

Jackson said nothing, and Jacob—embarrassed by his remark—began to cool.

After a moment's silence, Jackson, not to be deterred from his goal, began, "I have come upon very damaging information concerning Mr. Jaeger. He has plans, sir, of which I am fairly certain you are not aware. Plans which involve you—but of which you may not approve."

"And where did you learn his plans?" asked Jacob coolly.

"I'm not at liberty to disclose that just now. Let me simply say that I did learn of them from a source I consider most reliable."

"Yes, yes—no doubt," said Michaels. "And you think I know nothing of these plans, is that it?"

"I cannot speak for what you know or do not know. I only felt it my duty to warn you."

A harsh reply rushed to Jacob's lips, but he thought better of it, checked his tongue, and said nothing for the moment.

"Well, go on . . . go on!" he said finally.

"There are two areas actually," continued Jackson, "where Mr. Jaeger has rather far-reaching designs. In both cases he intends to use and build upon your reputation to further his own schemes. I have no doubt that you have been duped by him like everyone else. I can't for a moment bring myself to believe that you would knowingly have a hand in this . . ."

Jacob remained silent and simply stared absently out the window.

". . . the first of these concerns is the Greenville property. I know you both thought I was up to some conniving with the investigation for the article I wrote. But I can assure you I had nothing in mind whatsoever. But the more I scouted about the more I was intrigued by Jaeger's intense reaction. And Greenville seemed to be the center of it. I have recently learned that what he intends there is more than simply a center for Christian activity, as the public is being told, with some minor cooperation between various ministries. He, in fact, intends nothing short of a massive takeover of other Christian organizations with himself occupying the focal position of power and with you as a figurehead, symbolic leader. As I understand it, there are currently five organizations that have signed merger papers with ETW. But they have no idea of the extent to which they've actually relegated both their finances and their power structure over to Jaeger. They have essentially given away their right to govern themselves."

"I know all about the Greenville plans and these five ministries," said Jacob. "In fact, I'm making a public announcement to that effect in a few days. I'm afraid you're overexaggerating certain elements of it."

"No, sir," replied Jackson, "I'm not. I'm afraid it's you who does not understand the implications of what Jaeger has done. He has selectively fed you—and the others involved—only bits of the truth, just enough to keep you coming along with him. For instance, are you aware of his personal purchase of an eighty-acre ranch which borders the Greenville property?"

Jacob turned quickly around. "No, I wasn't aware of that," he said with growing interest.

"I've been there," said Jackson, "seen the property, spoken to the owners and the agent. I can assure you it's true. Which brings me to the other part of this news—what Jaeger intends to use this ranch for."

"Go on," said Jacob.

"He visualizes this as his 'command post.' That phrase has even been used to describe it. From there he'll control the activities of the massive conglomerate that will soon be under his dominion. And from that communications center he intends—"

Jackson hesitated. As he formulated the words he realized how incredible they must sound.

"I'm listening," said Jacob, now fully attentive.

"—he intends, sir, to launch a national presidential campaign behind a Jacob Michaels candidacy employing all the facilities of the largest Christian enterprise ever assembled. He already has contacts in Washington putting it together, I was there . . . it was in Washington I learned of this."

Jacob sunk into his chair and sat stunned.

Neither man spoke.

After a few minutes Jacob rose, left the room without a word. Jackson stood up, walked around the room, glanced at the volumes of books in the cases, looked out the window into the nicely trimmed backyard.

Within two minutes, Jacob returned carrying two glasses of juice, handed one to Jackson, and sat down once more. Still no word had been spoken.

At last Jacob said quietly, "It's not beyond Hamilton. He's clever enough to make it happen. What puzzles me is that he bothers with me at all. Why doesn't he just run for office himself?"

His voice had lost its cutting edge and was soft and sober. The fire had been drained from him.

"He'd never get far on his own" said Jackson. "Don't you see? You're his reason for being. Without you he's nothing. You are the man the people love. You are the face, the smile, the message. He perceives of himself as the force behind the face—"

"And he's not far wrong, is he?"

"I suppose not," said Jackson. "He knows that in most organizations it's those behind the scenes who generate the stuff of true influence. Jaeger is hungry for power, not necessarily the recognition of the public."

There was another silence.

"You're right . . . I see it in him," said Jacob slowly. Then his thoughts trailed off. "Ah, Jackson," he said at length, "you've dealt me a severe blow."

"I regret I had to be the one—"

"Quite all right. I'm glad to know. I appreciate your forthrightness . . . that you care enough about—about me to, well . . . to go out on a limb like this."

He paused, then looked Jackson full in the face. "And I must apologize for my insensitive words a few minutes ago," he said in a soft and sincere tone. "I behaved badly. Please forgive me."

"Think no more about it, sir," replied Jackson.

"Bob warned me," he went on, smiling to himself, "that all sorts of things would assail me the moment I tried to initiate changes in my life. He was sure right—here I find my own temper the first thing to come against me!"

"Bob?" asked Jackson, wondering if he meant Means.

"That's another story," replied Jacob. "One I hope I have the chance to tell you about one day. But for now, let me simply reiterate my apology, and my appreciation for your tenacity. It's cost you your job, your reputation temporarily. I tell you, it took guts to do what you did. You wouldn't be put off—by me, by Hamilton, by anyone."

"These are hard times for us all, Mr. Michaels," said Jackson. "The price I've had to pay might not compare with what's still ahead for you."

"You're right. What am I to do now? This is a very awkward situation indeed, considering that so much is already in the works. To withdraw now . . . well, there are many things to be thought about. One thing we need to do, at the soonest possible opportunity, is you and I both need to get together with my friend Bob. He'll be able to help us clarify what's to be done, I'm sure."

"If I might suggest again, sir—"

"Yes, my wife—you're right, Jackson, Elizabeth should be here, and Diana . . . I should have listened to you in the first place."

"I can tell them to come in," said Jackson. "I can let myself out." He rose to go.

"Jackson—" said Jacob. "Please . . . don't go—just yet. We need . . . well, I'd like you to stay—if you can."

"Of course, if I can be of any help," said Jackson. "Only, I didn't want to intrude."

"Think nothing of it, my boy. You've risked a great deal for this family. You're part of us now. I'd like you to help us try—somehow—to arrive at some idea of where we should go."

Jackson nodded and sat back down. Jacob rose, left the room, and soon returned with Elizabeth and Diana close behind.

"Elizabeth," Jacob began, "would you mind taking the phone off the hook? We have—that is . . . the two of us—we have something to tell you about, and I don't want us to be interrupted."

It was more than two hours later before anyone left the den.

73

Diana followed Jackson slowly outside to his car. Neither said a word.

When they reached the car she said, "Jackson, thank you—for caring about our family."

He was quiet a moment, then said, "I'm too emotionally drained to respond. I had no idea how your father would take it. For all I knew, he'd throw me out on my ear. It was hard to make myself come here like this."

"I'm glad you did. You've always been kind and thoughtful to me," she said. "But tonight I saw something different in you. There seemed to be a special feeling in your heart for, well—for all of us, for the whole family. The way you spoke to Mother, the respect I could sense toward my father, even in light of these hard things that are surrounding him . . . anyway, thank you."

Jackson smiled and nodded. Diana reached in the open car window, gave his arm a squeeze, turned, and ran back into the house.

Jackson drove back to his apartment slowly. Pervading his thoughts was the face of Jacob Michaels. It was, he discovered, a commanding face . . . forceful . . . a face that evoked a certain approbation and awe. He was a charismatic man, a man of stature who by nature towered over his peers. Was he presidential timber? He was certainly made of the stuff of heroes and mighty men of valor.

Jackson's initial response to the man so many months ago had been to consider all that a facade—a superficial gloss hiding the deeper reality of emptiness.

Now he wasn't so sure. The man seemed to be slowly changing, deepening. Notwithstanding his initial irritation and outburst, even his apology had seemed to flow out of some new reserve of personal fortitude and growth. The man, he realized, was gradually gaining his respect.

He'd been with Jacob Michaels through some pretty difficult times. He could now see that he was a man altogether different in every way from his antagonist, Hamilton Jaeger. He had displayed a momentary temper to be sure. And he was hardly skilled in dealing with the sort of stresses that were crashing in upon him now. Yet he had apologized and then listened openly and with a great sincerity. Jackson was coming to respect what he saw—that Jacob Michaels could listen when confronted, could respond to crises in a deeper way than scrambling to save his own skin.

Jackson sensed in him a sincere desire to do what was right. His spiritual conditioning may have been a little rusty. But through the last difficult months a dawning sensitivity seemed gradually coming to the fore. And in noticing it, Jackson discovered his own attitude softening as well. No longer was Michaels the enemy to be stalked but a responsive man with the need to be understood with compassion.

Jacob had been victimized by the ever-present danger of depersonalizing a public figure. The masses put such men on pedestals to idolize and deify them; the press to knock them down. But Jackson was coming to see that Jacob Michaels was simply a man—a man with all the universal human foibles and temptations, yet at the same time a man with unique strength of character.

As the image of Jacob Michaels loomed so dominant in his vision, Jackson found himself drawn toward him . . . into what sort of bond he could not have told.

74

In the absence of success with the telephone directory he had driven to the only two companies located in Janesville that seemed they could have anything to do with computers. The first, Wisconsin Electronic Equipment, had never heard of Jerome Bullinger. However, his persistence finally paid off in the personnel office of Technic, Ltd. Yes, the receptionist said, Mr. Bullinger worked for them as a computer technician. Fifteen minutes and a short tour of the plant later, and Jackson had at last met the elusive Jerome Bullinger and had arranged to meet him after work.

His first impression was different than expected. Bullinger hardly seemed as suspicious as he'd anticipated. He hoped the exterior would thaw even more over dinner.

"So how did you come to work for Hamilton Jaeger?" Jackson asked after they had ordered.

"He was looking for an assistant," said Bullinger, "someone to share the work load."

"Surely he had a full staff and complement of ETW secretaries to delegate to?"

"I think he hired me with more in mind than what they could have provided. He saw me as possibly his protégé, someone he could groom to take over in his position, I don't know . . . Hamilton was a different sort of guy."

"He confided in you heavily?" suggested Jackson.

"Too heavily."

"How so?"

"It went to my head. I realized I could move up fast, and I got too ambitious. I started playing the climb-the-ladder-at-any-cost game. And it ultimately cost me my job."

"Jaeger didn't want to share the power?"

"He soon knew he'd taken me too much into his confidence. I've thought about it a lot. It was uncharacteristic of him to share at all, so why did he with me? I still don't know actually. Must've just been the time I came along. He'd talk sometimes, reminisce, forget I was even there. That's how the thing about Michaels's affair slipped out. He never intended me to know."

"Michaels's affair?"

"I thought you knew . . . when he was in college—years ago. Before Elizabeth."

"That's explosive stuff. No wonder he didn't want that getting around."

"More perilous to Michaels than you may think. There was a child, then a full-scale cover-up engineered by Hamilton. Of course he worked for Henry's brother, Lance, then. It was a mess. And once he realized I knew too much, my days were numbered instantly."

Jackson's mind was spinning.

"But I was hungry for a piece of the pie." Bullinger went on, "I tried to use the knowledge he'd unwittingly given me as leverage. I should have known better, of course. Hamilton was the king of such machinations. I never had a snowball's chance in Palm Springs in a power game with him. He sent me packing quicker than you can snap your fingers."

Recovering himself gradually, Jackson asked, "He fired you?"

"It wasn't exactly that way," replied Bullinger. "I was foolish. I'd also inadvertently discovered his middle name. Something about that name made him crazy. He refused to let anyone use it to his face after Lance died—or so I'd heard. Lance had brought him into the ETW organization, and Hamilton learned much of his ruthlessness from him I gather. Lance had Hamilton do the dirty work—like when Jacob got mixed up with that girl. He looked up to Lance—he was a young and impressionable cadet back then. Lance had been his mentor, set him on track. Lance's death shattered Hamilton—left him emotionally stranded. After that, he went only by Hamilton, and then ultimately took over for Jacob in much the same way Lance had for Henry.

"One day I had the effrontery to sarcastically call him Bruce. He hit the roof, said no one ever called him that but Lance, and sent me from the room. Along with everything else, that was the last straw. He went to work, looked into my past—got some things on me—although nothing like what I had on him—but things that would make my parents cut me right out of their will if they ever found out. I had plenty on Hamilton—including some hidden discrepencies in ETW funds. But he would have blown the whistle

312

in a second to discredit me and save his own hide. I eventually was worried for my very life. So I quit and split, covering my tracks as best I could. I knew if he wanted to he could have made my life miserable for years to come."

Jackson's head was still reeling with the onslaught of so many incredible facts.

"You make ETW sound like a corrupt organization, but somehow there it is out in the world accomplishing so much good."

"No," said Jerome, "I would hardly say the organization is corrupt by any means. Maybe in this case a few bad apples *don't* spoil the barrel. Lance was greedy, no doubt . . . and Hamilton's the original spoiled apple. But Henry was OK. He was naive . . . never paid that much attention to Lance's schemes and was not close to Jacob in the early years. By the time he came to see things more fully, at least this is what Hamilton said one time, he wanted to make full disclosure about it all. But of course by then it was too late . . . too deeply buried in the past.

"Henry never did know about the pilferage going on. When he started making noise about 'repenting of our sins,' it was all so big, Jacob so respected . . . why, it would literally have taken the whole thing down. So he was humiliatingly shushed up . . . sent off to retirement, and to this day he hardly leaves that house of his. Hamilton made sure things went his way. Jacob never knew how cruelly he treated that old man. Jacob just left so much in Hamilton's hands. Elizabeth never suspected a thing. I suppose as years went by Jacob tended to forget he was blackmailed by Hamilton to keep silent. He never guessed even half of Hamilton's schemes or how he'd shamed Henry—there's a man you should talk to. Henry may be old now, but I couldn't help always having something of respect for him. He'd be able to tell you some things."

"You think he'd talk?"

"Probably not. He went into his shell and has never spoken a word to anyone. The only way you'll get him to open up is to talk about other things—the early days of his ministry. That's the track I'd pursue at least."

"I must say," said Jackson, "I was certain Jaeger had a few kinks in his nature, but I never imagined it was this involved."

"From what you told me at the plant, I assumed you to be knowledgeable about this. I thought that's why we were discussing it."

"I had some sketchy pieces here and there."

"I've probably put my own neck back in the noose by giving you all this."

"Don't worry, you're safe. None of this will get back to Jaeger."

"You did agree to strict confidentiality?" said Bullinger. "I may have come to my senses somewhat in the last couple years about my foolish notions back then. But I've still got a good job to protect and a past I don't want looked into. Hamilton could have my head on a platter in a moment's notice."

"Yes . . ." said Jackson, distracted again as the circle of new developments spun through his brain, ". . . certainly. Not a word. No one even knows I'm here. Besides, I wouldn't worry. You were rather difficult to find. Jaeger couldn't get to you if he tried."

"I don't want to take any chances," said Bullinger.

75

The drive home was only a couple of hours. But it was late, and Jackson chose to stop en route. About nine-thirty he pulled off the freeway and into the Colony Inn, which advertised cheap rooms and whose vacancy sign was still visible from the highway. He had to have time to reassess the new information he'd been bombarded with. He had thought he'd had inside information to share with Jacob Michaels earlier. Now he *really* possessed the inside scoop on the entire sordid history of ETW and the Michaels family. He had plenty of evidence to oust Jaeger, of that he was certain.

But what to do with the knowledge? he wondered as he lay trying to fall asleep. He felt as though he possessed a secret that was not his to have. After all, what prerogative was it of his to meddle in the internal affairs of ETW? Even if Jaeger deserved to be expelled, what right did he have to intrude? Yet . . .

how could he sit idly by and ignore his conversation with Bullinger?

What was ethically called for? No clear standard of right and wrong was visible—who would it benefit to make a public statement? Certainly there was a time for broadcasting the truth, but wasn't there also a time for concealing it? Knowledge of Jacob's past would wound Elizabeth severely. It could deal a deathblow to their marriage for all he knew.

Why was he—Jackson Maxwell, an uninvolved, unrelated, interfering, reporter—even part of the situation? Did he have a right to butt in? Did obligation or duty play any role in what was expected from him?

And then came the question he had hardly dared to form in his mind . . . the name *Bruce*—was it coincidental . . . could it be . . .

Jackson refused to face the mere suggestion. The emotions it raised were too deep. His innermost self was being turned inside out.

Names and faces tumbled over in his mind . . . confused . . . questioning . . . haunting him . . . leering at him . . .

"Who are you?" they shouted, "Why are you tormenting us? . . . What have you to do with us? . . . Get out, Maxwell . . . get out . . . get out . . . this is not your family, and you have no right to mock us with your questions, your insinuations, your relentless investigations! Get out, Maxwell . . . get out! You have no heritage with us . . . no place in our family . . . no right to be here!"

Then the name kept coming to him, pounding in his brain . . . "Bruce . . . Bruce . . . Bruce!" and with it came the distorted face of Hamilton B. Jaeger staring grimly at him . . . then reaching out with demonic realism and a huge, misshapen hand to clutch his ankle in the dark . . .

Suddenly, Jackson lurched forward! He was sitting—breathing hard. The motel sheet was drenched with cold sweat. He glanced around and was alone in the tasteless room. The clock read 1:23 A.M.

The dream had unnerved him.

One thing was for certain. Two people held the keys that would unlock his own past and reveal the full truth he had been searching for since this episode had begun six months earlier. As soon as possible, he had to speak with Sybil Macon again.

Then he had somehow to arrange an interview with Henry Michaels—whatever it took, whatever kind of story he had to write to get it.

He lay back down and spent the remainder of the night in a fitful sleep.

76

"Miss Macon . . . I'm the man who was in to see you about the Maxwell child—you know, the Maxwells in Quincy?"

"Uh . . . yes . . . ?"

"You were going to look into your files for some information for me?

"Yes . . . I vaguely recall—when did you say you were here?"

"It was three days ago. You were going to try to locate the original papers for me—we were talking about the possibility of learning the identity of the real parents."

"I do remember our conversation now . . . yes, it's coming back."

"I take it then you haven't found the papers yet?"

"No . . . you're right—not yet."

"It's terribly urgent . . . do you suppose you would be able to check into it today? Could I perhaps call you again this afternoon?"

"Doesn't leave me much time."

"It's already been three days . . . and it is imperative. If you could just check your files. If there's nothing there . . . then of course I'll understand it might take you longer."

"Yes . . . well, as long as we're clear on that."

"I am. I'll call you back about three this afternoon."

Jackson hug up the phone in frustration. Sybil Macon did not seem the type into whose hands you could dependably place your fate. She might never get around to looking. The records were more than likely lost anyway, or else misplaced in the jumble of her possessions, boxes, and footlockers.

In the meantime, he'd see about arranging an interview with Henry. He knew he was inaccessible to the public for the most part and his whereabouts was a carefully guarded secret—for personal reasons it was said.

He hoped Diana would be able to help.

For some time, even prior to six months ago, he had toyed with the idea of a feature article on Henry Michaels and his career as an evangelist. Nothing had ever come of it. Maybe now was the time to dust off the idea and have a go at it. Besides, he had to start making a living sometime. A well-done free-lance piece could command a fair price with any of a dozen magazines.

Since his retirement a decade earlier, Henry Michaels had rarely been seen in public. Yet his prominence had never been forgotten, and the aura surrounding him seemed in fact to grow as a result of his semireclusive lifestyle.

Henry had written six books and during the span of his career had lectured and preached on every continent of the globe, had been a sought-after conference speaker, convention personality, and missions board member. His books and tapes were circulating in twenty languages, and he held honorary degrees from a dozen colleges and universities.

Jackson considered that the most suitable approach might be simply to interview Dr. Michaels for an article. If doors opened in any other directions he would pursue them. But he had to lay the groundwork for a relationship first . . . ask questions later.

That afternoon he telephoned Sybil Macon again.

"I found the file," she said.

"And . . . ?" asked Jackson expectantly.

"They're so old . . . and the signatures are mostly unintelligible. I can hardly make them out."

"Please," said Jackson, "do try."

There was a hesitation at the other end of the line. "It looks like . . ." she said slowly, "Bruce has signed here where it says 'parental agent.' But I can hardly tell. It looks like *B* . . . just the letter *B* and then . . . let me see . . . B Garvey . . . or Janes or something. I just can't make it out. It's such a scribbled signature."

"What about any other names?" asked Jackson.

"Well, of course, my name's there . . . and the Maxwells—they're typed in, they didn't sign this document. Then there's a line labeled 'Father' and another 'Mother.' "

"Yes . . . go on!" said Jackson.

"The mother line is blank . . . the father line had an entry . . . but I tell you, I simply can't make it out."

"Please—stop saying you can't read it . . . just tell me what it says!" said Jackson in frustration.

"Young man!" said Sybil growing irritated. "I cannot read these names clearly! How often must I say it? Do you think I'm lying?"

"No, ma'am, I'm sorry," said Jackson.

"And just what is the urgency, may I ask? It's been buried for over thirty years already. I'm doing more than I am supposed to as it is," she said. "Give me one good reason I should be giving you this information."

Jackson was silent a moment, debating. Whatever he said could tip the scales of Sybil Macon's hardened visage either for or against him. He was so close. He couldn't let the information she at this moment held in her hand slip through his grasp.

"I'm the child," Jackson said. "I'm Jackson Maxwell. I'm trying to learn the identity of my blood parents."

"Oh—I see," said Sybil, "I thought as much. Well . . . if anyone has a right to this, I suppose it's you. But, young man . . . Jackson, I still can't help you. About all I can say is that your father's name appears to begin with an *M*. After that . . . I just can't say."

"What about if I drive down there and have a look for myself?" suggested Jackson.

"Better yet," said Sybil, "I'll send you a copy. Give me your mailing address. You should have it tomorrow."

"That'd be wonderful!"

Jackson hung up the phone.

77

The suspense was agony!

Every clue seemed to point in the same direction. Yet the thought was too incredible to believe. And without the confirmation of either the document in Sybil's office or a public declaration by Jaeger, nothing could be certain. And even if it were true, Jaeger would make no acknowledgment to help him. He would stop at nothing to thwart whatever plans Jackson had.

The mail wouldn't arrive until about ten-thirty the following morning. There was nothing to do now but sit tight. He would talk to Diana and try to get a session set up with Henry for the following afternoon. But the turmoil in his brain would have to remain with him through at least one more sleepless night.

And what if—unbelievably!—it turned out to be true?

What then?

Would he . . . *could* he . . . acknowledge his firstborn son without irrevocably damaging his reputation and career? Not to mention what the knowledge would do to Elizabeth and Diana!

Might it not be best to keep it secret? If he was the only one to know, why not keep it that way?

But what of the truth? Did he owe it to anyone—even himself— to bring it out?

It was all empty speculation anyway! Chances were a thousand to one against it! He would simply have to wait for Sybil's letter and put the aftermath out of his mind.

The next morning at 10:36 Jackson heard the mailman's jeep pull up in front of his apartment. Several minutes later he could hear the sounds of mailbox tops slamming shut. He dashed down the stairs and grabbed the contents of his own. Hurrying back up the stairs two at a time he shut the door behind him and frantically sorted through the letters.

There it was!

Postmarked St. Louis, return address stamped on the upper left, Sybil Macon, Adoptions—St. Louis, MO.

319

His fingers quivered as he tore at the envelope, nearly ripping the single sheet inside. His eyes scanned the signatures quickly . . . there it was just as Sybil had described it to him.

But she hadn't known what to look for!

He had inside information that only required confirmation. Yes—there could hardly be a doubt. The "parental agent" signature was scribbled to be sure—practically illegible—resembling the names Sybil had mistakenly suggested. But to Jackson there was no doubt. It was the signature of B. Jaeger!

Frantically he tried to make sense of the name on the line marked "Father." Sybil was right again. It was unreadable. But Jackson hardly needed more. The first initial was a recognizable *J* and as Sybil had said, the last name began with an *M*. All else was a blur except for the last two letters—*ls*.

There was no longer any doubt whatsoever. Jackson had seen the signature before on the bottom of a certificate of appreciation from ETW in Sondra's apartment—signed by the organization's leader.

Jackson dropped the papers on the floor and stood stunned.

How could it be? . . . Yet here was proof positive.

He sat down, stared blankly out the window and remained alone with his thoughts. It was several hours before he came again to himself.

78

He had arranged for Diana to take him to see her grandfather that afternoon. As he drove to the Michaels's home this time, all was changed. He waited for her in the car, hardly prepared to speak to anyone—especially Jacob should he have chanced to be there.

"You're not very talkative today," said Diana as they pulled out of the driveway.

"Sorry," replied Jackson, looking over at her. He gasped as the thought began to form. *She's my*—but he could not bring himself to say it. Then to Diana he added, "I've got a lot on my mind."

"Want to talk?"

"Not now," he said. "When the time is right." He drove on in silence. Meeting with Henry would be difficult too. He had to put himself in a reporter's frame of mind, concentrate on the interview. He had to block out the family situation, the new developments on his personal horizon—at least until there was some natural opening to bring it into the discussion. The timing couldn't have been worse.

They drove to a suburb on the outskirts of Chicago.

At length they arrived in front of a small, old home in the midst of what appeared an odd mix of former farm houses and city-built tract homes.

Diana led the way, and while Jackson waited in the kitchen she disappeared into the house. In about five minutes she returned.

"Grandpa's expecting you," she said. "He's in his study—through there, down the hall to the end, on the left. I'll wait for you in the living room."

Jackson made his way slowly down the corridor and found himself entering a bookcase-lined study with faded furniture and dim lighting. The afternoon sun pierced through the shrubbery in the yard, and a few beams of bright light exploded into the hazy room, revealing the frenzied but silent dance of millions of otherwise undiscernible dust particles. His eyes immediately took in the many books—oh, what a library!—the gangly, old, yellow-green sansevieria plant, the sort that could grow anywhere without much attention, the dusty windowsill, an oddly out of place baseball mitt stashed in a bookcase among a row of books, the pictures—whose faces he couldn't see—on the desk in front of the window, the ancient-model Underwood typewriter.

In the corner, in an antiquated oak rocker, sat Henry Michaels gazing quietly out into the afternoon. He rose and turned the moment he became aware the door had closed and approached to greet the young reporter.

Introductory pleasantries sufficiently exchanged, the elder Michaels resumed his seat and offered his companion a chair.

"Dr. Michaels," began Jackson, "as you may know, I've been doing some writing for my magazine on your son and the ETW organization. I've been hoping to broaden my approach with a possible story from your perspective—a through-the-years look at your walk with the Lord, the growth of ETW, highlights of your life . . . that sort of thing."

"Well, as you know young man, I permit very few interviews. I just don't know about such a story . . . why me?"

"People are interested in you. They're still reading your books as much as ever. Jacob's popularity keeps you fresh in the public mind. They want to know about you, what the really significant moments of life have been for you—what stands above all else."

Dr. Michaels said nothing for a moment.

"What I'd like to concentrate on," continued Jackson, "are those specific things you've done that capture the essence of what really bears fruit. It seems a reflective look at the past thirty or forty years would be the best way to grasp how the Lord is using ETW throughout the world today. You've been a leader in the Christian body for so many years. Your viewpoint is valuable. Yours has been a fruitful and productive life."

There was silence a moment. Dr. Michaels's thoughts seemed to drift away momentarily. The sun's beams into the room more than overpowered the corner lamp's sixty-watt bulb.

"So tell me," Jackson resumed, determined not to be sidetracked, "what do you consider those things in your life that mattered most? What is it you are most proud of as a Christian? What have been the times you feel God has used you most effectively to spread His kingdom?"

A sparkle passed through the eyes of the old man, obviously recollecting some of the memorable moments.

"China was wonderful," he sighed. "There was a week in thirty-four when so many came to the Lord . . . oh, that's a story in itself! And then . . . Ireland in fifty-eight. I was only there five days—teaching at a convention for pastors. My, but didn't we have a time! And of course when we first conceived the concept of ETW . . . we were so young, so full of life and exuberance, so ready to give our all."

His voice trailed off, clearly lagging far behind the reminiscing, yet vigorous, mind.

"I envy you, Dr. Michaels," said Jackson after a pause. "I mean—here you are eighty-two years of age and able to look back on your life and say, much as Paul did, 'I have fought the good fight, I've lived the life God gave me to live. I've made a difference. I haven't squandered my days.' "

He settled back in his mind the thunderous events of the morning, expecting to pull off the interview of the year as the elder statesman Michaels relaxed and began to share intimately.

An unexpected hush descended upon the room.

Neither spoke for several minutes. Dr. Michaels was clearly in deep thought. Jackson could wait. No matter if it took all afternoon—the rest of the day.

Finally the old man sighed deeply. "Yes," he said, almost wearily, "I suppose I may have made a difference in the kingdom. You might be right, I really don't know."

Another long pause.

Jackson sensed the emotion in the room shift. He felt a certain discomfort, yet had no word to offer.

"What matters most . . . ?" the aged saint began, then stopped.

His now soft voice sounded for the first time as old as his thin white hair.

He glanced toward the desk where several pictures stood. "You know my wife died seven years ago?"

He reached for a picture in a dusty wooden eight-by-ten frame. He eyed it for a moment—with noticeable emotion—then passed it to his young companion. It must have been forty-five or more years old—a young Michaels and wife, hand in hand, smiling, accompanied by a youngster—possibly four or five—all walking through a grassy park.

"Sometimes I think my wife mattered more than I knew," he continued as if uninterrupted. "I was so busy, 'serving the Lord,' as we say, that I was away from her far more than I should have been. Don't get me wrong. She was behind my work. It's just that . . . well, we never were really *close,* if you know what I mean. The last years were just too full. Maybe we were close, in a way, but certainly not like we could have been. I hadn't held her hand in years, brought her English toffee—she loved toffee!—really made sacrifices for things that mattered *to her* . . . You know, she always called me Dr. Michaels in public, Henry in private. But not once do I remember her calling me just plain Hank. We didn't have that kind of relationship. There was always a stiffness, a formality, I regret that now. How I wish that I'd accepted fewer speaking engagements, written fewer books, and . . . well, just given her more—of *myself.*"

He looked outside, then resumed as if thinking aloud, "She was from Vermont, the rugged forest country. Our whole marriage she talked about wanting to go spend a weekend there at a little cabin on a lake she remembered from her childhood. We talked about finding that cabin and renting it for a week or two—just the two of us . . . but—the curse of the busy schedule!—we never did. That was something she so wanted to do . . ."

He stopped, sighed deeply, stroked the back of his hand quickly across his eyes, in clear anguish from the memory.

"Things that really matter . . ." he continued. "Ah, what a heart-wrenching subject you've brought up . . . Do you see that house through the trees there? Across the way?"

He pointed, Jackson following his finger through the cloudy window.

"We've been here twenty years, neighbors. A man lived there, would have been seventy-nine now—three years my younger. He died five years ago—heart failure. Died unsaved far as I know . . ."

He paused.

"Can you imagine my grief over that man? I've wept several times since."

Jackson—by now somber, his pencil in his pocket and his notebook closed—swallowed hard. The old man was obviously fighting back the tears once more.

"Do you know I never once—not once!—really made an effort to get to know that man, express an interest in his life. Oh, one time I went through a gospel tract with him, in a shallow sort of way—making my perfunctory 'spiritual' call as a man of God, you know. But I never got 'inside' him . . . I was always too *busy*! That's been the plague of my life. Maybe I have furthered the gospel in some minor way . . . I don't know anymore. What difference have I made in the lives God put next to mine . . . my neighbors . . . my family? Not much that I can see. I was too busy . . . too important . . . too tied up . . . too active. Do you know the only thing my neighbor and I ever did together—I mean really did together!—was repair the fence that stands between our yards after one particularly bad windstorm. That's all . . . it disgraces me!"

He sniffed, then again.

Jackson sensed the grief yet was timid to intrude.

An article seemed altogether unimportant. He could feel a lump rising in his throat, threatening to loose years of pent-up unknown emotions. This was no mere distant compassion he felt for Henry. This was the very thing he had longed for, searched for. Yet now—for the moment—he had to continue to conceal it.

"Young man, would you mind handing me that box of Kleenex over there, by the couch?"

He blew his nose, dabbed his eyes, looked up, and said, "Forgive me. I know this must be awkward for you . . . not at all what you had in mind. I have these spells—more often now—when I really do get to wondering if I've devoted my life to things that, perhaps, didn't matter quite as much as I thought at the time. Down the street there's a family with two retarded children. Moved in about twenty years ago, kept them both at home rather than putting them into an institution. Commendable! They really serve those children. God will reward their diligence and love one day . . . count on it. Scraping by . . . all the money it takes to provide for them without assistance. It puts me to shame. They're Christians . . . we've talked a couple of times. They used to see me on TV every once in a while talking about all my exploits on the mission field . . . overseas . . . conducting crusades. They think I'm a great man—a leader. But do you know I haven't once been in their home—not that they haven't invited me. They have . . . several times. But I was always gone, or just coming back, or just leaving—something like that . . . I've never once even talked to those two wonderful, innocent children. I'm ashamed of myself! They're living the life of Jesus in down-to-earth and practical ways . . . Me? . . . I spent my life gallivanting around the world doing nothing but talking about it!"

A long silence followed.

Jackson had just summoned the determination to rise and leave, realizing now was hardly the time to dredge up further heartache with his own questions about his and Jacob's past, when Henry spoke once more—softly, almost to himself, his voice quavery and tentative.

"And my grandson, Richard—"

At the word a pang shot through Jackson's heart. With great effort he stifled any sound and quickly turned his face away. But Henry was too caught in his own grief to notice.

". . . that's his picture there, next to the one of Mother and Jacob and me."

He choked softly, wiped his eyes again.

He leaned toward the bookcase and moved a small Bible. It fell open where a letter was kept. No envelope . . . folded four times, the creases in the yellowed paper well worn, having been folded and refolded many times.

". . . not walking with the Lord just now. He shared with me some time ago that he doesn't really see what my 'life of service to God'—as he puts it—ever did for him. Said he loved his dad and me . . . just isn't interested in that kind of life for himself."

"I pray for him of course. I keep his first Bible—and this letter. He sent his Bible back to me when he was in college. Thought it might mean something to me, I suppose. At the time—in this same letter—he said he felt closer to me than to his own father."

The voice trailed off. He looked outside again, folded the letter, and replaced the Bible on the shelf, next to the baseball glove.

"Do you know what agony I go through over that? . . . realizing that my own son was so ill prepared to be a father? If it's true what they say about the test of a man's spirituality being his grandchildren . . . then I have failed. Of course, how could Jacob have known how to be a father? . . . I was his example . . . and I wasn't much of a father to him. All I taught him was to chase the empty phantoms of public acclaim. Is it any wonder he's gone following them as I did. I pray every day that he wakes up sooner than I did. But with Bruce poisoning his motives like Lance did mine . . I just don't know."

Here was the opening Jackson had hoped for. Yet it seemed so inappropriate to speak. His throat was dry. He wanted to reach out . . . to comfort . . . to somehow let Henry know that he was aware of the situation perhaps more than he realized, that he—

But no words would come.

"When the scandal happened," Henry went on, by now oblivious to Jackson's presence, "while Jacob was in college, I was so without backbone that I went along with the cover-up. Of course Lance and Bruce had already taken care of things by the time they let me in on it. But when I later came to my senses, they would have none of my let's-make-a-clean-break-of-it talk. And ever since it's broken my heart . . . to realize a lie is at the bottom of this family. We're all victims of money and celebrity pressures. And all the recognition and acclamation is powerless to change that rottenness at the core."

There was silence again. Jackson had to leave. A week earlier it would have been merely awkward. Today, however, he was an intrinsic part of every word. His own heart was being pulled inside out. Still Henry went on.

"You know . . ." he began again, following once more a different train of thought, "by the time young Dicky was born I was waking up. I gave him his first baseball glove—the same one Jacob had used when he was a boy. I gave it to Jacob one Christmas . . . but never played with him much. So when Richard was old enough—trying to make some amends I suppose—I dug it out of the attic. He and I used to play a lot together. Jacob never did with him much though . . . that's why I keep this old mitt . . ."

His hand reached out for it, ". . . as a reminder."

He could go no further.

The interview was finished.

The old mind tried to call into being happier times when a young son and father home for a few days could squeeze in a quick game of catch. "Just a few more tosses, Dad—please!"

"Sorry, son . . . got a meeting tonight. But I'll be back in five days. We'll do it again . . . then."

But now in the quiet of the study forty-five years later, the same father rocked quietly, alone in his thoughts. His vesseled old hand clutched the dried, gritty hunk of leather. A bony finger probed the thumb of the glove where another little hand had long ago scrawled the name J-A-C-O-B.

Sinking back into his chair, he gazed distantly out through the sun-filled window, rocking gently back and forth . . . the baseball glove pressed softly to his breast, a tear falling unnoticed down his ancient cheek.

Jackson rose quietly and left the room.

79

Diana was still sitting in the living room when Jackson walked through and out the door hurriedly. She followed him quickly along the sidewalk and away from the house.

"Jackson . . ." she called after him.

He kept walking without an answer.

She ran up behind him. "Jackson . . . is something wrong—what happened in there?"

She caught him and reached for his arm. He stopped and turned toward her. She saw for the first time that his face was red and his eyes moist.

"Jackson," she asked, "what is it?"

He simply shook his head—then clutched her and held her tightly to him, his body throbbing.

After a moment he released his embrace. They walked a short distance in silence. Then he said, "Diana, I just need to be alone for a few minutes—OK?"

She nodded and turned back toward the house. He walked on alone.

Twenty minutes later Jackson returned. "I'm OK now," he said to her. "I'm sorry. There's something I'm going through."

She said nothing, just nodded.

"I have to talk to your grandfather one more time. Would you mind waiting in the car?"

"No, of course not," she said, with a look of slight confusion as she rose.

When she was gone, Jackson slowly walked down the corridor once more. He entered the room. Henry was just where he had left him. Could either of their emotions survive what was to come?

"Dr. Michaels . . ." he began.

The old man turned around.

"I need just a few more minutes of your time. I know this is difficult for you. But . . . I think you'll understand—when I'm through."

Henry nodded his assent.

Jackson approached him but did not sit down.

With great feeling he began. "As I told you, I've spoken several times with your son. I've done some work investigating ETW, and . . . certain things have come to my attention recently—about the past, concerning Jacob and Jaeger, some of the things you alluded to a few moments ago."

He was rambling, brain muddled.

He took a huge breath, trying to calm his quavery voice and squelch the rising flood in his eyes all at once. "Dr. Michaels," Jackson went on, "I'm an adopted child. My folks live down in Quincy. I've been recently looking into my own background, my history—trying to learn what I can."

Henry perked up slightly. A trace of indistinct perception seemed to cross his face momentarily as he sat forward more intently.

"And certain facts have come to my attention, sir. I've spoken to the agent who handled the adoption—it was arranged privately, for reasons which . . . I think you yourself might also be aware. And . . . as I have looked into this, a certain . . . document, has come to my hands—"

The words faltered, his body nearly drenched with perspiration.

Henry was now standing, leaning toward him, his mind again sharp and attentive, eyes piercing Jackson's face. "Go on, young man . . . go on!"

"—and I have reason to believe," said Jackson, "that as a result of the affair you spoke of . . . that—" He was straining every emotion he presently possessed to continue.

"Yes?"

". . . that . . . well—that Jacob Michaels may be my father."

He collapsed in the chair

Henry bounded to him and knelt at Jackson's side, hands fumbling for Jackson's. "God love you, Jackson," he said, " . . . God love you!"

He was weeping.

Neither spoke for a minute or two. Then Jackson, regaining himself somewhat, said, "Do you think it's possible? . . . I'm thirty-one."

"Even as you were speaking I knew it was so," said Henry. "I can see it in your face . . . suddenly I saw Jacob in you. Yes . . the age is exactly right, and the eyes . . . the eyes . . ."

Jackson looked into the old man's face. Such a contrast with a short time ago. What he saw now were tears of joy streaming down the wrinkled face.

Jackson smiled.

Henry stood, then leaned forward to embrace him and welcome him into the family.

80

The den of the Michaels's home seemed so different this time, thought Jackson. How difficult it had been the last two days to keep silent . . . not to tell Diana . . . to refrain from giving Elizabeth the squeeze he longed to. But he must exercise prudence. All would work itself out in time. For now at least, the knowledge that only he and Henry shared must be carefully guarded.

He glanced over at Henry, calmly awaiting his son's arrival. The news had sparked something in him, brought him to life. No longer sadly consumed by the memory of what might have been, he now seemed exhilarated by what could be. In a mere moment of time, he had suddenly come awake after a long sleep. As the two of them had talked during the past forty-eight hours, trying to arrive at a workable strategy for handling the delicate information in the best possible manner, Henry had demonstrated great vigor and mental keenness. Was his enthusiasm founded on the hope of finally releasing the burden his heart had carried for thirty years and ridding the family of the deceit that had laid hidden so long?

After what seemed an interminable period, Jacob arrived home. His initial surprise at not finding Elizabeth—who was never gone at this hour—was further heightened by finding his father, whom he certainly hadn't expected. Jackson's presence completed the unnerving.

Jacob was progressing toward becoming a true man—indeed, a man of God. But the progress was slow, notwithstanding almost daily meetings with his friend Bob Means. For every battle won over the forces of self that had been so ingrained through his long association with Jaeger, there seemed a corresponding setback when he next returned to the office and the pressures of the organization.

Today he had been in Hamilton's company nearly the entire day, drafting the announcement and subsequent plans regarding the Greenville press conference scheduled with the other leaders for the day after next. He and Bob had prayed concerning many things. However, no leading had yet come which would have indicated a major change of direction for ETW. He could be forgiven his somewhat sour disposition in that his edginess partly resulted from the guilt of the knowledge that he was being led down the primrose path by Jaeger.

Jacob had sporadically experienced feelings for Jackson, even grown somewhat fond of him. He knew he could trust him. Yet there was something about his sharp nature that annoyed his former self. There were times, Jacob thought, when the best policy was to let well enough alone. So though he had believed what Jackson had told him several nights earlier, the inconvenience of the knowledge was insurmountable.

He had almost convinced himself that, even if Hamilton's methods were sometimes . . . well, unscrupulous and . . . yes, even underhanded at times, that he was still working for the overall good of ETW and therefore could possibly be, if not fully pardoned, at least excused his occasionally heightened zeal. He'd have plenty of time to exert his authority over Jaeger more fully later and to bring him back into a subordinate position. For now, maybe it would be best to go along, let Greenville evolve as it appeared to be doing, and just watch Hamilton a bit more closely.

His uneasiness stemmed from his own personal discomfort with such a plan. Yet he had all but assured himself this was the only way. Means had not pushed him toward any change. But his prayers were having their effect in the agitation of his friend's heart and the awakening of his conscience. Still, the soul of Jacob Michaels fought against the inevitable rebirth that was welling up inside him.

And tonight, to cap off what had been a dreadful day, he had a splitting headache besides.

Then here was the scoundrel again . . . with his father no less! What could the two of them want?

"Maxwell," he said taking the initiative, "what is the meaning of this? Am I to be greeted with meetings and messengers nightly when I arrive home?"

"I'm sorry, Mr.—sir," said Jackson, choking down the feelings that seemed determined to overpower him. He had not seen Jacob since learning the news. "I'm afraid—again, like last time—that it could not be helped."

"*What* couldn't be helped?" cried Jacob, quickly expending

what limited patience he had in reserve. "More urgent *news* for me, I suppose," he said bitterly.

"Walk gently, Jacob," said his father. "This young man is a man of honor and will do you no ill. But neither will he be put off—nor will I. We are here with something to say—and you will hear us out. It would be so much easier on you to do so with a calm spirit and open heart."

Jacob said nothing, just sighed and turned away, resigning himself to the inevitable. He hardly paused to take note of the new-found determination in his father's voice. The sooner he got it over and these two out of the house, the sooner he could have an Excedrin and lie down. The day had already been several hours too long.

"I'm sorry always to be the one bearing uncomfortable news," said Jackson.

"Why must you then?" said Jacob sharply.

"As I've said before, sir, the truth often demands to be told."

"Your truth is anything but pleasant."

"More unpleasant than even you think. Nevertheless, your father and I . . . we feel this is something the three of us need to sit down and discuss . . . together—as a family."

"Once again, you presume to tell me how to run my family's affairs!"

"I simply hoped we could discuss this calmly. I regret having found you in such a mood. But from the last time we talked I assumed you would perhaps be more open, seeing as how I have not misled you in the past."

"You assume a great deal, Mr. Maxwell!" shouted Jacob.

For all his angry outbursts, Jacob was in reality much closer to being able to willfully yield himself to God's will than he had ever been. To open oneself to God in a humble way requires a shattering of self that many never come within miles of. Jacob, however, was near the breaking point, as his uncharacteristic outbursts witnessed. The moment was nearly at hand, and God would have His way with him yet, though the inner tempests would continue to sputter even as the old life that fueled them died.

"Jacob!" admonished Henry sternly. "You are making an idiot of yourself. This young man bears you no malice. He comes with nothing but goodwill in his heart. He loves you! I can attest to it!"

"Loves me! How could he love me—he hardly knows me . . . nor I him!"

"Jacob! Sit down!" boomed the old man. "Say nothing, Jacob! . . . Don't you understand what we are trying to do is serious? Can't you tell? Look in his eyes . . . Don't you see it? Hasn't his age . . . his bearing, struck you as coincidental? . . Do you not yet understand? This young man here . . . this man is your son!"

Jacob rocked slightly. His hand groped for a chair, found one, and he slumped back. After a moment, he looked up at his father. Then his eyes sought Jackson, standing stock-still on the other side of the room. Then he glanced back at his own father again.

". . . my own grandson," added Henry, eyes now clouding with tears.

It was the first time he had used the word, and it brought the tears afresh to Jackson's eyes. He walked over and gently took his hand and eased him into a chair. The exertion had worn him out.

The relation already apparent between grandfather and grandson moved Jacob. The fight, the hostility, the resistance at last was subdued. He sat a broken man.

"You are certain?" he asked softly, after some moments which had been broken only by occasional sniffling in the quiet room.

Jackson produced from his pocket the paper he had received from Sybil Macon, walked over, and handed it to his father.

Jacob glanced at it briefly, then handed it back.

Jackson eyed him intently, searching his face for any sign. Would he welcome or disown him? His illegitimate position was not one that would be greeted with joy by most, especially by a public figure whose family could be disgraced, not to mention career and wealth toppled in a moment if the news came out.

At last Jacob stood, awkwardly, took two steps forward, and extended his hand to Jackson. He took it, looked into Jacob's face, and shook it firmly.

When they had each sat back down, Henry said, "Now we have to decide what is to be done."

"Who knows of this turn of events?"

"Only the three of us in this room," said Henry, "unless you count Bruce—Hamilton, that is—who knows only what went on years ago, but has no idea of Jackson's part in it."

"The women?" asked Jacob, "Elizabeth . . . Diana?"

"They know nothing," said Jackson.

"The woman—God forgive me, I can't even remember her name! Is she . . . that is, has she been located . . . is she involved—"

"No one knows anything about her, her whereabouts . . . anything. No attempt has been made to find her," said Henry. "We have come to you first."

Jacob sat silent. "You do realize," he said at length, "what public knowledge of this would mean?"

"I think we have some idea," said Jackson. "That's why we have said nothing and intend to do nothing except as a unit. We have to do what is best for all concerned, for you . . . for the organization . . . and especially for Elizabeth and Diana."

"Yes . . . you're right," said Jacob, softening toward Jackson, whom he could see was sensitively disposed and out for no personal gain.

"I don't want anyone hurt," said Jackson continuing. "For my part I could live with keeping it a secret indefinitely—"

"For my part," said Henry, "I can see no alternatives other than a full disclosure. For too long we've been living a lie. Are there degrees of lying? I don't think so. A lie is a lie. We've been authorizing a public falsehood, even if endorsing it with our silence. I know it would have implications . . . hurt Elizabeth temporarily. But no hurt is worth continuing a cover-up. We have a responsibility to let the light into this family—this ministry. We have a responsibility to ourselves and to the rest of the Christian body. We *have* to expose the truth . . . in humility!"

"I just thought it would never come up again," muttered Jacob half-inaudibly. "I'd nearly convinced myself it was just a dream . . . that it never happened in the first place."

"Lies always find us out," said Henry. "Jacob, the Lord placed us in positions of high responsibility. But we are only men. We trusted too heavily in ourselves . . . and in those around us. I trusted too much in Lance, even though I knew he was not always seeking the honorable way to do things. When he hired Bruce, I knew it was a perilous alliance. I could see it in his eyes from the beginning. But I said nothing. I stood by and did not attempt to stop them. But there comes a time, my son, when we must place principle above personal interests. I realize you have much to lose—

more than I do surely at this point. Nevertheless, we are God's men. We must stand for His truths. There is a standard to uphold. It is not, in the final analysis, even Lance and Bruce we must blame or accuse. It is ourselves, Jacob. We have sinned. We are weak! It was our responsibility to watch over those under us. We were the men in high places. We were the men God raised up the pinnacles of power to do His work. In our failing we take many with us. That's why we must submit to His humbling, so that the Lord may raise us up again . . . not to do His great world-renowned works . . . but simply to be His men and to demonstrate His character."

It had been a moving speech. The old warrior was now fully aroused to meet the coming challenges. Jackson and Jacob sat reflecting, each in his own way considering what Henry's words meant for them.

81

The following afternoon, in the same room, the trio of three generations was once more seated together. Diana and Elizabeth were also present. Henry and Jacob had previously—father and son together—determined that, painful though it would be, they should be told.

Jacob recounted the affair, breaking down twice, and confessed his remorse. Elizabeth—justifiably in tears—was openhearted toward him, as was Diana. Neither had seen Jacob shed tears in his life, and his doing so in their presence brought out the best in them, and in him. The compassion of all was clearly evident.

When the tearful session was over, Jackson rose, walked to his father sitting with hands covering his face, knelt down beside him, and placed his hands gently on his knee. Jacob's hand reached out and clasped Jackson's. Then Elizabeth rose, crying, followed by each of the others, and went to the spot where she could embrace them both in turn.

When the tears had dried, Jackson caught Diana's eye and motioned to her with his head. She followed him through the kitchen and outside.

They walked for a few moments in silence.

"Strangers no longer," said Jackson at last.

Diana laughed. "No identity doubts now," she said. She stopped and turned toward him. "Jackson," she said, "you have become very special to me . . . now even more so. I can't think of anyone I'd be more proud to be a sister to."

"Thank you," said Jackson, "I'll try to be a good brother to you."

They walked back into the house.

Beyond that moment, the only consensus agreed upon by the men of the family was that Hamilton must be removed from his position of what had grown to be near limitless power. It would be a gamble to divulge what they knew; there was no foreseeing how he might twist it toward his own ends. But even to Jacob, it was now plain that Jaeger's motives were rooted in self.

After the emotional session had ended, Jacob telephoned Hamilton and requested his presence at the Michaels's home—as soon as possible.

He arrived thirty minutes later, felt the vibrations in the room, saw the red eyes, sensed the drama, and immediately suspected the gathering clouds of imminent catastrophe.

"Hamilton," said Jacob firmly, taking the upper hand, "this is a family gathering to discuss the future of ETW, my own personal prospects . . . and yours. Certain facts have come to light recently that bear heavily on our outlook in all these areas. I will not bore you with the details. Suffice it to say that I am familiar with the substance of your clandestine meeting with Senator Montgomery in Washington last week and of your political aspirations on my behalf. I am aware of the basic gist of the legal documents you have had drawn up for your use in the Greenville merger deals, as well as the position—with all its implications—you have all along intended to occupy in the new order. Because of these areas where you have far exceeded your bounds and have kept even me in the dark concerning your activities, I—and the rest of the family here—I have been drawn to the inescapable conclusion that your presence in ETW is no longer serving the vision my father and I have always intended. Therefore it is our . . . it is *my* decision, to request your immediate resignation."

Hamilton shifted his weight in his chair but retained his composure.

"I take it, Jacob," he said, "that you've enlarged your family to include this . . ." he glanced at Jackson with a sneer, "this . . . reporter."

"That remains my concern, Hamilton," said Jacob.

"I don't know what he has been telling you, Jacob, or why you would suddenly value the word of a self-seeking and slanderous writer above the word of a trusted servant who has been with ETW for thirty years, but—"

"I fear the slander is on your side, Hamilton," interrupted Jacob. "I have come to know Mr.—er—Mr. Maxwell rather well in recent weeks, and I have nothing but respect for his integrity."

"Oh, no doubt . . no doubt!" said Hamilton with derision in his tone. "But, Jacob, I hardly need remind you that you alone do not have the power to fire me . . . if that is what this little inquisition is about. That is a matter for the board of directors to decide, and I have no intention of submitting a resignation, not now when my presence is all the more required."

"If you're referring to the press conference tomorrow and the acquisitions and mergers in Greenville—"

"Which are all signed, sealed, and delivered," interjected Hamilton with flouted confidence. "There is simply no way I could leave now, even if I wanted to. You need me, Jacob . . . now more than ever."

"I've already taken the liberty of canceling the press conference, Hamilton," said Jacob sharply.

"How dare you—without my being consulted!" shouted Hamilton.

"How dare I! Who's in charge here, Hamilton—you or me?"

"Of Greenville, sir," said Hamilton with unbridled contempt, "I'm afraid it is I who am presently in charge."

"Greenville has been put on temporary suspension, Hamilton," said Jacob, "as well as your political maneuvering. Everything's on hold right now. I'm backing off to reassess the priorities of ETW, which I shall be doing with my family alone!"

"You can't!" said Hamilton, the tide of his temper steadily rising. "I can see this fine little conspiracy now. But I warn you, Jacob, if you try to throw me out, I'll bring you down with me. Besides, I have the board on my side."

"Not when they know what we know about you," said Henry, speaking now for the first time. "You've given us all we need through the years, Mr. Hamilton Bruce Jaeger. I may have cowed under to my brother Lance, and then to you—back then. But no more!"

"You feeble old man," said Hamilton with disdain. "You never had any backbone. Lance and I *had* to take charge. There was a mission to fulfill . . . a sense of destiny you never had the guts to see. We had to do it!"

"Hamilton!" shouted Jacob enraged. "Do you dare speak so disparagingly to my father! . . . Get out! Either you resign or I'll have you publicly humiliated and fired!"

"Jacob," said Hamilton, his voice cold as steel, "I mean business. If you pursue this, I'll sing my song of your early college days. Your career is in my hands . . . remember?" He shot a cruel glance toward Elizabeth, then back to Jacob, as if in warning.

"Your blackmail worked back then, Hamilton. But no more! Don't you understand yet? It's over. They all know—Elizabeth, Diana . . . they know it all. The secret's out! You have no more hold over me."

"But the public doesn't know," said Hamilton, grasping at the last thread of his treacherous influence. "And when they know, it's all over for the influential Jacob Michaels. The mighty man will have fallen!"

"That's a chance I'll have to take," said Jacob calmly.

"Hamilton," said Henry, "you forget your own practices some years ago."

"I've done nothing more than what Jacob has done," he replied in the heat of wrath. "We stand or fall together!"

"I'm afraid that's where you're mistaken. Has that tidy sum that somehow mysteriously escaped from your 'Reserve Fund' so many years ago slipped your mind? I believe they call that embezzlement."

Hamilton's face turned white.

"Thought I didn't know about that, didn't you?" said Henry. "Just before he died, Lance gave me the book on you, Bruce. He

knew your kind. He had been greedy, but he'd seen worse in you
. . . the lust for power. He foresaw this day on his deathbed, and
he gave me some ammunition of my own. And as much as I find
anything even resembling blackmail distasteful, for the sake of ETW
and the good work it is doing and in the memory of my dead brother
whom I love whatever his faults, I will resort to using this knowledge
I have against you. For I also know that there wasn't just one instance . . . that it has continued. I do not doubt for a moment that
it has continued right up to this present day—that a close examina-
tion of your personal finances would uncover some large
unaccounted-for funds. The knowledge I possess could easily send
you to jail, Bruce. Jacob has been guilty of indiscretion . . . perhaps
immorality, and bad judgment. But he has repented and all will
turn out well in the end. You are guilty of worse, and as far as
I can determine no repentance is in sight. I fear all will not be
well with you, Bruce, until that time comes. Now . . . I believe
my son ordered you from his home."

Saying not another word, Jaeger turned and hastily strode from
the room.

82

There was no news conference the following day. Jaeger was
neither seen nor heard from.

Carson Mitchell, Tony Powers, Neil Pierce, Jerome McGrath,
Jeff Bahnes from Evangelism Radio—all in town for the announcement and subsequent meetings—were called into Jacob's office early
that morning. In a private meeting Jacob explained that there had
been major new developments that would affect the plans of ETW
in many respects. He declined further comment other than to
apologize for the last-minute cancellation and to beg their continued
silence on the matter. It could not be helped, he said, and he would
contact them each immediately once the crisis was past and a resolution arrived at.

One of Jackson's first orders of business was to talk with Sondra DeQue. He told her of all the events of recent weeks leading up to the final few days. She listened eagerly, and when he at last sighed deeply, signaling his completion of the incredible story, she approached and embraced him tightly.

"I'm happy for you, Jackson," she said. "I know what you've gone through has been hard, but at least now you can see a purpose in it all."

"But there's more news," he said after a moment. "I mentioned it to Jacob, and he agreed wholeheartedly with the idea—he wants to reinstate you at your former position—with full back pay!"

Sondra's eyes filled with tears. She kissed him lightly on the cheek and simply said, "Jackson . . . you're a dear!"

Some days later, when Jackson was alone with Jacob, his father said, "I know I promised that I would talk to your superiors about having you rehired at *News with a Vision*. But I would like—if you'd consider it—to offer you a position with us, serving with me. I would be proud to have you take over Hamilton's job, gradually of course, as my assistant."

Honored, Jackson declined a decision. "So much has happened," he said. "I'll have to think about it for a while. Think about it—*and* pray about it," he added after a moment's pause.

"Indeed!" replied Jacob with a serious nod of his head. "That is a perspective on decision-making that is unfortunately still foreign to me but one we must learn to incorporate into everything we do from now on. I'm afraid I've been a slow learner."

Jackson laughed. "A malady we all share!"

"Hopefully with people like you and Bob near me, I can start making the progress I should have begun years ago. I'm afraid I'm going to have to reorient my whole way of looking at everything, and I'm going to need help."

"I don't know how much help I'm going to be able to be. I've got plenty to learn about walking daily as a Christian too."

"You're miles ahead of me!"

"Well, I doubt that," replied Jackson. "I suppose there is a lot we can *both* learn from Bob."

"No doubt," added Jacob. "But from where I sit, even though you're my son, I still view you as someone I have a great deal to learn from—and one to whom I owe a great debt of gratitude for forcing me to confront the truth."

Jacob's brief speech left Jackson silent. Though his heart felt it would burst for sheer joy, there were no words to say. He judged it best not to reply for the moment, and let the tears in his eyes express the wellsprings flowing from deep within his being.

The family of five met frequently throughout the following week, sharing most meals, talking as they hadn't for years. The humbling pain had mysteriously breathed new life into every relationship, as if they were becoming acquainted for the first time.

Richard had been notified and was expected—no one knew for certain when.

Each knew weighty alternatives faced them. Toward week's end, a somber mood of quiet began to settle upon Jacob. All the others sensed that as the burden of decision was shifting to his shoulders a mantle of authority began to settle upon him in a spiritual manner in which it never had all his life. He was coming to apprehend in the spirit that direction was called for and that he alone would be the one who would have to point the way. The humbling realization brought with it the accompanying revelation that his leadership must no longer operate in a vacuum and that, as he sought the guidance of God, he also needed more than ever the prayers and encouragement and counsel and help of people he could trust.

Thus it was that after several more days, he called together those three with whom he now felt inextricably bound, both personally and spiritually. They met in his office on the sixth floor of the Luxor Towers. The time was 5:45 A.M. Present were Jacob Michaels, Henry Michaels, Jackson Maxwell, and Robert Means.

A sense of sobriety and import pervaded even their greetings and handshakes and preparations of coffee and tea. Each of the four knew momentous matters awaited them. When they were ready, Jacob spoke out. His voice was soft with humility, yet it resonated with purpose and a new authority. Even in the midst of his doubts and questions, it was clear God had laid His finger upon the man's heart for a purpose, yet undisclosed.

"I appreciate your all being here," he began. "More than that, I appreciate you, and what each of you deeply means to me . . ."

He paused and drew in a long breath, struggling with how

342

to embark on what he had to say.

"I really need your help," he went on at last. "There are so many decisions to make, so much I've been wrestling with inside, so many things I need for you to pray with me about. That is perhaps what we need to do most of all together—just pray, and ask God to show us what to do. I also need your advice and wisdom. I need to unburden myself. You are my closest friends. I know you will each understand, for you are part of all that has happened. I've spoken with Elizabeth at length this past week, and even asked her to be here this morning. But she felt it would be most appropriate for just the four of us to talk and pray, at least this first time. Perhaps this will become a regular thing for a while, as we try to discern what direction to go, and perhaps she and Diana—might we even hope Richard too in time—can join us later."

The others all nodded and expressed their assent.

"But for now," Jacob added, "here we are, and I want to just ask you to pray with me, and then perhaps we can discuss how I ought to proceed."

"We are honored to be part of this time with you," replied Means.

Jackson and Jacob's father nodded in agreement.

"Before we pray," Jacob went on, "if I could, I would just like to tell you as briefly as I can what my present perspective is."

He stopped for a minute. The others waited respectfully as he gathered his thoughts and then continued.

"Something you wrote in your second article, Jackson," he said, "has stuck with me ever since. You may think no one around here was paying any attention," he said, glancing in Jackson's direction with a smile, "but the Lord was getting at me through you, though I can't say I enjoyed the process at first!

"Anyway, do you remember that quote you wrote about the suggestion for ministry, that no one ought to enter the ministry until he had demonstrated that he could make some other living first?"

Jackson nodded.

"I haven't been able to get that out of my head. And what I find that I keep asking myself is—Have I ever really done an honest day's work in my life? You really raised some pointed questions, Jackson. Handouts, a life of ease, the donations from working people who can hardly afford it while I live . . . well, just look at how I live!" he exclaimed, gesturing widely about the expansive office. "I don't know whether you had me in mind specifically, but I tell you, your words struck root in my subconscious, and, boy—the Lord has really been working me over about this! Dirt under *my* fingernails? No way! Not since I was a kid!

"Look at me—look at all this!" He flung his hand again around the room. "A big fancy office! Why, we rent three floors in this building! All first-class—the expenses of ministry. Just like everything else about this organization, to the tune of half a billion dollars in assets—the most successful Christian enterprise the world has ever seen! And now all of a sudden, I'm questioning the very basis for it. Look at me! I'm the man the whole world looks to as Christ's representative—and what do I really know of the Christlike life? Nothing! I'm a man with sin in my life, a man who is barely a babe in really living spiritual truths. Why, all three of you are a hundred miles further down that road than I am! And yet . . ."

He paused, groping for words.

". . . and yet—here we are! Here I still stand at the head of this monster of an organization, with decisions to make, with thousands of people still essentially working for me, with so much going on . . . and . . . what do I do? For the first time in my life, suddenly I really *want* to be the man God wants me to be. I *want* to be the kind of leader that reflects Him. Maybe for the first time I truly desire that ETW be His organization, not mine, not my father's, not anyone else's. And yet—in the midst of all this, I can't help but feel incredibly hypocritical for being in this position at all. As I said, I'm such a babe in the woods. What right do I have to stand in front of people to speak, to say or do anything—until I learn a little more about this life of being a Christian in a *real* and daily way?

"I just don't know what to do. Naturally, I want to begin operating ETW as it should have been operating from the beginning. But another side of me says that in order to put things right, I need to get right myself first. That side of me is saying that the only right thing for me to do is to publicly come completely clean about the past, tell everything, and admit to the false priorities that have infected ETW for so long. I've spent more time in prayer this last week probably than in my entire life. And I must say, the realizations are anything but pleasant.

"It seems to me that truthfulness and honesty and integrity demand that I step down, that I take myself out of the limelight, remove myself from public leadership.

"All this has been weighing heavily on me for about a week now. I feel almost desperately caught in the midst of all this until I know what it is God would have me do. How can I presume to go on in this position I am in—writing, singing, preaching, and as the head of an evangelistic ministry of the magnitude of ETW—when down at the core, inside myself, inside my own heart, I am not yet a man of God?

"It seems I ought not only to step down, but that I also ought to remove my books and records from circulation. They don't represent truth. I have been mouthing spiritual words without character, without *life* in me to back it up, to give it meaning. I've thought I ought to go on nationwide radio or television and simply tell our supporters how things stand and tell them to cancel their future donations to ETW until they pray about what God would have them do. If that spells the end of ETW, so be it. If not, then perhaps it is time we began depending on God to supply our needs, not asking for donations.

"I've even found myself reflecting on the story of Zaccheus and how he determined to give back four times everything he had taken. I'll tell you, *that* one is really something to consider! A half-billion in assets we've amassed! How does that give glory to God and further the gospel? Maybe it does in some way, but I have to tell you, right now I'm not so sure. Do we seek to make amends? Do we try to give it back to the Adas and Ednas who have given to ETW through the years? Four times would be two billion dollars! Those are staggering amounts! Does God want us to make restitution? I don't know . . . I just don't know!"

He stopped and breathed deeply.

"You see what I mean—the questions are huge ones. You really struck some chords with that article, Jackson! And most of all, I find myself wondering if I myself am supposed to be in this sort of public position anymore at all. It seems that I should step down and then simply go to work somewhere to support my immediate family—with my hands. Get a job as a carpenter's assistant, maybe learn the plumbing trade, even digging ditches if it came to that. If God's going to make of me a true man, it seems the process has to start at the basement, the foundation, not way up here on the sixth floor in a luxury suite of offices where I don't belong and never have belonged!

"You said it, Jackson—the question is whether or not the man is worthy of the labor. And I'm not worthy of being the Lord's so-called spokesman any longer. If I ever am again, well . . . that's something only He can determine, and if it should come to that, I would hope to earn my wings, so to speak, by being a man out in the trenches of life interacting with real people with my sleeves rolled up and my fingernails dirty, just like you said in your article. What *would* happen to the gospel enterprise if its leaders did as you suggested? I don't know. It's hardly been done since Paul's time. But maybe it's time somebody tried it, and maybe it ought to be me who dives in and sees what might become of it. If the world never hears another word from the mouth of Jacob Michaels, at least I'll be living a life of integrity and will be supporting my family with my own hands. And maybe there's something more important in that, after all, than . . . than all this I've been immersed in for so long."

The office fell suddenly silent. Jacob was spent. He had used up a great deal of energy, and now he sat back in his chair as one drained. It was aging Henry who next spoke.

"Much of what you have spoken, my son, has been on my heart as well. Perhaps it has been there for years, I now think I am realizing. But I was so unaccustomed to listening to the voice of the Spirit that I scarcely recognized His attempts to get through to me. I cannot even guess when they began. I share your grief, your hurt, your bewilderment. It all weighs with dreadful heaviness upon me, too, because in many ways I also am responsible for the false priorities upon which ETW has been founded—the religious words, the staged conversions, without the depth of character to make it all real."

He paused, then added, "So I think it is time we do as you originally suggested. It is a practice we have carried on all too little in ETW, to our shame, and I think it is high time we place the direction for our lives into the hands where it should have been all along. I think it is time we pray . . . and ask God what *He*

346

would have us do."

The old man slipped to his knees. As if by one accord the other three in the room quietly joined him, bending knees to the floor, and began praying together, silently and aloud, for direction and wisdom from on high.

83

The quiet office looking out upon Chicago was still the only room occupied within the Luxor Towers, though signs that the city was coming to life could be heard in the distance. Faint streaks signaling the breaking of dawn were brightening the eastern horizon. None of the four men present, however, was conscious of the sounds outside or the coming light of day as they gradually resumed their seats.

Another ten minutes went by during which no one spoke.

Finally, it was Jacob's longtime friend, Robert Means, who broke the silence.

"If I may, Jacob," he said softly, "might I share some thoughts?"

"Certainly, Bob," replied Michaels. "I have been waiting, hoping you would have some words of wisdom for me."

"There is something so right in God's order, so powerful, so in line with how I believe He works, in the three of you being here with each other—father, son, and grandson . . . praying, sharing, seeking God's direction together as a unit, as a family, as three men of God. I have to tell you I feel very out of place among you— yet honored at the same time to be included with you in these wonderful and also momentus times. But positionally, in the manner in which God's authority works, I cannot help feeling somewhat like the odd man out—"

"Nonsense, Bob," said Jacob. "If anyone ought to be included in these decisions, it's you! You understand so much of these . . . these—I don't even know what to call them!—these principles of how to live and act and think like we're supposed to as Christians. You grasp them better than I probably will for years. You've been at it so much longer. We would be—what does the Bible call it?—like the blind leading the blind without you to hold the flashlight for us."

Means laughed. "Well, God does work that way too. So I'll try to hold the flashlight a while, as you say. Yet I still am humbled to be part of it. There are just certain principles of authority that are rarely understood, and I see visible evidences of it right here in this room. Authority is not a static thing. There's a flow to it. God's authority passes into men and then continues to pass on through them. God's power to impact the world in great ways comes as men and women are able to place themselves in the midst of that flow and then allow it to pass through them—both up and down. Authority and submission to authority are greatly mistaken to be two different things when in fact they are the same thing. It's all in the flowing of it. There's a flow both upward *and* downward that must operate simultaneously. And that's what I sense is happening here—a flow between the three of you through which God is going to work perhaps some things we do not yet see. I suppose that's a tangential observation, but it's something I feel going on that I'm a little awed by. That's why I perhaps feel peculiar presuming to give you counsel."

"Please, Bob—you *are* part of this with us, and we are hungry for anything you might have to share."

Jackson and Henry both added their words of encouraging assent.

"Well, there are several things that came to me as we were praying," said Means.

"I want to hear them all," said Jacob. "Even if it takes all day! I genuinely don't know what to do next, and I need all the advice I can get!"

"The first thing, I suppose, is just this. Being unsure about what to do is probably the best place you could be."

"How do you mean?"

"I mean, it's not until God gets us broken down to the point where we stop depending on our own intellects that He can begin to infuse His own guidance into our outlook. That's why I say your uncertainty is just where God wants you. It will force you into prayer—daily, urgent, questioning, humble, listening prayer."

"But what do I pray for?"

"I think God will show you. But whenever I've been in circumstances where I didn't know what I was to do, I found myself falling back on one very simple prayer. It was just this: *Show me, Lord, what You want me to do, and give me the strength and willingness to do it.* There have been many, many times when I've prayed that prayer over and over, for days, even months on end—when I've prayed hardly anything else. During times of drought and spiritual uncertainty, I always begin by praying that prayer. I pray it every day and have been for years. And the key is that if we *do* everything God does show us to do—however small . . . do it with *our* willingness but in *His* strength, then He will continually be showing us more of what He does indeed want from us."

"It sounds too simple."

"God's ways *are* simple. That doesn't make them easy to live by. But there isn't anything particularly complex about the life of obedience. Simple, but not easy, as the saying goes."

"OK, then after we've prayed that prayer, then what do we do?" asked Jacob.

"Again, I'd say the same thing as before—I think God will show you. What He shows you to do may be a little thing, but if you do it, He will show you more. I think there is every possibility that God has placed many of the thoughts in your brain you were sharing with us. You said you have been praying—well, those were the beginnings of His answers. *Keep* praying, and I will keep praying, and I know Jackson and your father will keep praying, and Elizabeth and others, and God will refine what He is saying to you. But I am confident you are already hearing Him as a direct result of the praying you have been doing these past couple weeks. You can expect to hear more as a result of our time this morning. And the more you pray, *Show me what to do, and help me to do it,* the more He will continually reveal to your mind and heart—that is, as long as you act on what He shows."

Jacob was silent a few moments, clearly pondering what Means had been telling him.

"So you think," he asked at length, "that God could be indicating His direction through all these thoughts I've been having—my feeling uncomfortable being at the head of ETW, the possibility of stepping down, the idea of withdrawing my books and tapes from the market, making a public confession, going to work with my hands, maybe even finding a way to give back some of the money we've accumulated . . . you think all this could be coming from God?"

"Oh, I think they're definitely coming from Him! That doesn't mean *every* single idea is from Him or that we shouldn't submit each to a great deal more prayer. Obedience doesn't mean a reckless, instant charging off after every thought that comes into our heads on the assumption that God put it there. God can give you direction through dreams, for instance. But indigestion or something you see on TV can produce dreams too. Not all the thoughts in your head are from the Lord. But some of them are. If we are continually praying, a good many of them will be. And we have to discern which ones are from Him and which ones are just thoughts our own brain is spinning out on its own."

"That's not easy," sighed Jacob.

"I can surely attest to that," added Jackson.

"Indeed!" Means laughed. "It *is* bewildering! Which brings us back again to the vital necessity of earnest prayer. We have to keep submitting these ideas to God, asking Him to show us which are from Him. He will then strengthen the ones He wants us to focus on, and those things that are from our own brains or indigestion will gradually die away. At least that's the way it's supposed to work! But nothing in the spiritual realm can be programmed to be the same every time for every person. There's a great deal of trust in God that it all depends on too.

"Anyway, to answer your question, Jacob, I do think much of what you are thinking about could be from God. And you must just continue to pray for further insight. The Lord may want you to step down but remain in some capacity. He could want you to make some restitution, but He will have to show you what kind and how to go about it. As to the matter of taking a job of physical labor—I can't speculate on God's intent. Now about what should be done concerning your books and tapes, the future of ETW—I just don't know, Jacob. I would not presume to offer *my* thoughts. It is God's mind you must seek, not mine. But I think the key to it all is your *willingness* to do any of the things. If I read you correctly, Jacob, I truly think if right now God spoke in some way

350

and made it clear to you that you *were* to step down altogether, to sell your house and cars and give away all the money from the sale and then move into a small apartment with just your wife, where you would support yourself with hard labor every day working for eight dollars an hour . . . and if no one in the world ever again heard the name Jacob Michaels in connection with books and sermons and songs and crusades and public gatherings and words of influence . . . I think you would do it."

Silence filled the office.

Even though Jacob had been hinting in the same direction, suddenly it sounded like an incredibly real possibility. The astounding import of Means's words seemed to jolt each of the four all the more wide awake.

Jacob leaned forward in his chair and cupped his cheeks between his palms deep in thought and reflection. At last he let out a long sigh, speaking softly as he did so.

"The implications of what you suggest, Bob . . . they're overwhelming . . . it would be so hard . . . so humbling. Just imagine what people would think."

"But perhaps life-generating and renewing and transforming at the same time," added Means. "God never asks us to do anything that *isn't* rejuvenating—that isn't the absolute best thing for us."

"It's so huge. Here I was thinking I ought perhaps to step down, but somehow the reality of what it could actually mean never sank in."

"But what I said is true—isn't it, Jacob?"

Again a long silence followed.

"Yes, Bob, I think it is," sighed Michaels at length. "I don't know—it would be so difficult, but yes . . . I think I would be willing."

"Then the battle is three-quarters over, my friend," said Means with a smile, his eyes dancing brightly amid restrained tears. "Because that willingness is all He requires. If you have that, He will give you the strength to do the rest."

When the silence was next broken, the voice was that of Jacob Michaels, speaking nearly inaudibly, yet with a brokenness of spirit that resounded with power through the heavenlies.

"Oh, God, I do ask You to show me what You want me to do. Make me willing, Lord. Make me more willing than I at this moment want to be! Give me understanding of what You want, and please give me strength to do it . . . no matter how hard it might be."

84

Jacob Michaels continued to pray.

As he did, he continued to seek counsel and suggestions from his family, especially his father and wife. The imperative continued to press itself upon him that the truth had to be told. He could not do so, however, without the consent especially of Elizabeth and Henry, both of whose lives would be equally affected in ways no one could foresee. The pros and cons of various alternative strategies were evaluated, and finally a consensus was reached. Only in a full disclosure would they be able to build a future based on truth and right. Doing so could greatly disrupt ETW's work on many ongoing levels, even before they knew what God's design for the future of the organization was. Likewise, it would gravely alter both Jacob's and Diana's positions as public figures. Yet everyone concerned welcomed whatever might be the result. For the first time in their lives, they knew God was ordering their steps, and though there was apprehension, there was no fear.

Whatever befell them, whatever God led them to do, they were prepared to adjust to. Whatever hardships He chose for them to encounter, whatever kindness and compassion was shown to them, they would look upon it all as a gift from God. In their hearts was the growing conviction that if God's people were to be united, and if the world was to believe anything they had to say, then truth had to begin with individuals and families and organizations and leaders taking the principles of God seriously enough to lay themselves on the line for the sake of them. Risk though it was, such was the price of integrity, of being God's people. For too long such had not been the undergirding foundation of either ETW or of the family of Jacob Michaels. They all agreed—now was the time to begin.

The upshot was an enlarged "family" gathering at the Maxwell farm in Quincy. The two families whose histories had become so intermingled had many relationships to form. Out of the changes emerged newfound strength of relational bonds and spiritual vitality. Never had Jacob seemed so real a person, so likable a man.

The spread on Ellen's table was sumptuous! The wife who had had no child of her own now had family aplenty and a heart full enough to minister to them all. Never had her cup of joy run so full!

Jacob had come to the conclusion that what was required was a full and bold public statement. He said he could only feel right in his heart by going all the way with it. He therefore made plans to videotape a personal message—to his followers and to all America—a message disclosing his own weakness, his repentance, and the priorities he was praying would be infused into his new attempts to walk as a Christian—living uprightly and scripturally in all the details of one's activities and relationships.

The segment was taped on the Maxwell farm. Sondra supervised the session for Jacob and spent four days with the family in Quincy.

Jacob's final request was that a full-length feature article written by Jackson ("Another notorious series?" he suggested; Jackson laughed.) appear as soon as possible after the taped television broadcast. In it he asked Jackson to disclose fully what had occurred and also to offer his own perspective, as the one who had not only been the catalyst but around whom the whole story in one sense centered.

"I'm not asking you to make public our relationship," Jacob added, "only to give what perspective you can as a writer to the whole thing."

"You don't think I would have reservations about being known as your son?" said Jackson.

"No, I think I know you well enough now not to be concerned about *that*," replied Jacob "*I'm* the one with reservations. I don't want to impose what I do in public onto you. It may at some time be appropriate for your readers to know who you *really* are, so to speak. But that is something we have to weigh and pray about. For right now, I'm concerned that nothing I do undermine your future as a writer. There is a great deal that I think is going to happen through your articles because of the hunger you have to see truth operating among God's people. I don't want in any way to prevent people from hearing what you have to say in the future."

"I understand what you're saying," said Jackson slowly. "But you do know that I would be proud to go on camera with you and be just as open about everything as you want to be about yourself?"

"Of course I know that. But I don't think it is wise for you to do so yet. There may be things God has for you to do that could not happen were you known to be my son."

"Well, I'll respect your judgment."

"Just like your name. I think, both for those reasons, and for the sake of dear Fred and Ellen, I would hope you would continue to go by Maxwell. I don't feel I deserve to have the son into whom *they* built such strength and virtue, go by *my* name."

Jackson sighed. "I hadn't really thought of all that yet. I will do nothing without consulting you."

After the videotaping session was completed and the lights and cameras turned off, everyone sat back to breathe an I'm-glad-that's-over sigh. It had been a draining afternoon.

Ellen made the rounds with the coffee pot and then said, "There's still pie in the kitchen."

Some took her up on her offer. Fred and Jacob were engrossed in some discussion together and didn't seem to hear. Suddenly Jacob could be heard roaring with laughter. But no one ever discovered the cause because immediately thereafter, Fred motioned to him, and the two left the house and went out back where Fred spent the next hour showing off—with accompanying detailed explanations—the hybrid tomato plant he was developing. Glancing out the window at the two heads together, Elizabeth felt a great surge of pride in the man she was coming to love all over again . . . kneeling in the black dirt, fingers turning over the loose soil, then looking up to question Fred about some technical facet of the procedure.

Jackson rose, caught Diana's eye, and they smiled. Just then Ellen walked in holding an unspoken-for piece of blackberry pie.

"Jackson . . . ?" she asked.

"No thanks, Mom," he replied. "I've had plenty . . . and I was considering giving some thought to the article."

He turned slowly and walked to the back of the house where his folks still kept his room as he had left it years ago. There on his desk sat the ancient manual Hermes—his first typewriter. They'd bought it at a secondhand store when he was sixteen and had given it to him for Christmas. He'd typed his first articles on it.

He sat down, fingers resting gently on the keys. How the feel of that typewriter took him back! He reached for a clean sheet of white paper . . . it was still in the top right drawer of the desk, just like always. He inserted it into the typewriter, shoved the carriage back to the beginning of the line, and started to type:

Today was a day of new beginnings—for many people . . . for two families . . . for the man Jacob Michaels. As probably one of the best-known Christian personalities the world has known, the life of Jacob Michaels has been constantly before the critical glare of the public eye.

Yet today, Jacob Michaels made a bold and daring declaration to the nation that told not of sainthood but instead of human weakness—and of that universal predicament of mankind called sin. But in his honesty, and in the integrity of that confession, Jacob Michaels has shown us—like David of old—that the path toward unity with God and with our fellow man does not lie in a life of perfection but in a life of humility, repentance, and openness to God's love and forgiveness.

There are no Christian superstars. Each of us is mortal. Forgetting that truth and seeking to raise ourselves too high, we inevitably fall. When we remember it, God is able to work His life into us.

"This is the story of that process in the lives of two men—father and son . . ."

Jackson fell silent and reread what he had just written. Yes, he thought, he did respect his father. He was no saint—only barely beginning to follow the principles of godliness.

Yet he was at last walking down the right road.

Jackson lifted his fingers and once again set them upon the keys.

85

The eternal round of seasons had once again given Illinois fresh birth. In its ordained time, spring brought renewal, warmth, and color to the land.

Nor was new life only to be found in the deep blue of the heavens, the greenery budding out of the trees, the bursting forth of colorful daffodils and tulips and crocuses, and the fertility in the fields of the Midwestern countryside. Gentle warming winds of the Spirit were blowing through ETW as well. The open confession of its head, followed by his daily attempts to step off the pedestal upon which most of his employees had placed him, had infected all three floors of the Luxor Towers with great hope and optimism. An energetic bouyancy was being breathed throughout the entire fabric of the organization that only a few months before had been inwardly floundering in stagnation.

Following the taped message by Jacob Michaels, all public appearances and meetings, including May's week-long crusade, had been canceled. But in all other respects the daily activities of ETW and its arms continued to function normally. While he prayed about what course of action to take, Jacob flew in many noted Christian personalities—and a good many who were neither noted nor leaders—in order to seek their counsel and ask for their prayers. Among them were most of the men, such as Mitchell and Powers, who had been involved in the Greenville plans, as well as certain men and women from diverse walks of life of whom no one had ever heard but who had been recommended as reliable and prayerful spiritual comrades of faith. He met with each individually over the following weeks and months, gaining a pledge of strict confidentiality. No one ever discovered the contents of a single one of those one-on-one sessions, but through them Jacob found himself opened to new vistas of awareness of the expansiveness of the Christian body. What a small part hc now realized he had occupied in it after all. How different were those times of fellowship, which usually ended with bent knees and moist eyes, from those he used to have with Hamilton Jaeger.

His former assistant did not set foot inside the Luxor Towers for another year. Jacob did not lay eyes on him throughout the entire spring, though in early summer word was announced that Jaeger had maneuvered his way onto the board of directors of an organization that had sprung up in Alabama whose purpose was purportedly the unification of leadership from a broad cross section of Christendom. The hope was that many small ministries and agencies, possibly even churches, would ally themselves to the parent organization, Evangelical Unity, Unltd., which would then send out discipling teams to help more closely align the smaller groups into a structure and format in harmony with the overall purpose and direction invisioned by the founders of EU.

As Jacob laid down the issue of *CO&M* in which he had read of the plans of EU, liberally sprinkled with pious quotes from the man labeled as the "former executive assistant to Jacob Michaels and second in command of all of ETW," he shook his head sadly. "Hamilton, Hamilton . . ." he sighed softly to himself, "what will He be forced to take you through before you learn?"

As for ETW, for several months Jacob continued to wrestle with what ought to be done in the area of finances and whether any changes or restitution should be undertaken. In the absence of clear leading thus far, he had authorized daily matters to continue in as normal a manner as possible, though he reviewed all major expenditures and curtailed a number of ETW's activities whose spiritual legitimacy he questioned. He had canceled all future book and recording contracts and with some of the funds set aside for the Greenville project bought all remaining inventories of each title. For the present, this stock would be stored in one of ETW's warehouses until Jacob knew what was to be done with it. He had thought of giving the books and tapes to struggling Christian schools to be used as a basis for fund-raising. Yet a part of him remained loath to see messages bearing his name going out into the public's hands at all. The subject remained one of regular prayer.

As yet he had not stepped down as head of ETW or taken a position as a carpenter's or a plumber's assistant—although he had contacted a few tradesmen discreetly to inquire whether they would be willing to take on a fifty-three-year-old apprentice. For the moment, however, he continued to infuse energy into ETW and viewed it as where God wanted him to remain, at least for the present.

He did sell two of his three cars and was now taking a bus into the city every morning. As he handed Jackson the check from the proceeds of the sale of the cars, he gave him instructions to find several poor families in Chicago and to see what could be done with the money to fix up their homes and apartments.

"Real people, Jackson," he said. "No agencies or governmental handout plans. Find some good families that we can help. After you've arranged it—make sure no one knows who's behind it—then we'll get a team together and go in and do the work ourselves."

Jackson agreed.

"And I want to be part of it, you understand," added Jacob. "I want to pound nails and fix leaks too. But they can't hear my name. The whole thing has got to be anonymous. If we can make it work with my car money—which isn't much, but at least it's personal and doesn't have to show on any books anywhere as having been donated—then maybe we can look into doing some projects like this on a larger scale. We've got to start small and see what God might develop through it. The homeless too—it's a huge mission field. We've got to see what we can do—a center where they can come to get food, some new housing . . . I don't know. But we've got to get involved in some of these areas. You look into the whole thing."

"I'll get right on it," replied Jackson enthusiastically.

As Jacob sat in the small office thinking about that interchange with his son of a day earlier, he was almost glad Jackson had decided not to take the job as his assistant. Now that he was back with *NWV*, their deepening relationship was able to move in broader avenues for being part of one another's lives than had they shared adjoining offices. Jackson would make the drive over to the Luxor several times a week, often to discuss with his father some story he was working on. Likewise, Jacob treasured the moments he spent praying with Jackson about his own dilemmas and quandaries, and he felt certain that the recommendations and insights Jackson was able to give carried an added dimension of legitimacy because he was still out there in the world, mixing with people who were observing ETW and Jacob Michaels from a distance.

The room where Jacob sat behind a small desk was probably barely one-sixth the size of his former suite up on the sixth floor—a suite now vacant on most days.

At his own request, for three months Jacob had not only been occupying the small "Correspondence" office where his friend Bob Means had spent the last ten years, he had himself taken on almost the entirety of Means's duties.

"What better place to get an inside look at the grass roots of this thing," he had said, "than right here in your chair!"

Means had heartily agreed to the plan, thinking Jacob meant for an afternoon or two. But after three weeks, Jacob was enjoying himself so much that he could hardly be found anywhere else in the building. He took every phone call into the correspondence section himself and was downstairs in the mailroom the moment deliveries arrived each morning, pouring through every handwritten envelope. Mere business others could handle. But any scrap of personal correspondence, all prayer requests, or questions of faith he grabbed himself, later in the day to answer with either a letter from his own hand or a phone call with his own voice.

Never had he felt such a sense of purpose. Never had he dreamed there was such a personal and rewarding aspect to the ministry of ETW behind the closed doors of the small offices he had all but ignored for so long.

"I can't believe all I've been missing!" he was heard to exclaim more than once. "You guys interacting with people have been doing the real work all these years. These people that write and call in are wonderful!"

He could hardly wait to get to the office every day and to jump into whatever interactions the Lord had for him. Any thoughts of public engagements and national visibility could not have been more removed from his mind.

In the meantime, he sent Means on excursions, for a day or two, sometimes for a week, throughout the vast empire of all that ETW had grown to become.

"I want you to visit the people and places and ministries we're involved in, Bob," he had said. "Don't tell them you know me. Just be a fly on the wall. Listen, observe, and pray—I want you to feel the pulse of what's going on out there."

"Am I looking for anything in particular?" his friend had asked.

"I want to know if we're doing any good, Bob. You know what I mean—*real* good . . . helping people, changing lives. Not the kind of stuff Hamilton Jaeger would be interested in—but the kind of thing you would have noticed a year ago that I would have been blind to. Are we helping any people who are *really* hurting? Does ETW's money buy any food for hungry children? Do people working for me lead anyone to Christ—personally, not like the conversionary scorecards we used to keep on every meeting for our PR files, but the kind of conversions that last and take root and really make a permanent difference? Do our people help struggling couples avoid divorce? What are we doing with our assets and resources to ease suffering in the communities where we are involved? Are we buying blankets and groceries to distribute in the skid rows of this nations' cities? Are we helping families in crisis and anxiety?

"What *are* we doing, Bob? Are we doing anything or only conducting meetings and running organizations? I've got to find out as much as I can about what ETW is really like. I can never see it because of who I am and what I represent. But if we are going to know how God wants us to proceed, then we've got to know as much as we can. So you go out there. You be my eyes and ears, Bob. You bring me back your thoughts, your prayers, your insights, your concerns, your recommendations."

Jacob glanced down at the scripture he had been meditating on before his thoughts had strayed to Jackson and Bob a few minutes earlier. He read the words once more:

> Brothers, if someone is caught in a sin, you who are spiritual should restore him gently. But watch yourself, or you also may be tempted.

Just then the phone rang. Michaels listened a minute, then let out a huge laugh that echoed through the walls into several offices in both directions. The conversation that followed sounded like an exchange between old friends who had not visited in years.

As he hung up the receiver, he heard footsteps approach from the outer office. It was Bob Means.

"I tell you, Bob," laughed Jacob as the two men shook hands, "that Mrs. Bloom is really something! I'm so glad you got me together with her!"

Means smiled and sat down in the one vacant chair of his old home. "I can see I'm still not about to get my office back!"

"Are you kidding? I love it here—this is the real center of ETW—these people. That dear lady—"

He pointed toward the phone as if Mrs. Bloom were still there.

"—ever since I had her come here so we could meet personally, she calls me faithfully once a week. We always pray together over the phone. She never fails to remind me that it was you who taught her not to feel uncomfortable doing it. Now she's teaching me. See how things come full circle."

"God's ways are big," said Means, "and always round. His principles never fail to come back upon themselves."

"So tell me, how were things out in Oregon?"

"God is at work."

"You say the same thing wherever you've been!"

"It's always true. God is busy everywhere."

"I'm learning to see it."

"And learning quickly."

"Not as quickly as I'd like. But at least being here in your old stomping grounds is speeding up the process. God's business really is in people's hearts, isn't it, Bob?"

"As I said, you *are* learning rapidly. That is a truth many people never see. There is much of both kinds of business going on out in Oregon—many exciting developments in people's hearts, but unfortunately a great deal of church folderol too. There are some things and some real opportunities we need to pray about."

"I want to hear everything," replied Jacob enthusiastically. "But right now I've been puzzling over a verse I want to ask you about. Do you mind . . . do you have time? I know you just got back."

"Of couse I have time," answered Bob. "I got home late last night. I'm well rested. Juliet and I had a leisurely breakfast together. I'm at your service."

"OK . . . well, you asked for it." He took a breath, then continued. "I've found myself wondering lately about the whole subject of restoration. I'm not even sure I know what the word means exactly, but it's been pressing itself on my mind, especially this Scripture—just a minute—"

He glanced down, found the verse, and read it to Means.

"See what I mean, Bob. It's obviously talking about me—a brother caught in sin. It seems clear, too, that he's talking to people like you and all the others he's sent to help me. I'm finding myself thinking about what exactly that word *restore* means. Not that I know much about studying the Bible, because I don't—but I've been trying in my own way to see if I can figure out if it has something for me to learn. I sense, Bob, that God wants to say something to me . . . I have the feeling that the key to what I'm to do next, the future, where ETW is supposed to go . . . that somehow there's something here in the meaning of this word that we need to get to the bottom of."

He paused and looked at his friend.

"Go on," said Means. "I'm curious to see what you've discovered. Remember what I've been telling you—it isn't a lot of knowledge or background you need to discover the secrets in God's word but a hungry heart that obeys the things you *do* find. I would place a great deal of confidence in what you discover in that book because your heart is hungry, and you're seeking to obey what you're shown. So go ahead, tell me what you've found."

"Not that much really," said Jacob. "When the word first started coming to me, my initial thought was in the sense of 'restoring' me—if I can use terminology like that—back to my so-called position of influence and prestige. I hope you understand what I mean, Bob. It's not that I was seeking the fame and fortune of it all again, its just that that is what came into my mind. I had fallen off the pedestal, so to speak, fallen from the high place where I had been, and so then came the idea of my being 'restored' there, and maybe having a new position of influence sometime in the future. I didn't so much *desire* that as it's what the word seemed to connote in my brain, because that's been how I've seen it applied to other men in my position. They fall out of favor for a while, then gradually climb back into the public eye, and they call that 'restoration.' "

He stopped. Means remained silent.

"But as I read through the Bible and put my concordance to its best use in years, it seemed usually to have to do with fixing broken things—a wound, a bone, a tree branch, eyes that couldn't see—or getting something back that was lost or missing—lost people, lost money, lost land—and bringing things back together, joining things that had been separated but that weren't supposed to be apart.

"Do you see what I mean, Bob? It doesn't seem to have much to do with someone in my position—I mean with putting someone back in a position of power, so to speak—as with joining or connecting things that have been severed. Yet you usually hear it used in the other way in reference to Christians and, you know, as I said, men in my position."

A smile had gradually been spreading across Means's face.

"So I've been waiting for you to get back so I could ask you about it," said Jacob. "And from that look on your face I can tell you've got something to say. So share whatever insight you have with me!"

"I was only smiling from listening to you, not because I was anxious to say anything. I think you've discovered the right track on your own. I think you're exactly on target. The Lord is revealing His truth to you. You don't need me to help Him."

"Still I'm eager for your insight."

"Well, I have given some thought and prayer to what you're talking about," said Means, "because I agree—it is sometimes misunderstood. You're not the first spiritual leader, Jacob, to fall from grace in the public eye. But what comes afterwards is something that I don't think's been got right very many times. Like you said, usually the whole emphasis is getting back into the former position as quickly as possible. However, I think there's a great deal more to it than that. You're right, restoration isn't about position at all—it's about healing . . . healing what has been damaged, separated, broken."

"OK," interjected Jacob, "I see that. But what is it that's been broken in my case? If it's not my reputation, my career, my position, the need to be put back together . . . then what is it?"

"The damage is far more widespread than just to yourself, Jacob. And that's why the restoration is on a far deeper plane than just you and your position. The separation is to the whole body of Christ. When one member falls, the whole body, because it is so interconnected, suffers."

"And so what is restoration?"

"I'm not sure I can say what it is entirely," replied Means. "But the glimpses I have tell me that it's got to do with a putting together, a making right, a joining, a healing of the entire body. That may come about in a very different way than just propping you back up where you were before. In a sense, your former position was an equal part of the problem, the damage, the brokenness, as was your fall. Putting you back on top might not restore anything at all. Restoration, in the sense I think God wants to achieve it, has to do with the knitting and joining of hearts into oneness, not with positions of visibility and authority. And of course, since we're talking about you, that process must begin in *your* heart."

"Go on," said Jacob.

"There are a couple books I've got to have you read," laughed Bob. "They'll clarify it all for you. But briefly I see it as a process— a process involving four parts. First comes repentance, then forgiveness, thirdly healing, and finally—after all the elements of the other three have done their cleansing and washing and regenerative work—will come restoration. True heart's repentance will always lead to forgiveness—forgiveness in both directions, both the sinner asking for forgiveness, and those who have been hurt extending forgiveness. And of course, in that process of repentance God's forgiveness covers it all. Out of the unfolding of this forgiveness flowing in all directions will blossom healing—again, in multifold directions.

"Finally, after all this has taken place—and the healing may be a long, slow process—restoration will come. But that restoration is not necessarily a putting back of things the way they were, but a healing of the wound within God's body. For all I know, your restoration in the coming years may just as well find you fixing toilets as preaching to congregations. I do know this—the healing of your heart that God is busily engaged in will lead to results years from now that neither of us can possibly foresee. But those results will be because you have been restored to God, and the parts of God's body have been restored to one another, not necessarily because you have been restored to your former position of influence."

Silence fell and lasted several minutes.

"I'm not sure I would want it in any case," said Jacob at length. "I continue to pray for God to disengage me further from the organizational aspects. I still wish you'd consider letting me make you president of ETW for a while."

"Not a chance, Jacob. The real work of evangelism is elsewhere, as you know yourself well enough by now."

"That's why I'm impatient to know what's to become of it all."

"He will show you what you are to do in His time."

"I eagerly await it."

"In the meantime, restoration goes on, though we perhaps do not see all its hidden facets. There is another Scripture I'm sure you are familiar with—hand me your Bible, I'll see if I can find it quickly."

Jacob handed Means the small Bible from which he'd been reading.

Bob flipped through the pages until he came to 1 Peter.

"Here it is," he said. "And the God of all grace, who called you to his eternal glory in Christ, after you have suffered a little while, will Himself restore you and make you strong, firm and steadfast."

He closed the Bible, thought for a moment, and then went on. "That's the process I see going on in you, Jacob," he said. "God is *Himself* restoring you and making you strong, firm, and steadfast. What else He may do with you remains to be seen, but it will be wonderful, whatever it is! Because it will have been borne out of *His* healing and restorative processes."

"I will look forward to whatever that is with patience," said Jacob, "though with eagerness as well," he added. "Who knows— maybe Jackson will write a follow-up article one of these days about Jacob Michaels the plumber!"

"And it will be a powerful article about the restoraton and healing of God's spirit!"

"Amen," said Jacob softly.

He glanced down at his watch. "Speaking of Jackson," he said, "he's coming over, and we're going to lunch together. Want to join us?"

"Thanks, no."

"How'd you like to man the desk for me?"

"Love to!" replied Means. "Anything I should know?"

"There are some interesting things in that stack of mail there you might like to look at. And Mr. Flynn said he'd be calling back today. He and I were praying for a neighbor of his he'd been trying to share Christ with, and he was going to call back and let me know how it had gone."

"Great, I haven't spoken with him in a long while."

The outer door opened, and in another moment Jackson's head poked in. "Ready . . . ?" he said, then seeing Means, his face brightened. "Hi, Bob . . . back from the West Coast, huh?"

"Come on, Jackson," said Jacob rising, "Let's get out of here. Bob's anxious to get back behind his old desk."

Jacob threw an arm around Jackson's shoulder, and they headed for the door, just as the phone rang behind them.

"That's probably Flynn now," said Means. "You two have a good lunch!"

Means picked up the receiver and began to talk amiably to the excitable Mr. Flynn, who had only an hour earlier led his neighbor to the Lord. Father and son walked down the hallway together, and Means's voice gradually faded behind them.

As they approached the elevator, Jacob stopped suddenly.

"You know, I haven't seen Sondra for several days," he said. "Go try to find her, Jackson. See if she'll join us—tell her lunch is on me! I'll just pop in here and say hello to Mrs. Peters."

Ten minutes later, Jacob Michaels, Jackson Maxwell, and Sondra DeQue emerged from the lobby of the Luxor Towers into the bright sunlight of a warm spring day.

All three wore smiles, and they were chatting freely.

The Jackson Maxwell Journals continue . . .

In book two, restoration within the Michaels family deepens, and the future of ETW unfolds in much different directions than any would have anticipated. Meanwhile, Jackson encounters fresh challenges to the truth as he tracks down a new assignment within the Christian body.